To De
Erosuy w
Mary C

# Fiery Fields

Historical Romance

*By Mary Carchio Anconetani*

Copyright 2003

ISBN: 1-58749-393-4

Earthling Press ~ United States of America

Fiery Fields by Mary Carchio Anconetani
Copyright 2003 by Mary Carchio Anconetani

Print edition 2003
ISBN: 1-58749-393-4

Electronic editions 2003
ISBNs: 1-58749-391-8 and 1-58749-392-6

Published by Earthling Press
A subsidiary of Awe-Struck E-Books, Inc.
Printed in the United States of America

www.awe-struck.net

Available in electronic and print formats

Editors Kathryn Struck and Dick Claassen

Cover art by Mary Carchio Anconetani based upon Leonardo da Vinci's *The Virgin of the Rocks*

# Chapter 1

May 1909

Teresa's anger almost blocked her fears. She leaned against the ship's railing and stared down at her weeping mother, nearly obscured amid the mass of emigrants on the Naples wharf. *I'm the one who should be crying,* Teresa thought bitterly. The more she struggled for control, the more her anger spread. It included the *Mostro,* which she viewed as the oldest, dirtiest ship afloat, not that she had ever seen others. In fact, she had never been out of her mountain village of Montaguto. Her anger didn't even stop at the brilliant sunshine. *It should be raining!* She clenched her fists, completely unaware that she had a stranglehold on the ball of black yarn in her hand.

"Exciting, isn't it?" a young girl standing beside her asked timidly.

"What?" Teresa responded more sharply than she had intended.

The girl recoiled. "Going to America, I mean."

"Sorry. I didn't mean to snap." Teresa judged the girl to be about her own age, seventeen, maybe younger. Although she was Teresa's height, five feet four, taller than most girls, she appeared smaller. Even the wisps of dark, curly hair at her temples seemed to protrude timidly from beneath the gray, woolen shawl protecting her head and shoulders. *How can she stand wearing it in this heat?*

Teresa wasn't used to such weather. The sirocco winds were rare in Montaguto. Montaguto, nestled in the Apennines thirty-five miles northeast of Naples, boasted balmy summers and mild winters.

Teresa pushed her own curly auburn hair away from her face and readjusted the white straw hat resting upon the loose bun at the back of her head. She had purchased the hat at dockside over the objections of her mother, who had wanted Teresa to wear a shawl like everybody else. "I'm not like everyone else," she had said with a toss of her head. "I'm going to be myself no matter what others think."

"I am Violetta Esposito," the girl whispered in Teresa's ear as if afraid someone would overhear. Her shawl slipped from her head, revealing the braid cascading down the back of her head. She quickly readjusted the shawl.

"I'm Teresa." She almost gave her maiden name, Tozzi, unwilling to call herself Martello. She didn't want to be Teresa Tozzi either.

A sudden breeze took possession of Violetta's gray woolen skirt, exposing her black, high-top buttoned shoes. They looked almost new.

Teresa failed to move her cramped toes in her mother's hand-me-downs.

"Are you traveling alone, too?" Violetta asked.

"Yes."

"Aren't you afraid of arriving in America alone?" She spoke nearly perfect Tuscan.

"Isn't someone meeting you?"

"Yes, my fiancé, Niccolo, and his mother, Giustina, in Nuova Yorka, near Mulberia Streeti." She shifted uneasily, then hopefully, "It sounds pretty, doesn't it? I mean, naming it after a sweet fruit like the mulberry?" Her dark eyes begged for reassurance.

"Yes," Teresa responded halfheartedly, but mentioning mulberries transported her to the solitude of her bedroom. Through the fluttering white muslin curtains, she could see the mulberry and endless varieties of other flowering fruit trees. Pink and white blossoms blanketed the mountainside all the way down to the Cervaro River. She saw herself running to the trees, showered by blossoms, her skirt billowed behind her.

Teresa longed to taste the succulent mulberries. *They are so perfect,* she thought, forgetting completely the ants they drew and the stains on her clothes. *Will I ever see Montaguto, another primavera?*

"Primavera."

"What?" Teresa resented returning to reality.

"Primavera, no, Springa, that's what it means. It's where Giustina wrote to meet them...a boarding house." Violetta shifted her gray ball of yarn to one hand. She withdrew a rumpled slip of paper from her white linen blouse and handed the paper to Teresa.

Teresa had difficulty reading it. *Signora* Delora Felice and Spring Street, New York City, were legible, but not the house number. She shrugged mentally and handed the note back; it had nothing to do with her.

"I can't wait to see it." Violetta blushed and looked down. "That is, if I wasn't so afraid of marriage and..." She blushed, replaced the note in her blouse and pulled out a photograph. "This is my intended. "She handed it to Teresa. She saw Teresa's eyes widen, and smiled. "Handsome, isn't he?"

"Yes," Teresa answered without removing her eyes from the sepia tone. The young man in a perfectly tailored brown suit looked ready for action. His dark eyes fascinated her; maybe it was because everyone complimented her on her own dark, almond-shaped eyes and long lashes. Whatever the reason, his were compelling. His dark, wavy hair, brushed neatly back, seemed to struggle for escape. A widow's peak pointed down his straight nose to his broad smile, revealing a perfect set of white teeth. It took an effort to turn the photograph over and read the inscription: "This is my son, Niccolo Giovane. February 18, 1908, on his twentieth birthday."

"I've never met them. Actually the letter was from Giustina, not Niccolo. They are distant cousins and my only living relatives, apart from Aunt Valentina. When Giustina heard from Aunt Valentina that Mama had died of typhoid, Giustina sent a letter to my aunt arranging the marriage." She flushed again. "I don't know why I'm telling you this...nerves or something." She tugged at her shawl.

Teresa handed the photograph back to her, fighting the temptation to place it in her own white muslin blouse. She fanned herself with the diminutive copy of *La Vita Nuova* she had been clutching as a talisman.

Violetta returned the photo to her blouse. "I hope Niccolo won't be disappointed in me. I was much younger in the picture I sent and the picture wasn't clear."

"You needn't worry," Teresa lied. "You are very pretty." She didn't lie.

Violetta blushed, "Who are you meeting?"

Teresa tried not to distort her face. "My...husband. I don't have a picture." The only picture she had of him had been their small wedding picture taken at the Montaguto church door. She had ripped the photograph into tiny fragments and flung them into the fireplace. Bitterly, she remembered her mother's words to her when she had forced Teresa to marry Rocco. "It is for your own good. Someone has to take you out of this misery. In the end, you will thank me."

"I won't!" Teresa had fired back. She had to stand her ground despite the pain she had seen in her mother's eyes.

"You need someone strong guiding you." Her mother had wiped the tears from her eyes with her bloodstained white apron. "You are too willful, too independent, too..."

Teresa knew it had been a mistake to have done so, but her temper had seized control. She had stamped her foot and shouted, "You can't make me!"

"Quiet!" Her mother's anger had returned in kind. "You will do as I say!"

"I won't! I hate you!"

*"Strega!"* Her mother had screamed and pulled Teresa's hair. "God and the Madonna will punish you! Lord knows I have tried my best. Do you think it was easy raising you without your father or his and my family's help? Too late, I see he was right. I should not have allowed the nuns to teach you reading and writing. 'Annunziata,' he said, 'you will make her lazy, too independent and give her unhealthy dreams!'" She had tried pulling Teresa's hair again, but Teresa had run out the door.

Teresa had run along the vine-covered stone wall, past the Blue Madonna shrine and into the orchard, trying to escape her mother's shouts of *"Strega!"* She had fallen to her knees beneath a mulberry tree and covered her ears.

Her mother called her *strega* whenever she was angry with her. That had happened more frequently as she had grown up. *"Strega,"* she'd yell when Teresa disobeyed, *"Strega,"* when she ran to the orchard to escape work, or when a boy smiled at her.

"Stop swinging your hips, you *male femmina!*"

Teresa didn't swing her hips deliberately to encourage the boys. Still, she had to acknowledge, she did spend a great deal of time brushing her auburn hair to bring out its sheen and pinched her cheeks to make them glow. *What's wrong with looking good?* she often wondered. As for disobeying, didn't her mother disobey her landed parents by marrying a tradesman? For eighteen years, Annunziata remained an outcast to them and the townspeople for having married beneath her class—the town's butcher. They had shunned Teresa's father, too, for daring to reach above his class.

*Butcher.* Teresa shuddered. Whenever her mother was about to kill an animal, Teresa would grab a book and a slate and run to the orchard. Reading and sketching were on Annunziata's complaint list.

"You lazy girl! I am all alone, and you are no help. All you do is read and draw pictures."

Teresa shouted back once, "One day I'm going to be a great writer or artist or...!"

"You?" Annunziata had laughed.

Teresa had tossed her head, "One day, everybody will know the name of Teresa Tozzi. You will see!"

"No, you will." Annunziata's lips formed a thin line. "Once, I too, was young and foolish, but I learned. I never wanted to butcher animals, but life is not always what you want it to be. I was only fourteen, but you are sixteen, old enough to know better. Stop dreaming!"

Teresa threw back her shoulders. "Dreaming about love can't be wrong."

Annunziata laughed, "Silly girl! You don't know what love is!"

"You do?" Teresa sneered. She regretted having said it for she had seen her mother recoil in pain.

"All too well. I learned that love has the twin demons, betrayal and pain."

"I hope you never know love. Love can steal your soul."

"But even in the Bible it says that love is beautiful and..."

"Look what love has gotten me." She waved her arms around, taking in the room. "Love is only for the rich. For us there is only survival. Love! Do you think marrying you off for love is easy, even if you are pretty? No man in Montaguto wants you without a dowry. They want a woman strong like a bull, who will work in the fields and bear their children without complaint. You are much too slender, too tall, too educated and put on airs with your Tuscan pronunciation."

Now it was Teresa's turn to recoil. It wasn't that she didn't know the Neopolitan dialect, she preferred the Tuscan that fell from her lips like poetry.

"Don't give me that look. I have heard them talk, even if you haven't. Until now, I have made life too easy for you. I don't have to tell you that other girls younger than you are working from dawn till dusk in the fields and even have families. We poor struggle to exist and we die too soon."

"...soon." Violetta's voice shattered Teresa's thoughts.

"What?"

"We will be sailing soon. See? They removed that thing."

"Gangplank," Teresa responded.

Violetta looked regretfully at the yarn in her hand. "I don't have anyone to throw it to."

"I'm sorry." Teresa didn't know what else to say to comfort her.

Violetta dried her eyes. "I don't mean to cry, but I'm all alone in the world except for Aunt Valentina, and she is too sick to see me off. Everyone says, 'you should be happy, Violetta. You are going to Niccolo Giovane in America who must be a millionaire by now.'" Violetta smiled. Her eyes glowed with excitement. "You know, I feel better talking to you. I can't wait to get there now. It must be better than what we had. We were close to starvation with the crop failures, not that we were farmers. My father was a cabinet maker and my mother a seamstress, but the farmers couldn't pay us anymore. The poor things had to give two-thirds of their harvest to the landlords."

Teresa wished she'd stop talking. She had her own problems.

"I thought it couldn't get worse," Violetta continued, "but when Papa and Mama died we lost everything. I hoped I would die too. It was a sin, like evoking the evil eye, but I couldn't help it. When Giustina's letter came it was resurrection."

Teresa felt ashamed of her selfish thoughts and put her arm around the apprehensive girl. "Things will be better in America, you'll see."

"Yes," she smiled, "who knows what joy awaits us?" Her face brightened. "I know. I'll throw the yarn to the winds and Mama in heaven. Oh, I'm so happy I met you. My luck is changing. First Niccolo, now you."

The *Mostro* trembled as her screws churned the water of the Tyrrhenian Sea. She blasted her warning and edged away from the dock. Somewhere on steerage deck, a tenor's voice rang out clear, powerful, mournful, *Santa Lucia...Lontano,*

Voices unquelled by tears joined him,

*The ship sails to find a distant shore.*

*We Neapolitans...circle the world,*

*Seeking our fortune, but...we yearn for Naples...*

The passengers crowded the railings to catch what would be for most the last they would see of their families, friends, the only world they knew. Each held one end of the yarn and threw the ball down to loved ones on the dock, who scrambled to grasp it. As the distance between ship and dock increased, the balls unwound until separation played out the wool. Indifferent winds carried the wool aloft, floating it as if in suspended animation...the last link severed.

Teresa stood motionless at the railing, unmindful of the beautiful crescent-shaped bay between the headlands of Sorrento and Posillipo; unmindful of the glistening, white stucco buildings and fluted terra-cotta roofs silhouetted against the azure sky. All she saw was her mother's face until it disappeared in the distance. Teresa tossed her head back defiantly and threw her ball of wool into the agitated water.

Even after the shoreline could no longer be seen and tears choked the song in their hearts, the immigrants remained motionless, clinging to the railings as if hoping the ship would turn around. Slowly, they began vanishing into the black of the ship's hold. Only Teresa and Violetta remained at the railing. Violetta faced home. Teresa turned her back to the shore. Then, as if the wind had blown the fire from Teresa, fear replaced anger, loneliness. Then fear closed in upon her, suffocating her. *Mama!* She spun around and looked toward shore—too late.

# Chapter 2

Steerage reeked of engine oil, disinfectants, body odors and urine, magnified by heat and humidity. Beads of perspiration formed on Teresa's forehead. Pounding engines, shrieking babies, and the babble of countless people hammered in her head. She didn't know what was worse, the stench, the heat or the noise. If Violetta had not been following so closely, she would have rushed back on deck.

Violetta, clinging to the back of Teresa's black skirt, spoke into Teresa's ear, "Maybe we'd better hurry and find our beds."

"You call these two levels of wooden shelves beds? There are only two feet between shelves." Teresa edged her way through the maze. "Look. The mattresses are burlap-covered straw! Even the animals at home have it better!" She'd never dreamed steerage would be so appalling. Yet, although she had known her husband for only a couple of days, it didn't surprise her he'd subject her to it, despite his supposed wealth. This stranger who had suddenly appeared from America hadn't fooled her.

"They can't expect us to sleep with men! It's indecent! Only those little boards will keep us from rolling together!"

"Let's not panic, Violetta. There must be some place without men. Yes, look!" Teresa pointed to the stern with her chin, "By that lady."

Suddenly, the ship began pitching and rolling. Teresa grabbed a bunk and closed her eyes, desperately trying to overcome the nausea. *Think of something else.* She hurried as quickly as she could to the stern, although Violetta's holding onto the collar of her white muslin blouse didn't help. The pounding engines and the stench of oil intensified, the closer she got to the exposed steering mechanism.

"Hello!" Teresa called.

The woman turned around and smiled broadly. Her motherly demeanor embraced Teresa like open arms. Teresa judged the rosy-cheeked woman to be two or three years older than she. *Should I speak to her in Neapolitan or Tuscan?* She guessed Neapolitan, and raised her voice. "May we share these beds with you?"

"Yes!" she shouted back in Neapolitan, and readjusted her white muslin blouse and black woolen skirt that had twisted around. "I'm Rosa Piacenza. Call me Rosa." Apparently satisfied with her appraisal of them, she leaned in, spacing her words for pauses in the steering. "We have to take turns...sleeping...if we can, with this noise. My husband, Peppi, wrote me to sleep with my clothes on, because...of," she looked at them knowingly, "the men."

*"Mama mia!"* Violetta shrank back and dropped her bundle.

"Now, now," Rosa's soothing voice was like a caress. "It can't be that bad. Peppi worries too much about me. We've got each other now."

"Yes," Teresa agreed, "stay calm. Just think of the good things waiting for you in America. Think of your handsome, rich fiancé, Niccolo." *If he is so rich, why did he have Violetta travel steerage?*

"I... Violetta staggered.

"Oh, lie down, *angela.*" Rosa helped Violetta recline on the coarse bedding. "Better?"

Violetta nodded and drew herself into a ball. "Are you traveling alone, too?"

"Yes," Rosa brushed the hair from Violetta's face. "I am going to meet Peppi in some place called Vesta Vergine."

"That's where I'm going!" Teresa couldn't believe the coincidence. "Do you know anything about it?"

"Peppi's last letter to me said that he was going to live in a real house this time. He's been working some terrible places. Once, in a place called Bostone, Mazzacuca, he lived in," her eyes widened, "a wooden box. Can you believe it? All I know is that now he is digging for coal," she widened her eyes again, "and he sets the explosives." She shrugged, "Who knows? He brags a lot. You know how men are. I'm talking too much. Tell me, why are you going to Vest Vergine?"

"To be with my...husband." Teresa hated saying his name; it was like invoking the devil. When he had been gone for a year, she had hoped that he had forgotten her. However, her curiosity overcame her abhorrence. "Did Peppi ever mention Rocco Martello?"

Rosa pondered for a minute. "No."

The *Mostro* pitched suddenly. Teresa and Rosa fell against the bunk. They laughed, but Violetta, green-faced, was about to become sick.

Teresa reached for an empty bucket tucked beneath the bunk.

"All right, *piccola.*" Rosa removed the shawl from Violetta's shoulders. She turned and saw a steward entering their aisle. "Young man, bring me some fresh water."

The steward returned with a rusty bucket of brackish water.

Reluctantly, Rosa dipped her handkerchief into the water and placed the handkerchief upon Violetta's forehead. "Better?"

Violetta nodded weakly.

"Soon you will be safe in America and everything will be wonderful."

"I'd feel better if I knew what kind of man I will be marrying."

Rosa pushed Violetta's damp hair back from her forehead. "Who knows whom we marry? Marriage is a mystery that unwinds like a ball of yarn after the wedding ceremony. Everything looks tidy, but if you are not careful it can become a tangled mess." Rosa shrugged. "Still, I could have it worse. At least Peppi doesn't beat me."

Violetta raised her head and looked around to see if anyone were listening. "Can you tell me what happens...that is...between a man and a woman when they get married? No one will tell me."

Rosa chuckled and reddened. "Only your husband can answer that."

"Everybody says that." Violetta, disappointed, turned her head toward the bulkhead.

Teresa would have liked to ask the same question, for although she had been married for nearly a year, she'd never had relations with Rocco. All she knew was what her mother had said, "You must obey your husband in all things, unless it is against God or the Virgin Mary. Remember, if you want children, you must put up with certain things." What she meant by that Teresa couldn't guess. "Tell me, Rosa," Teresa ventured, "Was your wedding night pleasant?"

"Oh, yes. Wasn't yours?"

"No." The very thought of it sent her heart pounding in rhythm with the *Mostro's* engines. In spite of her mother's repeated cautions, "Never tell anyone your secrets or problems because they only want to laugh at your expense," she found herself saying to this stranger. "Rocco got drunk and beat me." She bit her tongue and blushed with embarrassed annoyance.

"You poor thing." Rosa shook her head sympathetically.

Teresa shook her head, too, but in an attempt to dislodge her thoughts. Despite her effort, her mind returned to her wedding night.

She was standing at the foot of her bed, shaking with fear, unconsciously pulling at the pink ribbons on her white muslin nightgown. Teresa could hear Rocco's heavy footsteps pounding outside her door. The door burst open then slammed back against the freshly whitewashed wall. His powerfully built body, silhouetted against the light at his back, seemed larger than it was. He swayed. Drunk.

Too frightened to tremble, she remained petrified.

Rocco kicked the door shut, lunged at her and almost fell forward.

Teresa regained her senses and ran to the tight space between the corner of the room and the cupboard. She clung to the cavity as if hoping a door would miraculously appear behind her, allowing for her escape.

"Get over here!" He slurred his words between clenched teeth. Yellowish-brown tobacco spittle marked the corners of his mouth. "Damn it! Get the hell on the bed!"

She tried to move, but her legs refused to respond.

"I'm not telling you again!" His heavy hand grabbed at her nightgown. He staggered and fell, tearing her nightgown away from her body. "God damn it!" Rocco got up. Rage contorted his craggy face into a purple mass. The foul smell of wine mingling with tobacco on his breath nauseated her. She wanted to run, but fear immobilized her.

"I'll show you whose boss!" Rocco swung wildly. Teresa turned just in time. He hit the cupboard door. A circular spider-web crack marked the spot on the highly polished surface. His anger surged. "Goddamn you!" He swung again. This time the punch struck her breast. She screamed in agony and collapsed on the floor. Rocco bent over her, fire in his eyes. He raised his hand again, but reeled and passed out at her feet.

How much time passed, she didn't know. It seemed forever as she crouched on the floor, paralyzed with fear. She clutched her torn gown to her throbbing breast as if the gown would protect and soothe her.

A soft tapping at the door barely echoed in the room.
She didn't answer.

The door opened. Annunziata peeked in and saw Teresa
sitting in the corner with Rocco at her feet. Without a word, she
examined the bed sheets and then the floor. She eyed Teresa
suspiciously. "No blood?"

"No." Teresa examined her breast for blood. "No blood." Her
voice, barely audible, boomed in her head.

"What happened?"

"He hit me."

"I don't mean that. Why is there no blood on the sheet?"
Annunziata's voice was low, but the words flogged like a whip.
"You were not a virgin, so he hit you!"

"No, I swear! He...hit me for no reason. Look." Teresa
gestured toward the cupboard door.

*"Mama mia!"* Annunziata crossed herself and wrung her
hands. "What will everyone think? *Gesù,* help me." As if the answer
came from above, she ran to the kitchen while Teresa, in a stupor,
remained on the floor with Rocco's head only inches away. In
moments, Annunziata re-entered the room with a bucket of pigs'
blood she had saved for blood sausage and smeared the sheet with
the blood. She lifted the sheet and examined it. Satisfied, she hung
it outside the window for everyone to see.

"You're bleeding."

Rosa's words brought Teresa back to the present. "What?"

"There's blood on your lip."

Until then, Teresa hadn't been aware she had been biting her
lip.

# Chapter 3

A crush of people filled almost every inch of steerage deck. Children darted about. Howling, red-faced babies squirmed in their mothers' arms. Husbands and wives huddled together clutching their meager possessions as if fearing their hold on reality.

Teresa, having left Violetta in Rosa's care below, breathed the ocean air in deeply, trying without success to rid her nasal passages of the steerage stench. Black smoke from the smokestack swooped down upon them, sending the immigrants into coughing fits. Blessedly, the wind changed direction and carried the smoke to the leeward side. Teresa took her handkerchief from inside the sleeve of her blouse and wiped the tears from her eyes. Again breathing the refreshing ocean air, she wondered what she should do to occupy herself. Keep a journal? No, her thoughts raced too quickly. Instead, she looked at the upper deck.

Separated from the immigrants, a different class of women caught her attention. Beautifully dressed, they either strolled with colorful parasols or sat on deck chairs beneath protective, flapping awnings. No scorching sun or irritating cinders there. Then she became aware that these well-tailored, well-mannered people were observing the immigrants as if the immigrants were there for their amusement.

A beautiful young woman in a crisp white dress with navy blue piping around a large collar stared directly at her. Teresa felt strange, dirty somehow. It was a new experience for her. An almost obscure, carefully woven rip in her own black woolen skirt seemed too large to endure. Teresa ran her hand over it as if trying to renew the cloth. She threw her head and shoulders back and headed for the ship's bowels. *One day, I'm going to wear the best clothes, and have the best. No one and nothing will stop me!*

\* \* \*

Topside, wave after wave driven by a nor'easter smashed against the *Mostro*. The boiling ocean heaved and sank. A huge curling black wave with clawing fingers of white spume washed over the deck. Howling winds tore at the awning on the upper deck. It fluttered helplessly, bounced on steerage deck, and sailed overboard.

For nearly a week the storm trapped everyone in steerage. Vomit, human waste and rotting food scraps added to the disinfectant and engine oil stench. The immigrants, having never been to sea, believed the next pitch would send them to the bottom.

Teresa, as frightened as the rest, lay in her bunk and recited the Act of Contrition. "O, my God, I am heartily sorry for having offended Thee and..." Another wave almost hurled her into the aisle. *Why did I worry about Rocco? I'm never getting to America! Please forgive me, Mama, for the pain I caused you.* Another wave. She held on. *Dear Lord, make the ocean calm.* As if in response, the *Mostro* stopped its heaving. However, another torment followed. With each blast of the bellowing foghorn, the *Mostro* shuddered.

Cautiously, Teresa raised herself on her elbow and turned to Rosa. "Are you all right?"

"Yes, and you?" came her hushed response.

"I don't think I can stand another day's confinement. This was only supposed to take fourteen days. It's been fifteen. What on earth, do you suppose, is keeping us?"

"I wish I knew."

"How is Violetta?"

Rosa shook her head, "The *poverella* is so sick. It's not seasickness. With all those bowel movements, she can't last much longer."

"I'm telling that steward just what I think of this stinking ship!"

"No, Teresa," Rosa pleaded, "it will only make trouble for us."

Then the thought occurred to Teresa that perhaps they had stopped because they had arrived in America.

The hatch swung open. A blinding light streamed through as if it were a beam of light from God. Everyone fell silent and looked up.

A sailor yelled down, "You can come up now!"

The immigrants became almost boisterous in their excitement. "America?" someone called up.

"No!" the sailor yelled down. "A few more days yet."

Teresa's heart sank, not for herself, for she was in no rush to get into Rocco's clutches, but for Violetta. Her irritation grew. *I'm finding someone to help Violetta!* Trying to control her temper, Teresa made her way up on deck. A thick fog had enveloped the *Mostro*, preventing even a glimpse of the sea. Still, she was relieved to breathe fresh air. She tried to stop some sailors, but no one paid her any attention. At last she found a sailor who was willing to listen.

"If I were you," he advised, "I'd keep quiet about it. If she is that sick, they'll throw her overboard. They can't take chances with having an epidemic on board."

Teresa crossed herself as he walked away from her. Thwarted, she resigned herself to merely buying rice for Violetta.

A man with an accordion began playing a spirited tarantella. As if by magic, a clearing formed where Teresa thought it impossible. She started for the hold, but someone grabbed her by the arm and spun her around.

"Dance with me, bella," a steward said. It was more a command than a request.

Although she knew she shouldn't, she couldn't resist the temptation. She danced as she had never danced before, unmindful of Sister Margherita's words that rang in her head, *"Dancing is sinful. It will lead to bad things."*

\* \* \*

"She's dead!" Rosa crossed herself as she looked down at Violetta's limp body.

Teresa placed her hands over her face, trying to block the horror of it. "It can't be. She's too young. Why did she have to die, Rosa? She was looking forward to a new life in America, a life free from want, free from worry, free from pain. Tell me, why Violetta and not I, who hate going to Rocco?"

"Teresa! For shame!" Rosa crossed herself. "How can you question the will of God?" She crossed herself again.

"Mama! Wake up!" A child's voice rang out.

*"E' morta,* little one." A woman examining his mother shook her head in pity.

"God save us!" a cry went up. *"La pesta."*

A steward appeared from nowhere. He stood beside Teresa and nervously poked at Violetta's body with a stick. Finding no sign of life, he shrugged his shoulders. "She's dead, all right! Ricardo!" he yelled to another steward, "We've got another one! Get a stretcher." He reached for a rope hanging from a nail on a post and tossed it to Rosa. "Wrap the body in the blanket. Tie it good!"

Teresa watched the steward disappear among the throng and said bitterly, "Just a minute ago, 'it' was 'she,' and 'the body' was 'Violetta.' You would think that she never existed."

* * *

The *Mostro's* foghorn's constant vibrating wails broke the immigrants' palpable silence. Standing at the railing between the two lifeless bodies, Teresa felt that the only living thing in and on the ocean was the *Mostro* itself.

She focused her attention on the red, white and green Italian flags covering the two stretchers perched on the railings. Sailors in white stood on either side of the stretchers, while the Captain read the Scripture of the Dead from a well-worn Bible. The orphaned boy clung to a woman who held him tenderly and stroked his hair.

Standing beside Teresa, Rosa silently wept and said her rosary. Although Rosa had seen much death in her life, letting go of Violetta was difficult for her. Why this was eluded her, but the pain was real enough.

Teresa twisted her ring around her finger and tried to come to grips with her thoughts. For the first time in her life, she couldn't pray or cry. It surprised her. All her life her emotions had been close to the surface. Now she felt empty, as if her soul hovered over Violetta. It suddenly struck her that she was thinking of herself instead of Violetta. Shame swept through her. *Only a few days ago you were unaware of how little time you had. How much time has any of us? How much time do you have, Teresa Martello?*

The Captain turned to Teresa. "Name?"

"Teresa Martello."

"Teresa Martello, I commend your body to the deep."

Violetta's body slid silently from beneath the flag and plunged into the ocean, barely making a ripple in the still water.

Rosa, astonished, turned to Teresa.

It came as much of a surprise to Teresa as it did to Rosa. The name had escaped her lips without thinking. Had she decided, or had the decision been made for her? She didn't know, but it felt right, as if her soul had returned to her. Unobserved, she slipped the ring off her finger and tucked it into her bag.

# Chapter 4

Teresa and Rosa, grateful for having endured Ellis Island's ordeals, sweltered as they walked up Mulberry Street. Their shadows on the gray pavement followed, seemingly trying to avoid the sun, horse manure, and rotting waste baking in the gutters. Horseflies swarmed everywhere. People just as thickly overran the narrow, cobblestoned street. Pushcarts and horses forced people to submit to their power. Black awnings jutting from a storefront protected them from the blazing sun, but not from the humidity.

Rosa, almost dragging her bundle, expelled an exasperated sigh. "The nerve of that cab driver, taking us to that awful place. Seven women and a baby in one small room with only one window facing a filthy courtyard."

"Dirtiest place I ever saw." Teresa readjusted her straw hat and tossed back the long braid she now wore in the manner of a single girl.

"What do we do now?" Rosa tried to ignore how her body chafed with every step.

"I don't know; maybe find *Signora* Felice's place. It must be decent if Giustina recommended it." She tried to sound positive but, she remembered, Giustina also had brought Violetta in steerage.

Rosa hesitated, afraid of distressing Teresa, "What happens when they see you?"

Teresa shrugged. "Maybe I will find another place before they do. After all, the ship was several days late. They wouldn't wait around for Violetta."

"The very idea makes me shiver. It's like walking in a dead person's shoes." She shuddered, remembering that Teresa was actually wearing Violetta's shoes.

"You worry too much. For me, it was a Godsend." She bit her tongue, regretting having said it. It sounded callous. "Forgive me, Rosa. I didn't mean it the way it sounded. It's just a new start for me, free from Rocco, in a free new country. What could be better?"

Rosa shifted her bundle. "God willing."

"Another thing, if you don't mind, from now on, I'm speaking Toscano so that I won't give myself away. Can you forgive me?"

"Of course. I understand why you must. I'll get used to it."

Huge Clydesdale horses, pulling a heavy brewery wagon, rumbled past, interrupting a baseball game. Two boys jumped up and dangled precariously off the rear of the wagon. Yielding to the brewery wagon, a fruit peddler pushed his cart onto the sidewalk. A boy grabbed some fruit from the cart and darted up the street. The peddler cursed and chased after him. Four other boys, seeing their chance, grabbed fruit from the cart and ran in the opposite direction. As the brewery wagon turned the corner, other boys resumed playing.

"Get the hell out of here!" a policeman across the street barked at the boys. "I'm not telling you wops again." They scattered, dropping their bat.

"Ah, yer modders mustache, Clancy," a boy yelled at the officer.

Clancy picked up their bat and laughed.

Teresa saw a boy leaning over the building's edge above the man. Clancy, unaware, took off his domed helmet and fanned himself with it.

The boy held out a swollen paper bag. "Hey, Clancy!"

Clancy looked up. The boy released the bag, hitting Clancy square in the face, dousing him with water.

"You damn wop!" He dropped the bat and disappeared into the building.

Almost immediately, Clancy emerged on the roof and chased the water-bag boy. To Teresa's astonishment, the boy leaped across a five-foot gap to the adjoining roof. Clancy stopped at the roof's edge and shook his nightstick after the boy.

"Crazy boys in this country," Rosa said, astounded.

"Wild and crazy."

"Mind if we stop for a minute?" Rosa placed her enormous bundle on the pavement. "I think my arm is going to fall off."

"What is in that bundle anyway?" Teresa dropped her much smaller bundle.

"My clothes, table and bed linens; you know, my dowry. Didn't you bring yours?"

"My mother wanted me to, but I said, if a man living in America, the land of millionaires, can't supply them, who can?"

As they sat on their bundles, Clancy, still angry at having lost his prey, emerged from the building. When he saw Teresa and Rosa he sneered, "Mother McCrea, more wops. Is there no end?" He wiped his brow with his coat and strode down the street swinging his nightstick.

Teresa and Rosa picked up their bundles. When they reached a grocery store, they stood for a moment, studying the fruit stand. Although the fruits weren't as large as they were in Italy, they marveled at the enormous selection. Teresa pointed to the sign in Italian. "Listen, it says, *Vittorio Tomaso Malespina, Banker, Notary Public, Legal Adviser, Post Master, Steamship and Train Ticket Broker, Scribe, Money Exchanger, Job Recruiter, Licensee, Investment Broker, and General Store Owner.*"

Rosa's eyes widened, "My goodness, all that? He must be very important."

"Oh, my! Look at that exchange rate! A good thing we exchanged our money at Ellis Island. We would have lost half—"

*"Buon giorno."* A short, thin man appeared in the doorway, dangling a long, twisted, acrid-smelling *di Nobili* cigar from the corner of his mouth. He blew smoke in the air and smiled. His gold tooth glinted in a sliver of sunlight that found its way through a gap in the awning. With an air of superiority, he leaned against the doorjamb. "I'm *Signore* Malespina, the owner of this establishment."

"Do you know *Signora* Felice?" Teresa asked.

"Yes. Keeps a clean boardinghouse. Up the street, turn left." He pushed his derby back on his head. Black, thick, curly locks jutted from beneath its brim. Malespina took out a gold pocketwatch, wound it deliberately, and replaced it. He adjusted his polka-dotted cravat with its flashing diamond stickpin and thrust his thumbs into his pinstripe vest's armpits. Assessing the new arrivals he said, "You'd better let me hold your money. Many Italians are killed for their money, right in their beds."

Rosa gasped. The small hairs on the back of her neck stood up.

Teresa, however, having taken an instant dislike to Malespina and the disgusting way he looked at her, said, "We have nothing, but we will keep it in mind."

No longer interested in them, he re-entered the store.

Rosa, still frightened, said, "Maybe we should give him our money."

Teresa shook her head. "Maybe, but he could be another swindler like the driver."

Rosa looked at Teresa with admiration. "I never thought of it."

"We can't be too careful. Mama always said, 'Never reveal the bottom of your purse or your mind.'"

As they reached the corner, they saw two urchins approaching them. Teresa judged the boy to be about seven years old, and the girl, five. Tears had formed paths down their dirty cheeks. "Heavens! Have you ever seen such pitiful children in your life, Rosa?"

"Never! Such rags, the poor things!"

"Give us some money," the boy said. "We are hungry."

"Where are your parents?" Teresa asked.

The little girl scratched her matted hair. "Italy."

"Quiet!" The boy pulled on the girl's arm.

They astonished Teresa. "Why aren't you with them?" She winced at the sight of purple bruises on their arms and legs.

"I don't know," the little girl answered, brushing her cheeks with the back of her tattered sleeve. "Please, give us money!" The urgency in her voice was beyond hunger.

Both Rosa and Teresa drew some money from their bags and gave it to them.

"I want my Mama," the little girl cried, and looked beseechingly at Teresa as if Teresa could magically produce her.

The boy almost dragged the little girl into Malespina's store.

Rosa wiped the tears from her eyes. "What do you make of that?"

"I don't know. I can't believe that their parents are in Italy, but then if they aren't, why are they so dirty, and why those awful bruises? Something has to be done for them!"

"What can we do, Teresa, I mean, Violetta? After all, we have just arrived in America."

"I guess you're right." She sighed and continued on Spring Street. Teresa saw two boys fighting.

"Ernesto!" A pregnant woman on the fire escape of a three-story building shouted, but the boy didn't answer.

Teresa recognized Ernesto as the boy who had dropped the water bag on Clancy.

Both boys, now on the ground, swung at each other.

"Ernesto!" His mother, now on the front steps, waved the rag she had been using to clean the bay window. "Stopa!" she said, speaking to him in English. "No hit Stefano! If you no stopa, I tell you papa when he come home!" The woman waved her hand, showing a spanking was in order, but he didn't stop.

Teresa saw Clancy rounding the corner just when a boy did. "Clancy!" The boy yelled the alarm.

That did it. The boys, including the belligerents, sprinted up the street with Clancy in pursuit. When they were out of sight, Teresa asked, "Do you know *Signora* Delora Felice?"

"I am *Signora* Delora Felice," she said in the Tuscan dialect.

Teresa noted Delora's Tuscan dialect and was happy she had used it. She observed, too, that *Signora* Delora's gentle eyes belied her somber demeanor. Her black dress, relieved by a long, crisp, white apron pinned on just above the breasts with huge safety pins, testified to her cleanliness. Two knitting needles piercing the bun at the back of her head stuck out like exclamation points. "That boy!" She shook her head, still preoccupied with Ernesto's lack of obedience. "Almost twelve years old and still not obedient. That's what it is in this country. You give them everything and what happens? No respect. In Italy, he would be helping support the family, but here, I don't know. I should send him to work like other parents do."

A sign on the plate-glass window on the ground floor shocked Teresa into not listening. In large, red letters, in both Italian and English, she read: *"Giovane and Son Clothing Factory."* In a near panic, she searched the faces of the men within the factory, but Niccolo wasn't among them. She breathed easier.

*Signora* Felice, thinking that Teresa was impatient with her, stopped her litany. *"Sorry,* you wanted me?"

"Yes," Teresa nodded, "do you have rooms for us?"

Her eyes narrowed for a moment. "Who did you say you are?"

Teresa hesitated. If she said Violetta, Niccolo; if Teresa, Rocco. Giving still another name was out of the question. She didn't have identity papers. Teresa plunged in. "Violetta Esposito. This is my good friend, Rosa Piacenza."

*Signora* Felice's demeanor suddenly changed. "Oh, good. I was expecting you." To Teresa's surprise, Delora clasped Teresa to her breasts. Only her mother had ever done that. "I'm Delora. Please come in." She began to ascend the stone steps. "I don't take anyone without a recommendation." She pushed open the door and labored up the wooden steps in the dark hallway. The keys on a string hanging from her waist rattled rhythmically with every step. Still preoccupied with Ernesto, she muttered, "If he's not fighting in the streets, he is up on the roof with those disgusting pigeons. One day I'm cooking them."

Teresa knew it was an idle threat, for she could see the way her eyes radiated when she talked about Ernesto.

On the railroad flat's first landing, they crossed the hall and entered the front sitting room. The aroma of tomato sauce cooking greeted them. It was Teresa's first sense of home since leaving Montaguto. She looked about the room. White lace curtains hung limply at the bay window. The drawn shades didn't keep out the heat or street babble. Centered in front of the window was a faded red-brocade settee. To her left sat an upright piano with a clarinet case on top. Leaning against the piano bench was a classical guitar, beside it an accordion. It pleased Teresa, for a house with music suggested a cheerful, fun-loving home.

"My children and my husband, Rafaello," Delora pointed to an overstuffed chair to her right as if he were in it, "play music. Do either of you?"

"No," Teresa said.

Rosa smiled, "No, but I like to sing a little."

"Oh, good, Rafaello will be happy. He loves a good singer."

Rosa reddened and laughed, "I didn't say I was good, just that I like to sing."

"Well, no one here is a professional." She pointed to a windup phonograph with a long horn that sat on a mahogany sideboard to the mantel's right. "That's a talking machine. You put a cylinder on that spindle and music comes out of that horn."

If Delora had told them that a man was walking on the moon, she couldn't have astonished them more.

"You ladies may play it whenever you like. Not after nine in the evening, of course. Everybody goes to bed early. Another thing, all your entertaining will be done here. I don't permit men beyond this point."

Rosa smiled. "I can see *Signore* Malespina is right. You keep a clean house."

"The *Padrone?*" She shrugged without any comment.

An enormous black cat glided through the sliding oak-paneled doors on Teresa's right, jumped on the overstuffed chair and began washing herself.

"Don't touch the cat," Delora warned. "I'm the only one who can, and then only sometimes. Poor thing was almost starved when I found her. Isn't that right, Fortunata?" She tried stroking the cat, but Fortunata thrashed out, barely missing Delora's hand. She shrugged and pointed to the dining room. "That is where I serve supper and breakfast." Through the sliding doors, Teresa saw a massive mahogany dining table holding a white linen tablecloth that almost touched the floor. A little girl sat beneath the table, polishing the legs.

Delora pointed to the girl, "My daughter, Liza."

Liza stopped her cleaning, poked her head out and adjusted her wire-rimmed glasses over her tearful eyes.

"She is ten years old."

"Ten and a half!" Liza snapped back in Italian while hiding the gap where her two top teeth had been. Her high-pitched voice shook the glassware in the breakfront that stood against the wall.

"Liza is upset because the nuns chased her away from the church we went to."

Delora wiped a tear from the corner of her eye with her apron. "I told you not to go there. It's an Irish church. We have our own church now. I know it's not as grand, but you should be thankful that Giustina gave money for it."

"Not all the money," Liza corrected.

Delora's eyes narrowed. "Don't be disrespectful! She gave a lot more than we could. Why do you want to go to the other one anyway?"

"It doethn't look like a church. It'th only a thtorefront."

"It's not the size of the church that counts, but what is in your heart." Delora resumed climbing the stairs.

*"Signora,"* Teresa ventured, "is it true that they have murdered some people for their money as they sleep?"

*Signora* Felice shrugged. "It's been known. But not here. Only the best ladies stay here. Including you two, I have twenty." She stopped on the landing to catch her breath. Stale, musty air persisted in spite of all Delora's attempts get rid of it. *"Mama mia,* it's getting harder to make these stairs, being in a family way like I am."

*"Signora,"* Teresa rested her bundle on the landing, "we saw two children begging in the streets who said that their parents were in Italy. Is it true?"

"Yes, many of them. Terrible men kidnap them from Italy."
She used the English word. Seeing their puzzled look she said,
*"Rubare,* steal them to beg in the street."

Both Rosa and Teresa took in a quick breath of horror.

Delora shook her head with compassion. "If the poor things
don't bring back enough, they are beaten."

"Beaten? No!" Both Teresa and Rosa recoiled.

"Can't something be done about it?" Teresa asked.

Delora shrugged. "Sometimes I feed them; sometimes give
them money, when I can. They don't like coming here because I
scrub them before I feed them. Anyway, it's foolish to make
trouble. The authorities have deported people, some without cause.
People say the *Padrone* is one of the people who steal children from
Italy to work for him." Then, as if afraid she had said too much,
she added, "Even he couldn't be that bad."

Delora led them through a succession of hot, windowless
bedrooms, each with one bed, one chair, one chiffonier, and one
armoire. As they approached the last bedroom she said, "This is the
best room. It has a window facing the courtyard, like my bedroom,
so it's cooler and not as noisy. Don't close the door. It will stop the
light and air for the rooms inside, and besides, everyone must get to
the fire escape in an emergency." Delora smiled. "You can use the
fire escape just like a balcony back home."

The window was open, but its white lace curtain and shade
hung limply. Lemon oil almost masked a strong odor of kerosene.
The room had two double beds. Above each bed, a large wooden
crucifix hung on the pale yellow wall. Crowded into the room were
an armoire, a straight-back wooden chair and a chiffonier. On the
chiffonier, resting on a crocheted white scarf, an etched glass tray
held two hairbrushes.

"You are fortunate, ladies. I had six women in this room, like
other rooming houses, but I cut it to four. Six are too many. You
will share this room with Elena and Giuseppina...I mean Josephine.
She doesn't like being called Giuseppina. Anyway, they are working
downstairs in the factory and will be up at nightfall." She paused
and looked around. "I guess that's all." Then, as an afterthought,
"Please feel free to go down to the kitchen and make yourself some
coffee or ask Liza to do it for you."

"When is supper?" Teresa asked.

"At sundown. We eat in two shifts. Elena and Josephine will
tell you the time." She shrugged her shoulders by way of apology.

"It's because we have so many people living here, more if Giustina spends the night."

Teresa stopped breathing. *I'm done for!*

It was Rosa who had breath left to ask, "Will she be here tonight?"

"No. I haven't seen her for over a week. She is busy in her Paterson factory."

Teresa hoped Paterson wasn't too close.

"And her son?" Rosa asked.

"Niccolo? I see him now and then. He's such a good son. He helps his mother take care of the business in both factories, so he's too busy to come upstairs."

Teresa began breathing naturally again.

Delora checked the bun at the back of her head, seeing if any of the hairpins had edged free. "I guess that is all." She took a deep breath and left the room.

When she no longer could hear Delora's retreating footsteps on the linoleum floor, Rosa said, "You are lucky, but for how long? I don't see how you can manage it. You don't look much like Violetta."

Teresa looked at herself in the mirror over the chiffonier. "I don't, do I?"

Rosa studied her for a minute. "No, but you do have her full mouth and dark almond-shaped eyes. You're taller, not as slender, and your bust is fuller. There's something else, too. I can't put my finger on it." She pondered. "I have it. Violetta was unsure of herself; not you. No, I don't think you can get away with it."

"Well, at least we have a place to sleep tonight."

Rosa shook her head. "I thought America was a big place. Why do I feel so crowded?" She examined the bedding. "It looks clean, but it smells like kerosene."

"Maybe somebody spilled some on the mattress." Teresa lifted the shade, looked out the window and peered through the fire escape's open grillwork. Clothes hung limply on several clotheslines stretching from building to building. In the courtyard there were more motionless clothes on lines held up by wooden poles. In the courtyard's center sat four outhouses. Closer to her building, scrawny grapevines seized a grape arbor. Closer still was a small garden with several rows of tomato plants. In one corner was a fig tree, and joy of joys, a mulberry tree alongside the wall!

Something scurried across the yard. Fortunata? No! "My God! Rats!"

\* \* \*

Teresa and Rosa, too tired to undress, stretched out across the bed and fell asleep. Rosa slept soundly, but Teresa thrashed about as if she were drowning, experiencing a recurring dream she'd had since she left Italy:

Her mother called to Teresa with outstretched arms. Annunziata's pleading eyes bored through Teresa. Teresa tried reaching out, but the more she reached, the farther apart they grew. A black ball of yarn in Teresa's mouth prevented her from calling. Strands of yarn took on a life of their own, wrapping themselves around her until she no longer could reach out. This time, however, the wool pricked and itched maddeningly.

She didn't know what had awakened her first, the itching or the footsteps at the door. Two young women stood looking at her. She tried jumping up but the tangle of bedclothes prevented her.

The woman with the match spoke first, "Hello, I'm Elena."

"I'm..." Teresa hesitated, perhaps a little too long, "Violetta." In her daze, she'd almost given her real name. Trying to cover her hesitation, she struggled more than she should have, untangling herself.

"I'm Josephine."

Josephine was the most beautiful woman Teresa had ever seen. Her shiny, auburn hair heaped high in the Gibson-girl fashion and dark eyes with long eyelashes were a striking contrast to her smooth, porcelain-like complexion. Her features and straight body were almost too perfect. Josephine, aware of her attributes, had carefully altered her clothing to show her body to its best advantage.

Teresa wondered how she could accomplish looking as fresh and neat as if she had just gotten dressed. As for herself, finally free of the bed sheets, she felt as if someone had dragged her through an orchard. More than that, she became maddeningly aware of her itching arms and legs.

Josephine laughed. "I see our pets have welcomed you."

Elena picked up a spray gun. "We've tried everything to get rid of them." She sprayed the air with a fine mist. Kerosene.

"Delora and her daughter, Liza, boil the sheets with strong lye soap, but nothing helps. They are in the walls. The only way to get rid of them is to tear the building down."

"I guess I'll have to share this bed with you." Barely hiding her annoyance, Josephine sat on the bed alongside Teresa.

"Rosa and I could share this one. You and..."

"No. This is *my* bed." Her abrupt answer told Teresa that the subject was closed. Josephine unlaced her high-top shoes and pulled them off. "Oh, that's so good." She plopped back on the bed, raised her skirt hip high, exposing her well-formed legs, and fanned herself with her skirt. "After twelve hours a day, six days a week, I can almost ignore the bugs."

"Almost." The angular Elena unbuttoned her blouse's top buttons to let in some air. "Please make it rain, dear Lord." She collapsed on the bed beside Rosa.

"What is Delora like?" Teresa asked.

Elena yawned, "All right, but I don't know how that spy, Liza, could be hers."

"And her husband, Rafaello?" Rosa asked.

"A good man," Elena said. "He's a tailor. He plays the clarinet and..."

"He," Josephine interrupted, "drives me crazy with that talking machine, and operas. Who cares? The hero or heroine always dies at the end. Oh, I can't stand this! God made me for better things."

Elena laughed, "The queen hates being called Giuseppina. Think that will make Nick tumble and take you out of all this? Well, you can just forget him, anyway."

"What do you mean?" Josephine propped herself up on one elbow.

"Thought that would wake you," Elena laughed. "His mother isn't going to let him get serious with anybody who's been married before, widowed or not."

"That pinch-nosed skinflint Giustina? I've a word for her tha..."

"What are your plans, ladies?" Elena interrupted.

"Find work." Teresa stretched and yawned. "But there's not much I can do." She smiled. "I can read, sketch, do sums, make Mama and the nuns angry a lot. The only practical thing I can do is some hand sewing, but I'm not good at it."

"Tell them you are," Elena stated emphatically, "and don't worry about it."

Josephine yawned again. "There are a couple of openings downstairs, but you'll have to see the *Padrone.*"

"You mean Malespina?" Teresa asked, hoping it wasn't true.

"Yes," Elena said. "Malespina and the rest of the padroni have control of the jobs."

Josephine moaned. "Malespina takes a big bite out of your wages, but there's nothing you can do about it. She shuddered. "He makes my skin crawl when he looks at me. Boy, is he jealous of his wife, Marietta! Sometimes I think the *Padrone* could kill her or the men that go into the store. He's that jealous."

"He's mean enough," Elena said, "but I can't say I blame him. Marietta's a flirt."

"Forget them," Josephine said. "Tell me, Rosa, don't you want a job, too?"

"No. I'm going to be with my husband Peppi in Vesta Vegine, to..."

"What?" Josephine and Elena sat bolt upright and made the sign of the cross.

"What's wrong with Vesta Vergine?" Rosa sat up, alarmed.

Josephine spat out, "You are looking at two West Virginia widows..."

"Widows!" Teresa and Rosa exclaimed in unison.

"Delora lost three brothers there," Josephine said. "The whole side of the mountain came down on them. They gave the widows only a hundred dollars! They said we should be grateful. They don't have to give you anything. Maybe. Still, they gave anybody who wasn't Italian more than double that."

"Stop it, Josephine!" Elena implored. "You're scaring them."

"Isn't it true, Elena?" Josephine threw her hands into the air.

"Yes, but you'll give them nightmares."

"Don't go, Rosa!" Josephine said. "You'll never come back."

# Chapter 5

The oppressive mid-afternoon heat intensified Teresa's irritation. Refusing to be enslaved by Malespina, for three days she had checked every Italian sewing shop in the area. However, a wall of greediness and collusion kept her from the work she desperately needed. She kept repeating her mother's admonitions not to lose her temper, but Liza's incessant whining didn't help pacify her.

*"Thignorina,* H-o-w m-u-c-h l-o-n-g-e-r? We are getting clothe to Five Pointh thecthion. Mama thed to keep away fro..."

"Five Points?" Teresa asked absentmindedly.

"That'th where Worth, Baxter and Park Thtreet come together, but really it'th a one thquare mile thecthon with all bad people. Goodneth, everyone knowth that."

Teresa clenched her teeth, turned around and headed north on Mulberry. *Why can't I travel alone the way men do?* Teresa sighed, "All right, we're going to the *Padrone."*

"I told you tho. Didn't I? Mama told you tho, didn't she? If you had lithened, we would have thaved a lot of time and I wouldn't be so thirthty! I want lemon ithe and..."

*Think of something else before you pull her hair.* She thought of Rosa. It seemed much longer than three days since Rosa had left for West Virginia. *Strange that we formed so close an attachment in so short a time.*

Liza's irritating voice pulled her out of her thoughts.

"You're walking too thlow."

"Here's the money." But Liza couldn't wait.

Teresa approached the entrance to Malespina's store as if entombment were awaiting her. She stopped for a moment at the open doorway, took a deep breath and entered.

A tempting aroma greeted Teresa. To her left, in front of the display counter, were barrels of cured olives. Over the counter hung cured meats: salami, mortadella, and prosciuto, interspersed with provolone and scamorzo. On the counter were huge wheels of Parmigiano and Romano cheeses. Within the display counter were fresh cheeses. Between the counter and glass bins containing an assemblage of dried beans, pastas, herbs and spices was an attractive young woman waiting on an elderly woman. Although the young woman was slender, her astonishingly large breasts bulged at the cleavage. Teresa deduced that this was Malespina's wife, Marietta.

Teresa approached Malespina, sitting at the store's rear. He yawned loudly, not bothering to cover his mouth. A frail young man sat opposite him, Doric-column rigid. Clouds of cigarette, pipe and cigar smoke floated from a room behind Malespina. She peered in. A few men sat opposite a boy, about Ernesto's age, who was chalking figures on a blackboard. They made no sense to her: ATT 126 3/8 down 1/4, BALT & OH 112 1/4; another young boy chalked words: Win, Place, Show. In one corner, a glass-domed machine spewed strips of paper into a wicker basket. In the far corner, pigeons cooed in cages.

A pigeon appeared at a transom-sized window. Teresa wondered if it were one of Ernesto's birds, then remembered he raced his birds only on Sunday. This was Wednesday. The boy chalking *Win, Place and Show* scooted to the wall, stood on a chair, and retrieved a capsule from the pigeon's leg. He placed the bird in a cage, ran to the blackboard, and wrote *The Winner, Win: Sensation @ 5 to 1.* The men roared.

Malespina tilted his chair back on its hind legs and pulled the door closed. "Marietta," he yelled to the woman behind the counter and pointed to the man opposite him. "Give *Signore* Forte, Leonardo, another glass of red wine."

"No thank you," Leonardo said without moving an inch. His deep voice resonated, belying his frail appearance. "As I said, I am a teacher, not a laborer."

"I know, *Professore,* " Malespina's sarcasm telegraphed, "but I do not need a teacher of Italian, Italian history, literature or political science."

Leonardo stiffened in defiance.

Seeing that approach wasn't working, Malespina smiled. "I suggests you take the job in West Virginia. The work will be light and easy for you. Whenever you want, you may return and I'll find work somewhere else for you, at a reasonable fee, of course."

"How far away is it?" Leonardo asked.

"Not far, only a couple of hours. You can even come home on weekends." He pushed the paper forward.

Leonardo began to read.

Malespina's eyes narrowed. "You can read English?"

"Of course, and speak it."

He snatched the paper from Leonardo. "This is just a formality."

"No matter." Leonardo was unperturbed. "I have decided not to leave the area."

*"You* have decided?" Astonished, Malespina stood abruptly. "If you don't want work, don't waste my valuable time."

Leonardo calmly picked up his black fedora from the table and rose.

Teresa was as dismayed as Malespina at Leonardo's cavalier attitude, but Malespina quickly regained his composure. His eyes took on animal cunning. "Tell me, is there anything you can do, in a practical way?"

He shrugged, "I am an experienced cutter of ladies' garments."

"Why didn't you say so? Sit." Malespina sat again. "I have an opening at Giovane and Son." He shuffled through the pile of papers on the table and pulled out another form. "Sign this paper." He glanced up at Teresa. "Are you waiting for me, *Signorina?"*

"Yes," Teresa replied crisply, omitting the polite *'signore'* form of address.

His eyes narrowed slightly. It wasn't lost on him. "Be with you shortly. Marietta, give the *Signorina* some of our best wine."

Teresa saw Marietta's eyes flash with anger at being ordered about. Nevertheless, she reached for a glass behind her. "Red or white?"

"Nothing, thank you," Teresa replied. The offer tempted her, but she didn't want to be obligated to the *Padrone.* She paid for Liza's refreshments as Liza left the store.

When the elderly woman left the store, a handsome young man entered. He took great pleasure in watching Marietta move.

Marietta smiled broadly at him.

Malespina's attention turned sharply to Marietta. Furious, he puffed on his cigar as if he were sending smoke signals. Marietta, however, paid no attention to her husband's jealousy.

Leonardo completed his transaction and turned to leave. His dark, deep-set eyes were so piercing that his well-trimmed imperial beard was almost a surprising afterthought. He was small and grasshopper-thin. His bearing displayed a strong sense of arrogance.

Malespina, without getting up, motioned Teresa to sit opposite him. She sat, glad to get off her feet even if it were opposite Malespina. He tilted his chair on its hind legs and took a nail file out of his vest pocket. Never taking his eyes off Marietta, he cleaned his fingernails. He blew smoke in Teresa's direction. His lack of consideration vexed her, but she said nothing, unwilling to say more to him than she had to.

As the young man left the store, Marietta tidied the counter. Malespina cleared his throat pointedly and gave her a savage glare, but Marietta laughed. He turned to Teresa. "What can I do for you, young lady?"

"I need work," Teresa said simply.

"I don't usually do business with a lady. Where is your father?"

"He is dead."

"I'm sorry," he said without a sign of any real sympathy. "A brother, uncle, or cousin?" Gray smoke coiled around her.

"No."

He peeked at Marietta. She wasn't paying attention. He smiled broadly at Teresa, leaned in closer and, in an oily voice, asked, "All alone, my dear?"

Teresa backed away, resenting his familiarity. "For now," she said pointedly.

"Oh, too bad." His tone was unconvincing. "What can you do, my dear?"

"I can read and write in Italian, and do numbers."

He looked surprised. "Where did you learn that?"

"The nuns," she replied curtly, wanting to add, it's none of your business.

He shook his head. "That won't help in this country. You must have *other* talents," he smiled broadly and moved in closer.

"I can sew," Teresa replied sharply and looked at Marietta.

He drew back and became all business. "Machine or hand?"

"Both," she lied.

"Good." He looked through some papers on the table. "You're lucky. I have one opening left in the Giovane and Son Clothing Factory."

Teresa winced. "Don't you have anything else?"

He eyed her suspiciously. "Why? What's wrong with the place?"

"Nothing. It's just that..."

"Listen, my girl, you should be grateful. It's the best factory in New York. The Giovanes are fair, too fair if you ask me, and they keep a clean place."

From what she had seen through the window, it seemed clean. Conditions elsewhere were disgustingly filthy. The workers tossed garments to each other or over their heads to bins without bothering to see if they hit their mark. She hadn't seen any of that through Giovane's window. In other factories, she had seen a sign that read in Italian, *"If You Don't Come In On Sunday, Don't Come In On Monday."* Elena and Josephine got Sundays off.

Malespina got up.

Although she felt manipulated, Teresa said, "All right." *Maybe I can avoid meeting either Giustina or Niccolo for a while.*

"Good." He sat again. "Of course I can't do it without a fee." He smiled. His eyes narrowed, "But since you are such a beautiful young girl and all alone in the city, I won't charge you much." Malespina lowered his voice and leaned in closely. "This is our little secret."

As she expected, it was less than Leonardo's, but equal to Elena's and Josephine's.

\* \* \*

It was late afternoon when Teresa left Giovane's, but no cooler. Still, she felt thankful she hadn't encountered either Niccolo or Giustina. When she could, she'd get away, but the money she was going to get wouldn't take her very far. Suddenly she thought, *What if all America is like this, crowded and ugly?* She shuddered. *I'll face that, too, when the time comes.*

Teresa entered her stifling bedroom, climbed onto the fire escape and sat on the metal landing. In the relative quiet from the street noise, it would almost have been pleasant sitting there, except for the oppressive heat and humidity. Blessedly, a breeze blew in from the east, bringing the promise of rain, dispelling her pessimistic thoughts. She smiled to herself. *I'm such a fool, always thinking the worst. I should be happy. I have a job, I'm not going to Rocco and I haven't met either Niccolo or Giustina.*

She untied the laces on her high-top shoes, pulled them off and rubbed her aching feet. At first, Violetta's shoes had seemed to fit better than her mother's, but now they pinched as badly. Teresa hugged her knees and rested her head on them. *Thank God, peace at last.*

*"Thignorina,"* Liza's irritating voice inside the bedroom almost made Teresa scream. "You have a vithitor downthairth."

Near panic set in. "A visitor? Who?"

"Nick Giovane."

# Chapter 6

Rosa was the only woman among the sixty men in the three railroad cars. Too frightened to look at the twenty men in her railroad car, she clung to the basket on her lap and the bundle between her feet.

Until now, refusing Peppi's summons had never crossed her mind, but on the second day—traveling, frightened, gritty, tired and hungry—she felt like bolting. The locomotive's soot smarted her eyes and she tired of focusing on the scenery. Mile after mile of rugged mountains and valleys thick with forests and sun-drenched lakes drifted by. Endless. Overwhelming. She saw no beauty in the landscape, only frightening remoteness. She closed her eyes, but Elena and Josephine's terrifying accounts loomed larger until she almost panicked.

*Stop it! You are only tired and hungry,* she consoled herself. Delora had packed a basket with provalone, salami, coffee beans, wine and water, but Rosa couldn't eat in front of the men who had nothing. Despite her fears she felt compassion, so she withstood her hunger pangs and thirst.

When she thought she could no longer endure, the train stopped at a ramshackle hut on a wooden platform. Her tension spiraled when she saw a dozen armed men standing upon the platform. A man dressed in black from his derby to his shiny boots stepped forward. His tin star flashed in the sunlight. "All right," he said, in Neopolitan, "you wops! Get your asses off that train!"

Rosa struggled with her possessions as she disembarked.

"Mother Jones on board?" the man with the star asked a man who had been on the train.

"Nope, Sheriff," he replied gruffly. "Maybe we done scared the ol' bitch."

"Not that one," the sheriff said. "Probably on the next train, but I'll be ready for the old hag. You can bet your sweet ass!"

A black man on a speckled mare rode out of the woods.

"Hey, Sherman," the sheriff called to the man on horseback. "Take these wops to camp. Me and the boys'll wait for Mother Jones."

"Yesah, boss."

This was the first time Rosa had seen a black man. "Is he an Indian?" she asked a young man who had been on the train.

"No," he replied, "he's an *Africano.*"

Rosa and the workers followed the man on horseback along a spur in the tracks. Lush tree branches and vines formed a canopy overhead, closing out all but a few darting specks of sunlight. Thick vines spread from tree to tree, but none were grapevines, none of the trees, olive. *What do they drink with their meals? What do they cook with and use for ointments and lotions?*

Still it felt good to walk following the long train ride, and she was grateful for the clean, fresh air. However, another annoyance replaced New York City street noises, countless screeching insects and chirping birds. Their shrill calls became a torment. Apart from the gray squirrels and the chipmunks that scurried away with their approach, the only other signs of life were mosquitoes, gnats, and mayflies, thousands of them. Swatting them was useless. After about a mile of carting her belongings and food basket, she couldn't avoid dragging her bundle.

"Let me help." The young man's voice had a singer's rich timbre. He swung his mandolin over one shoulder and hoisted her bundle onto the other.

"Thank you. You're a Godsend." She guessed he was about twenty-one, maybe twenty-two years old. He was not as massive nor as strong as Peppi, not that he was a weakling; far from it, for he carried both her bundle and his suitcase without effort. He was taller, slimmer, and suppler than Peppi. His blond, wavy hair, olive complexion and smiling blue eyes made him far handsomer.

"I'm Francesco Santucci." Something comforting in his tone and smiling face helped relieve her anxiety. What's more, he radiated an excitement, a joy for life, that was compelling.

"I'm Rosa Piacenza."

"Why are you here?"

"I'm going to join my husband. And you?"

"The *Padrone* said they had some book work for me. I hope so. I've never done any hard labor."

"What did you do in Italy?" Rosa couldn't imagine Francesco doing hard labor. His bearing and Tuscan dialect marked him as a refined intellectual. She was happy that she had adjusted her ear to Teresa's speaking it.

"I was a student at the University of Bologna studying to become a surgeon, but unfortunately I was only able to complete one year."

Her eyes widened with astonishment. "Why did you come to America?"

His tone became somber. "My family lost everything in the crop failures. Our land had been in the family for many generations." His eyes darkened. "Even worse, my father and mother died in the epidemic."

"Oh, I'm sorry. May God rest their souls." Rosa made the sign of the cross.

"My father grieved because it was under his guardianship that our land was lost. But that's the past." He brightened. "People say that America is a land of opportunity. So, some day I will be a surgeon. I'm sure of it. And you, where are you from?"

"Pozzuoli, not far from the *Campi Flegrie* and the *Solfatara* volcano." She believed the legend that no bird could fly across the area and live because of the poisonous sulfurous vapors.

His eyes widened. He'd always wanted to visit the *Campi Flegrei*. It was one of the world's most geologically unstable areas. The poet, Virgil, had called the area the entrance to Hell. Francesco, although in America for a short time, had learned some English. He searched for the translation of *Campi Flegrei. Fiery Fields, yes, that's it. Fiery Fields.*

"Look," Rosa pointed. "Is that another train ahead?"

He squinted. "No. It's not on the tracks."

As they approached, she saw four grimy boxcars sitting on the tracks' northern side. South of the tracks, in a bowl, stretched a sunlit clearing worn smooth by countless feet. At the bowl's southern edge stood a large, freshly-painted green bungalow. Spotless windows ran along the veranda circling the bungalow. To the bungalow's left were a few vertically framed wooden shacks half the bungalow's size. Deep half-circle grooves on each rotting porch-floor marked the doors' paths. All the shacks listed to the side. Rosa, having lived in thick masonry walls all her life, assumed these shacks were for livestock.

West of the clearing, barely visible, was what looked like a denuded mountain on fire. Slag. For one frightening instant she was in the Fiery Fields with its natural steam vents and sulfur gasses. The wind gathered the black smoke in a spiral and swooped down upon her, gagging her. Blessedly, the wind changed direction, carrying the smoke away.

When the smoke cleared, she saw, south of the clearing, a Gatling gun on a ridge. Surrounding the clearing, a half dozen black men on foot stood guard, each armed with a Winchester rifle and a German shepherd. It was all the guards could do to restrain the frenzied dogs, eager to attack the arrivals.

The bungalow's front door opened. A barrel-chested white man strutted out to the veranda. He stamped his feet, kicking black dust over his brown boots. "Shut the hell up!" he shouted at the dogs. The dogs obeyed. He cleared his throat and spat on the ground. "How many we got?"

"Sixty, Boss," Sherman said, "and one woman."

"A whore." His voice was as cold as his eyes. Although he hiked up his trousers, the gun's weight kept them hanging beneath his protruding stomach. "I'm Big Mike," he shouted in the Neapolitan dialect. "You wops are here to work. No excuses, pissin', moanin', or leanin' on the shovel."

"Why all the guns?" Francesco asked.

"To see that you wops finish your two-year contract and..."

"Two years?" A cry of disbelief went up.

Big Mike took the gun out of his holster and fired it into the air. The report ricocheted off the mountains, scurrying screaming birds from the trees. Again, the dogs started barking. "Shut up!" he yelled. They obeyed, but whined their displeasure. "You signed a paper!"

The men stood in shocked silence.

Big Mike pointed with his thumb to a cabin. "These are all full, see? So we have sometin' very cozy for you." He gestured with his chin to the boxcars and laughed. "You're lucky you're not livin' in a wooden lean-to. This past winter, a couple of them up north blew over and killed every wop inside." Big Mike laughed until he began coughing.

*The poor men,* Rosa thought. Then fear attacked her. *Will I have to live in a boxcar? No. Peppi said he lived in a real house.* Still, her heart raced.

Mike finally caught his breath. "Okay, line up in twos! Sherman, hand 'em out." Sherman began handing out square-foot rags with numbers stamped on them. "You'll find needles and threads in them boxcars. Sew them on the back of your shirts. From now on, you'll answer to those numbers. Got it? I..."

The dogs began barking again, this time at something in the woods. As if in answer, came distant bloodhound yelps. Rosa strained to see what was approaching. All she could see was a man on horseback accompanied by several yelping bloodhounds. He was towing something from a rope tied to his saddle horn. *An animal? No. Mama mia, they are dragging a man through the thickets!*

The man on horseback stopped in the middle of the clearing. Like a wounded animal, the dragged man curled himself into a ball on the ground. His moans were so pathetic, Rosa started to go to his aid, but Francesco held her back. He shook his head no, pity clearly expressed in his eyes, too.

"Shut up!" Mike bellowed at the dogs. Again they submitted. "Good work, Randolph!" He yelled to the man on horseback. Then he turned to the new arrivals. "This is what happens to runaways. Gone for a week, but we caught him." His face turned even colder. "Nobody gets away. Remember that! Hey, Sherman, Randolph, put the wop in the shed."

Sherman and Randolph dragged the prostrate man to a shed near the edge of the clearing and threw him in. They secured the door with a rusty hasp and inserted a stick for a lock.

Big Mike descended the porch steps, divided the men into three groups of twenty and designated which boxcar they were to occupy. When he got to Francesco, he stopped and scowled. "Who the hell are you?"

"Francesco Santucci. The..."

"Wrong!" He looked at the number in Francesco's hand. "One-fifty-seven. Can't you read?"

"Of course. I have been to the University of Bologna, in Italy, studying to become a surgeon. The..."

"Eyetalian University? That doesn't mean shit in this country."

Undaunted, Francesco tried again. "The *Padrone* told me you had light work for me."

"Sure. Let's see you lift that light rock." He pointed to a rock three and a half feet in diameter. "Operate on that, Doctor!"

"Impossible."

"We don't use that word 'round here. Down!"

Francesco went down on his knees and strained, but couldn't budge it.

Mike laughed. "Try harder, you weaklin'! "He lifted his foot and stomped on Francesco's hand.

"Ohhhh. My hand!"

"Shut up, One-fifty-seven! Let that be a lesson to all you wops. I tell you what to do and when to do it. Get up, you bastard. Next time, I won't be so easy on you."

Francesco got up and tried to rub the pain from his broken hand.

Big Mike turned to Rosa. "Who the hell are you?"

"I am Rosa Piacenza, Peppi's wife."

He scowled. "Oh, that troublemaker, Forty-three. He's billeted in that there cabin." He pointed to the cabin closest to the clearing.

"Thank you, *Signore.*" She curtsied, grateful she didn't have to live in a boxcar.

Without acknowledging her curtsy, Big Mike entered his bungalow. Inside, a woman squealed with pleasure.

When Rosa opened her cabin door, an overwhelming mildew and body odor stench assaulted her. She stood aside for a moment, trying not to breathe. When the fresh air didn't dispel the odor, she held a handkerchief to her nose and reluctantly entered. Once her eyes adjusted to the darkness, she was sorry they had.

There were two rooms. In the center of the first room was a table, or rather, two stacks of upraised crates with two wide planks on top. Old newspapers covered the planks. Flies buzzed and crawled around the newspaper, searching for food scraps. Around the table, six upraised wooden crates passed for chairs. On the wall beside the door, six nails held six grimy jackets, so filthy she couldn't identify their color. In the corner was a potbellied stove. Black soot clung to the ceiling, walls and floor.

A doorway, minus a door, led to the back room. Two rickety beds almost filled the room. They had no mattresses, sheets or springs, only boards. Overwhelmed with despair, she collapsed in a heap on the bed's edge and sobbed.

"B-a-a-a-r-r-r-o-o-m!" An explosion shook the shack, flinging her to the floor.

Black dust dislodged from the walls filled the room, nearly choking her. The *Solfatara Volcano!* She ran out of the cabin and onto the porch. She wasn't the only one startled. All the men who had arrived with her were standing in the clearing.

"Don't worry, *Signora* Piacenza." Francesco, still rubbing his aching hand, called to her. "It's only the miners."

*"Signora* Piacenza!" A woman called to Rose from the next shack. "Welcome! I've heard so much about you from Peppi. I'm Concetina Grosso."

"Oh, thank God!" Elated, Rosa ran to the woman and embraced her as if she were afraid the woman would disappear. "I was afraid I was the only woman here." She wiped the tears from her eyes.

"No. We have five other women in camp. Six, if you want to count Anna." She rolled her eyes. "That one spends more time in Big Mike's bungalow than he does, but let's not talk about her."

A woman came out of Mike's bungalow, reinserted a few hairpins into the bun at the back of her head and straightened her skirt.

"That is Anna," Concetina tossed her head as she ushered Rosa into her shack.

Rosa wished she had taken a better look at Anna, but for now she occupied herself with comparing this cabin with hers. Although the shack was identical to hers, there were no foul odors. Replacing them was the welcoming aroma of tomato sauce simmering in a large pot on the potbellied stove. The shack was spotless. Concetina had covered the upright crates with flour-sacks. Although she had washed the sacks, the company's name and trademark, an eagle with stars, were still plainly visible. Hanging beside the door, Rosa saw six clean plaid jackets.

"Make yourself comfortable." Concetina motioned to a vertical crate. "You are having supper with us tonight."

When she saw the freshly made pasta on the scrubbed table, Rosa's eyes glowed with anticipation, but overriding her hunger was her concern for the man in the shed. "What is going to happen to that poor man?"

"No one seems to know. Some say they will kill him and bury him in the woods. Some say that they will whip him, wash him in brine and drag him off to jail."

*"Madonna mia!* Can't we do something to help him?"

"Believe me, if Mike catches anyone helping, they will get the same, or worse. So, don't try." Concetina took the pasta strands from the table and hung them along with others already drying on a pole that extended from one crate to another.

"Are there mostly Neapolitans here?"

"Just in this section. They separate Italians according to what part of Italy they are from. You know, Neapolitans here, Sicilians there, and so on. They also separate non-Italians, Irish, Polish, and so on. They say it is to keep the men from fighting, but I say it's so they can't organize."

"How can you stand this awful place?"

Concetina leaned in closely and lowered her voice. "My dear, you haven't seen the worst yet. There is going to be a strike."

"A what?"

"Of course you don't know. You just came from Italy. Everybody refuses to work." She removed the sauce from the stove and placed it on a vertical crate sitting beside the stove.

"Refuses to work?" Rosa had never heard of such a thing.

"You see, they pay the men less than half the money the *Padrone* promised. Out of that, they must pay for these shacks, the bosses, the *Padrone,* the railroad fare, their picks and shovels and for having them sharpened. Your husband even has to pay for the dynamite he uses."

Rosa's eyes widened. "Then he does work with dynamite!"

"Yes. He's good at it, or they would have gotten rid of him, because they suspect he is a troublemaker."

"Peppi? He was always so quiet back home."

Concetina shrugged again. "This is America."

"Why do the men pay the *Padrone?* After all, he lied."

"If they don't, there is no work. They come to America penniless and can't speak the language. The officials, to break the padroni system, ask them if they have signed a contract to a *padrone.* The men have to say they are without papers. If they say yes, the officials tell them their papers are not in order and deport them. Some say that is why they call us w.o.p.s."

"Is that what it means?"

"I'm not sure. Some say yes, some say no, but whatever it is, it's not meant kindly. You see," Concetina continued without a break in her cooking, "the padroni and bosses work together."

"They are treating the men like slaves."

"That's why the strike. What the bosses suspect is true. Peppi and my husband, Ubaldo, are leaders. Mother Jones is going to help us like she has helped miners all over the country." Then, as if she could read Rosa's mind she said, "When the *Padrone* told Peppi about this place, it sounded so wonderful that he sent for you. After he found out, the poor man wanted to write to you not to come, but no one here could write. The same thing happened to me."

"Was it the same for Anna?"

Concetina shook her head. "No, her husband knew. He brought her here for the men."

"What?" Rosa uttered an indrawn gasp. "She went along with it?"

"You'll see for yourself. She has taken another man since someone killed her husband. This other man has sent for another woman. I thought it was you. That's why I didn't speak to you at first."

"ME?" A shock ran though her.

"I realized my mistake when I heard your name. This other man, Rocco, tried to get me to do it, too."

"Rocco?"

"Rocco Martello. I thought you were Teresa Martello."

"Teresa!" Rosa stood up. "That scoundrel! How could he?" It was as if she had taken maternal custody of Teresa. She raised her voice more than she had intended. "I know," she bit her lip, "that is, I knew Teresa. A fine young lady!"

"Shhh. The men should be coming home soon. Please," Concetina cautioned, "don't say anything about the strike whenever you are around Rocco. We can't trust him."

*"Mama mia!"* Rosa looked up as if an escape plan could be found written on the ceiling.

Concetina softened her voice, too. "It could be worse. You could be living with twenty men in those vermin infested railroad cars."

"How many live here?"

"The same as yours, six."

"WHAT?" She stood up abruptly. "I'll be living with six men?"

\* \* \*

Although the trip had thoroughly exhausted Rosa, she couldn't sleep soundly. Peppi, however, was sleeping quietly beside her. The men coughed and wheezed so much, she wondered how she had slept at all. Still, Rosa was grateful that Peppi had removed one bed from the room so that they could have this room to themselves. Although the dispossessed men weren't happy about sharing one bed and the floor, they said nothing.

As she lay in the darkness, adjusting to the idea of getting up and starting breakfast, she reflected on her meeting Peppi the evening before. He had greeted her with a rare show of tears and begged for forgiveness for having brought her to West Virginia. She had tried to reassure him that things would be fine, but in their hearts they knew it wouldn't.

She sighed, lit the hurricane lamp, got dressed, and pushed aside the flour-bag curtain that Peppi had nailed up in the doorway. Carefully, she made her way around the men and looked through a provision box on the floor. *Only cornmeal? It's polenta, then.*

After the men had breakfast, she stood on the porch and watched them quietly make their way to the mine. They swung their hand-held lamps, forming a ghostlike river of light in a sea of darkness and disappeared into the woods.

Rosa reentered the shack and began mentally listing things she must do that day.

"B-a-a-a-r-r-o-o-m!" The shack and ground shook. Dust. "B-a-a-a-r-r-o-o-m!" More dust. She screamed with each blast, but there was no place to hide.

\* \* \*

When the committeemen heard that the sheriff had whisked Mother Jones off to jail, they knew they had to call a meeting. However, they needed a cover to keep Big Mike, the guards and spies occupied. They decided to have a party and sent a delegation to invite Big Mike.

He laughed. "I don't go to no party with wops. Besides, I need no invite. I go where I want."

On the evening of the party, a bright moon and oil lamps hanging on poles illuminated the area. Millions of shimmering fireflies brought their magical aura, transcending the blighted conditions. Even the boards placed on the ground, serving as a dance floor and a makeshift platform, glowed in the light. The platform supported the band that included both workers and guards. It surprised Rosa how well a concertina, a guitar, a mandolin, two harmonicas, and an empty gallon jug for bass notes could sound. Francesco, unable to play his mandolin with his swollen bandaged hand, sang.

It was the first time the women and miners had enjoyed themselves since they had left Italy. They danced almost with abandon, trying to release their anxieties.

Even Peppi appeared content. After dancing with Rosa, he swept her onto the platform. "Sing for me, Rosa," he pleaded.

"No," she protested, refusing to let go of his hands. "Don't ask me."

"Please, for me."

Rosa was going to continue to object, but the look in his eyes stopped her. She released his hands and stood up. "All right." She turned to Francesco and the man playing the concertina. "Do you know 'You Who Do Not Weep'?"

They nodded yes.

If Rosa had been back home, she would have had no qualms, but in front of so many strangers, her contralto voice refused to obey. Soon, however, the music and words carried her away. She closed her eyes and yielded to the conscious longing for home and the unconscious longing for a passion she had never known. Her warm, sensual tones sprang from the deep recesses of her soul, almost frightening her. She opened her eyes and stared into space:

"You who weep not, while you make me weep,
Where are you tonight? I need you..."

To whom she sang she didn't know, but why Peppi had made her sing was evident. As she looked about her, she saw that everyone in the clearing had stopped whatever they were doing to listen. The only people missing were Big Mike, Rocco and Anna. Big Mike, she knew, was in his bungalow. As for Rocco and Anna, she could only guess that they were at it again. While she sang, she saw Peppi and the committeemen slip quietly away.

Big Mike emerged from his bungalow, leaned against the porch rail and stared at her. Her flesh crawled. She closed her eyes, trying to shake the feeling and allow the music to carry her away. Francesco, unable to resist, joined in. Their voices pulsed and entwined as if they were lovers. Again the sensation that took possession of her was unsettling.

When they finished singing, Francesco jumped down and helped her down.

"Dance with me."

Rosa was about to say, "Let me ask Peppi," but caught herself in time; better for her to draw attention to herself rather than Peppi.

Francesco took her hand and they began dancing, a proper distance apart. She didn't have any difficulty pretending she was enjoying herself. Francesco's gaze evoked the emotions she had felt when they sang. Each beat of the music thrilled her and throbbed throughout her body. This completely new, delicious feeling was too wonderful to dismiss. She allowed it to grow within her and spur her laughter.

Her laughter thrilled Francesco and suppressed his pain and fears.

The music and laughter of the camp reaching Concetina's darkened shack contrasted sharply with the mood inside. Only the pale light from the moon illuminated the men's ghost-like faces. A shiver crept down Peppi's spine. Succumbing to such forebodings annoyed him. His exasperation with himself, the imbroglio he had gotten himself into, and the men's obstinacy hung in the darkness. "We are committed."

"But we don't have Mother Jones," the cook insisted.

"Do we have to hide behind an eighty-year-old woman's skirts?" Ubaldo challenged impatiently.

Peppi could barely contain his annoyance at Ubaldo's attitude. "She is not just any woman. She is a symbol the men respect."

"Whatever she is, we don't have her." Ubaldo curled his fingers into a fist. "We only have each other and some weapons."

"Weapons?" the cook laughed. "Like what? Stones and shovels?"

"Rifles," Ubaldo assured them. "Not many, just four. Someone sneaked them in."

"Four rifles and dynamite," Peppi added almost casually.

"Dynamite!" The men could barely keep their voices down with this discovery.

"Shhh," Peppi commanded. "I heard something." They listened.

"I don't hear anything," Ubaldo said. "You're getting jumpy. Tell me, how did you get the dynamite? They check you out at the end of each day."

Peppi laughed. "It was easy. One day when I went to the privy, I rubbed some of my waste around it and stuck it in my pants. They wouldn't come near me."

They all laughed.

"Where is it?" Ubaldo asked.

"Under this shack."

"What?" Ubaldo raised his shocked voice inadvertently.

"Don't worry," Peppi laughed. "It's safe without the detonator. I hid the dynamite here in case they searched my shack. That's where they'd look."

"Shhh," Ubaldo put his finger on his lips. "I think I heard something, too."

They listened, but all they could hear was the music.

"Now who's getting jumpy?" Peppi asked. He Got up, looked through the window and smiled at the sight of Rosa whirling around the dance floor. *At least she found something to be happy about in the mess I dragged her into.*

Rosa couldn't remember when she had felt so happy. Francesco's attentions made her feel desirable for the first time. She sighed, almost regretting that she must go back to Peppi. *Dear sweet Peppi, but not affectionate Peppi.*

"Barrrrooooom!" The explosion lit up the night sky.

Everyone ran in the direction of the explosion; everyone but Rosa. She remained paralyzed. Even Concetina's screaming didn't mobilize her. Rosa knew beyond any doubt that no one in the shack could have survived. Guilt assailed her, as if she had willed his death. *"Dio mio!"* she cried, and sank to her knees.

# Chapter 7

Teresa's heart beat wildly with dread. She squared her shoulders and entered the dimly lit sitting room. Nick stood looking out the bay window. Even in her nervous state, she marveled at how tall he was and how broad his shoulders. For the first time she didn't feel like an Amazon.

*Who is he talking to? Liza?* She looked around the room. *No. Thank God. She isn't here to tattle.* When he turned, to her amazement, she saw he was talking to Fortunata, tucked contentedly in his strong arms. Although he held the cat tenderly, Teresa could feel his surging power across the room.

"Good afternoon." His deep voice at once thrilled and frightened her. "I'm Nick Giovane." He tilted his head to one side, "Violetta?"

Teresa shifted uneasily. *Maybe he can't see me clearly in this light.* She avoided answering directly. "Please sit?" She gestured toward the easy chair that received the strongest light in the room.

Still holding Fortunata, he sat and stretched his long legs out in front of him. The light from the window intensified his good looks. Teresa caught her breath. He was even handsomer than his photograph. She sat on the settee opposite him, praying that the backlighting would obscure her face.

The silence amplified the incessant clock's ticking on the fireplace mantel and Fortunata's purring. A passing cloud darkened the room as large raindrops splashed against the windowpane. She heard Liza rushing to the back porch and almost immediately the clothesline pulleys creaked. Teresa closed the bay windows and returned to her seat.

Both spoke at once.

"You first," he said.

"All I was going to say was that Fortunata likes you. It's unusual."

He smiled. "That someone or something would like me?"

She laughed nervously. "No. What I meant was that even Delora can't touch her." Her voice trailed off.

*Damn it! Why in hell did Mama get me into this mess? The last thing I want is to get involved with a greenhorn clinging vine. How the hell can I duck out?*

The staccato beating of the raindrops quickened as the wind kicked up.

"I'm sorry Mama and I weren't here to greet you. Of course, the ship was several days late."

"Heavy seas and storms delayed us."

"I'm sorry. It must have been difficult."

"Very."

"Did Mama send you enough money for the passage?"

"Yes. Enough for steerage." She couldn't resist expressing her displeasure and pricking at that self-assured presence.

"Steerage?" His brows knitted. "I'm sorry. I didn't know."

She regretted saying it. Teresa looked down at her feet and searched for something to say. "You own the factory downstairs?" *You idiot. If he didn't, would he have his name on the front?*

"Not really. It's my mother's, but I guess you can say that, and a factory in Paterson, New Jersey. Do you know where that is?"

"No."

"It's in an adjoining state west of here. I guess in Italy they call it a province. That's where we've been for the past few weeks, catching up on our work and putting our new house in Totowa in shape." He hesitated. "Someday I'll take you there." *Why the hell did I say that? I'm not going to.*

Silence.

The rain cascaded in sheets on the windowpanes but didn't clear the air. Instead, the heat seemingly forced its way through the walls and hung in the room.

"I'm sorry, Violetta, but I can't...my Italian isn't very good."

"It's excellent." *That's not what he was going to say. What was it?*

"I've never been to Italy. It must be very beautiful."

"Yes, but you can't eat beauty."

"Things are difficult there?"

"Very."

"I'm sorry." *Why did I say that? It's not my fault.*

She shrugged, then as if she knew his thoughts, "It's not your fault."

Silence.

He felt he must fill the void with something. "Taking care of both factories and boning up is time-consuming."

"Boning up?"

"An American colloquial expression. It means studying extra hard. I'm trying to get into college and it doesn't give me much time for, ah, socializing."

She thought he emphasized socializing a bit too much.

He placed Fortunata down and got up. "Do you mind if I light the lamp?" Before she could answer he strode to the sideboard, lit the lamp and brought it close to her face. Their eyes met for the first time. He saw something flickering far back in those bright, intelligent eyes, a sort of reserve he couldn't place. "You aren't at all what I expected."

She tensed. "Not what you expected?"

"Different from the picture Mama showed me." He stared at her for what seemed forever, penetrating her soul. "Of course, the picture wasn't very good. Still..."

"I'm sorry you are disappointed." Why was she annoyed?

"On the contrary. You're very lovely." He deliberated, "Yes, very." *Those eyes look bright, but she's probably cloddish as they come.*

She blushed and looked away.

He returned the lamp to the sideboard. "Do you need money, or anything?"

"No, thank you. They hired me in your factory today."

"Good." He paused and looked at her.

She felt that he was struggling with something that needed saying.

Nick looked out the window for a moment, then returned to face her squarely.

She couldn't hide her nervousness.

A blinding lightning bolt illuminated the room, followed almost immediately by a crack of thunder.

Teresa recoiled.

"Don't be afraid of me."

"It wasn't you. The thunder startled me."

"That's not what I mean." *Oh, what the hell. Here goes.* He jumped in before he lost his nerve. "It was Mama who arranged the engagement, not m...that is, this is America. Things are done differently here. We don't have to get married simply because our parents want us to." He saw the relief on her face. "I thought so. I'm not what you expected, either."

"No," she said truthfully.

Why did that bother him? "Think of me as a...brother, or cousin, or friend. I'll never abandon you."

The room stopped shaking beneath her. This was more than she could have hoped for. At last she felt free, in control of her own fate!

"You are very quiet. Have you nothing to say?"

"I don't know what to say, except, thank you, Niccolo."

"Nick, please. Only Mama, Delora and Rafaello call me Niccolo."

"Very well, Nick. I am not ready for marriage."

"Neither am I. They arrange these things without our consent, don't they? It is not that I don't find you attractive. You are."

She blushed.

He looked at her again. Yes, she was. Not at all like one of those squat greenhorns. More like the women he was used to at school; tall, slender, and self-assured. "It's just that marriage is not for me." He smiled. "You should be happy. I'm not much of a catch."

"Catch?" Again he had used the English expression.

"No bonanza." He made a move as if to leave.

A lock of hair edged its way down his brow. She wanted to reach up and push it back and, for some reason, she wanted him to stay. To keep him from leaving, she asked, "What is it you wish to study in college?"

Nick turned, surprised that he wanted to stay. He sat in the overstuffed chair. "Engineering, although flight intrigues me."

"Flight? You mean aeroplanes?"

"Yes." She surprised him. "You've heard of them?"

"Of course." She felt insulted. "I may be from a small town, but I'm still on this planet."

"Sorry. I didn't mean that."

Again she felt sorry she'd sounded curt. "Still," she added quickly to hide her embarrassment, "the idea frightens me. It's so dangerous. I know that most new things are considered to have an element of danger, but flight has more than just an element."

"Perhaps that's part of the fascination. That and speed. I'm impatient with delay. Someday, perhaps, flying can save days. Maybe it's escape. At least, that's what my buddy, Bob, says. I don't know. Bob's thinking of going to England." Nick became animated. "He has some connections that can help." He colored at the idea of using pull instead of merit to get what he wanted.

Teresa sensed his excitement about flying and wasn't too sure she liked it. "How does your mother feel about flying?"

He laughed. "I haven't discussed it with her, but I can guess." He laughed again. "She'd say that it's just like me to keep my head in the clouds. She wants me to study law, or accounting." Nick shook his head. "Maybe she's right. A person can't get anywhere in this world without knowing the law."

"I don't trust the law. In Italy, everyone points to the statue of justice on the courthouse roof and says that's why you can't find justice inside. People say that in America there is justice." She shrugged. "At least, there's always hope."

"Yes, but it's difficult getting into college."

"I don't understand. Aren't your grades good enough?"

"On the contrary. I was class valedictorian, you know, tops in my class."

"Then, why?"

"They don't admit Italian-Americans to Columbia University."

"I'm sorry. That would bother me. However, you aren't poor. You have two factories and a home of your own. Why would you want more?"

He smiled. "They're Mama's. Besides, it's not as much as you think. Many people take their cut. Then people are always trying to stop us, or take it away."

"Even in this country?"

Nick nodded. "Maybe that's why Mama says to study law."

"I believe you should do whatever you want and not what someone else tells you. After all, you cannot live someone else's life, nor can they, yours."

\* \* \*

Teresa watched the dancing sewing machine needle closely to keep it from striking her fingers. *I'm going to die of boredom.* She glanced at the people in the tight quarters, all intent on their work, and smiled to herself. *I don't think anyone would notice.* Along with the monotony, she struggled with her discomfort. In the heat and humidity, the woolen lint found its pinching way into almost every part of her body.

Initially, the room had appeared spotless, but now that she had time to study it she could see that the white walls needed painting. The sculptured geometric patterns in the metal ceiling, once white, were outlined gray by the obsolete gas-jets' fumes. Clear, glaring, unsheathed light bulbs hanging from electric wires in the room's center were harsh, but still inadequate. The three dozen men and women crowded into three rows seemed dull and in need of illumination. They bobbed feverishly back and forth as they treadled, completely oblivious of her. That's what she thought, until the man beside her pulled an unfinished garment away from her.

"Give me a chance!" she said to him.

"Hurry up!" he commanded. "It's piece work. Every minute counts."

Teresa looked up as Nick passed by her. It was the fifth time he had passed her and for the fifth time ignored her. True, he was busy fixing the machines, but still, why ignore her? It infuriated her. Yet, she wasn't interested in him, so why should it? For another thing, why hadn't he introduced her to his mother? Giustina was in her office, at least that's what everyone said, although Teresa hadn't seen her. Teresa studied the translucent glass on the office door at the rear of the room; not even a shadow. Hadn't he told his mother she was here? If so, why didn't Giustina ask to see her?

The lunch bell rang. The machines stopped abruptly.

"Violetta!" Elena called. "Wait for me."

Teresa waited as the others finished punching out at the time clock.

"You're a sly one."

"What are you talking about?"

"Nick, of course. He's interested in you."

Teresa's mouth fell open in amazement. "Why, he doesn't even look at me."

"That's what you think. He must have circled your machine a dozen times this morning. Josephine has noticed it, too, and she doesn't like it. You should have seen the evil eye she's been giving you!"

"What nerve!" Teresa raised her voice a notch or two. "You can tell Josephine she can have him for all I care!"

"Whoa! I'm just telling you what she said. Josephine could be trouble for you if she sets her mind to it."

"What do you mean?"

"Josephine says you're putting on airs by speaking Tuscan and reading. She says it doesn't make you any better than us. You're just an immigrant too.'"

Teresa's eyes narrowed. Somehow she didn't feel like an immigrant.

Elena continued as if it were she who wanted the explanation. "Then there's church, for instance."

"I don't understand. I've been to church every Sunday."

"But not confession. She wonders why."

Teresa knitted her brows. How could she go? She'd have to confess her false identity, and Rocco. She knew she couldn't lie to the priest. Still, she must go with them this afternoon.

"Then there's the way you don't always answer to your name as if you don't know it. I told her that you are preoccupied. Josephine said, 'What could preoccupy a young girl that much?'"

"Tell Josephine to mind her business." Although she liked Elena, she wanted to say the same thing to her.

* * *

After lunch, Nick smiled broadly at Teresa in excited anticipation. "I added a small electric motor to your machine. It's an experiment. Do you mind?"

"Not at all." She looked at him blankly. All she could think of were Elena's words, "He is interested in you," and "It's as if you don't know your own name." For some reason, "He's interested in you," troubled her more.

"Be careful. It'll move very fast. Press on this lever." He pointed to a lever beside her knee, too flustered to say knee.

*Now I know why he was hovering around. It was my machine!* Slightly irritated at the thought, she sat and pushed it too much. The machine roared. The needle blurred.

"Try it again, less pressure this time. That's it!" He smiled. "I knew you'd be the one who could do it."

In no time she sewed so rapidly that the others crowded around her.

"Put one on my machine," a woman requested.

"Mine too," another said.

Then everyone clamored for the motors.

"Wait!" Nick protested. "It's just an experiment; besides, I don't have enough motors to go around. Be patient." He smiled and strode into the office.

Teresa watched the needle carefully, but as time progressed, she became careless. Like a shot, the needle pierced her thumb. She screamed, more from shock than from pain, for the needle had entered too quickly to be painful. The needle, separated from the machine, remained in her thumb. Teresa stared at her thumb. *No blood?* It surprised her.

Nick, hearing her scream, was by her side in an instant. His face was ashen with anxiety.

He took her hand in his to examine it.

A thrill ran though her and surprised her almost as much as the needle had.

"It's all right." He breathed easier. "The needle missed the bone." Without releasing her hand he led her into the office.

Giustina looked up from her desk. Teresa wondered how the angular woman had gotten past her without being seen, for the room had no other doors. A poorly applied patch of white plaster on the back wall and a transom marked the spot where a door had been. Wooden filing cabinets formed a wall behind Giustina. Opposite her desk was another desk at which Nick apparently worked. Alongside the door stood a table that once housed a treadle sewing machine. It now held a typewriter.

Giustina could see Nick's flushed face, "Well?"

"A needle in the finger."

Her eyes narrowed. "That new contraption of yours?"

"Afraid so."

She shook her head, "I told you it wouldn't work."

"I have to slow it down. Getting it right will take a while."

"You're always experimenting," the woman accused, shrugged, and went back to work. "You are so impractical."

Teresa felt foolish just standing there, but she couldn't think of anything to say. Although Giustina hadn't acknowledged her, she felt as if the woman were aware of whom she was. If so, why didn't Giustina welcome her?

"When are you reinstalling that back door, Mama? We need an emergency exit. We may regret not having it, someday."

Giustina made a gesture as if she were swatting a pesky fly. "Did you settle the contract with Harry Goldstein?"

"Yes. He's sending the material this afternoon."

"Did you call Stein and Stein? They owe us money."

"Not yet. Another thing, Mama, when are you going to learn to use the typewriter?"

"I don't have time to waste."

"You're going to have to hire someone soon. The work load is getting too big. What are you going to do if I get into college? You should think about using that adding machine, too." He gestured to the machine resting on the corner of his desk. "It'll help with the accounts." He opened the bottom drawer of his desk and pulled out a green metal toolbox.

"I don't need any new contraptions. I told you not to buy it. You're too free with money."

Nick rummaged through the tools until he found a pair of pliers. "This should do the trick." He smiled at Teresa. "It might hurt a little, but I haven't lost a patient yet."

Teresa looked away. He pulled the needle out with such a quick gesture, she felt no pain. Had his hands trembled or hers?

"Face it, Mama, you're going to need help. You can't work in two places at once. Another thing, this office is getting too small for our business."

"Big shot. This office was big enough for me and your father. Good thing he didn't live to hear..."

"Maybe a ticker tape, too," he continued, ignoring her objections.

"Ticker tape?" She laughed and shook her head. "What on earth for?"

"I could make money investing in the market."

"Or lose it. Forget it!"

Nick painted some antiseptic on Teresa's finger and wrapped it with a bit of gauze. He smiled broadly at her. "Sorry about this. I never wanted to hurt you. Don't use the machine. I'll be out there in a minute to unhook it." Nick tossed the pliers, tape and antiseptic back in the box and sat opposite Giustina. He picked up the phone.

"Don't be too long on the telephone," his mother admonished. "I have to make some calls."

"We can use another telephone, too. Hello, operator? Get me..."

Giustina got up, turned and opened a filing cabinet's top drawer. "Niccolo," she shook her head, "how could you let the files get in such a mess?" She closed the drawer, sat at the desk and studied Teresa for a moment. "Is there something you have to say to me?"

Teresa felt as if the woman were asking for something of her, but she couldn't imagine what. Again she felt foolish standing there, yet she still could think of nothing to say. "No," she said simply.

"I see. Then get back to work. We don't have time to waste."

Teresa thought she saw disappointment in Giustina's eyes, but she wasn't sure. She went back to work, ignoring the throb that had begun in her thumb, and wondered why Nick hadn't introduced her to his mother. *Maybe I should have introduced myself to her? Could that be what she wanted?*

* * *

The confinement of the makeshift confessional in the storefront church made it difficult to breathe. Teresa felt faint. Struggling for control, she rested her head on her clenched hands.

"Courage, my child," the priest prompted. His Irish brogue edged its way into his schooled Italian. "Remember, God loves you."

Her throat tightened. She swallowed hard. "I didn't show the proper respect for my mother." *Yes, that's the approach. It's not a lie, but it doesn't give me away.*

"How? Did you blaspheme?" His voice suggested that he had heard it all before.

"No. By separating myself from her." Still, noncommittal.

"Well, my child," he yawned, "how many of us have separated ourselves from our parents to come to America? We had no choice. Nevertheless, never forget the Ten Commandments tell us to honor our mother and father. Anything else?"

"...and..." her voice grew softer.

"What was that, my child?"

Teresa detected a note of compassion in his voice. She cleared her throat and tried disciplining her voice, "I said, I left my husband."

"WHAT?" He raised his voice despite himself.

Teresa flinched, frightened that Elena and Josephine had overheard.

He composed himself and began again, quietly, "It's a very grave sin! You have been wed to him in the sight of God and only by God are you separated."

"But he beat me, and..."

"That's no excuse. Perhaps you did or said something that provoked him." He expressed total conviction in his tone.

"No. Nothing!"

"Well, my child, your vows say for better or worse. Before God you are bound to him for life. You must go to him. It is God's will."

Suddenly her nausea left her. Her mother and the nuns had taught her never to question the scriptures or the word of a priest, but she could not accept what he was saying. Trying desperately to keep from screaming at him, she said, "Never, not for you or anyone! No matter what you say, I can't believe God wants it."

She dismayed him. "Then I cannot give you absolution!"

If the screen between them had suddenly burst into flames, neither of them would have been the least surprised nor less exasperated with each another.

"Father," she began, her voice calm and steady, "to be wed to him *is* a living Hell." She got up and left the confessional. Just beyond the crimson velvet curtain, she hesitated. If she walked out of church, it would arouse too much attention. She couldn't go to the altar and pray the customary penances. The priest hadn't given her absolution.

Elena stared at her, puzzled at her hesitancy. Josephine nudged Elena's side with her elbow as if to say I told you so.

Teresa thought she saw the curtain on the priest's side open a crack. *If you are watching me, Father, I can still pray, even if you haven't absolved me.* She threw her shoulders back and strode to the altar railing.

# Chapter 8

The driver helped Rosa onto the buckboard, threw her bundle into the back, and flicked the reins. The gray horse snorted and slowly pulled the buckboard. Trying desperately to keep the anguish at a safe distance, she kept her eyes away from the mound of dirt covering Peppi's grave. Big Mike swaggered out of his cabin and leaned against the rail. With a sweeping motion, he struck a match on the seat of his jodhpurs, lit a cigar and blew smoke in Rosa's direction as if in farewell to rubbish.

"Rosa!" Francesco shouted as he ran alongside the buckboard. "Please wait!"

Rosa pulled on the driver's arm. Reluctantly, he pulled on the reins and stopped the horse. "Why aren't you at the mines, Francesco?"

He laughed. "Meet Big Mike's new cook."

She laughed in spite of herself. "I didn't know you could cook."

"Neither did I, and what's better, neither does he."

They laughed again.

He took her hand in his. She tried to pull away, but he held fast. "Rosa, I can't let you go. I know it is not the time to tell you, but if I don't say something now, it will be too late."

She could read his meaning in his eyes. "You're right, Francesco. Now is not the time."

"Give me a chance, Rosa, please," he pleaded.

She felt shame and guilt at his attentions. It violated all that she had been raised to believe. True, she had not been married long enough to form strong emotional ties to Peppi; tradition, yes, obligation, yes, but not love. Still, all she could think of were Peppi's merits that loomed larger than life. The bull-like man had been unbelievably gentle, caring, and so very fond of her singing. Often he had said, "Whenever you feel happy or unhappy, sing. Life is too short to carry sorrow in the heart for even a moment." She didn't feel like singing.

"Rosa, please."

The tightness in her throat made it difficult to speak. She swallowed hard. "Francesco, don't you see, this is the time for mourning."

"Of course. Forgive me for being indiscreet, but it isn't as if I live next door to you. I can't wait for the proper mourning period to end. I may never get another chance." His voice, though raw with urgency, was like a warm embrace.

"Let's go!" The driver's voice tossed cold water on them.

"Yeah, let her go," Big Mike called to Francesco. "You can get any Eyetalian whore any time, anywhere."

Rosa saw the fire in Francesco's eyes. "No, Francesco," she murmured as she squeezed his hand. "Don't do something you will regret."

"I can't let that go unchallenged." Rage clawed at him.

"We have no choice. We are less than nothing in this country."

He didn't want Mike to destroy his last chance with Rosa, so he swallowed his pride and anger. "I won't let you go until you give me an answer."

"I'm going!" The driver flicked the reins and the horse started moving.

"I'm sorry. Forgive me, Francesco." She hung onto the buckboard's seat as it darted forward.

Francesco ran alongside. Trying to keep her from disappearing, he called to her, "Rosa, where you are going? What are you going to do?"

Rosa wondered too. She knew she was going to Spring Street, but then what?

\* \* \*

Teresa felt grateful that Liza had brought her to the library. She wandered around the stacks, touching the leather bindings, longing to know what knowledge they concealed. Although the library was only the size of a storefront, to Teresa it seemed enormous. Never had she seen so many books in one place.

For the first time in America she had found, if not privacy, a bit of silence. At work, chattering people and droning machines surrounded her. The street had constant pandemonium and Liza's whining. In the evenings, there was the chatter of Delora's family,

Elena, Josephine and the other boarders. Even at bedtime she wasn't alone. Sometimes she found a measure of quiet and solitude on the fire escape or on the boarding house's roof. The roof, however, had Ernesto's pigeons and the intrusion of almost anyone in the house.

"May I help you?" the librarian asked as she placed a book on the shelf.

*"Mi scusi?"*

*"Italiano?"*

*"Si, "* Teresa affirmed.

"I'm *Signorina* Elizabeth Rinaldi," the slender young woman announced. "Do you need any help?"

"Unfortunately I cannot read English."

"I am teaching English to immigrants. The class will begin in about fifteen minutes. Would you like to join us?"

"Oh, yes. Where?"

"Through that back door. Classes will be an hour long."

Teresa turned to Liza. "Will you wait for me?"

"An hour!" She made a rude noise with her tongue between her lips.

"Then will you meet me after? I'll buy you a lemon ice."

"All right," she agreed reluctantly.

As the smiling librarian walked away, Teresa asked Liza, "Will you help me with my lessons?"

"Aw, I don't want to."

"I'll pay you."

"All right," she said more readily and watched as Teresa disappeared into the back room.

The hour flew for Teresa, opening a new world for her. When she and Liza arrived home, Teresa urged Liza to help her immediately. Before long, Teresa found herself wishing she had a teacher with more patience and front teeth. Still, there was so much that even Liza could teach her, although grudgingly.

"No!" Liza exclaimed with irritation in her voice. "I told you before, the wordth thound the thame, but we thpell them differently. Look," she wrote as she spoke, "to, two, and too. We have a lot of wordth like that."

Teresa sighed, determined to learn, and without an accent, the only way to get ahead. If only the rich can have love, then she would get rich somehow. But money meant more than love to her; it meant power, independence, never being forced into a box again.

\* \* \*

Teresa, returning from her most recent lesson at the library, needed to be alone. It had only been two weeks. Still, she wondered if she would ever learn this strange language, despite the encouragement her teacher had given her that evening. She climbed the stairs to her bedroom and found Rosa, fully clothed, sleeping on the bed. All her anxieties vanished. Teresa couldn't resist waking her. They hugged, cried, and hugged again. "Let me look at you." Only then did Teresa notice that Rosa was completely in black. "What happened?"

"They killed Peppi."

"Killed? My God! Who? Why?"

Rosa looked away. As quickly as she could, she related what had happened.

When she had finished, Teresa said, "You're keeping something from me. What is it?" A confusing rush of anticipation and dread whirled inside her.

Rosa avoided looking into Teresa's eyes. "Some believe that Rocco did it."

"ROCCO!" *Bound to him for life.* She felt her heart beating against her ribs as if it were trying to escape.

"He is the only one missing. Some believe the explosion killed him, too, but..."

"You don't."

"I don't know. All I know is that they found the other bodies, including Anna's."

"Anna?"

"His kept woman."

It didn't surprise Teresa that Rocco had a kept woman. "I don't believe he's dead." Then a frightening thought surfaced. "What if he comes here and asks Malespina for a job?"

She shook her head. "I don't know. All I know is that I must get some sleep."

Allowing Rosa to get some sleep, Teresa climbed out onto the fire escape to absorb what Rosa had told her. She sat against the railing and gazed at the mulberry tree that struggled for existence in a confined, hostile space. *Well, this isn't home, but I could have been in West Virginia.*

Shouting coming from Delora's bedroom below her broke her thoughts. In all the time she had lived there, she had never heard Delora and Rafaello argue. Rafaello, a good-tempered man, kept his silence while Delora only mumbled her displeasures to herself.

"Rafaello," Delora's irritation telegraphed, "how could you ask that anarchist to live in a house with women?"

"Leonardo is a good man. Everybody at the club thinks he is a genius."

Teresa wondered if it were the same bearded Leonardo who worked in Giustina's factory.

"I'm not surprised," Delora scoffed. "They are a bunch of idiots in that club! All they do is eat, drink, and talk politics as if they understand it! Be sensible. Where is he going to sleep?"

"With Ernesto."

"Ernesto! Never will I have that skeleton in bed with my son."

Teresa couldn't hear Rafaello's response.

"WHAT!" Delora shouted. "Are you crazy? You expect me to feed him and clean up after him for nothing?"

Rafaello edged closer to the window. "He doesn't have money."

"What do you mean he doesn't have any money? What does he do with the money he gets at Giovane's?"

*It is Leonardo!* Teresa raised her eyebrows.

"He gives it to the working man's cause."

"More stupidity." Rafaello couldn't lead her astray. "I can't believe you! Without thinking, or asking, you..."

"Quiet!" Rafaello shouted with a rare show of tenacity. "What is done is done!"

\* \* \*

Teresa sat at the library table and studied her English lessons, thankful that Liza, at the other end of the table, was quiet for a change. She sighed and thought about Rosa, who had moved to Totowa, a suburb of Paterson, to work at Giustina's factory. Teresa needed her to confide in. *I can feel that Rocco is alive and could sneak up on me any time.*

"Violetta."

A male voice shot through her. "What? Who? Oh, it's only you, Nick." Her face expressed such relief, it surprised him.

"Only?" He smiled. "I don't know whether I should be glad or not with that greeting."

"I'm sorry. Of course, I'm glad to see you."

"Shhh," the librarian cautioned.

He moved in closer and lowered his voice. "Why were you so frightened? Who did you think it was?"

Liza looked up quizzically.

"You're mistaken. You startled me, that's all."

He leaned in closely. "What are you studying?" Their cheeks nearly touched.

She felt a thrill. "English. How did you know I was here?" she whispered.

"I didn't."

She blushed. *You fool, as if he were here to see you.*

"I'm doing research. I've been admitted to Columbia University." He didn't hide his joy.

"Congratulations. But I thought they wouldn't admit Italians."

"I hated to do it, but I changed my name."

"Oh, my, what did Giustina say about that?"

"I didn't tell her."

"Shhh!" The librarian was more insistent.

He lowered his voice to a mere whisper. "Tell me, what do you do on Sundays?"

"Mostly go to church, study, and..."

"How about going with me to a museum, or something, before I have to buckle down?"

Teresa knew it would appear unseemly to spend the day alone with a young man. A bad reputation was not something she wanted. She turned to Liza and asked with anticipation, "How about going with us?"

Liza screwed up her nose as if she smelled something bad. "I don't wanna."

Teresa failed to hide her disappointment. "I'm sorry, Nick."

"How about the Botanical Gardens?" Nick asked, unwilling to give up.

"No, it'th boring." Liza drew the words out.

"How about the zoo?"

Both looked at Liza, who thought for a minute, evidently enjoying her moment of power. Then, her face brightened up, "Will you buy me thome ithe cream?"

Nick smiled. "Sure. Whoever heard of going to the zoo without ice cream? How about this Sunday?"

Teresa's heart fell. "I'm sorry. I can't. My friend Rosa is coming to visit."

"Bring her along."

"I don't know if she'll come. She is in mourning, but I'll try."

The librarian approached them. "Nick, you have spent enough time at the library to know the rules."

"I'm sorry, Miss Rinaldi. I'm going. I came to thank you in person for the generous and kind thing you did for me. Did you receive my letter?"

"Yes, but there is no need to thank me. You deserve it. You were one of the best students I ever had. By the way, if anyone asks, I do not know what you are talking about." She smiled and went back to her desk.

Teresa looked puzzled.

Nick smiled. "Not only is she a librarian, but she teaches English at the high school I attended." He leaned in even closer and whispered. "So that I could get into Columbia, she changed my records to read Nicholas Young. It means the same thing. I don't know whether she can get into trouble for it, but she did it anyway. Not many people would have done it."

* * *

It was a relief for Rosa not to see the endless column of gray row-houses. Cheek to cheek, they crowded the bare Paterson streets. Although the houses in Totowa were also gray, they were set back, maple trees lined the sidewalk, and narrow alleyways separated the houses.

Rosa clanged shut the black wrought-iron gate within the waist-high concrete wall leading to her lodging house. Against the gray stucco house, a climbing cluster of red seven-sisters roses clung to a white fanned trellis, the only touch of color on the entire street. She liked the front porch with its two-person swing, but she loved the backyard garden that, although small, returned her to her peasant roots.

Rosa was grateful to Giustina for arranging these lodgings. Here, her landlords were kind and easy-going. She didn't mind having to share her small, immaculate room with two fifteen-year-old twin girls. A horse and buggy killed their parents, confirming her fear of horses. Even in her village in Italy she had feared horses, but in America, the horses seemed to run wild through the streets, multiplying her fears. Why the haste? It seemed to her that Americans were in a race with time.

Rosa climbed the cement steps and was about to unlock the front door when she heard the gate clang behind her. She turned abruptly and almost collided with Francesco.

"At last! I had a devil of a time finding you." He took her hands in his.

"How did you find me?" She couldn't hide her delight.

"I pried your Spring Street address out of Concetina."

"Is she all right? Where is she?"

"I don't know. She left the camp shortly after you did. Anyway, I went to *Signora* Felice's. Your friend, Violetta, told me you were here."

"How did you escape?"

"It's a long story. May I sit?"

"Of course." She gestured toward the porch swing. "I can't let you in the house. No one is at home."

"I understand." He sat on the swing. "Come," he tapped the seat with his good hand.

Rosa sat beside him and to her surprise found herself trembling.

"There was a cave-in."

*"Dio mio!"* Her eyes jumped up to meet his.

"Everybody in the camp ran to the disaster except me. I ran toward the railroad tracks. When I got to that shack they call a depot, I hid under it and waited forever for a train to stop."

"What courage."

"Not courage, survival." His eyes looked haunted. He took a deep breath. "Did I tell you that you look lovely?"

She blushed. "Please continue."

"You look lovely," he repeated and tried to take her hand.

She laughed and pushed him away. "I mean with your story."

"Well, at the end of the day, almost starved, I heard the dogs baying in the woods."

"Oh, my God!" Her hands covered her mouth. Her eyes reflected the terror she was sure he had felt.

"I prayed harder than ever that a train would come soon. God must have heard me, for one did. In the confusion of men getting off the train, I crawled onto the metal braces between the wheels. The dogs were getting closer. I could almost feel their breath. Again I prayed, this time that the train would leave quickly."

"Thank God. It did!" she gasped.

He sighed. "I regretted leaving my mandolin behind. It had a tone almost as beautiful as your laughter."

Her head spun in a whirl as if she'd tasted one glass of wine too many; she put the back of her hand to her cheeks that felt on fire. She got up and leaned against the railing.

He followed her.

Trying to keep her head from spinning, she asked, "Surely, you didn't travel under the train for two days?"

"You're right. At the next stop some Pinkerton men put Mother Jones on board. I sneaked on board when the conductor wasn't looking and asked her to help me. Would you believe it? She even gave me some money for the fare. That's one great lady. The first chance I had, I sent her the money with a little to spare." Then Francesco took a deep breath. "Enough about me. I know it's still too soon, but may I call on you?"

She picked at the gray paint peeling off the railing, needing time to gather her thoughts. "No, Francesco. You can see that I am still in mourning."

"I understand, but you know that I cannot leave you, don't you?"

She didn't answer. Rosa found him disturbingly attractive. Never had she felt such an exhilarating response to any man.

He put his arm around her waist and gently turned her toward him. This time she didn't resist. She felt the warmth of his body close beside her and trembled.

"I think we could love each other." His voice was husky.

Rosa didn't answer. The blood rushed to her cheeks. She felt him tremble.

"Can you give me any hope at all?"

"Just give me time, Francesco, please."

"That's all I ask, *cara.*"

She felt his hand tighten on her waist just when she saw the twins walking up the street. Reluctantly, she pulled away from him. "My roommates are coming." Her voice quivered. Flustered, she ran her hands over her long black skirt. "Uh, Francesco, uh, what are your plans?"

He sat on the porch swing, stretched his legs out and crossed them at his ankles. "Besides marrying you? Well, work in a dye shop."

"Dye shop? Oh, *caro mio,* from..."

His eyes shone. "Say that again."

"What?"

*"Caro mio.* It sounded so wonderful."

Her flush rose higher over her face. "What I wanted to say was that I hear the dye shops are horrible."

"It won't be forever. When I've saved enough money, I hope to go to medical school. Of course, I can't be a surgeon." He looked at his disfigured hand. "My hand didn't heal properly, but I can still be a doctor."

Rosa's pain for him was almost as deep as his, but she didn't know what to say to comfort him. After a pause she asked, "Where are you staying?"

"In a rooming house not far from the dye shop. Close to you, *cara,* but not close enough. May I see you next Sunday?"

"I won't be here. I've promised to visit Violetta in New York."

"May I come along? She is such a beautiful lady. I'd love to see her again."

Rosa felt a twinge of jealousy, a new experience for her. She almost said no, but scolded herself for her foolishness. "Yes, but we must have a chaperon."

\* \* \*

In the embrace of good weather, throngs of people converged on the Botanical Gardens, eagerly leaving their cramped dwellings and enjoying the fresh air and sunshine. Both Teresa and Rosa, however, were sure God had arranged the day and the Gardens just for them.

This was their second outing. On their first, they had visited the zoo. Today, to please Teresa, Nick took them to the Gardens. Liza had balked at first, but when Nick pointed out that they didn't need her as a chaperone, with all the people in their party, she changed her mind.

They walked for hours with Liza and her brother, Ernesto, leading the twins. Rosa and Francesco followed them; a few feet behind strolled Teresa and Nick. Teresa could see that there was something special happening between Rosa and Francesco and wished that she, too, could experience the same feelings. Francesco looked like a man who had been given a second chance at life, as he truly had. As for Nick, he kept a respectful distance from Teresa. He was easy to be with, seeming to sense her every mood and not trying to infringe on her privacy. She sighed wistfully.

"What's wrong?" Nick asked.

"Absolutely nothing. Thank you for giving me such a marvelous day. I'll remember it fondly always."

"The pleasure is all mine. You've given me new insight into what I'm seeing. Another place you must see is the Metropolitan Museum of Art. I'd like to take you there some day."

The prospect brought excitement to her eyes. She had heard about the museum from the librarian, and ever since she had fantasized about it. "Oh, that sounds simply wonderful. Could we please?"

Nick felt the need to be alone with her, and added quickly, "Or perhaps Central Park. Why waste the beautiful weather? We could take the mechanical traction lines up to the park and then go rowing on the lake." To his disappointment, she called to Rosa, who turned and waited for them.

"Nick has a splendid idea. He'd like to take us rowing on the lake in Central Park."

"How marvelous!" Rosa said.

"Done!" It troubled him that he found himself happier than the idea merited. "We'll do it next Sunday."

They fell into silence. For a frightening moment, Teresa thought she saw Rocco in the crowd.

Nick sensed her uneasiness. "Something is bothering you. I could see it at the library and I think I just saw it again. Won't you tell me what it is? Maybe I can be of help." He studied her eyes intensely, wishing she would confide in him.

"Nothing is bothering me, Nick, especially today." His thoughtfulness touched her. Teresa lifted her eyes slowly and looked at him.

He sensed something had come up behind her eyes. "Is it because I didn't insist that we marry?"

"No." Her answer was a little too abrupt. She could see the discomfort in his face. "I'm sorry, Nick, I didn't mean it the way it sounded. I'm not ready for marriage, that's all."

"Is there something else?"

"No. Please, let's not spoil the day."

"All right, but remember, as I said before, you can count on me anytime."

She knew that he meant every word of it and wished with all her heart she could tell him everything.

He could see that she was not one for confiding and was learning not to question her unduly. *Why,* he wondered, *must she always hide her feelings?* The mystery increased his fascination with her.

\* \* \*

The following Sunday, Rosa, Francesco, Nick and Teresa were rowing on the lake in Central Park. Francesco and Rosa were in one rowboat, Nick and Teresa in another. The twins had come down with colds and decided to stay home. Rosa braved convention and traveled to the city alone with Francesco. They hadn't invited Liza and Ernesto, because the youngsters couldn't swim.

Teresa, holding a white silk parasol that she had borrowed from her landlady, leaned back on a pillow in the boat's stern and trailed her hand in the lake. She smiled, remembering how pleased Delora had been when she saw how lovely her youthful white silk skirt looked on Teresa. Teresa had lengthened it with a bit of satin and taken it in slightly. An occasional breeze rippled the skirt as she watched the sunlight flashing over the waves that Nick created with his rowing. A flock of geese skimmed the water, landed a few yards away and bobbed like corks. Farther down the lake she saw two white swans speed toward the geese. At the last moment, the geese flapped their wings and flew into the air. They circled and landed on the lake, but this time farther away.

It was all too wonderful for her. Teresa couldn't remember when she had felt so calm and joyful, not even back home under the fruit trees. She stole a glance at Nick as he slowly rowed the boat. How handsome he was in his red and white striped blazer and straw boater hat. She wondered if he had purchased them for just this occasion.

Nick never took his eyes off her, finding her more radiant than ever. "You're so quiet. What are you thinking?"

"Just how perfect these days have been. I can't thank you enough."

He smiled. "Don't thank me; I've enjoyed it, too."

This hold she had on him began to disturb him. A small voice within him whispered, *"Run!"* Yet, he couldn't keep his eyes from the way her hair glistened in the sunlight. He wanted to reach out and touch her. *What the hell's gotten into you?* The redness of his face had nothing to do with the sun or the strain of rowing. Nick tried to shake the spell and look at her through cold eyes, but the image of something unflattering wouldn't come. He rowed faster, unconscious of the fact that he was forming blisters on the palms of his hands. *Nobody is going to trap me. This is absolutely the last time I take her out. Absolutely!*

Unmindful that he was splashing some water into the boat, she, too, was feeling disturbed about their relationship. *What are you getting into, you fool? I mustn't get too close to him. This is the last time I'll have him take me anywhere. Absolutely!*

# Chapter 9

Josephine threw money on the chiffonier and startled Teresa out of her reverie. "Eighteen hours, for six days, and half a day Sunday, and I haven't earned any more money! That witch keeps cutting the price for each piece! How can I buy the clothes I need?"

"Clothes?" Elena struggled to put her skirt into the overstuffed armoire. "You're taking all the room now!"

Josephine eyed her scornfully. "You're happy the way you look. I'm not. Without the right clothes, I'm stuck here."

Elena ignored Josephine's unflattering appraisal. "Complain to Giustina."

"Maybe we could talk to her." Teresa was barely listening as she folded her undergarments. Her thoughts were of Nick. Teresa hadn't heard from him for a week. Why did it annoy her? Wasn't it what she wanted?

"Talk to Giustina!" Josephine scoffed. "Do something she understands. Go on strike." She thought a minute. "Isn't that what you're saying, Violetta?"

Teresa thought she saw something flicker in her eyes. "I said talk, not strike. How about talking to Nick?"

"Waste of time," Josephine sneered. "He lets Giustina run everything. Talk to the workers, that's what."

"Who, you?" Elena derided.

"Yes," Josephine tossed her head and smiled, pleased at her own reflection in the mirror.

"What are we going to do for money, if they agree?" Elena sneered.

"Elena is right." Teresa rubbed her aching feet. "I don't even have enough money to buy shoes."

"Working for Giustina, you never will," Josephine said. "Walk out. Right, Violetta?"

Again Teresa thought she saw a flicker in Josephine's eyes. "We should think twice before we do anything. Remember Rosa's husband."

"That's true," Elena agreed, "but this isn't West Virginia and Giustina doesn't have any explosives."

"No," Josephine grimaced, "but one look from her can kill you."

They laughed so hard they were afraid they might bring in the curious.

Elena giggled, "Ask Giustina to join us."

Josephine placed her hand on her hip. "Go ahead, laugh. I'm going to the workers."

"All right," Elena agreed, not really believing Josephine would.

\* \* \*

Teresa, too, thought the idea would dissolve, but Josephine wasted no time speaking to the workers. What surprised her more was that they were open to the idea. However, they wanted Teresa as a negotiator. They didn't like Josephine, and they didn't trust Leonardo. But Teresa didn't want to get involved, especially with Nick as the objective. Nevertheless, it angered her when she thought about the degrading working conditions. The more she deliberated, the more she thought Nick must be aware of what Giustina was doing. Yet, she couldn't believe it. Now, sitting in the library with Liza, Teresa regretted not having been firmer about speaking to Nick. *I'm going to talk to him.*

"Hello, dark eyes." Nick's cheek nearly brushed hers. "We meet again."

Her face felt on fire. "Nick!"

"How's your English?" He shifted two heavy volumes onto his hip.

"Progressing with difficulty." *Now's my chance.* "Nick I..."

"Sorry, dark eyes, can't stay. I have a class. See you soon." He waved his hand and disappeared out the door.

\* \* \*

A week passed, during which, to Teresa's relief, everyone stopped talking about a strike. Grateful that cooler heads had taken over, she relaxed at her machine. When Nick marched past her, his face filled with rage, foreboding shot through her. *Good Lord, he's heard about the strike! I should have told him!*

He slammed the office door shut behind him. Almost immediately, she could hear him shouting at Giustina, but the noises of the machines prevented her from hearing what he was saying. The door swung open. The translucent glass nearly shattered as the door struck the wall. Without looking at her, he stormed out of the factory.

Giustina, stony-faced, appeared in the doorway and motioned Teresa to enter. Everyone watched Teresa as she walked into the office. Giustina closed the door. The floor began shaking beneath Teresa.

Apart from the needle incident, this was their first confrontation, despite Teresa's having worked there for two months. True, Giustina had been at her Paterson factory most of the time, but when she had been at Spring Street, Giustina had never walked around the factory. Teresa linked it to her mother's words of advice. "If you get too friendly with your workers, they lose respect for you."

"Sit down, my dear." Giustina pointed to Nick's chair and sat rigidly in hers. Despite the tender words, Teresa knew that Giustina was struggling for control. "You have been secretly seeing Niccolo, haven't you?"

*Good! It's not about the strike!* Still, she knew what Giustina was implying. "That's not correct, *Signora.*"

"No?" Giustina drew out the word. She gave Teresa a piercing look. "Haven't you been meeting at the library, going to the zoo, the gardens and park together?"

"Again, that is not exactly correct."

The woman's fixed stare unnerved her. "Then suppose you give me the 'exactly correct' version, my dear."

Teresa wished Giustina would stop using the familiar address in that tone of voice. It pierced like a needle. She had sensed it when they'd first met, but now Teresa had no doubt that this woman was a formidable opponent, cunning, perhaps even ruthless when she wanted to be.

Giustina crossed her arms. "Whenever you're ready, my dear."

"Yes, we were at the zoo, gardens, but with Ernesto, Liza and four friends of mine. At the lake, with Rosa, Francesco and a hundred or more other people."

Giustina ignored the barb. "And the library?" Her long thin nose pinched white.

"It is true," Teresa's voice flashed a note of truculence, "that your son and I have been at the library at the same time; however, we were not there for any secret meetings. I have been going to the library to study English." Her anger hung in the air.

"Don't be rude."

"Sorry, *Signora,*" Teresa said without being sorry, "but I don't like your suggesting I have done something wrong. Surely you're not suggesting Nick has."

"Leave Niccolo out of this."

"Pardon me, but isn't it Nick we are discussing?"

She sidestepped. "Tell me something about your background. What do your parents do in Italy?" Her blank eyes gave nothing away.

She searched her mind. "They are both dead, but you know that."

"A slip of the tongue." Giustina's cautious eyes missed nothing. "What did you say they did?"

"I didn't, but my father was a cabinet maker and my mother a dressmaker."

"Any living relatives?"

Again she searched her mind. "Aunt Valentina, but I'm not sure if she is still alive." Why ask? *She knows the answers. She is testing me!*

"Yes, Valentina." Giustina searched through the papers on her desk. "Ah, here it is. I received this letter from her today." She handed Teresa the envelope. "She is concerned about your well-being. Why haven't you written? I know you can write." Her eyes expressed challenge.

"Perhaps my letter got lost," she lied. "I should have written again, but when I didn't receive an answer I assumed the worst. May I keep the letter?"

"No. Valentina wants you to send a picture to relieve her anxiety and lessen the pain of your absence."

Teresa nearly panicked. *How can I? She'll see I'm not Violetta. Giustina knows! No. She's only guessing. Somehow I'll have to delay sending a picture.* "I'll send one when I have enough money to have my picture taken." Teresa turned the envelope over and noted the address.

"Maybe we can do something about that. Niccolo has a camera." She wrote a note to herself. "Perhaps next week. Meanwhile, tell me, are you God-fearing?"

Teresa felt almost as tormented as the picture of the crucified Christ hanging on the wall behind Giustina. "Of course."

"Have you attended church every Sunday and on Holy Days of Obligation?"

"Yes."

"Confession?"

"Yes." Not exactly a lie. Not every week, but she had been.

"Have you ever been married or divorced, Violetta?"

"No." Safe again. Violetta had never married, and she, Teresa, had never divorced.

"Are you a virgin?"

Her body tensed with hostility. She stood up rigidly. "What right have you to ask me such an outrageous question? You are not my mother!"

"That is an evasion. Are you?"

"Of course!" Giustina so outraged her that she stamped her foot and struck her hand on the desk.

"Calm yourself. Such a display is not becoming for a young lady. One must maintain control, always. Didn't your mother ever tell you that?"

Teresa was about to blast another sharp retort when Giustina motioned her to sit.

She sat. She didn't know why. This time Teresa's arms were crossed.

"You are angry?"

"Yes!"

"Good. I like anger. People reveal things they shouldn't when they are." Then, almost as an afterthought, "And they work harder, too."

Teresa was becoming increasingly angry with herself for allowing Giustina to keep her there.

"Are you studying anything else?"

"No. *Signora,* why all these questions? My affairs are none of your business!"

"They are, since I was the one that gave you the money for your passage and if you intend to become my daughter-in-law."

"But I don't!" Struggling for control, she said, "I know you sent the money, but I have no intention..."

"Yes, yes, I know all that. He told me that. Nevertheless, when you didn't come to me after your arrival, I thought you were also rejecting me. It was your place to come to me as your elder, not mine to go to you, but I accepted it. I saved you from starvation and you withdrew from your engagement. It was like misappropriating my money. Still, I gave you employment."

"I wasn't rejecting you. I didn't know you existed until shortly before I left for America," she said inadvertently. She hoped Violetta hadn't known about her.

Giustina knitted her brows. "None of your relatives spoke about me, ever?"

"No." Teresa prayed it was the right thing to say.

"Strange!" She almost looked hurt, but it passed so quickly Teresa wasn't sure she had observed it. "Well, whatever you thought or I thought, since then you have been seeing Niccolo behind my back. This is not proper behavior for a young, single lady. I don't know how they brought you up, but it is unacceptable to me."

"I assure you, I am not seeing Nick behind your back."

"Good. I hate sneaks. I have your word that you have no intention of marrying my son?"

Teresa was annoyed at Nick for having placed her in a position that forced her to behave uncivilly. She wanted to shout, "Not even if he were the last man on earth!" But she controlled herself. "Pardon me, but isn't that why you brought me here?"

"True. I don't have anything against you personally. From all reports, you are a hard worker and you tell me you are religious. Both attributes are very commendable, but," she picked up a pencil and tapped it on the desk, "when I sent for you, it was fulfilling a family obligation. I did what I thought best. When Niccolo told me you were not interested in marrying him, I was relieved, especially after he said he was not happy with the arrangement. He needs to move up in the world, not down."

The affront was so contemptuous she didn't know how to respond. She rose, stretched herself to her full height and drove her nails into the palms of her hands, *"Signora,* I wouldn't dream of lowering your or his exalted position."

Giustina either didn't notice the barb or didn't think it worth answering. Instead she continued her interrogation. "Niccolo said you did not need money."

"Correct." She thought she saw relief in Giustina's face. "And when I can, I intend to repay the steerage fare."

A smile came to Giustina's lips. Teresa's offer obviously had come as a welcomed surprise to her. "That won't be necessary."

"Nevertheless, I will." Although she was not obligated to do so, she didn't want this woman to have any hold on her.

"Fine. You won't see Niccolo behind my back?"

Again it was an insult to her and to Nick. Still, she controlled her temper. "Yes, *Signora.* I, for one, have never done anything to encourage him," she bit out.

"Good. As I said before, deception is the one thing I can never forgive."

# Chapter 10

As Teresa savored the aromas filling Delora's kitchen, her heart raced. She would be seeing Nick soon. It had been two weeks since she had seen him and since she'd had the confrontation with Giustina. Today was a celebration for Ernesto's twelfth birthday. In the spring Ernesto would be confirmed in the Catholic faith with Nick as his Godfather.

She looked around as she added the marble-sized balls of shredded chicken into the simmering chicken soup. Elena stirred an enormous pot of tomato sauce brimming with tightly wrapped braciolas. Josephine and Liza were conveying an assortment of delectables to the dining room sideboard: fruit, nuts, homemade cookies and Delora's pride, a three-layer birthday cake filled with vanilla and chocolate pastry cream.

Delora heaped flour on a kneading board, stopped for a moment and looked at her husband. "Rafaello."

"Mm?" he asked, concentrating on the stream of ruby wine flowing from the jug into the cut-glass decanter.

"You invited Leonardo, but *please,* no politics. I don't want him to upset Niccolo."

Rafaello smiled. "Niccolo is no baby. He can take care of himself."

"Regardless, he is an honored guest in this house." She made a well in the flour mound.

"You worry too much."

"If I don't, who is going to?" Delora rapidly beat the eggs with a fork, emphasizing her anxiety.

"Calm yourself," Rafaello said in his quiet way. "You will make the ravioli dough tough." He finished pouring the wine and wiped the decanter. "I'm surprised Leonardo didn't go to the Labor Day parade today like the ladies boarding here. He is so strong on politics."

"Leonardo makes a lot of noise, but a free meal comes first." She rolled out the dough until it was almost paper thin. "I don't trust him. He can't hide his foxy face behind that beard."

"Still," Teresa said, "Leonardo's kind. He's not charging me anything for the English lessons."

"He has an ulterior motive," Delora scoffed.

"I can't imagine what," Teresa said. "All I know is that I'm grateful. I can use every penny. For one thing I want to repay Giustina for my passage." That slipped out without thinking. It sounded like boasting.

"Repay? Why?" Josephine almost wrinkled her brow in astonishment.

"I feel I should."

Josephine reconsidered and scoffed. "Ha! It would be worth it, if only to see the look on that cheapskate's face." She edged her way around the kitchen, making sure she didn't get anything on her clothes.

Delora gave Josephine a cutting look, but Josephine didn't seem to care that she had offended Delora's friend.

* * *

Teresa looked around the table. Elena seemed to envy Rosa and Francesco who gazed at each other as if they were alone in the room. Rafaello, at the head of the table, beamed at his children, Liza and Ernesto. Leonardo, sitting opposite Nick, apparently trying to avoid eye contact with Nick, munched on nuts. Teresa, relieved that Giustina had stayed at home, complaining of a backache, had only one annoyance, Josephine. Josephine, sitting beside Nick, lost no opportunity to touch him.

Delora, on the other hand, smiled, happy that not one word of politics had been spoken.

Rafaello picked up a bottle of anisette and walked around the table filling everyone's cordial glass. "This toast," he began as everyone rose, "is to yesterday, today, and tomorrow, but most of all to honor. Yesterday, we left Italy, but let's never forget our proud heritage. Today, in our new country, we work hard to make a better life for our children. Tomorrow is for our children, in this glorious country of opportunity. As for honor, it is better to have honor without life than life without honor. Ernesto, Liza, remember always to carry our family name with honor."

Nick colored and thought to himself, *I had to change my name to get into Columbia. I had no choice.*

Teresa, too, colored and thought to herself, *I had to change my name to get rid of Rocco. I had no choice.*

Rafaello raised his glass, "Godspeed, my children."

Everyone but Leonardo raised his glass in tribute. He scoffed, "Yesterday, today and tomorrow. Old country, new country. You're a fool, Rafaello."

Rafaello's face blanched; Delora's reddened in anger.

"In the old country," Leonardo continued, not paying the least attention to their consternation, "your father nearly died fighting with Garibaldi in the *Risorgimento.* What good did it do him? Nothing. Without a murmur, he and all the rest planted and reaped wheat, but never ate white bread; cultivated the grape, but never drank wine; raised animals, but never ate meat. In this country we labor long hours for greedy capitalists. Tell me, does the past comfort you? Does the present honor you? Does the future promise you anything?"

Rafaello remained stunned that Leonardo would turn on him after all he had done for him and embarrassed at how Leonardo belittled him before his family and friends. *Still,* he reflected, *I can't upset my guests. It must wait. I'll evict him. No. Leonardo is an intellectual. He doesn't really mean anything personal by it.*

Delora, indignant, was about to answer for Rafaello, but standing in the doorway was Steve, Ernesto's friend.

"Hello, everybody!" Steve, hair plastered down, fidgeted in his new, full-length blue serge suit. The only blemish to his sartorial splendor was a black eye. He placed his banjo case down and smiled.

Delora swallowed her anger and embraced Stefano. "Happy birthday!" *I can't make a scene and ruin the meal. I'll talk to Rafaello later.*

Liza's face lit up when she saw Steve. Everything about him was perfection, including his black eye. *How brave he was standing up for himself against a bully.*

Teresa lit the candles as everyone began singing Happy Birthday to both boys who took turns blowing out the candles.

As the candle wax essence circled the room, Nick asked, "How is it you didn't march in the parade, Leonardo?"

Leonardo flushed from the unexpected question. "Meaningless Socialist nonsense. Socialism, Capitalism, Fascism, they are all alike. We must do away with all forms of government and bankers."

"More coffee, Leonardo?" Delora asked, hoping to change the topic, but he wasn't finished.

"The bankers create wars to add to their profits. We struggling workers fight their wars, thinking it's for a grand cause. They aim their rhetoric at the youths who believe they are invincible. Carl Marx is right. *'It is a case of the destruction of men for the production of goods.'* In Russia the masses are on the verge of a great revolution. It will spread. *'A great flame follows a little spark.'*"

"Francesco," Delora interrupted, trying desperately to change the subject, "tell us again how you escaped."

"Well, I..."

"Dante also said," Nick interjected, "'Thou shalt prove how salt is the taste of another's bread and how hard is the way up and down another man's shoes.' Anarchists think that people can survive without leadership and will voluntarily cooperate for the common good. Unfortunately, people aren't that way. Anarchists would destroy a nation. Socialists want to divide everything. In short order, everything would revert to the same competent people. Although the idea sounds wonderful, it'll never work. Another thing Socialists don't understand about economics, profit and loss..."

Leonardo, annoyed at being upstaged by Nick's surprising knowledge of Dante, raised his arm, stopping Nick in mid-sentence. "You Capitalists are all the same. All you worry about is profit, as if profit were a mistress."

Everyone else at the table recoiled.

Nick, although obviously vexed, spoke softly, "Leonardo, there are ladies present."

Leonardo, however, was unstoppable. "The ladies, my dear fellow, should know what is going on in the world. People like you are exploiting them in the workplace."

"Rafaello." The edge in Delora's voice did nothing to rouse Rafaello. He simply shrugged his shoulders and smiled, obviously enjoying the confrontation.

"I see." Nick's eyes narrowed. "How are we exploiting them?"

"The women work as hard as the men, but don't get paid the same, although I don't have to tell you. Just look at your own factory."

"Mine?" Nick's color deepened.

"Yes. The hours they keep and the pay you give them is disgraceful. Ask Violetta. She will tell you.

Nick stared at Teresa.

"Yes, ask her," Josephine agreed with a satisfied smile. "She's in on it."

Elena gave her a cutting look.

Teresa's mouth opened in astonishment. She looked at Josephine who did nothing to hide her self-satisfied expression. *So that was her motive, to discredit me in Nick's eyes.* It infuriated her, but somehow she managed to keep her temper.

Leonardo persisted, "You and your mother treat them no better than whores..."

The women gasped. Rafaello choked on his pipe, sending him into a coughing fit.

Nick, more upset by his disappointment in Teresa than by Leonardo's profanity, pounded the table. The glasses and demitasse cups jumped. "I'll thank you to keep a civil tongue in your head!" He stood up abruptly, almost toppling the chair.

Leonardo, frightened, jumped up and stepped back from the table.

"Gentlemen," Rafaello interjected, "enough politics. What do you say we play some cards, or some music? Yes, that's it, music. Come on, Leonardo, join me. I like the way you play guitar. Ernesto, Liza, come. Steve, get your banjo."

Everyone hastily rose from the table, trying to dispel the charged air with activity. Leonardo scooted to the corner and almost disappeared in the overstuffed chair. The musicians began tuning up. As the ladies cleared the table, Nick strode out the door.

"Nick," Teresa, close on his heels, called, "Wait!"

Josephine started after them, but Rosa blocked her way.

Elena handed Josephine a dish. "Get in the kitchen! You've done enough damage for one night."

"What do you mean?" Josephine tried to bypass Rosa, but Delora grabbed her arm. "Let me go!"

Rosa slid the dining room doors closed and leaned against them. "Sit down, Josephine, before I pull your hair out!"

"How dare you?" Nevertheless, Josephine, stunned by the assault, sat.

\* \* \*

While a full moon cast shadows, uniting the knee walls, aviary, and air vents scattered across the rooftop, distant building lights seemingly merged with the stars. Soft yellow lights from the skylight pushed through the darkness. A stillness and calm pervaded the rooftop as if the pigeons had asked all noise to stop so that they might sleep. However, the calm didn't reflect either Teresa's or Nick's emotions. They stood silently against the retaining wall, staring blindly at the building across the way. The lighted apartments formed a huge multilevel stage with the people as actors, oblivious of their audience.

Rosa, singing a Neapolitan love song, broke the silence. Her rich tones drifted through the open rooftop doorway.

"Who's singing?" Nick asked quietly, without turning to her.

"Rosa. It is the first time I've heard her sing, but I'd recognize her voice anywhere."

"Such feeling."

"Yes," Teresa agreed. "Francesco must have persuaded her to sing despite her mourning period."

"Love can work wonders—sometimes."

They fell silent, each afraid to say what was really on his mind. They allowed the music to swirl over and around them, like a vine tying them together. The music stopped, breaking the spell.

Without turning to face her, he asked, "What were Leonardo and Josephine talking about?"

"I'm not sure, except that since you've stopped managing things at the factory, things have changed."

"How?"

She began, feeling her way slowly. "The workers are increasingly agitated. Despite the longer hours their take-home pay hasn't increased."

"Violetta, we're in a competitive market. It's not a pleasant pastime. Whatever Mama is, she's a shrewd business woman who knows what the market will bear."

"Maybe so, but the workers feel abused and wonder why you haven't stepped in to help."

"Is that how you feel?"

"In a way. It affects me too."

"I'm sorry you feel that way."

His voice was gentle, but it stung. She was glad he couldn't see her redden.

"The business is hers. Even before Papa died, Mama managed it all alone. Papa wasn't a businessman, so he let her do whatever she thought best. She's made the business pay and grow. Work is everything for her. Except for Delora, she doesn't have time for friends. I tried to make things easier for her by bringing in labor-saving machines, but she finds them too time-consuming to learn, or too dangerous, like mechanizing your machine. I suggested shorter hours and fewer days. She went along for a time, but the business began to falter. I guess, like Papa, I've no head for business. How can I trample on all that she's done for me and the business, which supports me too? Still, it doesn't explain why Josephine said to ask you about it."

"The workers wanted me to be a spokesperson, but I didn't want to get involved."

"Good. Will you keep me informed?"

"I can't promise you that. I'm not a spy."

"I respect you for that. Let's keep it at that for now. By the way, I told Mama that you could read and write in English and Italian and are good with numbers."

"With numbers and read and write in Italian, yes. In English? Like a six-year-old."

"I believe you are better at it than you think. Anyway, Mama wants you to work in the office."

"Me?" He astonished her.

"Yes. She needs help since she has two factories to worry about."

"I don't understand. I thought she didn't like me."

"Mama?" His surprise was genuine. "That's not true. She likes your spunk. She believes you to be honest and genuine, someone she can trust. Believe me, Mama doesn't say that about many people."

Teresa shivered. It wasn't the cool night air that had settled in that bothered her so much, but Giustina's evaluation of her. Was it her sense of guilt or her lack of trust of Giustina?

"Cold?"

"A bit."

He removed his jacket and placed it around her shoulders. The warmth of his body had transferred to the jacket. Teresa trembled again. This time it wasn't from Giustina's evaluation nor sense of guilt.

"Still cold?"

"No. I'm fine. Thank you." His spicy aftershave essence floated toward her.

Francesco and Rosa began singing together. Teresa and Nick again grew silent, allowing the intoxicating Neapolitan love song to wash over them.

Unable to look at her, his voice grew soft as a caress, "Violetta..."

She, too, couldn't bring herself to look at him. "Yes?" she asked, her voice barely audible.

"What does Leonardo mean to you?"

"Mean?"

"Do you love him?"

Teresa couldn't help laughing. "Leonardo? No, I don't love Leonardo." She paused, afraid to ask her next question. "And Josephine? What does she mean to you?"

Now it was his turn to laugh. "Josephine? Absolutely nothing. She's much too bold." He touched Teresa's hand.

Shafts of electricity coursed through her veins, taking her breath away.

He turned her to face him. The moonlight shone on her face, setting it aglow with an unearthly radiance. "You're very beautiful."

"Beautiful? Me?"

"Yes, breathtakingly beautiful. Don't you know that? Turn around quickly sometime and you'll catch men, and even some women, staring at you."

Nick took her into his arms. His jacket fell from her shoulders. "You're bewitching," he whispered softly. He kissed her tenderly on the lips then her eyes, mouth and throat.

Was it the floor shaking or her legs? As his warm caresses enveloped her, she couldn't help responding, allowing all the emotions she had repressed her entire life rush forth. Then, fear took possession of her. Fear of what? She didn't know. She tried pushing him away, but he held her fast. "Nick," the throaty sound of her own voice surprised her, "please stop."

It was as surprising to him as to her, and yet he found himself saying in spite of himself, "You love me. I know you do." He kissed her throat again.

The blood rushed to her head. "Wait, please." She felt faint. "We mustn't."

"Why not?"

"I...promised," was all she could think of saying.

"Promised? Promised who?" Her words didn't register. He kissed her eyes.

"Your mother. I promised her I wouldn't be alone with you."

"What does she have to do with it? It's only between you and me. I think...I think I love you." The thought surprised him as much as it did her. "Someday, I'll want to marry you," Nick blurted out, amazed at his own impetuousness.

"Marry?" Until this moment, she hadn't thought of Rocco. She froze and pushed him away more urgently. "Nick, I can't."

"I don't understand. Why not? You love me. I know you do."

"Please, not yet." She sought desperately for an explanation.

"When?"

"Neither of us is ready. Nick. Please don't say anything about this to Giustina."

"Whatever you say, *cara.*" He took her into his arms again and kissed her.

"No, please, you're making my head spin." Nevertheless, she wished she could remain in his embrace.

# Chapter 11

Teresa thought the priest eyed her suspiciously as he entered the confessional. *You're becoming paranoid.* It was a new term she had learned from the librarian when the librarian had mentioned Sigmund Freud.

She stared at the new confessional with its intricate religious symbolic patterns cut deeply into its solid oak front. The new, hard oak genuflecting board felt as if it, too, had deep carvings in it. The discomfort she felt on her knees, however, was nothing to the discomfort she felt at having Giustina beside her. That was new, too, beginning three weeks ago when she had started to work in the office. Whenever Giustina was in town, she insisted upon attending church with Teresa. Teresa reflected, *Perhaps Giustina believes it will ensure my honesty and loyalty.*

Whatever the reason, Teresa couldn't escape going into the confessional. What was she going to say to the priest? If he did recognize her, would Giustina overhear his angry lecture? She could tell Giustina that she felt ill and had to go home. It wouldn't be a lie. The incense and flickering candle essences, coupled with the dread of entering, did make her feel ill. However, it would only delay the inevitable. *Never mind, try thinking of something pleasant.*

She thought of the evening on the rooftop. Her head spun even more. *Why didn't I tell him I would marry him?* True, she would be spending her entire life living a lie as Violetta, but that hadn't bothered her before, so why now? She knew the answer, fear of detection. *In God's eyes I'm married. But Rocco is dead!* Why didn't she believe it? *Stop it! Think of something else.* She thought about the promise she had made to Giustina. How could she tell Giustina that she had gone behind her back? Yes, that was it. Nevertheless, she knew deep down that Giustina wasn't her real problem; she was.

Then, other doubts began to creep in. *Why haven't I seen Nick since that night on the roof? Has he been too busy with exams, or is he annoyed with me for not being eager to marry? Maybe he's had second thoughts?* She was so deeply involved with her thoughts that she didn't notice it was her turn to enter the confessional.

Giustina eyed her suspiciously. She nudged Teresa in the side and stuck her chin out toward the confessional.

Teresa entered, knelt and began, "Forgive me, Father, for I have sinned. I..."

"So, it *is* you." His voice wasn't friendly. "Have you returned to your husband?" It was more an indictment than a question.

"No."

"Oh," he moaned. "My child, what can I say to convince you that you are sinning?" His words were drawn out as if she exhausted him with her lack of obedience.

"They have told me that an explosion killed him."

His voice softened and compassion replaced his cold demeanor. "I am sorry, my child. May God rest his soul. I will pray for him, as should you."

Teresa wanted to say, *Never!* but said instead, "Father, a man wants to marry me."

"You have these thoughts so soon?" The screen between them did nothing to filter out his disapproval. Then, sorry for his lack of civility, "May God bless your union."

Should she tell him about her double life? She must tell someone or go mad.

Sensing her hesitation, he asked, "What else, my child?"

"I'm not who people think I am."

"Only God knows who we are. We are a mystery even to ourselves."

"That's not what I mean."

"Go on, my child. God is listening."

"I have changed my identity."

"WHAT? WHY?"

Teresa recoiled, fearing that Giustina heard. She wanted to scream at the priest, "Control yourself!" Instead, she plunged forward. "To escape my husband's grasp, I changed my identity with that of another woman who died during the crossing." Teresa said it all in one breath, fearing she would lose courage in the middle. She thought she saw him coming nearer the screen. Instinctively, she backed up as far as she could.

"My dear, you are full of surprises." Teresa could almost see his eyes narrow with disapproval. "Have you told your intended?"

"No."

"You must." His tone was cold and distant. "You cannot go on living a lie."

"But I may lose him."

"Better now than later, my child. A marriage based on a lie is no marriage."

"You ask too much."

"It is not I who ask, but God."

Silence.

"Will you tell him?"

Silence.

"Think of it in this way, would you like it if he held some secrets from you?"

Teresa thought a bit. "No."

"There, you have it. So, will you tell him?"

She trembled at the very thought. "I will pray for guidance, Father."

"Good, and so shall I. Anything else?"

"Father, will you please do something for me?"

"What is it?"

Teresa now rationalized that although her mother had forced her into a horrible marriage, it was not through malevolence, but necessity. It wasn't that her mother didn't love her, she concluded, for hadn't her mother scrimped to send her to the nuns for an education, unheard of in Montaguto? "I would like to send some money to my mother in Italy each month. Would you do it for me?"

"Of course, but why don't you do it?"

"Not yet." Teresa bit her lower lip. "She believes that I died during the crossing."

"That is awful! Think what your poor mother must be going through. You must write to her that you are alive and well. *La mamma l'anima, chi la perde non la quedagna.*"

She had heard the proverb, "One's mother and one's soul—when lost can never be restored," often, mostly from her mother. *But if Rocco is still alive, he could learn I'm alive through Mama. I can't, not yet.* "I will, but meanwhile please don't tell her or anyone where it came from."

"All right, but this secrecy and deception will hurt you in the end."

For a second Teresa shivered at his words, but she shrugged them off.

## Chapter 12

Giustina sat with her back to the silent factory and watched the glistening raindrops creep down the transom-sized window in her office. A sudden gust of wind vibrated the pane, pelting rain against the glass in a failed attempt to penetrate it. This section of Manhattan was never pleasant for her, but when it rained, it almost became intolerable. The dank odors and walls seemingly closed in upon her.

In the fading light of day, with all the workers gone, the factory had a ghostly presence for her. Despite the unusually warm day for October, she shuddered as she studied the plastered area. *I should put that door back in. I'll lose the wall space, but coming and going without the workers knowing it would be worth it. It will keep Niccolo from bothering me, too.* Still, she didn't want to give in to his every whim.

She listened to Teresa's rhythmic tap-tap and smiled to herself. *Smart move getting her,* forgetting completely that it had been Nick's idea. *Maybe I should tell Niccolo to go after her. She's smart, ambitious, trustworthy, and a virgin.*

Giustina found herself increasingly relying on Teresa. Teresa answered the telephone, handled the less sensitive correspondence and best of all, added tedious columns of figures, something Giustina hated. She knitted her brows as she considered the ledgers. *Still, I must keep the ledgers locked away. Can't have her learning too much about the business. Why didn't I insist Niccolo study law or accounting? He never listens to me. He could be such a help to me. She* looked at Teresa with renewed interest. *If they get married, I wouldn't have to pay her and maybe I could even trust her with the ledgers. The only problem now is errands. I can't take someone away from the floor, and hiring someone else is a waste of money.* "Violetta?"

"Yes?" Concentrating intently on her typing, she didn't look up.

"I want to send you out on errands, but you can't go alone."

"How about Ernesto?"

"He's too young. I need someone like you."

"He could go with me after school. It would keep him out of trouble, too." Teresa shook her head, still concentrating on her typing. "It's not good for him to work in Malespina's back room."

Giustina's eyes brightened, "Mmm. He could remove spots, tie the smaller bundles and sweep the floor." She played with the bun behind her head as she was apt to do when she was thinking.

"Getting Ernesto away from Malespina will keep Niccolo from those stock tips Ernesto has been feeding him."

"I thought Nick was doing well with them."

"Worse yet. It can trap you and leave you penniless." However, Giustina's own problems took her away from Nick's. "I could hire Liza instead. She would be cheaper."

"Not with Delora in a family way."

"Too bad. Well, at least we are three and a half weeks ahead of schedule. Increasing the time the workers have been putting in and those motors that Niccolo finally added to the machines have saved us a lot of time."

"I'm glad. Then you can give me a raise."

"A raise?" She raised her voice several octaves.

"I'm still not making what I did on the floor."

"Because you are no longer productive. You should be paying me for teaching you new skills."

That hurt, but Teresa had to admit that Giustina's argument had merit. She was learning a lot. However, its drawbacks were the loss of money and friends. Apart from Elena and Leonardo, no one spoke to her, convinced she had become Giustina's spy. What bothered Teresa most was the constant surveillance. Now that Nick no longer was able to take his mother to Paterson every night, Giustina slept in Liza's room. Day and night Giustina watched her; if not Giustina, Liza; if not Liza, Josephine. Now it would be Ernesto, too. She almost regretted having suggested hiring him.

Generally, however, Teresa was content. Another advantage was that the workers had called off the strike. It would have placed her in an impossible position between Nick and the workers, and in a financial crisis, too.

Their thoughts so absorbed the two women that they wouldn't have seen a shadow move across the frosted glass on the office door even if the light had been favorable.

In the dim light that glowed through the plate glass window, a figure crept closer to the office door. He held his breath and listened. Satisfied, he selected a bundle of skirts and took a glass bottle filled with kerosene from his pocket. It was all he could do to pull out the cork between his chattering teeth. Carefully, to avoid getting any on himself, he poured the clear liquid on the bundle. With the grace of a predator, he reached overhead and took a handful of tissue-paper patterns from a wire that stretched from pillar to pillar. Struggling, he finally managed to tuck the patterns under the cord of the tightly wrapped bundle. He clustered more patterns on the wires directly over the bundle, then stopped and listened. The tapping of the typewriter reassured him.

"Violetta," Giustina yawned audibly. "I think we should go upstairs. It's late."

He almost bolted for the front door. His heart beat a rapid cadence against his bony ribs. *Don't pass out.* Perspiration dripped from his long, thin nose.

"Not yet," Teresa answered without looking up from the typewriter. "I'd like to practice some more."

"All right." Giustina smiled with patronizing pride at the girl's ambition.

The shadowy figure breathed easier, but his tension and trembling were not relieved. He took a wooden match from his back pocket, lifted his foot to strike the match on the sole and almost fell. He slumped against a post and succeeded in striking the match. It burst into flame, scorching his bony fingers, forcing him to drop the match onto the bundle. He jerked his fingers into his mouth to soothe them. Slowly, the match began to take hold of the paper patterns, slower than he had expected. The fire burned the patterns but refused to ignite the bundle. He shoved more patterns under the cord.

Giustina stretched and rubbed the small of her back with both hands. "Looks like it stopped raining. Good. I can't sit here a minute longer. I'll leave you to lock up." This was the first time she considered allowing Teresa to remain behind without vigil. She dropped the keys on the desk, reconsidered, and removed the ledger drawer key from the ring. Then she slipped the key into her purse and tossed the other keys back on the desk. "Keep the keys with you and open a half-hour earlier in the morning. Harry Goldstein is sending another shipment of cloth. Be sure to check the manifest. Harry's honest but you can't trust anybody. I...Shhh. Did you hear something?"

The petrified man held his breath.

Teresa stopped typing and listened. "No. I don't hear anything. Maybe it's Nick?" Her heart fluttered in anticipation.

"No, Niccolo isn't coming."

"It's not like you to be so nervous. Anything wrong?"

"No. I just had a *presagio*. That's all."

"A premonition?" Remaining alone now seemed too forbidding. Teresa sprang to her feet and covered the typewriter. "You're right. It's late. Let's go."

Giustina pulled the cord to the overhead light as Teresa opened the office door.

Teresa smelled the smoke before she saw it. "Fire!" she screamed. Then she saw the man escaping through the front door. *Leonardo?* Black smoke billowing from the bundle didn't give her time to dwell on it. Tiny fingers of fire grabbed the patterns and felt their way along a cord. Flaming pattern pieces flew into the air, barely missing the patterns suspended on the line. As if disappointed, the pieces floated listlessly to the floor. Teresa reached up, tore the patterns from the line and threw them left and right, but they swirled back at her. Lashing out at them with both arms did no good, for they merely floated out of reach. "Call the fire department!" she screamed at Giustina who stood petrified in the doorway.

Teresa grabbed a fire bucket sitting beside the office door. "Call the fire department!" Teresa screamed again and rushed to the bundle. With a sweep of her arms, she hurled the water at the bundle. The flame subsided, but it created more smoke. "Giustina! Don't stand there! Call the fire department!" she screamed, but Giustina stared blankly at her.

Teresa pushed past the immobilized woman, ran into the office, picked up the phone and frantically jiggled the hook. "Operator! Fire! Giovane and Son Clothing Factory, Spring Street. Hurry!" She dropped the long-necked phone so quickly it toppled off the desk and crashed to the floor. "Get out of the way!" She pushed Giustina aside and tugged at the bundle that showed signs of life again, but it refused to budge. "Giustina! For God's sake, help me!" Smoke filled her lungs, sending her into a coughing fit.

Giustina came out of her trance and ran for the nonexistent back door. Seeing only the transom window, she panicked again. The only way out was past the smoldering bundle. Suddenly, she remembered that this was the factory that she had spent more than half her life building from nothing. She ran into the office, grabbed another water bucket, raced back to Teresa, and tossed the water, hitting Teresa squarely in the chest.

The shock of the cold water hitting her took her breath away. Recovering her breath forced her to inhale more smoke, sending her into another coughing fit. Gasping, she ordered Giustina,

"Help me move the bundle!" However, with the added water weight, moving it was impossible. The smoke surged thicker than ever. "It's no use, Giustina. We've got to get out!"

"No! I won't leave my factory!"

"If we don't get out soon, we never will! I can squeeze through the transom, but you can't. Get out now!"

"No! I must save my factory! You go."

"Not without you! Let's try again."

They strained with all their might, but the soggy lump clung to the floorboards.

"Mama! Where are you?" Nick's voice rang out.

"Here, Nick!" Teresa called. "Near the office door. A bundle is on fire!"

He emerged through the haze. "For God's sake get out of here, both of you! I'll handle it!"

"No," Teresa insisted, despite the tears stinging her eyes. "Not without you."

"Let's not argue! We're wasting time. You push. I'll pull."

They pushed and tugged at the bundle. Nothing.

"Wait!" Nick grabbed a dry half-made skirt, threw it down and rolled the bundle on top of it. The bundle barely missed a sewing machine. He threw another half-made skirt on top, but it created more smoke. "Okay! Push!" He grabbed the end of the skirt at the bottom and pulled.

Slowly they began moving down the aisle.

*Please, dear God,* Teresa prayed, *don't let it snag on a machine or another bundle!* For what seemed forever to her, they dragged it past one machine, then another, and yet another. The smoke from the bundle was so thick she could barely see Nick's face although he was only inches away from her. Teresa thought her strength would give out before they could reach the door. At last, they reached the front door just when she thought she would collapse.

"Out of the way!" Nick shouted. With a mighty push he toppled the smoking mass out the door. Again and again he toppled it until it rested in the gutter. He straightened up just in time, for fed by the increased oxygen, flames shot from the bundle. Each of them gasped for air and collapsed on the wet front steps. As their breathing returned to normal, they heard the clanging bells of the horse-drawn fire engine up the street. Within seconds the horses snorted to an abrupt stop. A fireman jumped down and connected the hose to the fire hydrant while another fireman held the hose.

"Hey, Sam," a fireman called to the man holding the hose, "turn the hose on the factory! There's some smoke coming out."

"No!" Nick shouted after them as they started into the building. "The fire isn't inside! It's just this bundle." He rubbed his soot-covered hands together to ease the pain that pulling the bundle had caused and rushed over to the man with the hose.

"We've got to go inside anyway, Tony, to make sure," a burly fireman said as he swung an ax over his shoulder and entered the building.

Nick hated how non-Italians called all Italian men Tony. Nevertheless, he contained his anger and turned to Giustina. "What happened? How did it start?"

Giustina cleared her throat a few times to rid it of smoke before she could answer. "It was deliberate!" Giustina's fury burned brighter than the fire.

"Deliberate? Why? Who?"

"I don't know, but we saw a man running from the building, didn't we, Violetta?"

At first all Nick noticed was the black soot peppered over Teresa's face and shirtwaist. Then, in the streetlights' glow, he could see her breasts through her clinging shirtwaist. Clearly visible were the dark areolas that framed the taut points of her nipples. Her heavy breathing thrust them tantalizingly at him. He felt a curious tingling shock that aroused a yearning within him. Nick wanted desperately to reach out and touch her. Suddenly, he felt ashamed, took off his jacket and placed it over her shoulders. Again the thought of marriage flashed through his mind. *Why not? I like everything about her.* Nick took a deep breath, trying to come to grips with himself. *What were we talking about? Oh, yes.* "Did you see who it was, Violetta?"

Teresa was about to tell him of her suspicions, but thought, *What if it wasn't Leonardo? I could be destroying an innocent man.* "Everything happened so fast and it was so dark, I couldn't tell who it was."

\* \* \*

Two days after the fire, the stench still lingered throughout the building, constantly reminding Teresa of the frightful experience. Josephine and Elena and the other boarders, trying to escape the stench, were on the rooftop. In the basement, overriding the stench with zinfandel grape redolence, Rafaello, Ernesto and Steve crushed grapes for wine. Liza and Delora were doing the dishes in the kitchen.

The oil lamp sitting in the middle of the dining room table formed a soft yellow glow around Teresa and Leonardo, seemingly isolating them from the others in the house. Sitting opposite Leonardo, she tried to keep her mind on her English lesson. However, two other thoughts kept her from concentration: the possible loss of work and Leonardo. Dare she confront him with her suspicions? She felt ambivalence toward him, grateful for his teaching, yet unnerved too.

Leonardo sensed her intense scrutiny and looked over his wire-rimmed eyeglasses. His stoic face revealed nothing, but although his speech was as proper as ever, his shoulders were not as straight. "What's wrong?" His voice was hoarse.

"Nothing." Nevertheless, she continued staring, this time at his bandaged thumb and forefinger.

Leonardo's eyes twitched. He placed his hand in his lap, keeping it from her view, and cleared his throat. "Something is. What is it?" His question expressed more challenge than curiosity.

"You know many people. Who do you think...?"

"Whom," he corrected.

*"Whom,"* she said through clenched teeth, do you think started the fire?"

His brows knitted into a frown. "How should I know?" His answer was curt.

"It nearly killed Giustina and me. I don't understand why anyone would want to do that." She paused for effect. "Do you? For what purpose?"

"Don't ask me." He looked down, but even in the dim light, she could see his face had reddened.

Teresa pressed on. "I know Giustina is too abrasive and interested in profits to be compassionate, but still, she has given many people work." She paused again. "You and me."

"I," he corrected again.

"You and *I!* I haven't done anything to hurt anyone." Even as she said it she thought of her mother and a sharp pain pierced her.

He tapped the table nervously with his pencil. "You, my dear, have done nothing." He averted his eyes. "Giustina, on the other hand, and her pompous son are boils on the backside of humanity!"

The remark against Nick stabbed at her. She had the sudden urge to reach across the table and slap him. It surprised her.

"Yes indeed, I can see why someone would want to set the fire!"

Her eyes widened at the sudden realization. "It *was* you, wasn't it?"

"You are crazy!" His words were strong, but his voice lacked conviction. "I would not hurt you for anything, but many people would stop at nothing for the cause."

"The cause?" He amazed her. "Killing innocent people?" For the first time she saw how really warped his thinking was. Delora and Nick saw it. Why not she?

Leonardo leaned back in his chair. His rigid posture restored, he began speaking as if he had been rehearsing for years. "There are no innocent people, only two sides, management and workers. Management is the enemy. Workers are the soldiers in a battle for survival. In this battle, the workers are expendable for the..."

"Stop!" She sprang to her feet and slammed her book on the table.

The sharpness in her voice startled him. He almost toppled his chair.

Teresa began gathering her books and papers. "Fortunately, the fire killed no one and the factory didn't burn down." She was so angry she trembled. "Not only would those people you are so in touch with be out of work, but this entire building could have gone up in flames. It could have killed Delora, her family and all the boarders. Even if the fire didn't kill them, they could have lost what little they had." She stamped her foot. Her voice rose in pitch. "Delora and Rafaello took you in, gave you a place to live, fed you, cleaned up after you without asking for one penny. Is this the way you repay them?"

He started to say something, but she held up her hand. "Don't say one word. Even if the factory didn't burn down, you had your way. The smoke ruined the entire shipment! It could close the factory and throw everybody out on the street!" She headed for the door.

Leonardo got up and wagged his bound finger at her. "If I were you, I would not go around telling people what you think I may or may not have done. It could be dangerous! Very!"

She turned. "Don't threaten me. You needn't worry, Leonardo, I won't betray you. Not because of your threats. They don't frighten me in the least, but because you have been my teacher. I owe you a great deal for that, but don't betray me either."

"Oh! *Aiuto mi!*" Delora's scream stopped Teresa in her tracks. She rushed to the kitchen to find Delora on the floor gripping her stomach while Liza stood by helplessly wringing her hands and crying.

"Liza!" Teresa ordered. "Get the midwife! Get Mrs. Gallo!"

# Chapter 13

Harry's office on the four-story building's top floor was nearly six times as large as Giustina's, but five times as cluttered. Going from the almost pristine outer office into his was a shock. It was so unlike the Harry she had seen at Giustina's.

An old dressmaker's dummy stood beside the entrance. Several yards of white satin cloth hung on one shoulder and spread around its base. Sketches hung askew on the walls, nearly obscuring the polished mahogany surface. The only open spaces were the corner windows. Bright sunlight streaming through the glass gave the room a cheerful air despite the clutter. For some reason, Teresa suspected it was Harry who gave the room that feeling, not the sunlight.

Harry smiled broadly, got up quickly from behind his desk, grabbed his fawn-colored jacket from a coat rack beside him and put it on. The perfectly tailored jacket fit snugly around his tall, straight, supple body. He tugged at his vest to keep it where it should be. Harry, a clean shaven, urbane gentleman, looked almost half his thirty-six years despite the gray at his temples. His spicy aftershave scent, the same as Nick's, floated in her direction.

"It's so good seeing you again, Violetta. I was just thinking of you." His masculine eye swept over her entire figure, taking in every detail. He swept a sample book off a chair. "Please sit."

Although it was a straight-backed wooden chair, she couldn't remember being more comfortable. Harry's influence again. She pulled some papers from a leather briefcase just as the intercom buzzed.

"Please excuse me, Violetta." He sat on the desk's edge and reached back for the button. "Barbara, I asked you not to interrupt me now."

As Harry spoke to his secretary, Teresa picked up a silk garment someone had draped across the chair beside her. The tag pinned to the garment told her that it was a sample. Although the fabric was top quality, the sewing wasn't. She frowned.

Harry finished his conversation and saw her disapproval. "Something wrong?"

"Well, it's not my place to say."

"Go ahead. I'd like hearing what you have to say."

"Well, this garment was poorly done. The seam allowance is too small and hasn't been finished properly." She walked over to the window for better light. "Look at the stitching." He stood beside her. "Too few stitches." She fingered the material. "This silk is much too fine for sloppy handiwork. Giovane's craftsmen can do better, and..." She stopped when she saw him smiling. "I'm sorry, but you asked." She smiled and returned to her seat.

He laughed. "I did, didn't I?"

Seeing an opportunity, she asked, "Why don't you have us make a sample for you?"

"Let me think about it. Meanwhile, how is the current production going?"

"We've been working these past three weeks far into the night using both factories to make up the time, but I'm afraid we'll be almost two weeks short of the delivery date."

"Two weeks?" He sat hard at his desk. "Phew! That's not good at all!"

"I know, but if you can stall your distributors, I'm sure they won't be disappointed. Our quality will please them very much. You know we do excellent work. Frankly, our garments are worth more money. I'd say they are worth at least three cents more a garment. Look at it this way; if you go to another manufacturer, it will take even longer to complete the shipment. Nick mechanized our machines." She shrugged. "It would be worth your while to wait. Don't you agree?"

Harry laughed. "Quite a saleslady, aren't you?"

She blushed. "I have been rambling on, haven't I? Anyway, Giustina sent these revised contracts for your approval." She handed the papers to him, but to her disappointment, she left without an agreement.

* * *

The following evening, a hint of snow hung in the still, crisp air. Inside the factory, everyone worked feverishly, but it did little to take the edge off the cold, damp room. Still, they worked without complaint, knowing that it meant survival, for them and the factory. Nick almost flew from machine to machine repairing, replacing snapped belts and oiling the motors. Within the office, a bleary-eyed Teresa's fingers flew across the adding machine's keys while Giustina worked on the ledgers.

Giustina removed her eyeglasses and rubbed her eyes. "When are we going to hear from Harry? He's taking too long." With an accusatory note in her voice she asked, "What did you say to him yesterday, Violetta?"

"Just what you said I should." Although Teresa was frightened that she had gone too far in her suggestions, she bristled at the implication that she had done something wrong.

"Then why hasn't he signed the papers?"

Teresa was about to say, *Next time, do your own dirty work,* but Giustina's incessant monologue saved her.

"Even if he waits, I'll need two cents more to show a profit. I should have told you to tell him that. No, you should have realized that for yourself."

Teresa didn't trust herself to speak.

Giustina wasn't finished complaining. "Fine time for Leonardo to run off, just when we need him." The telephone rang. "Hello, Giovani and...Harry, I was just talking about you." She sat at her desk.

The factory noise increased as Nick entered.

Giustina placed her hand over the mouthpiece. "Close the door, Niccolo! Sorry, Harry. What did you say?"

Nick sat on the edge of Teresa's desk. "Mama has you doing double duty, sewing during the day and office work at night. It must be wearing you out."

Giustina glared at Nick over her glasses, but neither of them noticed.

"What about you? Going to college and dashing from New York to Paterson can't be easy."

"I'll survive, if my grades do. I haven't seen you at the library lately."

"I haven't had time, so it can wait." She laughed, "I haven't even had time to spend that twenty-five cents a week raise your mother gave me on clothes and shoes. Guess I'll just have to save my money until we finish the shipment."

"I hope you don't save it at *Padrone's,*" he said as he began linking some paperclips together.

"No," she shook her head. "I don't trust him." She was too embarrassed to say she pinned her money inside her clothing.

Giustina hung up the phone and laughed, startling Teresa. Laughter wasn't one of Giustina's strong points.

"Something wrong?" Teresa asked.

"Wrong?" Giustina looked puzzled at the question. "No, nothing. Harry Goldstein is willing to give us the extension on the order, thanks to you."

"Me?" The compliment was even more astonishing.

"Yes. He said you charmed him when you were in his office. Because of you, he agreed to wait, and he's willing to give us three cents more per garment! *Brava,* Violetta!"

Teresa's mouth hung open; she was unable to come to grips with all the praise.

"That's not all. He said he is going to let us bid on some silk dresses. I've been trying to get that bid for a long time, with no luck. How did you do it?"

Teresa shrugged. "The sample I saw in his office was pitiful. I said our people can do better work. That's all."

"Why didn't you tell me this before?"

"Because Harry, I mean Mr. Goldstein, said he wanted to think about it. No use building false hopes."

Giustina clapped her hands. "He's going to send us some silk, a sketch and a pattern. We'll make the dress and you can deliver it to him, Violetta."

"No." Nick's eyes brightened. "That's not good enough. Violetta is going to model it for him."

"What?" Teresa took a quick breath, utterly astonished. "Me!" Today held no end of surprises for her. "Isn't Josephine a better choice?"

"Josephine?" Nick looked puzzled. "No, you. Wait! I've seen some of your sketches. They're good. We'll make one of them up too."

Now it was Giustina's mouth that hung open in disbelief.

He spun the linked paperclips around his index finger. "Too bad Leonardo isn't here. He was our best cutter, but Salvatore is almost as good."

Nick's excitement transferred itself to Teresa. "Elena should be the one to make up the sample. She is our best. Another thing, I've often wondered why we don't bypass the primary contractor and get the work direct. Maybe even do some designing ourselves.

Not on Harry's, I mean, Mr. Goldstein's, contracts, that wouldn't be ethical, but there would be a lot more money in it if we went direct." Teresa caught Giustina staring at her, wide-eyed. "Did I say something wrong?"

"No," Giustina smiled, "just the opposite. Maybe we should look into it."

The door opened and the floorlady poked her head in. "Nick, another snapped belt."

"Right!" Nick turned as he was about to leave. "By the way, Mama, don't you think we should give Violetta more than twenty-five cents a week?"

Giustina's eyes narrowed at Nick's lack of business sense. When the door closed behind him, Giustina started to say something and changed her mind. Then she said, "You know, Violetta, it's all right with me if you see Niccolo." *Maybe you can give him some business sense.*

Teresa didn't know why, but she resented Giustina's statement. Perhaps it was Giustina's assumption that it was Giustina who was in control of her relationship with Nick, much like her own mother controlling whom she should marry. Whatever it was, she smoldered. *Not much chance of anything happening between Nick and me, anyway. He hasn't said anything to me since that night on the roof. It must have been the wine.* Her temper was beginning to win out, but fortunately Giustina changed the subject.

"I wish Niccolo had more time to help me with the accounts. Running two factories so far apart is not easy. Maybe I should let him buy that automobile he wants. It would save us a great deal of time. Time is money."

*Let him? He's a grown man. Why doesn't he buy one if he wants one?* Then she thought, *Maybe I'm not being fair to him. Giustina must have complete financial control.*

The door swung open. "Afternoon mail!" Ernesto shouted as if they were both deaf, dumped a pile of mail on the desk, and dashed out. Teresa checked the mail. A black-bordered letter from Italy addressed to Violetta stopped her short. It was from a priest in Violetta's village. She tore open the end and pulled out the letter:

It is with deep regret that I must inform you that your Aunt Valentina has died. Fortunately, with God's blessing, it came in her sleep. May God have mercy on her soul.

Although she had never known Valentina, Teresa thought she should feel remorse, but she didn't. All she felt was relief at not having to worry about detection from that source.

The telephone rang. It was Giustina who answered it. "Harry? Is something wrong?" Her eyes narrowed. "Oh, I see...Thank you....Yes, I'll tell her." She hung up and remained motionless, totally stunned.

"What's wrong?" Teresa asked anxiously. "Has he changed his mind?"

"No. Just that I can't believe it. He has given us three tickets for a performance of Bellini's *La Sonnambula* at the Metropolitan Opera House. He said a business associate gave him tickets for this Saturday night."

"Why would he do that?" Teresa's eyes were wide with bewilderment. "Mr. Goldstein told me once that he loved the opera but couldn't get tickets." She knew Rafaello would have given his soul for a ticket.

"Harry has five tickets, two in the orchestra and three in a box. He was insistent that I should give you one." She eyed Teresa suspiciously.

"Me?" If she hadn't been sitting, she would have fallen. "The opera? But...I don't have anything to wear to the opera!" was all she could think of saying.

"Since it's his idea, we'll get something from him. He must have many samples."

\* \* \*

Delora's house swarmed with activity. Rafaello's new Victor phonograph blared a recording of the soprano, Luisa Tetrazzini, singing *"Ah! non credea mirati"* from *La Sonnambula.* Her voice overpowered the voices behind the closed dining room doors. Everyone was delighted to help Teresa dress for the opera, everyone except Ernesto, Rafaello, Josephine and Fortunata. Fortunata slept on top of the upright piano, unperturbed. Ernesto lay on the floor doing his homework, wondering what the fuss was all about. Rafaello, uncomfortable in his new easy chair, did his best to hide his envy behind the newspaper. From time to time he looked at the sliding doors and bit on his pipe stem. He wasn't the only envious one. Josephine, face down on the bed, sobbed bitterly. Between sobs, she promised herself that someday she'd get even with Teresa.

Rafaello looked up when Nick and Giustina entered the room. To his surprise, Giustina was almost attractive in her beaded black gown.

*"Permesso?"* she asked, but didn't wait for permission to enter.

*"Si,"* Rafaello rose to greet them.

*"Buona sera."* Nick, looking resplendent in his rented white tie and tails, bent down and ruffled Ernesto's hair. "Hello there, kiddo."

Ernesto got up and playfully lifted his arms in a boxing position.

Nick laughed and took a defensive pose. "Not today, kiddo. Is Violetta ready yet?"

Ernesto returned to his sprawled-out position on the floor when Giustina sat. "It's a lotta fuss for nothin', if you ask me."

"Nobody's asking you," Rafaello snapped. He lowered the volume on the phonograph, sat and replaced his pipe in his mouth. "Get some anisette for our guests."

"Just a little anisette," Giustina instructed.

Nick shook his head, "Nothing for me, thanks." He sat on the settee and tried to keep Fortunata from rubbing against his black evening clothes as he waited impatiently. Nick looked toward the dining room door.

"Do you like opera?" Rafaello asked Giustina.

She shrugged. "My husband, God rest his soul, loved the opera. As for me," she shrugged again, "why waste the money?"

"Do you know the story of *La Sonnambula?*" Rafaello asked, aching to tell her the story of the sleepwalker.

"Yes," she stifled a yawn, "I saw it in Milano. I..."

The doors to the dining room slid open, framing Teresa as if she were a portrait. Behind her, peeking to see the reaction, were Delora and the other women. Teresa's white, beaded, off-the-shoulder gown that Harry had gladly offered for the evening shimmered in the flickering gas lights. One tiny white beaded shoe peeked out from beneath the gown. Harry had even provided a delicate tiara to wear in her hair that she had piled high upon her head. Teresa's cheeks glowed.

Nick rose to his feet, his mouth wide with admiration. Teresa's beauty so stunned Rafaello that his pipe fell from his mouth, jettisoning its tobacco over his vest. Quickly he brushed the embers off before they could ignite his clothes. Giustina struggled with her cordial glass to avoid spilling her sticky drink. Even Ernesto stood in awe.

"Do I look all right?" Teresa asked with genuine concern, for no one said anything.

"All right? Why...you're stunning," Nick stuttered. He took the white evening wrap that Harry had provided and placed it around her shoulders, envious that it was Harry who had clothed her. He kicked himself for not having had the foresight to bring her flowers. *But then,* he rationalized, *that would have been overkill. She's more beautiful than any flower.*

Teresa glided from the apartment to the horse and carriage, floated from the carriage to the entrance of the opera house, and glided into the lobby. No one, least of all Nick, would have guessed that she felt ill at ease. She had never seen so many lights, colors or jewels, or so many beautifully dressed people. Being a part of it for even one evening thrilled her.

Nick escorted her on his arm, feeling intense pleasure at being the lucky one to have her in his possession. Giustina trailed behind them, almost forgotten.

"Good evening," a man's voice behind them said.

Teresa turned to see Harry impeccably attired in evening clothes. His smile seemed to outshine the lights around them. "Good evening, Harry," she answered and wondered if shaking hands were proper. She didn't see any of the women in the throng doing it. She decided it wasn't.

Giustina acknowledged the greeting with a polite nod. He kissed her hand. Nick extended his hand. Harry took it, but his admiring eyes never left Teresa.

She flushed.

"You look radiantly lovely, my dear, as always." He kissed her hand.

Nick sensed Harry's intense interest in Teresa and felt threatened, so much so that he felt like punching Harry. He'd never felt that way before.

Harry turned to a stately older woman standing beside him. "May I introduce Mrs. Williams? It was she who was kind enough to give us the tickets for this evening's performance."

They exchanged polite greetings and grateful indebtedness just as the bell for the performance sounded.

With renewed pride, Nick led Teresa up the stairs to the dress circle. They entered the plush box along the side of the horseshoe curve. Teresa sat beside Giustina, completely unaware that many in the house were training their opera glasses in her direction, among them Harry. Nick, sitting behind her, leaned over to her. His warm breath on her neck and shoulders sent a fire through every nerve in her body. He whispered, "When are we getting married, *cara?* Don't have me wait too long."

\* \* \*

A week later, Teresa felt ill at ease entering Harry's outer-office wearing the sample dress she had designed. Neither she nor Giustina had heard from him since opera night. Teresa took off her overcoat and pulled at the high, stand-up collar of her black georgette-crepe silk dress. She straightened the bishop sleeves and looked down to see if all the steel buttons from the high neck down to her hemline were intact. They were. The only things she felt comfortable in were her black leather pointed shoes with T-straps and high heels. Excluding the evening slippers, they were the first pair of shoes that had fit her since she lived in Italy.

Ernesto placed a box containing the evening dress and a box containing the sample dress that Harry had requested on a chair beside him. Then he plopped down in the straight-backed chair preparing himself for a long stay.

Harry's secretary hung up the phone and looked up. "My, how lovely you look, Miss Esposito. I wish I had the figure to wear a straight-line dress like that."

"Thank you." Teresa put her hand on her black, silk-covered, brimless hat and fluffed the feather hanging to one side.

"I'm sorry. Harry was called away on an emergency. I tried to reach you, but you had already left. He's been so busy lately that he hasn't had a chance to get in touch with you." The short, stocky older woman looked genuinely sorry. "He left a note for you." She searched her desk. "Ah, yes, here it is."

Teresa opened the envelope and read:

*Sorry I couldn't get in touch with you sooner. Permit me to tell you again how enchanting you looked the night of the opera. I hope to see you soon,*
*Harry*

# Chapter 14

### December 1910

The wind whirling the snow about the transom window in Giustina's Spring Street office intensified Teresa's shivering. She tried clearing her throat, but its raspiness made it impossible. Sucking on the horehound drops that Delora had given her only helped a little. Sitting at her desk, she found herself reliving the evening at the opera and Nick's proposal, but the warmth of remembrance failed to keep the chill from her bones. Although he had repeated the proposal during the months that had passed, she was able to persuade him to wait. Teresa wondered if she had done the right thing.

Giustina peered over her eyeglasses. "You look feverish. Go to bed."

"But it's only ten o'clock in the morning. There's still a lot to do."

"I'll finish it."

Giustina's sudden concern surprised her. She thought cynically, *Maybe Harry's being sold on the sample silk dress and the added three-cent revenue on the replacement garments has something to do with it.* Still, she had to admit that Giustina had been kinder to her since the fire. She sneezed.

"Go to bed," Giustina directed.

"All right." She started to leave, but the ringing of the telephone stopped her.

"Get that, Violetta."

She sat again, suddenly annoyed at having to stay. "Giovane and Son. Rosa? What's wrong?" Rosa's phoning was so unusual, it frightened her.

"Nothing, just the opposite." Rosa's voice was joyous. "I'm calling from the corner drugstore. I couldn't wait to tell you. Francesco and I are getting married."

"Wonderful! Congratulations!"

"Do you think it's too soon?" she asked, afraid she was disgracing herself.

"Of course not." Teresa didn't hold with some arbitrary conventions, or perhaps it was just that she wanted to see Rosa happy, no matter what.

"I can't believe this is happening to me."

"When are you getting married?"

"May thirty-first. Will you be my maid of honor?"

"I'd be delighted!" *Would bearing witness with a false name make the marriage legal?* She tossed the thought back.

"I'm working in a silk mill as a winder. You know, twisting the silk on spindles. It's tiresome and doesn't pay much, and to tell the truth, the noise is driving me crazy. The clickty-clacking machines make my ears chirp, just like I had crickets in them. Even worse, the foreman, the pig, pinches the women's backsides. I..."

"That's outrageous!" Teresa's shocked voice made Giustina turn around and stare at her. "Why doesn't somebody report him?"

"We'd get fired. This job was the only thing I could get when Giustina ran out of work. I don't know why I complain. It isn't dynamite." Rosa shuddered at the memory of West Virginia.

"Still, you must be happy planning the wedding."

"I am. It is going to be a small, simple wedding. Will you design my dress? I can do the sewing."

"I'd love to!"

"Francesco is going to ask Nick to be the best man."

When she heard Nick's name, Teresa flushed a bright red. *What would it be like to marry for love? I never had the choice.*

\* \* \*

The following evening Teresa sat sketching at Delora's dining room table. Josephine and Elena sat beside her watching with interest while the same bug that plagued Teresa had chased the other ladies in the boardinghouse to bed. Rafaello snored in the living room. At his feet, Ernesto played with a crystal radio set Nick had given him for his birthday. Delora, in her bedroom, softly sang *'Ninna Nanna'* to her sick child.

The Italian lullaby brought back tender childhood memories to Teresa. Tears welled in her eyes. She wiped her eyes and blew her nose. A sudden gust of wind shaking the window panes in the living room brought her back from the memory but not the pain inside.

"Whatcha doin', Violetta?" Liza asked as she entered the room from the kitchen.

"Designing a dress for Rosa's wedding. You can be a big help if you hold my pencils." She handed Liza several colored pencils. "Let's start with light blue."

"Blue for a wedding dreth?" Liza screwed up her face as she handed Teresa the pencil.

"This is not Rosa's first wedding, honey. Besides, we have no choice. She's using rejected factory silk. She got some white and lilac striped silk for me too. Because it was rejected, we didn't have to pay much..."

"Rejected thilk?" Liza's nose wrinkled again as if she smelled something bad.

"It's not as bad as it sounds. They only have minor imperfections."

"Ith it thoft and delicate?"

"Very. Like a spring breeze kissing your sweet pink face."

Liza smiled at the compliment.

Teresa found that if she paid attention to Liza, she responded favorably. Liza had opened her heart to her. Although she was a bright girl, the non-Italian teachers gave her a difficult time. Caught between two cultures, Liza found herself confused and belligerent. Teresa hadn't encountered the prejudice for herself, but she intuitively understood. "Tell you what, if we have enough silk left over, we'll make a dress for you. How's that?"

Liza's eyes glowed with excitement. She leaned across the table and watched Teresa sketch.

Teresa completed three sketches. One was a two-piece tailored suit, another a fitted bodice with a three-tiered skirt. She began another.

"What is wrong with thoth?" she asked, impatient to see what her dress would look like.

"I want to give Rosa a choice."

"Do one for me," Josephine prodded, "one that will show off my figure. Something sensational like black velvet."

Teresa pursed her lips, "Remember, Josephine, it's the end of May. Don't you think a light color and material would be more in keeping with the season?"

"No. That's what I want."

"Mmm." She tapped her pencil on the paper. "How about this?" Teresa quickly sketched a straight, ankle-length dress with three quarter length dolman sleeves. "The dress itself will be a pale gray silk and it will have black silk trim here, here and here." She marked a black empire cummerbund and a banded v-shaped plunging neckline." For modesty, Teresa inserted white silk inside the v-neck opening. "The dress will have less black, be more in keeping with the season, and still be striking."

Josephine tilted her head to one side and squinted at the sketch. "It's too plain."

Teresa squinted as she reexamined the sketch. "Fine, how about if we have a false split in front and gather it at each side with a pannier? Then you can wear long black silk gloves and a large black hat with a wide brim. With black silk shoes, gray stockings and a long-handled black parasol, it would be very dramatic, wouldn't you say?"

"Maybe," she said, obviously interested but unwilling to give in too soon.

"Make one for me?" Elena asked. "One piece, but please, not as fancy as Josephine's. Cream-colored silk, if Rosa can get me some."

"Something like this?" Teresa sketched an ankle-length dress with tan silk-velvet dolman-style sleeves.

"I like it. What is yours going to be like?"

"I'm not sure yet."

Josephine's eyes narrowed. "Trying to top us?"

Elena laughed, "No one can top your dress."

Josephine placed both hands on her hips. "What is that supposed to mean?"

"Only that with your face and figure in that dress, Josephine, even the crown jewels would come in second."

That brought a smile to Josephine's lips, but she wasn't to be put off. "Show me what you have in mind so far."

"All right. It's going to be a simple one-piece dress with lilac satin accents. I think I'll make it a narrow dress with no hobble; I don't like feeling confined. Something like this." She began sketching. The empire waist had a wide lilac belt. "The skirt will have six panels and the seams will be bound with lilac satin."

Josephine smirked, "You're right, it is simple. Put a little mystery and fire into your clothing, Violetta, or you'll disappear. Why have a good figure if you don't show it off?"

"Oh, Josephine," Elena threw up her hands, "you don't know plain from elegant. As for mystery, you leave nothing to the imagination."

Josephine put her hands on her hips, "What do you mean?"

"Figure it out for yourself."

# Chapter 15

## May 31, 1911

Nick waited impatiently in front of Delora's house for Teresa, Elena and Josephine. The clear sky and balmy breezes of a perfect May day did nothing to lessen his impatience. He polished his second-hand Model T Ford's headlamps for the third time. The gleaming headlamps reflected his face and new white boater hat, but he didn't notice. So that Teresa's first sight of his new car would be the interior with its flawless black leather, he had lowered the black top. Now he regretted it. Although he had proudly beamed when the adults inspected the vehicle, the boys were another matter. He had tolerated them, realizing the fascination it had for them. Their bouncing on the seats had been no problem. The boys on the running board rocking the auto had been bearable. However, not the boy honking the horn. Nick readjusted his new navy-blue blazer and yelled, "Out! All of you!"

The boy honking the horn stuck his chin out. "Ahh, whatcha tink ya got here, a gol' mine, or somptin? It ain't so hot. I seen better."

"OUT!" Nick flicked his polishing cloth at him as the boy climbed out.

"Ah ya modder's mustache!"

Nick smiled inwardly, recalling how often he had said the same thing to a pompous adult. *Have I gotten that affected? Hope not.* Yet, he had to laugh at himself after he checked to make sure his new white trousers were still in pristine condition. *Guess I am.* He climbed into the car and began wiping off the fingerprints that were everywhere. An admiring gasp from a cluster of people made him face the building.

Josephine, Teresa and Elena were standing on the stoop.

*"Quanto bello,"* a woman called out.

Most eyes were on Josephine, who stood in front of Teresa and Elena. Josephine struck a pose as if she were on a glamour magazine's cover. She placed a hand on her hip and planted her parasol to one side. However, Nick's eyes were on Teresa, finding her so captivating that he forgot his impatience and his automobile.

"Nick!" Teresa called out. "It's beautiful! Use it in good health."

"Congratulations!" Elena called out.

"Yes, it's beautiful." Josephine reddened at not having said something pleasing about Nick's automobile before Teresa had. She tossed the notion aside and started to walk down the steps.

"Wait!" Nick jumped out of the auto as if he were leaping the high hurdles. "I must escort such beauty." He took Josephine by the hand, and with a flourish, walked her down the steps. To her consternation, he ushered her into the back seat and handed her a long white duster. "This will keep you clean." He turned and made his second run.

Josephine snapped open her parasol and sat hard, not bothering with the duster.

Nick, oblivious of Josephine's vexation, escorted Elena to the back seat and handed her a duster that she promptly put on. Nick's movements were so flamboyant that he drew laughter and applause from Teresa and the crowd. He took off his hat and bowed to the group, then made a dash for the steps and whispered, "I saved the best for last." Slowly, so that he could enjoy holding her hand, he escorted her to the auto and helped her put a duster on. Once he'd safely seated her on the front seat, he ran to the front of the auto and cranked it up.

Josephine poked Teresa in the shoulder with her parasol, leaned over, and whispered in her ear, "Don't think this means anything, my dear. The day isn't over yet."

Teresa ignored her as she placed a white silk scarf over her hat. For her, it was one of those days when nothing would dare go wrong. The thought cheered her immeasurably. Nick, in a sweeping motion, put on his duster, reentered the auto and beamed at her. She smiled in return. The torment of not seeing him during the winter months melted away now that she sat beside him.

As for Nick, all the way up Broadway to the 125th Street ferry slip, he found it difficult to keep his eyes off Teresa. Almost before he knew it, he drove into the middle section of the wide, shallow-bottomed ferry and parked, the last auto in the double row of vehicles. Taking Teresa's hand in his he suggested, "Let's go to the passenger section." He pushed open the white frosted glass door leading to the passenger section and allowed the ladies to pass into the cabin. The aroma of brewing coffee greeted them, but they declined his offer of coffee, finding American style coffee too watery.

Josephine and Elena had taken possession of a bench alongside the batteries of windows, but the dark-paneled waiting room felt too confining to Teresa. She never wanted to be confined under any circumstances. "Do you mind if we go outside on the upper deck, Nick?"

"It's liable to be a bit breezy," he cautioned.

"I don't mind. I want to breathe the fresh air."

She and Nick climbed the steps to the upper deck. Josephine, seething, jumped up, threw her black silk scarf over her hat and scurried behind them, cursing her hobble-skirt and Teresa under her breath. Elena remained where she sat, not willing to get mussed by the winds. When Teresa and Josephine stepped outside, a sudden strong gust forced them to cling to their scarves and hats.

As the ferry chugged across the Hudson's choppy water, Teresa looked down-river at Ellis Island. She shuddered, remembering how close she had come to deportation. It hadn't frightened her then, but now, contemplating it was inconceivable. It wasn't her living condition; it was Nick.

Nick moved close to her, so close she could feel the warmth of his body. "Cold?"

"No. It's just that awful Ellis Island."

He placed his arm around her waist and whispered, "That's past. You've got me now."

She smiled at him.

"Want me to open your parasol?"

"Yes, thank you, Nick."

Josephine edged close to Nick's other side and placed her arm inside his, preventing him from opening Teresa's parasol. "It's too windy out here."

Nick laughed. "Those feathers look as if they want to fly away. Why don't you go inside? You don't want to lose that pretty hat."

"I'd rather be here with you." Josephine smiled broadly at him. The vessel swung north, away from Ellis Island. She pulled on his arm. "What is that building?" She pointed with her parasol to an obscure building on the Jersey side.

"I'm sorry. I don't know."

"And that one?" This time she pointed to a building on the Manhattan side.

Out of courtesy, he had to withdraw his arm from around Teresa to shield his eyes from the morning sun. "Got me again, Josephine," he laughed. "Guess I'm not much of a guide."

They remained quiet for the rest of the trip up the Hudson. As the ferry swung left, Nick turned to Teresa, "Looks like we're getting close to the Edgewater slip. We'd better go back to the auto."

Josephine tried to move ahead of the others, but Elena, guessing Josephine's motive was to sit beside Nick, refused to give way no matter how hard Josephine pulled on her arm or poked at her with her parasol. Infuriated, Josephine pinched Elena's arm when they sat.

"Ow, what's that for?" Elena pretended innocence.

"As if you didn't know," Josephine answered through clenched teeth. "Don't do that again! Who do you think you are?"

\* \* \*

Nick stopped in front of the church and kept the motor running. He took Teresa by the hand and asked eagerly, "Why don't you come with me to pick up Mama? We'll pass the Great Passaic River Falls. The spring rains have made it spectacular."

"Sounds lovely, but it's late. Rosa must be worrying"

"I'll come." Josephine edged closer to the auto.

Elena blocked Josephine from reentering the auto. "We can't, Josephine. If you hadn't taken so long getting dressed, we would have had time."

"She doesn't need me," Josephine protested.

"It wouldn't be right," Elena insisted.

"I guess she's right," Nick agreed, although disappointed at not having Teresa with him. He jumped into the shaking automobile. "I'll be right back." With a flourish, he doffed his hat and honked the horn as he drove away.

\* \* \*

Teresa saw all five members of Delora's family sitting in the front pew. Despite Teresa's repeated assurances, Rafaello had insisted that he and his family leave their home early so that they wouldn't be late. She knew they had been sitting there for at least an hour. Teresa smiled to herself, recalling Delora's reaction when Rafaello had suggested they buy a used automobile,

"Are you crazy? Want to catch up with death?"

Teresa was happy that Rosa was getting married in a church that Italian immigrants had established. This was a proper church with a long aisle that led to a white marble Romanesque genuflecting rail and a snow-white marble altar. She smiled at Francesco who anxiously paced up and down. "Rosa?" she asked, pointing to the vestry door left of the altar.

"Yes." He pointed with his chin. "Please see if she's all right. Where's Nick?"

"Picking up Giustina. He won't be long."

He nodded impatiently and fidgeted with his tie.

It was all Teresa could do to keep from giggling at his nervousness. *Is this what it means to be in love?* Teresa entered the vestry where Rosa, doing her share of pacing, looked charming in her blue dress. She held a white rose bouquet with white ribbon streamers that curled gracefully to her knees.

Father Palmiotti, in his officiating vestments, smiled. "Hello, Teresa."

"Hello, Father," she smiled in return.

Rosa gave her a big hug and almost knocked Teresa's hat off. "I'm so happy you are here. I was worried."

Teresa held Rosa at arms' length. "You look lovely."

"Thank you." Rosa smiled and gestured toward the church. "Is everybody here?"

Teresa knew she was asking about Francesco and smiled. "Yes, everybody's here except Nick and his mother. They should be here any minute."

"I hope they hurry. The service should have started by now. Father Palmiotti has another wedding after mine."

Five minutes passed, then ten. Rosa's impatience mounted with the priest's. "Oh dear, I hope nothing has happened to them."

"You know Giustina's late for everything but work. Let me look in the church again." She peeked out the vestry just as Nick and his mother entered the church. Teresa turned and signaled to the priest.

Quickly, the priest strode to the altar and motioned to Rosa to enter. He conducted the service so hurriedly that it was over before Teresa had time to enjoy it. After the ceremony, the round of hugs, kisses and best wishes for the bride and groom lasted longer than the ceremony.

Everyone but Nick and Ernesto walked to Rosa's boarding house down the street. Ernesto, however, wanted to know how everything worked under the hood. Nick proudly gave the wide-eyed young man a tour of the engine. Now, at Rosa's boardinghouse, impatient to see Teresa, Nick jumped to the pavement almost before the auto came to a complete stop. He ran along the alleyway to the rear of the house. His heart raced when he saw Teresa standing at the grape arbor entrance that Rosa and Francesco had entwined with red roses and white ribbons. The white streamers swayed gently in the breeze.

Beneath the arbor Rosa had covered a picnic table and benches with white linen. Sunlight danced among the shadows as a gentle breeze rustled the young grape leaves. Behind the arbor, the landlord stood cooking chickens and sausages on a stone fireplace while a guitarist and an accordionist played Neopolitan love songs. The guitarist, however, concentrated more on Josephine than on his music. Josephine, welcoming his flirtations, glanced at Nick, hoping he would notice. Nick, unconscious of her efforts, peered into his new box camera, arranging everyone into groups, but his primary target was Teresa.

At dinner, they dined on antipasto, chicken soup, ravioli and huge platters of barbecued sausages and chickens. Fresh asparagus and lettuce from the landlord's small garden graced the table. After the meal, Teresa, sitting beside Rafaello, sipped her demitasse coffee laced with anisette. Too full to indulge in the rum-flavored wedding cake, candied almonds or fresh fruit, Teresa smiled as the accordionist began playing a rousing tarantella.

The guitarist took Josephine by the hand and spun her in the lively dance. She laughed shrilly, hoping to capture Nick's attention. Instead, Nick took Teresa by the hand and led her to the front of the house. As they strolled slowly down the street, Teresa's spirits soared above the maple trees lining the street.

Nick stopped and turned her toward him. "How is it you look lovelier each time I see you?"

Teresa smiled as the blood rushed to her cheeks.

He kissed her palms. The thrill rushed through her and brought a smile to her lips. "Your smile makes my heart leap with joy." He wanted to take her in his arms in the middle of the street but knew convention forbade it. "It's been a long time since we were alone. Do you remember the time we kissed on the roof top?"

Her knees trembled as she recalled the evening. "How could I forget?"

"Since then I've asked you repeatedly to marry me. Each time you said you needed time. I've been struggling to give you time, *amora*. Several times I called you at the factory to ask you again. Each time I hung up, afraid your answer would be no. Then I called just to hear your voice."

"That was you? I wondered who it was." She laughed, delighted to know his secret. It made her feel closer to him.

"Yes, I'm sorry if I frightened you," he teased.

"You didn't frighten me," she whispered.

"Day and night I see your face before me. I can't escape even in my dreams. You're driving me mad. I can't wait any longer for your answer. It's time for a decision. Will you marry me?"

Teresa longed to say yes, but nagging thoughts of Rocco tormented her. She believed he was dead and she was free. Nevertheless, she couldn't begin to think about a marriage with a lie. How could she tell him she wasn't even Violetta? Afraid of losing him, she hesitated.

"Violetta?"

"I..." Her voice faltered. "You know so little about me. You see..."

"I can't figure you out." Nick's expression changed from disappointment, to disbelief, to annoyance. His jaw tightened. "What are you trying to say?"

"Nick, what I have to tell you isn't easy for me. Please, try to understand. You see, I have somethi..."

He shook his head, not listening. "I've been making a fool of myself. I can see now that you are trying to tell me you don't love me." The Italian proverb, *He who is patient, is not in love,* shot through his mind. Obviously, *then*, she wasn't in love with him. Confused and feeling rejected as a man, he left her and strode to the rear of the house. Nick was so angry he could barely see his mother, who was talking to an aloof Josephine. "I'm going for a drive. I may be gone a while."

Giustina's eyes narrowed. "What's wrong? You don't look well." She was about to touch his forehead to check for a fever.

He brushed her hand aside. "I'm fine!" For some reason, her gesture made him angrier. He needed a woman now, a woman who wasn't his mother.

"I'll come with you, Nick." Josephine tried to slip her hand through the crook of his arm, but he pulled away. Undaunted, Josephine trailed behind him with rapid, mincing steps, again cursing Teresa for hobbling her. "Wait, Nick."

Teresa, unbelieving, watched as Josephine entered the auto by herself. Nick adjusted the choke and cranked the engine up, jumped into the shaking vehicle and drove abruptly away.

Josephine, ecstatic at being with him, didn't notice the anger clearly displayed on his face. She laughed as she snuggled up beside him. Nick, oblivious to her attentions, remained silent as he drove to the crest of the hill overlooking the Great Falls. He stopped abruptly and got out of the automobile.

Josephine stepped out of the shaking auto, stood beside him and stared at the racing water. Too afraid even to touch the black wrought-iron fence that protected them from the gaping drop, she gasped in wonder.

Heavy snows and spring rains had swelled the river upstream to nearly overflowing its banks. Angry water cascaded down the precipice, roaring its power with uncontrolled violence. Framing the raging falls to her left was the dark, redbrick power plant that collected the force for the factories. To the right of the falls, craggy black rocks formed a massive wall, seemingly defying the falls. A footbridge on top, connecting the rocky walls containing the falls, seemed too frail a link to her. Above the footbridge, the rushing waters generated a plume that soared like steam from a mammoth boiling pot.

Nick, his body rigid, stared at the water that rushed down as if trying to arrest the movement of the huge column of white water. He wanted desperately to feel as if he could control something. God, why did he feel so out of control? The water, too, plunging out of control through the crevice, struck a huge, protruding rock at its base. The water swirled around and around the rock in confused circles, licking and caressing the rock that seemed to welcome its caresses. It hypnotized him, making him feel outside himself. He preferred it that way.

Josephine, faint with the fury swirling around her, begged, "Nick, take me away from here. It's making me dizzy."

He didn't hear her.

"Nick?" She tugged at his arm.

"What?" He turned to face her, for the first time fully aware of her presence. The wildness in his eyes at once frightened and excited her.

"Take me away from here." She tried wrapping her arms around him, but he took her roughly by the arm and almost pushed her into the automobile.

"Where are we going?"

"Do you care?"

"No. I'd go to the ends of the earth with you." She moved closer.

He drove recklessly, silently, to his mother's house. Josephine laughed wildly, reveling in the excitement. She could sense his reckless madness, but didn't care. Boldly, she reached over and stroked his muscular thigh. Her breast rested against his arm.

The falls' roar followed them for the four blocks in a turbulent chase. Both in their own thoughts, they didn't hear the roar, and would they have cared if they did?

Nick came to an abrupt stop in front of his mother's house, nearly sending Josephine over the windshield. "Get out," he snapped and jumped out, ran up the gray stone steps, unlocked the door and entered. She followed as quickly as her skirt would allow. Once inside, he kicked the door shut, grabbed her in a powerful grip and kissed her hard on the mouth.

Josephine felt anger in his passion, yet she opened her lips to his, clung to him, eager for his touch. "I've waited so long for you," she breathed. Then more boldly, "Take me."

Nick swept her up in his arms and strode to his bedroom. All he wanted was release from his confusion, to prove that he was a man whose needs couldn't be ignored. Frantically, she undressed herself, flinging her clothing around the room. Finally she removed the pins from her hair, shook her head to let her hair cascade. With outstretched arms, she reached for him. "Take me, Nick! Take me now!" He climbed onto the bed. She arched her hips to meet his and cried out as he thrust forward with the piston-driving strength of his body. "Oh, God! Nick! Nick!" she shouted.

When he reached his peak, he felt as if he were cascading down the Great Falls. With a fevered groan, he collapsed on top of her.

Josephine, in a daze of triumph, couldn't be sure, but she thought he whispered, *Violetta.* Only then did she notice he hadn't even removed his trousers. No matter! He was hers. She had won.

\* \* \*

In the two agonizing months that had passed since Rosa's wedding, Teresa hadn't heard from Nick. Now, alone in Giustina's office, she came to a decision. His long absence had done the trick; she would say yes to him, but she'd have to tell him the truth first. *I can't hide forever. Rocco is dead, so what is there to hide from? If Nick loves me, he will understand. He does love me. I feel it.* Now that she had decided, she felt almost like singing.

She got up from her desk, opened the door to the factory and looked around again to check for Giustina. No one looked up. On damp days such as this, mingled with the cleaning-fluid benzine, a hint of smoke remained in the air. *Where on earth is she?* Teresa hadn't heard from her for three days. Giustina never stayed away without calling the office.

Stranger still was Josephine's disappearance, also for three days. Josephine had been acting oddly ever since Rosa's wedding. Sometimes she wore an enigmatic smile. Sometimes she cried, but neither Teresa nor Elena could get Josephine to confide in her.

Teresa closed the door and returned to her desk. *Why wait to hear from Nick? What would be wrong if I called him? Maybe he still feels rejected?* The ringing telephone startled her. *Maybe it's Nick!* Her heart jumped in anticipation. Quickly, she answered, "Giovane and Son...Rosa!" Teresa telegraphed her alarm over Rosa's rare phone call. "Is everything all right?"

"Oh, yes. Violetta, I never dreamed that being married could be like this."

Teresa smiled to herself, pleased at Rosa's buoyant happiness. "Where are you?"

"Our new house in Totowa. You should see it. It's lovely. It has two bedrooms, so you must visit. The only thing bothering me is that it's not a two-family. It'd help pay expenses." She finally stopped her excited rambling and began to giggle. "Francesco insisted we put in a telephone because..." she giggled again, "I'm in a family way."

"Wonderful!" Teresa felt torn between joy for her friend and envy. "You must be overjoyed. You've always wanted children. How does Francesco feel about it?"

"Thrilled, but I'm sorry we put the down payment on this house. It bothers me that he can't go to college yet. Francesco would be such a good doctor, but money will be very tight, especially since I must leave my job when I start to show. Still, we praise Heaven that he survived his escape from West Virginia and has lived to create a new life."

"Things will work out. They always do. This year was a happy year for you with your marriage. Next year will be even better with the baby."

After Teresa spoke to Rosa, her resolve to call Nick strengthened. She called the Paterson factory and was told that Giustina and Nick were at home. *At this time of day? Is Giustina sick? Nick?* She called Giustina's home. Nick answered. His voice sounded so strange she almost didn't recognize it. "Nick?"

"Yeah?" He blared. "Who is...?" He paused abruptly. "Oh, Violetta." His voice softened.

She rushed in before he could say anything that would stop her. "I didn't say what I meant to say when you asked me to marry you." His silence surprised her. Her body tightened. After all, he hadn't spoken to her since Rosa's wedding; maybe he had changed his mind. She took a deep breath and plunged in, "I know I took a long time to say yes, but there was a problem I hope you will understand." Her courage began to fail her. She paused, hoping he would say something to bring it back, but he didn't. "Nick, have I made a mistake in calling you? I mean, do you still love me? Because I...?"

"Violetta," there was a catch in his throat, "it doesn't matter anymore who loves who. I married Josephine today." He blurted it out and hung up.

The click on the other end was as loud as a rifle shot. Teresa sat back, stunned. It took a moment for her to realize that it was all over. She hung up the phone, put her head down on the desk and sobbed. All her pent-up emotions twisted inside her. *Why did he marry Josephine?* She answered her own question. *Because, you fool, you thought he would wait forever. Just look in the mirror. How can you compare yourself with the beautiful Josephine? You gave him time to choose her over you.* Her head reeled with confusion. *But if he didn't love me, why did he ask me? Did he love Josephine, too?*

She sobbed with abandon, promising herself, *I'll never allow someone into my heart again. The pain of rejection is too great. Oh, why were these feelings inflamed in me only to be smothered?* Her mother's words flared up at her. *I hope you never know love. Love can steal your soul.* She wanted to strike out, but at whom? She didn't know.

"God, help me!" Teresa felt consuming anger at her mother for forcing her to marry Rocco and at Giustina for arranging Violetta's marriage to Nick. She felt angry with Violetta for dying, at Nick for making her fall in love with him, at Josephine for taking him away. Most of all she felt angry with herself for allowing it all to happen to her.

The ringing phone startled her. She didn't answer it. After a time, it stopped, as did her tears. Teresa got up, brushed the strands of hair off her face, and went out the newly installed door to the back yard. She raised her face, permitting the drizzle to cool her burning eyes. The mulberry tree in the corner beckoned her, but somehow she didn't feel the nearness of home she had when she had first stood beside it. All she felt was consuming loneliness. *There is nothing left for me here. Hearing his voice on the phone or seeing him come through that door and knowing he isn't mine would be too cruel. No! I can't be reminded every day of my foolishness.*

Then the realization struck her that she couldn't continue to live at Delora's either, too close and yet too far from Nick. Still, where could she live? Work? For some reason, the Stein and Stein Clothing Factory came to mind, the firm that Giustina didn't like. It wasn't because their factory was dark and filthy or that it was near Five Points. It was because they held back payments until Giustina feared they wouldn't pay at all. Thinking about practical matters, although it didn't ease the pain, kept her sane.

The phone rang again. This time she answered it, her voice lifeless, the echo of a dead girl's voice, "Giovane and Son Clothing Factory."

Giustina's voice registered remorse. "Violetta, I'm so sorry. I tried talking him out of it. After all, why marry her? She was trapping him into giving her a soft life. He said he had no choice with Josephine in her condition. He's too good for any lying fake. I had begun to hope that he would pick you, now that I have come to know you. You are so good for the business. You didn't run away from the fire. You know how to handle Harry Goldstein. You would have been a good daughter-in-law. Where did I make a mistake? Niccolo has always been such a good boy, but now, I don't know, he can't even finish college without my help..."

Teresa stopped listening. Giustina just continued to be Giustina. Teresa raised herself to her fullest extent, placed the mouthpiece over her heart so that Giustina couldn't hear and said, "I don't need anyone but myself. With or without him, I'll make it!" That's what her head said, but her heart said something else.

# Chapter 16

## March 1912

Josephine, furious, could barely see Nick's face as she sat on the settee in their living room. She placed her empty wine glass on the end table beside her, nearly upsetting the cut-class decanter on the table's dusty surface. Housekeeping wasn't what she had thought marrying Nick would be all about. She yanked her pink chenille bathrobe across her body. "It's two-thirty in the morning." Her speech was thick with drink. "Where were you?"

"Out!" He edged past her and slumped in the maroon easy chair in the corner of the room. Nick shoved his gray woolen gloves into the black overcoat's pocket.

She had detected the stench of liquor on his breath when he had passed her. "You've been drinking again!"

"You haven't?" He pushed his gray fedora back on his head. "I can't remember the last time you were sober."

"At least I do my drinking at home."

"I prefer a pleasant atmosphere."

"It's up to you to make it that way, Niccolo." She dragged 'Niccolo' out, knowing he hated it.

He tried to ignore it. "For Heaven's sake, when the hell are you pulling yourself together? It's been almost four months since you lost the baby."

"That's not what's making *you* drink," she spat at him. "You started drinking the day we got married. Why?" The accusation hit home and she knew it.

"Do you really want to know about me? I thought you only thought about yourself." He leaned forward. "Let's not argue, Josephine. I've something to tell you. I've come to a decision. I..."

"You, you! It's always you!" She wasn't listening. All evening she had been tormenting herself about his absence. Why wasn't she going places with him where she could show herself off? When she'd married Nick, Josephine had visions of going to lovely places with lovely gowns not made from rejects. She'd seen herself riding in a shiny automobile, arriving at splendid mansions with Nick at her elbow.

"I know you're upset over having lost the baby, but it's time to move on."

*Upset? Glad! Who needed a brat tying me down and twisting my body out of shape? Should I tell him?* Josephine wanted to hurt him, but instinctively knew it was going too far. Yet she couldn't let things go. She blurted out, "You leave the house early in the morning and don't come home until late at night. Sometimes you don't even bother, and when you do, you sleep down here on the settee. All I've done since I've married you is sit alone in this dreary house." The evening of the opera and Teresa's fancy dress loomed in her head. She could bear it no longer. "You don't love me! You love Violetta."

"Not that again."

"Yes, again and again." She wished that she had done something to ruin her rival, her enemy.

"For God's sakes! Stop for a minute and listen!" His carefully rehearsed declaration stuck in his throat.

"Why don't you go to her and get it over with?" Then, as if it were a sudden revelation, she got up and swayed before him. "You *have* been going to her, *haven't* you?"

Nick's eyes, alight with fire, looked up at her. "Take care, Josephine, take care!"

Nevertheless, she couldn't stop herself. "That's why you haven't touched me for so long. You've been going to that *putana...*"

"Watch your filthy tongue!" Nick couldn't control himself any longer. "Violetta is not a *putana*. You are, for what you did before we were married!"

Josephine, astonished, knew he meant every word. A scream ripped her throat, "You bastard!" She picked up the glass vase, a wedding present from Giustina, from the mantel and threw it at him, barely missing him. The vase crashed to the floor, shooting glass in every direction.

The rage within him exploded with equal force. Slowly, deliberately, he got up from the chair and came face to face with her. "All right, you asked for it! Yes, I love her. I've always loved her. I never loved you! You trapped me!" The words were sudden and raw. He regretted having said it. It was heartless, but it was too late. He knew he had played a part in allowing this farce of a marriage, but he no longer cared. With long strides, he headed for the front door.

"Where are you going?" In panic, she shouted after him, her dreams shattering, just like Giustina's vase. "Nick! Don't leave!" She grabbed his arm. Nick jerked it away, forcing her to release her controlling grip. He slammed the door. A diagonal crack in the glass insert sliced the glass in two.

Josephine fell in a heap on the floor and wept bitterly. "Nick," she moaned from deep within her soul. *Oh, Madonna mia, what will happen to me?*

* * *

At the Great Falls, Nick made a U-turn and parked facing the downpour. He sat with the engine running, trying to calm down. The cold, crisp night sharpened the roar of the falls and echoed in his brain. Heavy black shadows cast by a full moon on the craggy rock surface closed in upon him, mocking him.

You're seeing things, kiddo. He pulled out the gold pocketwatch Josephine had given him from his vest pocket and flicked it open. Quarter after three. Without thinking, he wound the spring almost to the breaking point. The watch, a piece of glitter like Josephine, meant nothing to him. He shoved it into his coat pocket.

His trembling transcended the cold night. Nick reached for the silver flask tucked in his overcoat's side pocket. Empty. "Shit! What have I become?" He tossed it onto the back seat. Tucking the woolen blanket that rested on the seat beside him around his legs didn't help. The cold trapped within the blanket made him colder. The sweater in the black satchel on the rear seat tempted him, but that meant taking his coat off and repacking everything. He looked behind him at the folded top. "Why the hell didn't I fix that thing?"

His mind wandered back to the day he had thrust himself into Josephine's body. Ten? *No. Eleven months ago? I am a bastard. I used her. Hell, she used me, too, but it was still damn unfair of me. Well, I paid for it.* "Hell, she never even tried being a wife." *Shit, I'm talking to myself. I should have told her I was leaving.* He had meant to, but his anger had won out. He felt like a coward. *I should go back and tell it to her face.* Nick checked his watch again. Twenty after three. *No. She'll keep me there until it's too late.*

*Well, Nick baby, if you stay here any longer, you'll be part of the scenery until June. But where the hell can I go? It's too early to go to the pier. Mama? No. She'd only carry on something fierce and it's too close to Josephine's.* He whisked off the blanket, put the car in drive, made a U-turn and drove down the hill.

A compelling force led him to Teresa's boardinghouse. Nick knew the way; he sat there many nights. He even knew which windows of the four-story brownstone were hers. Soft yellow lights shining through those windows illuminated the nearly deserted street in rectangular patches. The only sign of life on the street was a horse-drawn milk truck. The milk truck rattled past just as the lights of the windows went out.

Nick, cold sober now, cursed himself. "What the hell are you doing here, you fool? What good is sitting here doing you?" A tangle of emotions tormented him. Knowing he was near her filled him with joy, and yet a deep sense of loss stung. "Shit!" Nick almost drove off but stopped when he saw Teresa emerging from the building. His heart pounded as he watched her chatting with her three roommates. "Violetta!" he shouted over the engine's whine.

"Nick!" Stunned, she stopped halfway down the brownstone steps.

"Get in!" he invited as he opened the car door.

Still astonished, she asked, "Is there something wrong? Rosa? Her baby?"

"Stop asking questions. Get in."

Frightened that something dreadful had happened, she got into the car. Her shocked roommates watched with their mouths open. "Please," she urged them, "start for work without me. You have to get there on time." She turned to Nick. "Something dreadful has happened, hasn't it?"

"Nothing. I just wanted to see you," he pleaded.

"Heavens! At this hour? What will people say?" She glanced at the retreating girls.

"To hell with them." He placed the woolen blanket around her legs and drove off.

She held onto her large black hat, trying to thwart the wind's insistent desire to possess it.

"Where are we going?"

He didn't answer.

"I have to go to work."

He didn't answer.

Trying desperately to force laughter over tears, she suddenly found the whole thing ridiculous. "Are you shanghaiing me?" she laughed nervously. It had been such a long time since she had seen Nick, she wanted to reach out to him, but she also needed to protect herself.

Without turning to her he said, "I've left Josephine. I'm sailing for England. Today." He paused for effect.

He'd so stunned her that she let her hat go. It climbed as if striving to be the first to greet the light of day. She sat staring at him, riveted, amazed.

"Don't you have anything to say? Talk to me, Violetta!"

"What can I say?" A barrage of questions hit her at once. "When did you decide this? Poor Josephine. What did she say? How does Giustina feel about it? Why...?"

"I've been thinking about it a long time. When my friend Bob told me about his plan to go to England to do some flying, I saw my chance to get away." He shrugged. "All Josephine and I do is fight. It got so bad tonight, I told her I never loved her."

"What?" She placed her gloved hand over her mouth. "Oh, Nick, how cruel."

"I know. I just blurted it out in anger." He shook his head as if admonishing himself. "It's too late to take it back. I haven't told her or Mama I'm sailing for England."

"But the poor things will worry about you. Don't you see that?"

"I'll call them from the pier."

Compassion tore at her. "What is going to happen to Josephine?"

"She'll be okay. The house is free and clear. It's a two-family, so there's an income, and she has a generous allowance. Besides, she's good at taking care of herself. She's proven that to me. I..." He stopped. "Let's not talk about her."

It was more than financial considerations that troubled Teresa. She knew how much Josephine had wanted him. Teresa placed the blanket around her head and shoulders and tried to keep out the thought that she might never see him again. Although he wasn't hers, she longed at least to know he was near. She looked at him, trying to think of something that could change his mind. "Still, flying! It terrifies me."

He shrugged it off. "I've been taking lessons for quite a while. I love it."

"But do you have to go all the way to England for it? Why not stay here?" she pleaded.

"The farther the better."

She wanted to say that it sounded like running away but felt she was a fine one to talk about that.

"I had to see you before I leave. Who knows when I'll be back, if ever? I've been a fool. I want you to know that I have never stopped loving you."

"You mustn't say that." She really wanted to say that hearing it served as a painful reminder that she loved him, too. "You're married."

"In name only. Let's not argue. I don't have much time."

They had arrived at Pier 53 on the North River where the Cunard Line had a ship waiting. The venders, the passengers bidding farewell, the smells of the sea, all tugged at Teresa's memories, magnifying her anxieties, both tangible and intangible. She loathed boats and trains; they always meant saying goodbye to someone she loved. Teresa tried to think of something to calm herself. "What are you going to do about the automobile?"

"I thought I'd have it shipped to Josephine...no, Ernest. He's only fifteen, but he knows more about the engine than I do. He's been doing all the repairs on it for me. "

"He'll be thrilled, but I don't think Delora will be."

After arranging the auto's shipment, they returned to the pier and stood beside the wooden retaining fence at the dock's edge. Teresa looked up at the ship's imposing hull, shivered, and wrapped the blanket more firmly around herself, wishing the blanket were Nick.

"Violetta, *mia cara,* "his voice, warm and tender, took the chill out of the air, "I may never see you again, unless..." He hesitated, "No, that's asking too much."

"What?" A desperate hope raced through her.

"You could come with me." It was more a question than a statement.

She had a wild urge to say, *Yes*! How simple it would be to surrender. What joy*!* Then reality and a sense of shame struck home. "I can't. You'd be committing adultery." How could she commit Nick's soul to perpetual torment? She felt she had enough to atone for without adding that sin to the list. "No, I can't," she repeated more to convince herself than Nick.

"I'm sorry. Chalk it up as just another selfish thing on my part." He turned her toward him and took her by the shoulders. "At least you can tell me you love me, can't you? I need to know."

"What good does admitting it do? Nothing can come of it."

"Maybe so, *cara,* but at least let me kiss you goodbye." He bent down; his lips touched hers, surprisingly soft and sensitive at first, then hard as he permitted his emotions to take possession of him. His kiss, full of passion and need, transmitted itself to her, a wild hungry need that they couldn't fulfill. Nick felt her love for him even if she withheld the words.

As they clung to each other, she trembled in his arms. Tears filled her eyes.

Her tears tore at him. "I've made such a mess of our lives. What we could have been to each other if only...I'm such an idiot. I didn't go to Josephine because I loved her. Can you believe that? I haven't done anything right, and here, in my selfishness, I'm making you cry again. I tried staying away, but I didn't have the strength to see it through. Forgive me. I'm so muddled up. For my sanity, I've got to get away. I..."

Teresa kissed him on the lips to keep him from talking. She couldn't help herself. "Nick, I do love you with all my heart. You've never heard me say it. I've never even said it to myself. Nick, I think I loved you even before I met you, from the first time I saw your picture, b..."

"My dearest, that's all I wanted to hear." He closed his eyes and turned his face heavenward. "Thank God!" Then he gazed at her. "But it's making it harder for me to leave."

"I can tell you that I love you only because you are leaving. There is so much I should have told you long before now. Oh, why did you have to come back into my life now, just as you are going away?" she cried, with longing in her voice. The ship's final boarding whistle vibrated through them. "Give me one last kiss and go, please, my darling. You're tearing me apart."

His very soul was in that kiss. Reluctantly he let her go and ran up the gangplank, forgetting completely his promise to call Josephine and his mother.

With a shuddering sigh, Teresa watched him disappear in the crowd. Tormenting herself, she searched the crowd above until she saw him edge his way through the throng and strain against the ship's railing. Teresa attempted to hide her pain for Nick's sake. She waved. He, amid the gaily colored streamers, waved frantically. A young man at his side patted Nick on the back, but Nick paid no attention to him.

Tears flowed down her face despite her deliberate attempt to smile. A sudden wild urge seized her to run up the gangplank to his waiting arms. If they hadn't removed the gangplank, she would have. Powerless, she watched the ship slowly back away from the dock. As a last gesture, he threw a streamer to her. She scrambled to grasp it, but it fell short.

*"Come back to me, mio amore,"* she whispered to the winds as the ship edged away. She feared that no matter how much she beseeched the winds, Nick wouldn't return to her, ever. *No! Mustn't think it. I couldn't bear it.*

Long after she could no longer see the ship and the last of the well-wishers had left the dock, she stood there and wept. Colored streamers, played out, fell into the murky waters.

Only then did it occur to her that they'd fire her at Stein and Stein's for not going to work. Then, too, when her roommates reported to the landlady that she had gone off with a man in an automobile, she'd have to move. Where? Delora's? No. Rosa's? *Yes, Rosa will take me in and can probably find a job for me at the silk mill.*

\* \* \*

Josephine paced back and forth and looked out the window at every turn hoping to see his automobile. She hadn't slept much in the three days since Nick had left. Beside herself with fatigue and worry, she picked up the telephone in the hall and called the silk mill where he worked as a technician. Not there for three days. Josephine called Giustina's Paterson factory. Not there. It took a supreme effort for her to call Giustina on Spring Street. She knew Giustina hated her for marrying Nick, but then again, she felt that Giustina hated everyone except herself, Nick, and that *putana.*

"Oh, it's you." Giustina's voice was less than cordial. She could hear that Josephine had been drinking. "What do you want?"

She got to the point quickly. "Is Niccolo there?"

"It's Saturday. Isn't he working?"

Josephine didn't answer. She stared at the cracked glass in the front door without seeing it.

"Well?" Giustina asked impatiently. "What is it? I'm busy."

Josephine hesitated for a moment. Then before she lost her nerve she blurted out, "When was the last time you heard from him?"

Giustina audibly showed her impatience with Josephine. "Have you two quarreled again?"

Josephine wanted to scream at her, "Mind your own business," but repeated the question instead.

"I haven't seen him or heard from him for three days. Why?"

Josephine ignored the question. "Have him call me when he gets in touch with you." Without saying goodbye, she hung up. She looked out the front door to check for the auto. Still not there.

"Where are you? You've never been away this long. If you come back, I'll be good." Josephine had made that promise before and broken it. Anger swelled within her. "You're with that *putana,* Violetta, damn you! All I have been doing since we got married is wait around like a ninny. Not anymore! I'm going to face Violetta where she is working! Where did Elena say Violetta is working?" The more she struggled with the factory's name, the further off it flew. "I need another drink." Josephine reached for the bottle on the end table. Empty. She missed in her attempt to replace it on the table. It rolled off and onto the floor. *Kitchen. That's where I put that other bottle.*

Josephine staggered into the kitchen and opened the icebox lid. Melting ice had almost completely imbedded the bottle of wine. "Where the hell is that icepick?" The room spun. When she regained some of her composure, she saw the rusty icepick on the wooden table amid the dirty dishes. She stabbed at the ice as if it were Teresa. Bits and pieces of ice flew about, striking her face and settling themselves in her unkempt hair. Finally freeing the bottle, she tugged at the cork with her teeth and took a long swig. She wiped her mouth with her sleeve, sat at the kitchen table, pushed the clutter away and rested her head on her arms.

Her head cleared a little. *Stein and Stein's. That's where. If Violetta isn't there, then they're together in her room doing...!* The thought ate at her. "I'll scratch her eyes out!" She stabbed at the wooden tabletop with the icepick with such force it embedded itself in the surface and rocked back and forth. Josephine got up abruptly, knocking the chair over.

She headed for the front door and stopped when she saw her reflection in the hall mirror. It surprised her. *I can't go out in my night things.* Hanging tightly to the railing to keep from falling back down, she climbed the stairs. *I need another drink to settle my nerves.* She started to go down, then remembered why she was climbing. *I'll get it when I've finished dressing.*

Without realizing it, she put on the same dress that she had worn to Rosa's wedding. She tried combing her hair, but neither the brush nor the comb would smooth out the tangles. Resignedly, she simply twisted it into a loose bun at the back of her head and stuck in a few hairpins. Josephine put on the same large black hat she had worn to the wedding. The delicate aigrettes, once sweeping, were now twisted and flying in all directions.

*Why is it so warm in here? I need a drink to cool me off.* She staggered down to the kitchen and took another swallow of wine directly from the bottle. With the bottle still in her hand, she walked out the front door. Not stopping to put on an overcoat, close the door, or look where she was going, she stepped into the street.

The horse saw her before the buggy driver did. The animal reared up. His hooves swung in the air and came down on Josephine, killing her instantly.

# Chapter 17

### February 1913

Teresa, Francesco, Rosa with her baby, and twenty-five thousand striking mill workers tried to shield their eyes against the drizzle. They looked up at the white and green trimmed Botto house's balcony with apprehensions. Since the mill owners owned almost everything in Paterson, the strikers were forced to climb the long, steep hill to the adjoining town of Haledon. The mayor, a Socialist, permitted them to meet there. Fearlessly, the Botto family, Italian immigrants, also on strike, had opened their home to the I.W.W. leaders.

Teresa, having listened to the never-ending speeches, knew they were in for a long strike. She thought about Josephine. Although she knew she had done nothing directly to cause her death, she felt as if somehow she could have prevented it if she hadn't loved Nick so much. It was irrational, she knew it, yet the guilt persisted.

The drizzle changed to sleet. Teresa pulled the woolen shawl tighter around her head and shoulders, barricading herself against the elements and her consuming thoughts. She looked at Rosa and the baby that Rosa carried in her arms. Teresa opened her black umbrella and placed it over Rosa and the baby. A sea of black mushroom-shaped umbrellas popped up around them and swayed with the shuffling, poorly-dressed, undernourished striking workers.

Survival brought them out on strike, not some grand cause. Silk workers were the lowest paid employees of the top twenty-five industries in the United States. Working fifty-five hours a week, the men made only $10.59, the women, $7.17, and the girls under sixteen, $1.85. It hadn't taken them long to realize they couldn't pay their bills. When the mill owners had ordered the weavers to work four machines instead of two, it had been unacceptable. It was far too dangerous and heralded layoffs.

Teresa hated the monotonous work as a winder that paid less than Giustina had; still, she'd had no choice. After leaving Stein and Stein's, Teresa had been lucky to find work in the mill. Now that they had been on strike for a month, she was at her wit's end for funds. Although Rosa had begged her not to pay rent, Teresa knew they needed the money.

As for Rosa, frustration and exasperation filled her as the young, blue-eyed, black-haired Irish beauty, Elizabeth Gurley Flynn of the I.W.W., began to speak.

Unmindful of the stabbing sleet, Elizabeth Gurley Flynn leaned forward on the railing and waved her fist in the air. "Do the employers spend their millions in Paterson? Does the Silk Association have its banquets here?" She waved her fist again. "No, they dine in the Waldorf-Astoria...Do their wives and daughters buy their gowns, their furs, jewels or automobiles in Paterson? Whenever did Caruso or Tetrazzini come to Paterson, though there are thousands of their countrymen here who would go without food to hear them...?"

Although she electrified her English-speaking audience with her eloquence, it meant nothing to Rosa.

Amid cheers, Elizabeth Gurley Flynn ended her speech and introduced Carlo Tresca as the next speaker. Although Tresca was the last speaker and many could not understand Italian, few left. They preferred to stand in the freezing rain, hoping against hope that by some magic the strike would be over by the time he finished speaking.

When he did, the light faded from Rosa's eyes. "I don't trust these union people. All the union means is no money and more trouble. The union here or in West Virginia, it's all the same." For the first time, she noticed that Teresa's umbrella was over her. Ice had begun to form around Teresa's head and face. "Violetta! Keep the umbrella over yourself! You'll catch your death."

"I'm fine. I like the coolness of it," she lied.

"So do I," Rosa lied in turn.

A gust of wind turned the umbrella inside out, yanking it out of Teresa's hand and sending it over the heads of the crowd.

"We both got our wish." Teresa smiled as they began their long walk down the slope. The rain and the feet of the crowd turned the slope into a slippery quagmire.

Francesco took the baby from Rosa and held onto her arm while she lifted her skirt out of the mud.

Rosa knew what Francesco was thinking. "No food for my family." However, that wasn't the only thing troubling her. Another door had closed on his dream. He had sacrificed everything for her. One day, just before the strike, she had looked into the dye shop where Francesco was working. What she saw was unbearable. The steam was so thick she couldn't see beyond the man in front of her. Fumes from bleaches, acids, and other chemicals stung her eyes. Filthy water ran underfoot, forcing the workers to wear rubber boots or wooden clogs. She never told him she had been there. It would have hurt him to know that she had witnessed his degradation. She glanced at him now as the freezing rain collected around the rim of his bowler. *Francesco, amore, forgive me.*

His lips were drawn into a hard thin line, "I'll have to take that coal mining job in Colorado."

Teresa hoped she hadn't heard right. "I don't understand." Teresa's voice wavered as she struggled to keep from sliding down the slope. "Where did you hear about it?"

"The *Padrone.*" Rosa's voice reflected her trepidation.

Teresa's eyes widened with concern. "You can't be serious! You know you can't trust him."

His face reddened. "I know, but it's different this time. He showed me a newsletter describing the place. The camp has two schools, one for us and one for our son. Who knows? Maybe I can do some teaching. The place even has an opera house."

Rosa shook her head. "It sounds wonderful—too wonderful." West Virginia's horrors were always with her.

"Do you have the newsletter?" Teresa asked.

"No. He said it was his only copy and needed it to show other workers."

Teresa shook her head in disbelief. "Sounds suspicious. Please don't go. The strike can't last forever."

Francesco laughed bitterly. "Neither can my money, Violetta. Every time I try to get work, they slam the door in my face when they hear I'm on strike."

Rosa, trying to block out the thought of Colorado, asked Teresa, "What are you going to do?"

"I don't know. I hate working as a winder."

"Maybe Giustina has something for us." Rosa looked at Teresa imploringly, as if Teresa had an admission ticket to Giustina's factories.

"Yes, Francesco," Teresa said, not thrilled at having to go to Giustina with her hat in her hand. "Please wait until we can find out."

"What do I know about sewing?" Francesco scoffed. "Even if I did, how can I?" He looked at his roughened hands.

"Maybe she knows of something else," Teresa suggested.

\* \* \*

Rosa and Francesco waited impatiently as Teresa spoke to Giustina over the phone. Giustina's tone was that of a mother reprimanding a child. "I wondered when you would get around to me. You can start working tomorrow in my Spring Street factory, but not at the same salary. I can't afford that. Business is off and you haven't been doing my office work. I'll be wasting time bringing you up to date."

Just what Teresa had expected. She almost felt sorry she had called. Teresa heard her mother's voice in her ears. "When you are at the bottom, you must suffer the pressures from above." Teresa bit her lip and charged forward. This time it wasn't for her; pride had nothing to do with it. "Anything for Rosa and Francesco?"

"For Rosa, yes, in my Paterson factory, but not for Francesco. She can start tomorrow. I'll call the floorlady. Next time, don't wait so long."

Again there was that irritating tone of censure. Again she bit her tongue and said with as much dignity as she could, "Francesco needs a job or he'll have to go to Colorado."

Giustina laughed. "Don't tell me; let me guess. Malespina showed Francesco that ten-year-old newsletter. Tell him that company is now the Colorado Fuel and Iron Company Works and belongs to John D. Rockefeller. There are no schools and no opera house." She laughed again. "Tell him to ask Malespina to show him the date on the letter."

Teresa couldn't help thinking about what Giustina had said to her once, "The more money you have, the more respect you get." That wasn't true of Malespina. She wondered if it were true of John D. Rockefeller. She finished her conversation with Giustina and told Rosa about the job in the Paterson plant.

Her face lit up for the first time in weeks. "And Francesco?" Rosa asked anxiously.

Teresa hesitated, then reluctantly, "No." She watched helplessly as their faces sank. Trying to give them hope she said quickly, "But..."

The telephone's ringing interrupted her.

"I just remembered," Giustina said, as if there had been no interruption in their conversation, "one of my Paterson workers told me that her husband just died. He was a janitor. What school was it?" Teresa could almost see Giustina playing with the bun at the back of her head. "Oh, yes, School No. 5 in Totowa. It may not pay as much as he was getting at the dye shop, but it's not the hell of the vats. Tell him to go right now."

Teresa smiled, nodded to Francesco, "Yes."

He picked up the baby and swung the giggling lad over his head.

\* \* \*

The gray March sky through Harry's office windows had no influence on the sunshine within. Nothing had changed much in the room; however, Teresa reflected, much had changed in her life and yet appeared the same. Again she was working for Giustina and living at Delora's, but Nick was no longer in her life. Teresa missed Rosa's. She missed, too, having a bed all to herself. Nevertheless, working at Giustina's had its blessings; it was interesting, sanitary, and had no lecherous foreman. Here, too, she could venture outdoors on errands despite being accompanied by Liza.

Harry got up quickly and smiled broadly at Teresa as she entered. He reached out and took her hands in his. "It's been so long since I last saw you. You look even lovelier than I remembered."

Now, as she looked at Harry, it puzzled her that during the four weeks since she had returned to work for Giustina, Giustina had never sent her to Harry's office. Other places, yes, but not Harry's.

"Where did you get that charming dress?" He swung her gently from side to side to see it from different angles.

"It's the one that I designed the time you had Giustina bid on those silk dresses. At the time, Nick thought you would be interested in seeing it. I know the dress is out of season, but Giustina thought you might want to see it."

"I'm sorry I didn't see it before. It's fine in both design and execution, but you already had the contract based on the other dress. You were right. Giustina's people did an excellent job. Please sit." He swept a book of samples off a chair for her. A book flew apart. A brightly colored yellow swatch, brighter than anything she had ever seen before, caught her attention. The adjoining page called it Tango Yellow. Harry sat at his desk. "I asked her to send you here last month, the moment I heard you were working for her. She said you were too busy. Didn't she tell you?"

"No." Teresa tried to hide her annoyance with Giustina. *What does Giustina have up her sleeve this time?*

"Well, anyway, it's good seeing you again." His warm smile swept her in.

"It's good seeing you too." Teresa sat on the edge of her chair. Assuming a businesslike attitude, she pulled some papers from a briefcase. "Giustina sent me with the contracts you wanted her to sign."

"Thanks." He took the papers and laid them on his desk without looking at them. "May I offer you some coffee?" He turned toward the door, about to call his secretary to bring some.

"No thank you. I still haven't gotten used to American coffee," she said politely.

"I'm sorry to say my secretary can't make a good cup of coffee, let alone espresso." Harry sat behind his desk and leaned back. "I've been looking at the sketches you dropped off a couple of days ago."

Teresa flushed, thinking about how she had dropped them off while on another errand for Giustina. She wasn't sure why she had dropped them off. It had been forward of her.

"Why didn't you come in to see me when you dropped them off?"

"I didn't want to bother you. You're much too busy." She lowered her eyes to hide her embarrassment.

"Nonsense. I always have time for you." He lifted one of her sketches out of the pile and looked at it. Despite the seeming disorder, he apparently knew where everything was. "They have great potential, just as the dress you're wearing does. They're innovative, yet they display good taste in their simplicity."

"Thank you." She flushed with excitement, hoping he would use them.

"You need only a little schooling and guidance." He placed the drawing down amid the clutter.

"Oh, perhaps I should take back that thank you." She laughed, but her disappointment showed through, despite herself.

He smiled. "I didn't mean it the way it sounded. What I meant was that yours is the kind of work that schooling helps. Others I've seen will never be worthwhile, no matter how many years of training the designer gets." He thought for a moment and looked as if he were seeing something in the future. "There is going to be a dramatic change in fashion shortly." Harry shrugged his shoulders. "That's not what I want to talk to you about, Violetta." He placed his hands behind his head, leaned back in his chair and fixed his penetrating eyes on her. "I like the way you work. You're accurate, punctual, and are always cordial, no matter how rude a person is to you."

She colored. "Thanks again."

"Why don't you join our little company? We're a growing concern. I need someone like you to help with that growth. You're trustworthy, smart, willing to learn, and reliable. I admire your quiet efficiency. You've only been in this country for a short time and already you speak English like a native."

Now it was her turn to sit back, but she was too astonished to assume Harry's relaxed posture. Was this why Giustina hadn't wanted her to see Harry? If so, why now? She knew the answer. Giustina needed to have the contracts signed, but more than that, she needed more work and knew that Teresa was her best avenue of getting it from Harry. *Maybe that was why she asked me to wear the dress. Or is there something more?*

"Well, what do you think?" His eyes glowed.

"I never thought about such a move," she said, still trying to analyze Harry's offer.

"I think I can guess what you're making now and can give you at least five times as much to start." He got up and sat on the front edge of the desk. His knee almost touched hers. "I'd like to send you to the Parsons School of Design." He saw her brighten. "I see you've heard of the school."

"Of course."

"You'd be a great help in that area, too."

She wanted to jump at the chance; however, she suspected that Harry was, or at least had been, interested in her as more than just an employee. He had asked her out once. She had refused. It annoyed her even now that he, a married man, would do that. It was immoral and insulting. Would he be hiring her because he expected more? "What would I be expected to do?"

"You'd be my Girl Friday."

"Your what?" Her skepticism was plainly visible.

He laughed. "An all-around person who does all sorts of work."

"A secretary?" She ventured, still skeptical.

"Much more. Barbara will be reporting to you." He smiled as he pushed some papers beside him on his desk. "For one thing, you would help me straighten out this abominable office. I'm hopeless at it. Barbara can't organize properly. When she did, I couldn't find anything and worse, neither could she."

They laughed.

"Sometimes you might have to do some traveling for me, or hold the fort while I travel. I have clients and associates here, Chicago, Los Angeles, France, and Italy. Sometimes I may call upon you to help me entertain my clients."

Again her suspicions telegraphed. He raised his hands defensively. "It's not what you're thinking. I know I asked you out, but believe me, this will be strictly a business arrangement, nothing more. You see, when I entertain customers, I need a companion or associate for the evening, you know, for dinner, or a show, concert, or opera. Entertaining clients is good business. It calls for someone who is attractive, intelligent and personable."

"I don't understand." She looked at a picture in a gold frame on his desk. A lovely young woman in an easy chair held an infant in her arms. "Why can't your wife accompany you?" It was the first time she had asked him about his personal life, and Giustina had never been informative. That was the one thing she respected about Giustina; she never gossiped.

Harry's face darkened. He got up, faced the windows and placed his hands in his pockets. It took him a few minutes before he answered, and then in a subdued voice. "My wife, Robin, and my children died four years ago. An auto accident. It had been raining. Robin swerved to avoid hitting a dog, lost control on the wet pavement and..." His voice trailed away.

"Oh, God, I'm so sorry." Her hands covered her mouth involuntarily. She shifted uneasily, not knowing what to say or do. Her heart went out to him. Until now, she had been aware only of his power, which had seemed almost rigid. Now he had gained a new dimension for her, one in which his momentary show of weakness had exhibited a greater character strength than she had been aware of.

Harry leaned against the window frame for what seemed an eternity to Teresa. Finally he straightened up, turned around and cleared his throat. "Sorry, I didn't mean to get emotional. I still feel it as if it happened yesterday."

"There's nothing to be sorry for." Teresa's voice was gentle. "It is I who should ask for forgiveness."

"Not at all. You didn't know." He said it as if nothing had happened, but his eyes had a pained, faraway look in them. "I need someone who will understand that we will be working strictly on a business level, no entanglements. Will you do it, Violetta?"

She hesitated. "I don't have the kind of clothing to wear to such functions."

"That'll be easy. You'll be modeling our latest fashions. With your face and figure, you'll be a knockout."

She blushed. "There's something else." She thought of Liza, waiting for her in the outer office. "I can't walk in the streets without an escort."

"Oh yes, Liza." He reflected for a moment. "I know you're a young lady with high morals. May I ask you, do you really think you need an escort to keep you that way?"

She bristled. "Of course not! It's not my lack of moral character. It's what my culture dictates. A single girl may not travel without a young person at her side. It just isn't done."

"I see. That is a problem. I could assign someone to be your escort, but that won't always be convenient. A young child tagging along when we entertain a client at the theater or opera wouldn't be exactly kosher. You understand that expression, kosher?"

"Yes."

He thought for a moment. "Maybe you're right. I don't want to ruin your standing in the circles you travel in."

She felt deeply disappointed at having lost such a wonderful opportunity and sudden annoyance at having to have an escort as if she were an unruly child.

"On the other hand, in the circle I'll introduce you to, should you choose to join us, we're not that provincial. You will be leaving that confining circle behind you and crossing into a more sophisticated one. It's entirely up to you. Do you dare? Do you have the courage, Violetta?"

Teresa reflected: *After all, what have I that's so wonderful? Who do I have to worry about? Rosa and Francesco will like me no matter what. Nick is out of my life forever. Mama will never know. Do the rest matter? I'd be a fool to refuse his offer. The increase in salary means I can send more money to Mama and even help Francesco, if he'll let me. Money seems to be the answer to everything in the world. This may be my chance to get it and gain complete control of my life.*

"Well? What do you think?"

"I'll have to give Giustina a few days notice. We're in the middle of some bookkeeping and I don't want to leave her suddenly. It wouldn't be right."

"Fair enough. That's the way I'd want you to treat me. I'd expect nothing less. Let's say two weeks. Is that ample time?"

"I think so." Teresa's heart was bursting with excitement and wonder at it all. The full impact of what he was offering her began to hit home.

"Good. Oh, by the way, how many languages do you speak?"

"Only two. Italian and English."

He tapped his chin with a pencil as he thought. "You have a good ear for language. That's something I can use. We'll have to get you French and Yiddish tutors. We deal with many Jewish clients. Maybe German, too." He sat at his desk and searched the clutter. Finally finding a pad, he made notes. "Can you dance?"

"Dance?" Her voice was breathless, "Yes. The tarantella. Is that what you mean?" she laughed.

Harry laughed too. "Not quite. I'll get a tutor for that, too." He wrote it down; then without looking up, he added, "A new dance craze is sweeping Europe and America called the tango. It started in Argentina. Many of my clients and their wives are mad about it."

"You want me to learn the tango?" He shocked her. The tango scandalized the women in her circle.

He smiled. "It's not as bad as you think. Anyway, this dance craze will be responsible for dramatic changes in fashion. A woman will need room to move. The blouse, for instance, should be full-sleeved, and more than likely, silk or satin. Perhaps the blouse could be in one piece, the seams from the shoulder to the wrists. Trains are out. I'll be happy to see those go. Some of your sketches with hats had horizontal aigrettes. They could blind their male partners. They're out, or placed vertically on the hat. The shoes will be pointed and lengthened to exaggerate the long, deliberate steps.

Even men's fashions will change. I've already had my dinner jackets cut long, and..." He saw her wide-eyed expression and stopped. "Sorry. I'm talking too much."

"Not at all. I'm fascinated." Her head spun as if he had whirled her around a dance floor for hours. "I've had no idea that all this was happening. Anything else?"

"Lots," he smiled at her enthusiasm, "but we'll talk more about that later. Oh, another thing, you'll have to move from Spring Street."

"What? Why?" she gasped.

"I can't call for you there with my buyers. You see, this business is nothing more than marketing. Do you think people need all these fashions? Hardly. Marketing makes people believe if they don't have them they'll be less than nothing. They think that they'll never have money, love, or status. Designing and manufacturing a garment aren't enough. Apart from selling it to the public, you have to sell the buyers who'll market it for you. If you don't, you can't go any further. They must believe you're a winner. We do that by selling ourselves, looking avant-garde, and prosperous." He saw her eyes widen in disbelief. He smiled. "Not a pretty picture, is it?"

"No."

"That's why I suggest you move uptown to the West Side."

"What?" He dismayed her. Just when she thought she had absorbed everything, he'd hit her with this incredible proposal. "I can't afford that! That's high society."

"You can, with what I'll be paying you. We're in luck. Right in that area, I've got an apartment house with an apartment that's just been vacated. It's being redecorated but should be ready soon. You can have that apartment for a reasonable rent."

Misgivings flashed through her. *What will people say if I move into this man's apartment building?* "Are you living in there now?"

He smiled. "I see you still don't trust me. No. My apartment is two blocks away." He looked about the room. "I plan to move this operation to 7th Avenue. It's going to be a big area for the garment trade. At least, I hope so, because I just purchased a large building there. What do you say?" He looked her straight in the eyes.

She threw caution aside. "Yes, but remember, Harry, I'll only take this job if we keep our relationship on a business level."

"Then it's settled." He got up and shook her hand. "You won't regret it." Harry laughed, feeling the same happy anticipation. He said jokingly, "Now I can have a decent cup of espresso."

"Did Giustina know you wanted to hire me?" It occurred to her to wonder.

"No." He looked genuinely puzzled.

# Chapter 18

## August 1914

The glass and chrome clock on the mantel chimed six o'clock. *Harry will be here in forty-five minutes.* Teresa looked around her Upper West Side apartment's living room to see if everything was in order. It was.

Although Teresa had been living in the apartment for nearly fifteen months, she hadn't completely adjusted to the Art Deco decor. She liked the clean lines and openness, yet all the white, glass and chrome felt cold. Why she had let Harry's decorator take control was beyond her. Teresa hadn't even balked at the two white sofas flanking the huge white marble fireplace. At times she hated sitting on them, afraid of marring their pristine, shot-silk surface. She had tried to rebel against Marcel *Duchamp's Nude Descending the Staircase* that dominated the area above the mantel. The cost had shocked her, but Harry had argued, "It's part of the business, like a building, or a sewing machine. The apartment must convey the right avant-garde image, since we use it to entertain our customers."

Although she had relented, at times she felt as fragmented as the painting. The decor wasn't the only thing troubling her; it was her life style, complete with a live-in maid. Teresa felt removed from her past, an important part of herself. Still, she immersed herself in her work with a passion reserved for the lover she never had. Many days were long and fatiguing; however, she enjoyed them immensely, although some days were filled with stress, not all work-related.

Today was such a day. The priest had delivered her mother's monthly letter. They were in response to the money that Teresa sent her mother. Having to face Annunziata's letter and censure from the priest for her secrecy distressed her. Teresa took the letter into her bedroom. It was when she received the letters that her bedroom screamed white the most. The walls, the satin bedspread, the rug, the dressing table, and the highly polished marble dressing table top were all Harry's choice.

She lifted her dress so that she wouldn't crush it by sitting at her dressing table. Trembling, she opened the letter though she knew what it would say. It seldom varied.

Thank God I am well. Things were difficult for me before these gifts, but with them I am well in body if not in mind, for I am alone in this world. Please convey my gratitude to my silent benefactor and, I beg you, have her make herself known to me!

It always said "her" not "him", as if her mother knew the benefactor was Teresa. Why Teresa still hadn't made herself known, she didn't know, only that some voice within her said not to. Teresa carefully slipped the letter into a white satin sachet with the other letters and tucked the sachet into the dressing table's bottom drawer. She said a silent prayer for her mother's well-being, took a tremulous breath, and closed the drawer, but the voice from within the drawer refused to remain silent.

Trying to silence the voice, Teresa took Nick's gold framed picture from the bottom drawer. It was secure from prying eyes. Nick was hers alone. She kissed the picture. Teresa performed this ritual first thing every morning, last thing every night, and in stressful moments.

The clock chimed the half hour. Teresa quickly placed the picture in the drawer and reentered the living room. She checked herself in the full-length mirror hanging in the entrance hall to see if the new gown that Harry wanted the customers to see was all right. Yes, except for the purple silk-satin cummerbund around the high waistline. She moved it slightly to the right and readjusted the light purple silk underbodice and lilac silk-chiffon overdress. Teresa sighed, wishing she could sit properly. It had been a long day, but she didn't want to crush her gown before Harry saw it.

To calm herself, she picked up the copy of the *New York Times* that her maid, Sofia, had neatly folded and placed on the glass entrance table. She opened the newspaper but failed to notice the letter fluttering to the floor. All she saw was the shocking headline:

Ludlow, Colorado, Massacre
Eleven Children and Two Women
Killed in Bloody Coal-Mining Strike

Teresa shivered and closed her eyes. *Madonna mia, Rosa's family could have been there!* It took a minute for the knot in her stomach to loosen. She was happy that Francesco had finally accepted a loan for his tuition. *If he can't be a doctor, at least he can be a teacher.* Teresa had wanted to give him the money, but his pride wouldn't allow him to accept it. She had offered Rosa a position, but Rosa didn't want to travel to New York and leave her family every day.

Teresa opened the newspaper. A small article in the far left corner caught her attention.

Leonardo Forte Deported

Leonardo Forte, an Italian immigrant, convicted of inciting a riot and fomenting sedition both here and in Boston, has been deported. Accused of instigating....

"He hasn't changed." Teresa folded the newspaper. It was then that she noticed the letter on the floor. *That Sofia! No matter how often I tell her to keep letters separate, she still forgets.* A tingle of delight ran through her; it was Nick's bold handwriting! She sat on the sofa, ignoring the crushing of her dress. This was his first letter in a long time. Nevertheless, she kept writing, following his movements and address changes through Giustina. When Giustina had become angry with her for leaving her employ, Teresa had relied on Liza. Her hands trembled as she opened the letter.

April 16, 1914

Dear Violetta

Rumors are everywhere that England will soon be at war with Germany. Here, at the aerodrome, we feel sure of it. I believe that was the reason that they accepted me, an Italian-American, in the Royal Flying Corps. They need fliers desperately, any fliers.

Teresa trembled at the thought of Nick going to war. He was so impulsive, so unafraid of danger. She had known it even before she met him. His picture had told her as much. *Dio mio, please, no war!* Teresa crossed herself and began reading again.

I like the English, although they're not as warm as Italians in their relationships. I miss that. Still, thank God for Bob's friendship. He's aces. Not that I haven't made friends, I've made a couple at the aerodrome. Not friends, exactly, comrades. I've discovered that in England, too, prejudice exists against Italians. They like me well enough until they hear my real name, Niccolo Giovane. At first I thought it was just class distinction, you know, having the right family ties, the right schools and all that goes with it. Then I realized it was my lineage that stood in the way. Perhaps

I should have kept my Anglicized name, but that would have been living a lie. I'm done with deception.

The bonding factor of flying isn't enough to welcome me into their homes. It's just as well. Mama always said that friendships bring heartaches and problems. Maybe she's right. Right or wrong, apart from Bob, the only real friend I have is my aeroplane. Bob said that kind of friend could be fickle.

I know it sounds strange, giving one's affection to a machine, but the aeroplane gives me a feeling of freedom. Maybe escape is more accurate. Initially, I thought it was escape from Josephine, but now I don't know. All I do know is that in the air nothing exists but me, the aeroplane and the sky. It's a wonderful sensation. You should try it. I believe you'd love it too.

That brings me to you, Violetta. Your warm letters have meant a great deal to me. I haven't responded because I needed time to think. Ever since Josephine's death I've been confused about many things. Josephine wanted my love. All I wanted was to give her protection from society. What we gave each other was misery. I try not thinking about the mess I've made of things, but it's always there. The way she died, good Lord, how awful! She was a beautiful woman. Day and night, I think about it and the terrible things I said to her before she died. We were both to blame, but I didn't have to be cruel.

Enough of my moaning. When I received your letter yesterday, I finally came to a decision. Violetta, this is the most difficult letter I've ever had to write. I'm not sure whether it was your letter or the threat of war that did it. In any event, I have decided to let you go.

A shock wave ran through her. Teresa felt as though the entire building had moved. Had she read it right? Desperately hoping she hadn't, she reread it and found it doubly disturbing. Her anxiety made her continue to read.

The last time we saw each other I asked you to wait for me, but please, my lovely Violetta, that was wrong and unfair. I may never return to the States. Only God knows. Thinking you are waiting for me would eat me up. Believe me, you'd be better off without me. I've hurt many people. I'm just that kind of guy. Forget me and forgive me, Violetta.

Nick.

Teresa crushed the letter in her fist and felt as if her heart were being crushed. Knowing that even the connection of words between them wouldn't exist was difficult to accept. Her bitter tears didn't ease her terrible consuming pain.

The clock chimed 6:45. Harry.

At first she didn't care. She would tell him to go away. Teresa needed desperately to be alone, to reason it all out, but something made her move. Whether it was a sense of commitment or just the thought of Harry's sweet, disappointed face, she didn't know. However, try as she might, she couldn't stem the tears. Her entire body tightened with the extreme effort to control herself.

She rushed into the bathroom, filled the basin with cold water and then remembered her dress. Quickly, she removed it and hung it behind the door. After placing a towel around her shoulders to protect her underbodice, she immersed her face in the cold water. It didn't shock her out of her anguish. She repeated the ritual. Still no release. Mechanically, she patted her face dry and applied some face powder, the only makeup she allowed herself. The water had turned her hair into ringlets that she couldn't straighten around her face. *No matter.*

She dressed and returned to the livingroom just as the doorbell rang. Teresa picked up the long cream satin gloves and purple purse resting on the sofa. A quick check through the peephole confirmed it was Harry, immaculate as ever in his white tie and tails.

\* \* \*

The opera was another performance of *Bellini's La Sonnambula*. Again, Luisa Tetrazzini sang the title role. Teresa was in the same box seat in which she had sat when she had first seen the opera with Nick. This time, however, she wasn't at the railing and Nick wasn't behind her. Gripped by the poignant music, she allowed her tears to flow unchecked. Losing Nick again was more than she could bear. *Is my life only a dream,* she wondered, *or are my memories only dreams?* She reflected on her lost opportunities, hopes, dreams of love. *Love! O God, where is it? Why have You denied it? Please, God, let this burning earth beneath me stop shaking. Take me out of this fiery hell.*

# Chapter 19

## September 1917

To everyone's relief, rain had kept the pilots grounded. Now, the celestial beauty of sunlight streaked puffy cumulus clouds belied the thousand tragedies happening below. Nick, flying over France toward his next mission, an important railway depot, breathed in his fleeting freedom as if it were something tangible. His white silk scarf flapped behind him, silenced by his biplane's drone. Four bombs in the rack beneath the fuselage waited patiently; he tried not to think about them. Others in his squadron seemed aloof, but he knew that they were trying to suppress the same nightmares he excused as fatigue.

His Royal Flying Corps squadron had seen three years of battles. It was no secret a combat pilot's life expectancy was only forty to sixty hours. Nick had flown well over that. For that reason he was glad he had told Teresa not to wait. Without a parachute he had two choices, jumping from a great height or going down in flames. Nevertheless, he engaged enemy planes in his flying coffin with reckless abandon, becoming a dashing hero to the English. He, however, viewed the medals and accolades with revulsion. Receiving a medal for killing was ludicrous. Bravado didn't drive him. He didn't know what did. He wondered if his comrades were right to call him Straitjacket Jack. It amused him that it had taken all that notoriety before they had given him his commission. They wanted their officers from the correct schools like Eton, Oxford, or Sandhurst.

He peered down at the infantrymen wallowing in trench muck. Here and there, gunfire smoke traveled skyward. *Poor devils. Don't wave back anymore, do you? Didn't take long to learn that these crates can drop bombs or machine-gun you into oblivion.*

Trying to take his mind off their hell, he watched the silver streaks skimming over the twin rails coldly pointing the way. Just behind the streak, his Camel biplane's shadow formed a cross stalking him. That image hadn't occurred to him before. *Ah, you're thinking too much. Target's dead ahead. Keep your mind on it.*

Nick kissed the gold cross hanging around his neck and patted his leather flight jacket's pocket. Tucked away in the pocket was Teresa's picture, the only thing keeping him going. He glanced at Bob, flying escort on his right; Bob didn't look back. "Holy Mary, Mother of God, pray for us all!" Nick took a deep breath and dove to within fifty feet of the ground. He could see the panic on the men's faces as they ran in a futile effort to escape. *Don't think about it!* He released the first bomb, hitting the rails. Rails and ties shot skyward like toothpicks. Now over a supply-shed, he dropped the next two bombs and pulled up quickly, almost stalling the plane. The shed exploded with unbelievable force. All the elements in nature catapulted within inches of his craft. "Shit!" *We're creating another fiery field and we're the only fools who dare fly.*

Over the target again, Nick let the last bomb go. He wheeled left, but he wasn't free. Two Fokkers shadowed him. Nick knew he could outrun them, but they were too close for comfort. One Fokker let go a blast. Bullets slapped his plane. He looped and had the Fokker in his sights. He let go a volley. The German pilot recoiled in pain. For some unknown reason, Nick did, too. The Fokker sputtered earthward, trailing spiraling black smoke. The other Fokker! "Where the hell are you?" Nick searched the sky. Above and to his left, Bob had the Fokker in his sights and let go a blast. Bits and pieces of the Fokker nearly struck Nick's plane. Nick dipped his wings in thanks and headed for home. Tears filled Nick's eyes, bewildering him. These battles had never bothered him before, so why now?

He wiped his eyes roughly with his gauntlet and checked his instruments. The fuel gauge read lower than it should. He tapped the gauge. No change. Bob, alongside him, pointed to the rear of Nick's Camel. Nick looked over his shoulder. Fuel formed a trail. *Shit! Not enough fuel to make it back to the aerodrome!* His only hope was landing somewhere in friendly French territory, but where? Below him, where a farmer had once neatly furrowed rows, now only shell holes in haphazard trench mazes grew. He could see where the infantry had rebuilt some trenches after repeated bombings. Enemy trenches? Nick couldn't tell; how the hell could the poor guys in the trenches?

The Camel sputtered. "Keep going, baby!" Nick tapped the gauge again, a useless maneuver, he knew. "This is it, Violetta.

Help me look for a landing spot for this crate." Behind the trenches, an abandoned pasture appeared promising, a little rough, but no craters. However, tall cypress trees at the end loomed large, and beyond them a wooded area. "Shit! Too damn short! Even if I land okay, can I stop before the trees stop me? No choice." He edged the plane down, closer, closer. Touch down. His Camel bounced a couple of times, then moved forward with vicious momentum. The trees towered larger and larger as he sped toward them. "Stop! Damn you, stop!"

* * *

Teresa removed her white fur evening wrap and tossed it on the sofa. She collapsed on the plush cushions, carefully keeping her evening gown's front slit closed. As modest as it was, it was the first time she had worn a slit to the knee. It was no longer considered shocking, but she still felt uncomfortable wearing it. Teresa wanted to kick off her long tapered tango shoes but felt it improper. Although she always enjoyed Harry's company, she wished he'd leave so that she could get to bed. "I thought those stubborn buyers would never stop dancing the tango."

"No one in the room could keep his eyes off you. You look ravishing."

She laughed. "It was you captivating them." Teresa wasn't drunk, exactly, but she felt a warmth that made her glow with tenderness toward Harry. She laughed again. "When I took my first lesson, I was shocked. I thought the church was right in condemning it. I never thought I'd find it so fascinating and delightful." She returned to the evening's purpose. "I'm sure they'll sign the contract in the morning."

"Thanks to you. You're wonderful with all our clients." He relaxed, settled back on the sofa opposite her.

"I don't do anything differently."

"Ah, but I am a man, rough around the edges."

"You?" She smiled broadly as she looked at him. Not a hair unsettled, unlike Nick whose lock always begged for her attention. "That's not the way I'd describe you."

He looked deep into her eyes. "How would you describe me?"

"You're the most polished, articulate man I have ever known."

"Thanks for those kind words." He sat forward on the sofa's edge and leaned toward her. His fringed scarf swept the glass coffee table separating them.

Teresa felt a little uncomfortable at his scrutiny, sensing that somehow he wanted more. Then she scoffed at her imaginings. *It's just the wine spinning around in my head.* Fatigue edged through her as she leaned back. She was sorry she had given Sophia the night off. Sofia would have gone into her protective mode and shooed Harry out the door.

"We've been working together for what? Four years?"

She thought a minute. "It hasn't seemed that long, and yet it must be. So much has happened: Parsons, a partnership in the firm, and my own house of design."

She hated Giustina and Delora's manner toward her. They didn't say they thought she was Harry's mistress, but she felt that's what they believed. *I haven't changed that much. For Heaven's sake, both have been in this country much longer than I, and yet they've remained so provincial. With all Giustina's business shrewdness you'd think she'd understand. If anything, she's more provincial than the rest. Oh, well, forget them, they don't matter.* She felt that way about Giustina, but Delora was another matter. She respected and loved Delora too much. How she felt about herself, she wasn't sure. "If I didn't go to Giustina's factory sometimes, I'd think my life belonged to someone else. Sometimes I don't feel like the same person."

"You aren't. You've matured, become more sophisticated."

"Thanks to you."

"No. You've done it all yourself."

She knew he was skirting the issue. His nervousness began transmitting itself to her, making her almost afraid to hear what was on his mind.

Harry sat on the coffee table and took her hands in his. "Violetta, during all these years, I've kept my promise to keep our relationship businesslike, but I can't any longer. You must know I love you."

She tried to remove her hands, but he held fast. He was so close she could smell his aftershave lotion. Nick's lotion. It was disconcerting.

"I've waited, hoping you would give me a sign that you shared my feelings. Every time I see you I want to take you in my arms and kiss you until you say you love me."

She got up and tried to move away from him, but he rose, refusing to release her hands. "Harry, don't. You know I love you as my mentor and respect you more than anyone else I know. You've done so much for me. I can never thank you enough, but..."

"Nonsense. It's I who should thank you. You've been invaluable in making my once mediocre business more than double, but it's not the business I'm thinking about. It's you."

"I don't love you in the way you would like, apparently." She felt him flinch and felt sorry she had been so tactless.

Still, he didn't release her hands. "There's more than one kind of love between a man and a woman. There's comfortable love, the kind that grows with maturity through the years. Then there's the passion of youth."

"I can't settle for comfortable love."

"I know you believe that now, but someday you may learn to see the difference. Passion doesn't last. Sometimes it even turns to hate. It can tear you apart, drive you insane and even possess you until you are in someone else's control. Passion without tenderness is hollow, even cruel."

"Maybe so, but..."

He released her hands. "I know I'm much older."

"Somehow I don't think of you as older. Dear Harry, I don't know what to say." She walked to the window and looked out over the city. It had begun to rain. The city lights shimmered in the raindrops glistening on the window pane. "Have you ever known that kind of love, passionate, I mean?"

"Yes." He wanted to say, "For you," but held back. "I've known both, and that's why I can tell you it can be misery. Although I didn't have a passionate love for my wife, our love and tenderness grew with the years. Trust and understanding went a long way toward making it a good marriage."

*Should I tell him I was married before?* She had wanted to tell Nick, felt she'd had to, but not with Harry. She stared into the darkness, feeling that if it were clear enough and she looked hard enough, she could see Nick all the way in Europe. *Oh, Nick, my darling!* Still gazing into the darkness, she asked Harry, "Isn't there a love that includes both?"

"Yes, but if you're holding out for that, or think you can conjure one up, good luck. Tell me, is there someone else? I've never seen you with anyone else."

Even after all the time, separation and rejection, a fire swept through her every time she thought of Nick. She still loved Nick, a deep, burning love that would last forever. After all this time she still waited to hear from him. But, obviously her many letters had meant nothing to him. Her heart sank. It would be so easy if she loved Harry. What was there about her that made everything so difficult? Without turning she said, "No, there is no one else."

A smile moved across his face. "Then, Violetta, I believe I can make you happy. In time I believe you could learn to love me. We're good together. Our relationship now is like a marriage. After losing my family, I felt dead. When you first came into my office, I knew that you were what I needed to make me human. You have brought hope to my life. I now have more wealth than I know what to do with. Let me indulge you with all the luxuries I long to..."

"Harry," she almost felt insulted, "it's not money driving me." It was the first time she realized it. "I..."

"Forgive me. I didn't mean to imply that in any way. That's not what's in my heart. What I meant was that it would please me to give you whatever you have dreamed of."

*Everything but Nick. I believed, once, that money would give me what Mama said only wealth could bring. Now that I have money, I have pain, but no love.*

"Please say yes. I want so much to call you darling." He took her into his arms and kissed her.

Teresa tried to resist, but he held fast. Suddenly she responded to Harry's kisses as if he were Nick. With her eyes closed, she allowed his kisses, his aftershave, to consume her. Teresa found herself kissing him with a passion she hadn't known since Nick had kissed her on the dock. It was Nick's arms around her, Nick's mouth on hers, Nick's body against hers, Nick's love consuming her. Never mind what her conscious mind told her. It was Nick whose arms encircled her.

Harry had hidden his feelings for so long that, with a rush, they filled his entire being. Overwhelmed, he lifted her in his arms and carried her into the darkened bedroom. He placed her gently on the bed as if he were afraid she would fade from him. Uncharacteristically, without regard for his clothing, he tossed his things on the floor and began undoing her dress. She found herself helping him. The white satin bedspread felt deliciously cool and soft on her skin.

Harry kissed her breasts as if he worshiped them. She felt her willpower slip further and further away. Tingling delight shimmered through her, sensuous, pervasive. *Nick.* Then, almost without her consent, tears filled her eyes and moistened her cheeks.

"What is it, dearest? I haven't hurt you, have I? That is, I haven't done anything yet."

His concern burned her conscience. "I can't. Forgive me, Harry, but I can't." She hid her face in her hands.

Harry moved slowly away from her and sat on the edge of the bed. He placed his elbows on his knees and hid his face in his hands. "I'm the one who should ask for forgiveness. I took advantage of you. I'll wait, my dear, and hope you'll come to me on your own. I'll continue loving you and hope it's something you can't resist."

Teresa's heart ached. She wanted to take him in her arms to comfort him, but she knew instinctively it would be the wrong time. For the hundredth time, she asked herself, *Why am I never able to accept love when it's offered to me? Is it my fate to yearn for something only after it's taken from me? My whole life seems to have been a dream, an illusion, a sham. Has my experience with Rocco affected my life that much, or has Nick? Somehow, I must kill this love for Nick.*

This wasn't the first time Harry thought about Nick in relationship to the woman he loved, but it was the strangest. More than once, he had seen her looking at Nick's photograph on Giustina's desk. Is it Nick she loves? *You fool, why wouldn't she love that handsome, young, dashing flier?* The notion ate at him. By contrast, he felt old, colorless; much worse, a shirker. Without telling anyone, he had tried to enlist, but the services wouldn't accept him. They needed the military uniforms he manufactured. To appease him, the army had offered him a commission so that he could wear a uniform. Harry had refused, despite the remarks from people demanding to know why he wasn't in uniform. He felt he wasn't endangering his life as so many others were; therefore, he hadn't the right to wear it. He wondered briefly if Teresa felt he was a malingerer, but he knew better.

# Chapter 20

## November 1917

The Indian-summer sunlight streaming through Giustina's plate-glass window failed to bring the workers a sense of well-being. With their men at war, all they felt was anxiety. Giustina, however, felt buoyant. Nick had written that he would return soon. She didn't know when, but each passing day brought increased excitement and anticipation. In a rare spending mood, she had bought him an automobile. True, the four-seater Studebaker coupe was two years old and not as sporty as some other autos she had seen whizzing past, but it was sensible. If nothing else, Giustina was sensible. This car had a hard top and glass windows. *He'll thank me in the end.*

So great was Giustina's eagerness to see him, she ignored the machine noises and had her desk moved to face the open office door. When she saw him, she would show him the books, have him take her to dinner and move in with her. Then the thought flashed in her mind: *Why is he coming home? The war isn't over. Something is wrong! No!* She refused to allow the thought to persist.

When a shadow crossed her desk, she looked up smiling with anticipation. Her face fell when she saw Teresa. Her disappointment wasn't only that it wasn't Nick, but that it was Teresa. Too well-dressed, in that tailored tan silk suit, not in keeping with her class. Outrageous, traveling the streets unescorted. Worse yet, living in one of Harry's apartment houses! Every Sunday, Giustina gave thanks Nick hadn't married her. *I'll see that he goes to church with me and gives thanks. No more of that "Leave me alone, I'm a grown man, Mama."*

Another thing bothering her about Teresa was Teresa's insistence that she drop Malespina as a hiring agent. *Easy for her. She doesn't have to worry about his connections. How dare she order me around?*

Occasionally, Giustina regretted having accepted their work. Now was one of those times. *Why did I put all my eggs in one basket?*

*Very risky! Still, what choice do I have? I can't manage two contractors by myself, not contracts this size.* Suddenly fatigue struck her.

Teresa closed the office door behind her. When Giustina glared at her, she misunderstood Giustina's displeasure. "I hope you don't mind my closing the door, but the noise makes it too difficult to hear."

She wanted to scream at the girl, *Yes, I do mind, but that would entail an explanation.* Giustina didn't want Teresa to know that Nick was coming home. Not until she informed Nick about the girl first.

Teresa placed a manila envelope on the desk. "These are the contracts for you to sign. You'll need to use both factories for this contract, so you can't take on any other work."

"Of course," she snapped. This time she was annoyed at being told the obvious. *I'll bet Violetta thinks I should feel gratitude for the work. Why should I? After all, the work came from Harry, not her. Besides, it's our quality, not their charity.* "I am thinking of expanding. With all this work, two factories are not enough." *Now why did I say that?* She hadn't thought of it before.

"Good idea. Perhaps we can form a merger. I was thinking of investing in a factory and..."

"You were?" Surprise and skepticism were clearly written on Giustina's face. *How did she get all that money so fast? It took me nearly all my life to get where I am.* Her eyes narrowed. *I'm right! Something is going on between those two! Go into business with her? Preposterous!* Nevertheless, the idea of expanding appealed to her. Without thinking she spoke her thoughts. "Before I can expand, I'll need someone I trust to help in the office. Now that Nick is coming home, I..."

"He's coming home?" Her temples pulsed with anticipation.

Giustina's blunder caused her to knock Nick's picture over. "What?"

"Nick is coming home?" Teresa's heart leaped at the thought. She picked up the picture and placed it so that she could see it.

Giustina's mouth formed a tight line. She moved the picture away from Teresa's view to show who had possession. "I guess so, someday, but..." The telephone rang. Giustina, grateful for the interruption, answered the phone and turned her back on Teresa. It was an unquestionable sign that the session had ended.

Teresa didn't care. All she could think was, *Nick's coming home!* She nearly floated out of the factory. Once on the sidewalk, she stopped to cool off, but the caressing breeze didn't quench the fire burning within. Although she hadn't heard from him after that painful letter, she still allowed her fantasy free rein. Teresa could almost feel his arms around her, his lips upon hers. She looked up and down the street. *Don't be silly. Giustina didn't say today...but then...maybe. He won't want to see me...but he might. Oh, you're such a fool! Stop being absurd and go home.* However, she couldn't. Not yet.

She looked at the plate-glass window. No, she didn't want to go back into the factory. *Delora? Yes, Delora. Since Ernesto's been in France, I haven't heard anything about him.* Teresa prayed he was safe. She started for the steps and stopped. *No. Go home, you fool.* However, the pull was too great. She rushed up the stairs to Delora's apartment. A delaying tactic, but she didn't care. Feeling Nick's presence, she didn't want to let go.

Teresa heard the weeping before she saw them sitting side by side on the settee. Delora clutched Liza to her ample breasts. Fortunata, uncharacteristically, rubbed her cheek against Liza's leg as if wanting to rub Liza's pain away.

"What is it?" Teresa asked, afraid of the answer.

"Ernesto wrote Liza that Stefano is dead."

"Oh, my dear Liza, I'm so terribly sorry." Liza had grown into a lovely young woman. Whether it was maturation or Steve's love that caused the change, she no longer was the brat that she had been as a child.

"I told her that she is only seventeen," Delora said, "and will find someone else."

"Never!" Liza cried.

Teresa struggled for something comforting to say, but all she could say was, "If I can do anything, let me know." It was pathetically weak and she knew it. She kissed the top of Liza's head and walked quietly out of the room. Could she ever love another man the way she loved Nick? No. The pain, still fresh in her heart after having lost Nick to Josephine, confirmed it for her.

Absorbed in thought, she opened the front door. Her feet stopped abruptly before a pair of shiny brown leather puttees and a cane. Her first thought was that Ernesto had magically returned home. She looked up. Nick! He had grown so thin. The war had left its mark on his sunken eyes, those magnificent eyes she looked longingly at so often in his photo. "Nick!"

For a split second Nick didn't recognize Teresa. Her hair had been straightened and bobbed, but it was more than that. She no longer had that lost look about her. When recognition sank in, his face lit up. He slid his arm from the sling, wrapped his arms around her and kissed her.

People on the street stared at them as they embraced on the stoop. Teresa and Nick didn't notice, nor would they have cared if they had. He didn't want to let her go and she didn't want to leave his arms, ever. Finally, reluctantly, they parted.

Nick held her at arms' length. "Darling," he murmured, "how wonderful you look." He tilted his head to one side. "What happened to all that beautiful, soft, wavy hair I loved so much? And your clothes make you look so different." He continued to study her. "You've changed, Violetta. You're more sophisticated." He closed his eyes and ran his fingers through her hair. "I'm not sure it's the you I remember."

She brushed aside the disapproval that he tried unsuccessfully to conceal and touched his sling with her fingertips. "Your arm, your leg, are you all right?" She searched for the handkerchief in her purse.

"This old fly-boy? Of course. They're a bit stiff," he tapped his leg with his cane, "but that's all." He took a handkerchief from his pocket and handed it to her.

Then she saw the small scar at his temple. She ran her fingers over it. "And this? Is this all right too?"

He touched it and tossed if off with a shrug. "Just a graze."

"Giustina is in her office, longing to see you."

"Never mind her. She'll keep. It's you I wanted to see. I can't believe my luck that you're here." He pushed her back into the hallway. As the door swung shut, he pushed her against the wall separating the hall from the factory, dropped his cane and took her into his arms.

Teresa shifted closer to him, clinging to him, unleashing her pent-up hunger for him. His lips at her temple, on her eyes, then upon her mouth, were warm, demanding. No longer was her kiss like the kiss on the rooftop, young, innocent. Passion seized her. The electric sewing machines' pulsing on the wall ran through her, intensifying her heart's throbbing. Her feelings grew more intense, surging through her body. She wanted desperately to welcome him into her body, but a small inner voice brought her back to her senses.

Teresa pushed him away, trying to regain control. "I...I...my breath."

"I know," he said, his voice thick with emotion. "Isn't it wonderful?" For a moment, he thought his legs were going to buckle under him. He took a deep breath, trying to ease his pounding heart, and leaned back against the wall. He held her hands. "Your hands are so beautiful." He kissed her palms, failing to notice the two-carat diamond ring on her finger.

She smiled through her tears. "That lock still refuses to stay in place." She pushed it back. "You look so good to me."

"Have you any idea how good you look to me?"

*Change the subject or I'll give myself to him right here.* "I...I wrote you several times, after receiving your letter, but you never..."

"I know. I wrote you several times, but each time I tore up the letter. It seemed too inadequate somehow. But your letters meant so much to me, *cara,* more than you'll ever know. I always had your picture and last letter near my heart." He touched his breast pocket. "They saw me through some rough times."

She could see the pain in his eyes. "Things must have been difficult for you. I'm so sorry."

"Let's not talk about me. I want to know about you. I peeked through the window, hoping by some miracle you'd be in the factory. When I didn't see you, I decided to take a chance and see if you were upstairs. I had to tell you how much I love you." He whispered her name, "Violetta. How I love saying your name, *cara.* It's so like you, a delicate flower." Nick tried to kiss her again, but she held him back. He smiled and touched her cheek to make sure she wasn't an apparition. "Listen, *cara,* I have some plans. With the money I made on investments and selling my house, and with Bob's money—they sent him home before me—anyway, we've bought an old aeroplane. Actually it's a combination of old planes that Bob's been knocking together. We're planning to start our own mail service."

As he spoke, his tired eyes grew large and sparkled with excitement. "There's some flat land in New Jersey that's a great place for an airfield and..." He laughed. "Listen to me. I'm flying too high. None of that is what I wanted to say." He tried to kiss her again, but she held him back. "Violetta, can you forget my crazy letter? I didn't want you waiting for a man who might be killed or maimed." He laughed nervously. "Why is it I faced death without fear and now I'm dying with fear? Please, *cara,* say yes, that we can start over."

She had heard the words in her dreams so often that they seemed unreal now. Again, tears clouded her vision, this time not of happiness, but of deep sorrow. Teresa hungered for him, but she knew she couldn't continue the cycle of pain that had been part of her life for so long. "I'm sorry, but it's too late."

"Too late?" His smile stiffened into an expression of panic. "Did I really do something that terrible when I wrote that letter? You're not married, are you?"

"No, but..."

He expelled air forcibly, expressing his relief. He put his arms around her. "Don't scare me."

"Nick." She pushed him away. Unable to meet his eyes she said, "I'm not married, but I'm engaged."

"What? No! Who?"

"Harry Goldstein."

"You can't be serious." It was only then that he saw the diamond ring on her finger. It stung him mentally and physically. He'd never thought of giving Josephine an engagement ring until she had asked for one, and even then, it was only a half-carat. He didn't have money for more and he knew that his mother wouldn't lend him any. He still couldn't give the woman he loved a ring as large as the one she wore. His emotions ran from low self-esteem, to jealously, to anger. "Harry's old enough to be your father!" he blurted out.

"Maybe so, but he's been so good to me. I can never thank him enough for all he's done and—Nick, you've been gone for so..."

"Gratitude is no basis for marriage. Anyway, what's he done to earn your gratitude?"

"Harry gave me a job and then he..."

"A job! Is that all? You mean you're marrying him to say thanks for a job?"

"No! That's not what..."

"Forget work. Once I'm settled, you won't have to work. It won't be long before Bob and I have a going concern." He tried to take her in his arms again, but she pulled away.

"No! Please let me go. I don't want anybody taking care of me. I enjoy my work and can stand on my own two feet." That's not what she wanted to say, but she didn't know what else to say, she was so confused.

"Violetta, apart from the difference in your ages, there is the cultural difference. What about your Italian heritage? How can Harry understand and become part of it? How can you put that all behind?"

"I left a lot more than that behind when I came to America."

He held her arms. "Let's not discuss that now, *cara*. I know you love me. You couldn't kiss me that way if you didn't."

"If only I had heard from you a little sooner, even one letter, but now it's too late for us. How can I do that to Harry? You can't ask me to. Please, let me go." She pulled away from him, blindly opened the door and ran out. *Oh, God, why did I wait here to see him? The way I live my life always tempts fate.* The reality around her was not as good as her dreams had been.

It had turned sharply colder. A stiff wind from the east pushed against her, but she didn't notice. All she could think of was how desperately she wanted to say yes. Nevertheless, because she knew so well what life could do, that exasperating voice within her whispered, *When he hears Giustina's lies, he'll never want to marry me.* Pain filled the emptiness that her withdrawal from him had left. Teresa closed her eyes tightly for an instant. *I can't bear to know he'll think badly of me.* Scarcely able to see her way through the tears, she ran to the nearest subway station.

# Chapter 21

Rocco wasn't in the habit of reading the *New York Times* or, for that matter, any newspaper's society page. He picked it up off the subway car seat to stuff into the window's cracks of his Five Points room. It was then that Teresa's picture announcing her engagement to Harry caught his eye. He spread the page out on the table in the middle of his closet-sized room and stared at it. Why is she familiar? After all, he had never had contact with anyone in society. He brought the paper closer to the bare light bulb hanging from the ceiling and began to read:

The lovely couturier, Violetta Esposito, is the owner of the House of Violetta, a couture on the fashionable Upper West Side...Her life reads like a rags-to-riches story. She emigrated from Italy in 1909 aboard the *Mostro* via steerage and is now a co-owner in the Goldstein Esposito Clothing Factory...

"Never heard of her." Rocco had developed the habit of talking to himself from living alone. "1909? That was the year I got fired for dynamiting the shack in West Virginia. The bastards tell me to get rid of those troublemakers and then go berserk because I blow up a company shack!" His voice, coarsened by cheap alcohol and cigars, echoed around the nearly empty room and seemed to be mocking him. "This stinkin' hole ain't no better than those lousy shacks." The under-stuffed mattress behind him stank from years of misuse.

"What the hell made Anna go to the shack? Shit, I could have moved from this stinkin' hole and lived decent if I had one like her and one like Teresa. Why the hell did Teresa die on the *Mostro*? Shit! I lose my job, my whore, my wife and—the *Mostro*?"

Rocco looked at the picture again. "Teresa?" He took their wedding picture from his wallet and placed it beside the article on the table. In the newspaper, she looked older and her hair was different, but to him the pictures compared favorably. Rocco was very familiar with his wedding picture, having shown it often to prospective johns to tantalize them. "If it is Teresa, the rotten bitch cheated me!"

He balanced his straight-backed wooden chair on its two hind legs. "This'll be too good to miss if it is." Rocco poured himself another glass of red wine, took a swig, and pulled a face. "It would mean no more rotgut, but the best wine, best food and the best whores for me. I can even buy back my revolver from Malespina. Mmm, he might know where she lives. No. Getting those brats from Italy was enough of a partnership." In desperate need of money, he considered blackmailing Malespina. "It'd be easy." He glanced at the chest of drawers beside him. "Good thing I kept those papers. They could send Malespina away for good." Then he shuddered, thinking about Malespina's long-reaching powers. "No. If it is Teresa, she's my way out. The bitch must have a telephone."

He tore the article out, went into the dimly lit hall and lifted a dog-eared telephone book dangling from the wall telephone. "No. Don't call her. See her face. Then I can be sure it is Teresa, but where?" He pulled on the wallpaper hanging in strips as he contemplated. "Her apartment? Goldstein and Esposito's? The House of Violetta?" He tore out the pages containing the addresses.

"Yep, you sure have come up in the world, Teresa." He laughed, "All the better for me."

\* \* \*

Teresa sat at the vanity table in her bedroom absent-mindedly brushing her hair until a static charge lifted the strands. She felt miserable. *Why is there always some pain with any joy I get?*

Tonight she and Harry were to dine without clients to come between them. She was glad she had given Sofia the night off. Doing what she must do with another person in the apartment would be much too difficult.

The ringing doorbell stabbed at her heart. Teresa got up and smoothed the white-satin evening gown over her slender hips. Dreading the task before her, she walked slowly to the door. She looked through the peephole.

Harry struggled with a champagne bottle in one hand and a corsage box in the other. Under one arm was a long box that probably contained long-stemmed white roses, her favorites. He had stopped giving her violets, saying they really didn't suit her. Tucked under the other arm was a five-pound box of chocolates, also her favorites.

*God, what am I doing to this very special man? One word will wipe that sweet smile from his face.*

Harry rang the bell again with the bottom of the bottle and almost dropped everything. "Honey, let me in before I have a catastrophe out here."

Her hands shook as she opened the door.

His smile faded when he saw her eyes glistening with tears. "What's happened? Are you okay?"

"I'm fine. It's just that I must talk to you."

"Sounds ominous, kid." He always called her kid when he thought she was too concerned about something or when he was afraid of losing her. That concern had crossed his mind often since she had said she would marry him. He placed the packages on the entrance table and followed her to the couch. "What is it, honey?" He sat beside her, took her hands. "It can't be that bad, can it?"

"Harry, please don't say anything until I've finished. This is too painful and far too difficult..."

"Painful? Difficult?" A hard knot formed in the pit of his stomach. "As bad as all that?"

Teresa got up, walked a few paces, returned and knelt at his knees. She took his hands in hers and looked into his eyes. They had suddenly grown old. If she didn't say it now, she never could, so she blurted out, "My dearest, I can't marry you. It wouldn't be fair to you."

It was only then that he noticed that her engagement ring was no longer on her hand. The black velveteen box it had come in rested on the coffee table. He tried to take his hands away, but she held fast. "I knew it was too good to be true. How could a lovely young woman like you love me?"

"I do love you, Harry, but I'm not *in* love with you. You've known that all along. How I wish I did. Things would be so much simpler." She closed her eyes to spare herself from the pain she saw in his. "Once you asked me if there was anyone else. There was always someone in my heart but not in my life."

"I don't understand."

"It's a long story."

"I'll listen. I've nothing else to do. Nothing that matters anymore, anyway."

Her heart went out to him. "You see, I loved him ever since I came to this country; no, even before. God, that seems so long ago. At the time, I didn't know it. It wasn't until he said he loved me that I realized it. Then, for a very long time, I thought he didn't love me, and I questioned my own feelings. Now he has returned from the war and has asked me to marry him. I've been so confused, but when I saw him, I realized..." She closed her eyes to ease the pain. "Oh, Harry, although I want to make you happy because you are so special to me, I want to marry him. Can you understand...?" Her voice faltered.

Then it struck him, "Nick?"

"Yes. Can you forgive me?"

Harry went to the window and stood with his back to her. Seeing him with his shoulders slumped, looking as he had looked when he had told her about his dead wife and children, was too painful. She could see his face reflected in the glass. His eyes were closed tightly as if holding back agonizing thoughts from his consciousness. He remained silent for a long time, too long for her to bear it any longer.

"Harry, I'm so very sorry." Teresa, huddled on the floor, hid her face in her hands to keep the sight of his grief-stricken face from her. She wept silently, struggling with her sense of guilt at giving him such pain. *How selfish. I'm thinking only of my needs, my wants, my desires. Maybe I should give in to convention; after all, many women have married without love, willingly, like Rosa and her first husband. But oh, my love, Nick!*

Harry turned, saw her on the floor and forgot his own misery. He knelt in front of her, took her face in his hands and kissed her eyelids. "My darling, don't cry. I love you so much that I can't deny you anything. All I want is your happiness. You know that." He lifted her off the floor and took her in his arms. It was all he could do to keep his own tears away.

She wept openly and trembled in his arms.

"Promise me one thing, my dearest Violetta, keep me as your friend. Whenever you need me, I'll be here and..." He couldn't say anything more.

* * *

"Don't dare say anything against Violetta! I won't have it!" Nick, his white-knuckled hand on the front doorknob of his mother's home, could barely contain himself. He wanted to put his fists through the door's etched glass.

Giustina had never seen Nick so angry, not even when they had argued about his marrying Josephine. She placed her hand on the front door, trying to keep him from leaving. "Use the brains God gave you. How do you suppose she climbed so fast? The little she knows about business, I taught her. Tell me, what is she doing for Harry for him to be so generous? File? Type? Answer the telephone?"

"You never liked her. That's why you're saying all these outrageous things." He pushed her away from the door and stormed out, shattering the etched glass in the door as he slammed it shut behind him. Nick cranked the engine of his auto. The crank kicked back, almost breaking his arm, but his anger was so intense, he didn't feel the pain.

All the way to Teterboro, Giustina's words prodded him, nearly driving him mad. He sped across the empty field, kicking up a cloud of dust behind him. A stiff wind swept the dust into the waving marsh grasses at the end of the runway. He didn't notice it or the other rickety hangars beside the one he had rented. All his head said was, *Not Violetta, she's too good, too pure.* Yet, nagging doubts gnawed at him. She was extremely prosperous for someone so young and inexperienced. *No! Not Violetta! There is nothing deceptive about her. Nothing! I'd bet my life on it!* The scar at his temple began to throb.

Still, could he blame her if she had wandered. After all, he hadn't been too fair with her. Hadn't he abandoned her for Josephine? Hadn't he ignored her letters? God! Had he pushed her to become someone he no longer knew?

He drove up to the hanger, hopped out and yanked the hanger doors so hard they rebounded, nearly hitting him as he entered. The sharp wind swept bits of paper into the shed and stopped at Bob's legs.

Bob, standing on a stack of milk crates tightening the nuts on the engine, yelled, "Close those damn doors!"

Nick slammed the doors shut.

"Whoa! Want to bring down the bloody shed?" The patch over Bob's eye almost blended in with the grease on his face. "What's eating you?"

"Nothing!"

Only a woman, Bob reflected, could cause that much anger. "Why the hell don't you marry her and get it over with? You're driving us both nuts."

"Mind your own business. I don't mind yours!" he yelled.

"Good!" Bob answered with equal force. "Glad to hear it!" Prudently, he changed the subject. He patted the two-seater's fuselage. "This hodgepodge will hold together, I think. How does she look?"

"Fine." Nick's mind was still too occupied with Teresa. He opened his leather jacket, releasing some heat his anger had generated. "Did you get that mail service set up?"

"Fell through, for now anyway. We've always got barnstorming."

"Shit!" Nick kicked the ground. "You're kidding! Not that bloody awful circus stuff? It's degrading." He pushed back the lock of his hair that had strayed almost into his eyes.

"Just kidding, but what else have we got? The army doesn't want me, and as for you, it's dragging its feet."

Bob sat on the milk crate and stuck out his stiff leg. "Have you tried Mum?"

"Forget it. Mama'll never part with anything for flying."

Bob climbed back onto the milk crates. "Oh, listen, you got a phone call from Violetta. Her number's on the wall beside the phone."

"Why the hell didn't you say so before?"

"Skipped me mind." He resumed tightening the nuts and began singing without thinking,

Come, Josephine, in my flying machine...

"Cut that! Sing something else!" Nick yelled over his shoulder as he entered the office in the back corner.

Bob began singing,

"There's a long, long trail a-winding,

Into the land of my dreams,

Where the nightingales are..."

*That guy's tenor voice is damn irritating.* Nick found Bob's careless scrawl penciled on the wall beside the phone. "What the hell is this, a six or an eight?"

"Did you say something?"

"Never mind," Nick called back as he cranked up the phone, taking a chance at its being a six, and giving the number to the operator. When Teresa answered the phone, all the doubts his mother had instilled left his consciousness.

"Yes," she said simply, "I will marry you, if you still want me."

"Want you?" He almost dropped the receiver in his excitement. "Of course I still want you! Now and forever! When?"

A thrill rushed through her. "When I can get my trousseau ready. How about two months?"

"Two months? No. I'm not taking any chances on your getting away. How about tomorrow?"

She laughed at his impatience. "That's impossible. We need a license and a blood test and..."

"I can fly you to Gretna Green, Maryland. We can get married there right away, no waiting. Just pack a bag for the weekend."

She laughed again, "I couldn't possibly. Giustina would kill us."

"Forget her. Only we are important."

"Don't say that, Nick. You'll regret it. We must post the banns and do it properly. I want a white wedding gown with a gossamer veil and, well, the whole works."

"All right, darling. Whatever you say. Where are you now?"

"The House of Violetta."

"Give me the address and don't move. I'll meet you there. No, better still, it'll be faster if you meet me at Mama's Spring Street factory. We'll tell her together."

Overjoyed, Teresa hung up the phone, although she wasn't too eager to face Giustina with the announcement.

Nick hung up the phone and began to sing along with Bob. Funny, he had never noticed what a splendid voice Bob had.

\* \* \*

Four blocks from Giustina's factory, Rocco walked with an unsteady gait. Too much wine had done its mischief. The brisk air did nothing to correct the alcohol's effects, nor did it awaken his better judgment. He belched, rekindling the taste of the cheap wine in his dry mouth. Rocco laughed aloud, "For once, I'm saved."

A few heads turned and looked at him with curiosity.

"What are you looking at?" he barked at them.

They quickly continued to go about their own business.

The receptionist at the House of Violetta had told him that Teresa was on her way to Giovane and Son. He was annoyed, for he wanted the money for his rent and his gambling debts to

Malespina. It had crossed his mind to skip town but he didn't have enough money for that. Then there was Marietta, his latest conquest. "She could be trouble. Ah, I can handle her until I'm through with her, but if Malespina ever finds out he'll kill me." He smiled. "Once I get the money all my troubles will be over." Then doubt crossed his mind. "What if it isn't Teresa? I could get into trouble. Shit! It's got to be. It's about time things went my way."

\* \* \*

When Teresa entered the office, she found Nick sitting on the edge of the desk, impatiently waiting for her. On the desk beside him sat a box of long-stemmed white roses. He had been disappointed not to find violets, but he forgot all about the flowers when he saw her. He took her in his arms, backed her against the closed door and kissed her. It was such a passionate kiss that it startled her at first, but then she melted into him. Again the sewing machines' vibrations reverberated through her, intensifying her sensations. So consuming was it that she didn't feel the doorknob turn.

"Who locked this door?" Giustina's voice chilled their ardor.

"Nick," Teresa breathed, "let me go. Your mother's trying to get in." She pulled away from him and tidied herself.

"Come in, Mama. No one's locked the door."

"What is going on here?" Giustina asked as she entered, not even trying to hide her suspicion and disapproval.

Nick placed his arm around Teresa's waist. "Violetta and I are getting married in two months. We'd like your blessings."

The color drained from Giustina's face. Her lips formed a thin, colorless line. She closed the door and leaned against it. "When did you decide this?"

"Today." Nick gave Teresa a squeeze. "Isn't it wonderful?" It pleased him that Teresa no longer had the engagement ring on her finger.

"And what about Harry?" Giustina's tone of voice said more than any incriminating remark could have.

The hackles rose on the back of Teresa's neck. She fought for control. After all, Giustina was Nick's mother. Screaming reproaches at Giustina would only hurt Nick, the one person she never wanted to hurt, and in the end, it would only backfire. As calmly as she could, she said, "We called off our engagement. It was a mistake to begin with."

Giustina stepped away from the door and came within inches of Teresa's face. "What other mistakes have you and Harry made between you?"

Nick could feel Teresa's body shake with anger. He held her tighter. His nose pinched in rage. He asked, "What's that supposed to mean?"

"Niccolo," she shook her head, "can't you see, she is not the girl you left behind when you went to England?"

His face flooded with anger. "Take care, Mama, take care!"

Nevertheless, she couldn't stop. "Even a blind man can see she's hiding something."

Still trying to remain calm, he said, "Mother, the years have changed us all, even you. Violetta is the only woman that I can completely trust. It's good finally being free of doubt. Don't try changing that."

"How do you think she got where she is? By her wits alone?"

Teresa couldn't restrain herself. She pulled away from Nick. "How dare you? If you mean that there has been anything between Harry and me besides business, you are wrong! Harry has been very much a gentleman, and I have never ever given myself to any man. Do you hear? Not to any man! If..."

The door swung open. Rocco swayed in the doorway.

The blood drained from Teresa's head and she fainted into Nick's arms.

Nick, alarmed, swept everything from the desk with one arm and gently placed her on top.

Her reaction proved it for Rocco. She was Teresa! Triumphant, Rocco became more brazen. "Get your hands off my wife!" he shouted.

"Wife?" Both Nick and Giustina stared at him, utterly astonished.

It was Giustina who recovered first. A sly smile crossed her face. "I knew it. All the time I knew that little *strega* was hiding something. Didn't I tell you?" It was all she could do to keep from laughing out loud with vindication.

"Who the devil are you?" Nick's eyes pierced Rocco's.

He pointed at Teresa with a shaky finger. "Her husband. That's who."

"I don't believe you!" Nick's anger hung in the air like a sword.

"Who the hell cares what you believe? She's Teresa Martello, my wife."

Nick sighed with relief, "Listen, fella, this is Violetta Esposito."

Rocco pulled out the photograph from his pants' pocket. "Then who is this?"

Nick looked at the likeness closely. Although desperate to deny it, he could detect the resemblance.

Teresa slowly stirred. When she saw Rocco, she tried to jump up, but her trembling forced her to steady herself against the desk. "Rocco! I thought you were dead." Teresa's involuntary reaction confirmed Rocco's claim.

"Me? Dead?" he laughed. "Not yet."

Nick shifted uneasily, a clawing dread ran through him. "Violetta, who is this man?"

"I tried to tell you so many times, but..."

"You mean he *is* your husband?" His tension increased.

"Yes, but in name only."

"Hah!" Rocco's voice cracked with a scornful laugh.

"My mother forced me to marry him. On our wedding night, in a drunken stupor, he beat me and collapsed on the floor. In the morning, without consummating the marriage, he left for America."

"Don't give me that!" Rocco growled. "I saw the sheets!"

"You saw what Mama wanted you and everybody else in town to see, but it was just blood from a animal she had butchered."

"It doesn't matter. You are my wife. As my wife, you owe me and are going to pay." He grabbed the picture from Nick's hand and shoved it into his pants' pocket.

"She owes you nothing." Nick towered over Rocco. "Get the hell out before I kill you!" He drew his fist back threateningly.

"Niccolo!" Giustina shouted.

Teresa held onto Nick's arm. "Nick, don't!"

Rocco backed up and reached in his pocket for his revolver, but realizing it was gone, his bravado left him. He staggered out of the office, wove his way through the row of silent sewing machines and out the front door. The workers, having heard the commotion, had stopped working and were listening intently.

Giustina closed the office door, but not before glaring at the workers, who quickly put their heads down and resumed working. She faced Teresa. "Imposter!"

Teresa, her face white and drawn, ignored Giustina. "He's dangerous, Nick. He's a murderer."

"Murderer?" Giustina sat hard. "My God!"

"He killed Rosa's husband and others. Everyone believed he died in the explosion, too. That's why I was so sure I could marry you."

Nick looked at Teresa as if seeing her for the first time. "What do I call you, Violetta or Teresa?"

"Either. I was Teresa Tozzi before I married Rocco Martello, but so much has happened since, I don't even remember that girl anymore." As quickly as she could, she explained her changed identity. "I was so terrified of Rocco. When I heard that his intention was to use me for other men, I felt vindicated."

The shocking revelation, coupled with her lack of faith in him, angered Nick. "What bothers me is that you didn't trust me enough to tell me the truth. I..."

"Now do you believe me, Niccolo?" Giustina interrupted triumphantly. "What else is she hiding?"

"Please believe me, Nick, there is nothing else. Can't you see how frightened I was at being detected? Why do you think I repeatedly refused to marry you? Then the events in our lives made it more difficult to..."

"Why should we believe you?" Giustina tugged at her skirt, an obvious dust-off motion. "You have been living a lie for all these years."

Teresa could read the confusion and anger in Nick's face. "I don't blame you for being angry and suspicious."

"I don't know who you are anymore."

In truth she didn't know who she was either. She felt like a displaced person. "Nick, I wouldn't blame you if you rejected me. You know I love you. For many years I've kept my silence." Her voice trailed into tears, for she could see he was unbending. "Oh, Nick, my life defeats me. I feel as if I have awakened from a dream to a nightmare that's just beginning. What am I going to do?"

"I don't know. I need time to think," he said and walked out of the office.

Rocco, however, knew what he wanted to do and didn't wait. Cold sober now from the adrenalin racing through his veins, he went straight to the nearest courthouse.

* * *

The court issued the summons to Violetta Esposito, Teresa Martello and Teresa Tozzi. Like a whirlwind, it hit the newspapers. Teresa's pictures were printed side by side: the wedding picture, supplied by Rocco, and the announcement of the engagement. Newspaper after newspaper asked:

*WHO IS THIS WOMAN?*

*If this is not Violetta Esposito, what has happened to the real Violetta Esposito? Is foul play suspected? Neither Harry Goldstein nor Violetta Esposito could be reached for comment...*

Swarms of reporters entrenched themselves around her building, factory, and House of Violetta. At work, her employees besieged her with questions. Finally, at her wit's end, she barricaded herself in her apartment. She removed the telephone receiver from its hook and told Sofia to admit no one. She remained huddled in her white satin bathrobe, as if trying to become invisible, on the white sofa.

Harry, unable to reach her by phone, rang her doorbell and knocked on the door. "Violetta, it's me, Harry. Let me in."

"Go away, Harry, please."

"I'm not leaving, so you'd better open the door."

"All right, Sofia, let him in and take the evening off."

Sofia took her coat from the entrance closet, let him in and left the apartment.

Teresa tugged nervously at her bathrobe. Not that she was immodestly dressed; she wasn't. She was too distressed to be concerned about modesty.

Harry strode quickly to the sofa, sat beside her and took her in his arms. "It's all right, kid," he tried to reassure her. He held her tightly until she stopped weeping. "Would you prefer that I call you Violetta or Teresa?"

"Whatever you like."

"Like to talk about it?"

"I do owe you an explanation." As succinctly as she could, she recounted her story. When she finished, he gave a low whistle.

"You poor kid, you've been through it, haven't you? Bearing it all by yourself all these years must have been tormenting. Why on earth didn't you confide in me before this? Never mind. I'll get my lawyers on it. In no way is that bastard getting his hands on your money. You do realize it's all about money, don't you?"

\* \* \*

Two days passed before Teresa saw Nick. She had been in torment for him. Time and again she found herself questioning and re-questioning her feelings about him and his feelings about her. Time and again she questioned her actions since leaving Italy.

Nick, trying to escape his torment by test-flying his biplane, was unable to concentrate on anything. Who was this woman he was sure he loved? He tried unraveling what she meant to him, but his deliberations wouldn't form neat columns. Nick knew he loved her, but she hadn't loved nor faith enough in him to confide in him. True, once having decided to change her identity, she had to go all the way. Her fear of Rocco was evident. Fear was something he understood. He'd understood the full meaning of fear ever since he had crashed and spent time in the bloody trenches. Nick had to admire her courage and strength in taking such a drastic step. She'd built a new life essentially by herself.

"What the hell! Was that a noise in the engine?" He listened intently for a couple of minutes. Nothing. "Your nerves are getting to you."

Giustina's words suddenly filled his head, blocking anything else from his conscious thoughts. "What else does she have to hide?" Harry? No. He refused to believe it. After all, she hadn't gone with him to England when she so easily could have. Again his mother's words, "You didn't listen to me about Josephine either. This one, too, is twisting you around her little finger, casting a spell over you."

Not for the first time his resentment against his mother and her constant meddling welled up within him. He spoke aloud as if his biplane were a person in whom he could confide. "Mama brought her here to marry me, then tried to poison me against her! Why?" His mother's last words to him when he had stormed out of the house had been, "If you marry a divorced woman, you are no son of mine! I'll have nothing more to do with you!"

He swung the aircraft around and headed for the landing field at Teterboro.

"Shit! What do I care if she divorces that bastard? I wanted to divorce Josephine, so what's the difference?" He landed the aircraft and drove it up to the hangar doors where Bob was waiting. Nick climbed out of the cockpit.

Bob tossed the newspaper he had been reading on the ground. "How'd she do?"

"Fine," he said absentmindedly.

"Give me a hand pulling Jenny back in."

"Sure."

Almost without thinking, Nick picked up the newspaper. The blaring article about Teresa struck him between the eyes. "Oh, God, she must feel as if she's getting it from all sides." He ran inside to call her.

"Hey, Nick! What about the bloody plane?"

But Nick didn't even hear him. The incessant busy signal and his heart told him he must go to her, and fast.

\* \* \*

Five minutes earlier Nick would have encountered Harry leaving Teresa's apartment building. It wouldn't have done much for his resolve if he had. Her apartment would have been a culture shock to Nick and another source of confusion about who she was if it hadn't been for the pathetic, lost girl who answered the door.

"Oh, Nick," she sobbed, tugging at her robe, still trying to relieve her distress.

"Darling, please forgive me for not staying with you and adding to your worries. I just had to get away to think and adjust to so many things." Nick swept her up in his arms and carried her to the sofa where he sat with her on his lap. He kissed her eyes and mouth, trying to stem her tears. Nick wanted to comfort her, not conquer her, yet his desire and kisses grew more intense. Trembling in his arms, she responded to his kisses. After a while, Teresa forced herself to pull away. "No. We can't."

"Aren't we alone?"

"Yes. I gave Sofia the night off, but that's not it. It's not right."

He yearned to make love to her, but her reluctance confirmed his faith in her virtue.

She got off his lap and went to the window. He followed her and placed his arms around her waist. They remained quiet as they watched the raindrops slowly roll down the window pane. Rain always evoked a sensual feeling for Teresa. That same feeling as she leaned against his firm body, combined with his warm breath against her cheeks, tugged strongly at her. Again she forced herself to pull away from him. "Please, *mio caro,* you are making it difficult for us both."

"Sorry." He accepted her feelings.

"What am I going to do, Nick? In no way am I allowing Rocco into my life. I'd rather die first."

"I wouldn't let you. I'd kill him first."

She caught her breath in fright and placed her hands on his lips. "Please don't say that."

He kissed her hand. "We'll figure something out. You'll divorce him. Desertion is a reason for divorce."

"I can't claim desertion. If anything, I deserted him. Even if it were true, the marriage took place in Italy. The laws are different there, but even here, the Catholic Church won't allow divorce except for adultery. Although I know he's an adulterer, I don't think it applies to men. Oh, Nick, part of me has always dreaded the nightmare of Rocco. I didn't know what to fear, but somehow I knew that he could destroy any happiness I might achieve. This can't be the end, can it?"

"There has to be something." He tried to take her in his arms, but she resisted, as if she knew that not even Nick could comfort her now.

She bit her lower lip and dug her nails into her palms for self-control. "Right now, it would be safer for you if you were to stay away from me."

"I'll stay on this side of the room," he said, misunderstanding her meaning.

She smiled. "I don't mean that. What I mean is, there's no telling what he might do if he found a man in my apartment. I am so afraid of Rocco. Look how clever he has been. Who would have thought that awful man, who's always defied the law, would use the courts the way he has. He's dangerous and cunning, like a snake."

"For the first time, Vi...Teresa, we've got a chance for happiness. I'm not letting anyone or anything come between us."

He held her face in his hands and looked intently at her. "We could sail for England, get married there and be done with all this."

"I've had enough running away. He's not going to control my life anymore. Then there are my businesses and my workers. Can I leave them to swing in the breeze? No, too many people are depending upon me."

"But I..."

"No, Nick." Tenderly, she pushed back the unruly lock of his hair. "Thank you for your help, but this is something I must do myself. I have learned to stand on my own two feet. Now there is more reason than ever to do it. Nick, I want to be worthy of you. I want us to have a real chance at a future."

"All I was going to say was that I don't see what claim he has on you. You are in this country as Violetta. The ship's documents verify Teresa died during the crossing."

"Of course!" Her eyes brightened. "Maybe we'll get lucky."

# Chapter 22

Curious bystanders, reporters and photographers packed the stifling mahogany-paneled courtroom. The hissing radiators added to the suffocating sensation for Teresa. Trying not to look at either Rocco in the witness chair or the black-robed Judge Rivers on the dais, she stared at the wall clock behind the judge. She reflected on what her lawyer, Ben Reichbach, had said about Judge Rivers. "We're lucky. He's fair and a woman's rights supporter."

Despite the assurances and Judge Rivers' seemingly compassionate face, Teresa's anxiety mounted. Ben's approach to the case bothered her. It wasn't aboveboard. Concerned that she'd have to take the witness chair, she twisted the handkerchief in her lap. If she did, she'd have to tell the truth. Although she had been living a lie, she didn't think herself a liar. She glanced at Ben, who crouched over his legal pad, then at Rocco's lawyer, David Goodman. The plump man, his head tucked on his chest, appeared to be asleep. Somehow she didn't feel comforted.

Directly behind Teresa sat Nick, with the ramrod posture he had developed in the Royal Flying Corps. From time to time he reached out lovingly and touched her shoulder with an air of ownership, but she was too tense to notice.

Giustina, sitting behind Nick, was equally inflexible, but for different reasons. *How stupid he is reaching out to this fallen woman who has fallen even further by being in court. Disgraceful! None of my family has ever been in court.*

Harry sat beside Nick, wanting to strike at Nick for touching Teresa. Behind them sat Delora and Rafaello. Even with Liza's translations, their fear of civil authorities interfered with their comprehension. However, with all their discomfort, they remained out of loyalty to Teresa. Near the double door entrance roosted a contented Malespina. He leaned back and admired his new gray spats and congratulated himself on his decision to pay Rocco's legal fees. It wasn't charity on his part; it was protecting his investment. *At last,* he thought, *I'm going to get the money this deadbeat owes me and have a neat profit. But I'm keeping an eye on this bastard to see he doesn't skip out on me.* He smiled. *As if he could.*

Rosa and Francesco, on the opposite side of the room, having never been in a courtroom, had settled uneasily on the hard wooden bench-like seats. Afraid of the establishment, Rosa feared for Teresa's safety. Adding to her concern was her guilt for leaving her child in someone else's care. Then, too, there was the embarrassment of appearing in public during her pregnancy.

"Take your coat off, Rosa. You'll roast in here," Francesco said, trying to help her with it.

"No," she whispered. "I'll show if I take it off."

"You're not showing yet," he insisted, and forced her to remove the coat.

They sat again. Rosa, red-faced, clutched her coat to her stomach. She leaned in close to Francesco. "There's Malespina," she whispered.

"I know," Francesco whispered back.

"Poor Teresa could use a friend to hold her hand. Isn't there some way we could be nearer to her?"

"With all these people, it's lucky we even got into the courtroom."

"So many people and reporters!" Rosa complained. "How can Teresa stand it?"

Until now, Teresa hadn't found the reporters objectionable; they were part of the business. Now, however, they had changed in their attitude and manner toward her, becoming overbearing, even vicious at times.

A photographer, who had been leaning against the side wall, crept forward. When he was squarely in front of Teresa, he jumped up and took her picture. The flash blinded her and nearly panicked her. A fine rain of magnesium oxide and smoke followed the flash. She waved her handkerchief to clear the air.

Judge Rivers banged his gavel. "Young man, sit! Try it again and I'll charge you with contempt of court! Want to blow us all up? That goes for all you reporters and photographers. None of that nonsense or I'll clear the court!"

The self-satisfied reporter sat against the wall and smiled contentedly; he had gotten his exclusive.

Shocked out of her lethargy, Teresa forced herself to look at Rocco as he slouched back on the witness chair. *What's the matter with me? This is my life we are dealing with here. Concentrate on what Rocco is saying. Look calm and confident, as Ben said. What else did he say?* "Think of Rocco as the pretender. You are the innocent victim. I know he is your husband, but it's up to him to prove it. So just sit there, look pretty and keep your mouth shut. Remember, you don't want him to get all your holdings. It wouldn't be fair to you or your employees."

She constantly repeated to herself, *Hold your temper and your tongue.*

"I tell you," Rocco leaned forward and pointed with outstretched arm, "that crazy Teresa Tozzi is my wife. I claim my right as a husband; all her businesses and properties are mine." He leaned back, crossed his arms and jutted his chin out as if dismissing Ben.

Ben, expecting this behavior, couldn't be rushed. Slowly, he paced back and forth. Finally, he stopped in front of Rocco. He leaned his grasshopper-like frame in close. "Tell me," he pointed to Teresa, "what proof do you have this is Teresa Tozzi? None," he answered for Rocco.

Rocco stuck his chin out. "I have the wedding picture."

"Yes, Exhibit A, one very small picture. The girl in that picture looks nothing like the girl in this courtroom."

"Well, she changed her hair and..."

"We have with us Exhibit B," Ben interrupted, "the *Mostro's* log, written in the impartial Captain Giuseppe Cantata's hand. It states that Teresa Tozzi died at sea. How, then, can you claim she is alive?"

"She switched with..."

"Tell me something else," Ben interrupted again, "where is the proof you were even married to Teresa Tozzi?"

"I tried getting the documents from Italy, but a fire destroyed them."

"A likely story."

David Goodman opened his eyes and said quietly, "Objection." It was the first sign of life she had seen in him.

"Sustained," the judge agreed. "Counselor, we have no jury here to play to."

"Sorry, Your Honor." Ben walked slowly to the table where Teresa sat and winked at her, but she took no solace from his attempt to ease her apprehension. "Your witness, Counselor," he said to Goodman and sat beside Teresa, confident that he had already won the case.

Slowly, deliberately, Goodman rose and opened a brown leather briefcase. With utmost calm, he took out documents, turned to Rocco and asked nonchalantly, "Do you know Mrs. Annunziata Carmela Maria Tozzi?"

"Of course, she's my mother-in-law." Rocco, still too annoyed with Ben to calm down, held his chin out to his own lawyer as if he were an adversary.

"Your Honor," Goodman approached the bench. "I'd like to enter these letters into evidence as Exhibits C, D, E and F, and a photograph as exhibit G." He handed the letters and the picture to the judge.

Ben snapped to his feet. "Objection! What is Counselor for the Defense pulling? What are these documents? I demand the right to examine them!"

Goodman responded, "They are letters to Mrs. Annunziata Carmela Maria Tozzi in Italian, her response in Italian, their translations, and the defendant's photograph."

Teresa's mouth fell open. Her blood drained from her face. It was all she could do to keep from fainting.

Goodman handed copies to Ben.

Ben, with knitted brows asked, "Why were we not informed before this?"

"Your Honor," Goodman explained calmly, "the response only arrived in this morning's mail."

The judge looked them over. "I can see no reason they cannot be entered."

"But Your Honor," Ben demanded, "we have not had time to examine them."

"Overruled," the judge said. "Let's get on with the case, gentlemen. Tell me, counselor Goodman, do we have other surprises to look forward to?"

"No, Your Honor."

An angry Ben turned to Goodman and asked, "Where did you get the address from? The plaintiff?" He pointed to Rocco.

"Initially, yes, but we contacted the Italian Consulate in New York who confirmed it. We then contacted the regional government in Avelino, Italy. It was no easy task finding the small town of Montaguto." Goodman looked at the judge. "In the letter, my clerk asks Annunziata Carmela Maria Tozzi if she had a daughter named Teresa and if that daughter had ever been married to Rocco Martello. Further, he asked if the woman in the picture taken from the newspaper, announcing the engagement to Mr. Harry Goldstein, Exhibit G, is her daughter Teresa Tozzi."

Ben, now furious, asked, "How do we know the picture you sent was the one in the newspaper?"

"I'm glad you asked," Goodman said with a triumphant note. "We had the picture and letter witnessed by a notary public. Let me read Exhibit F, the translation of her response: "Dear Counselor Goodman," he began, melodramatically,

Your letter comes as a great shock. Yes, my daughter, Teresa Tozzi, did marry Rocco Martello on the date stated in your letter. One year later, she left for America. The authorities told me my daughter died at sea. I have no other daughter. Losing a child is brutally painful. No greater pain exists in the world.

The girl in the picture is so unlike my daughter, yet there may be a resemblance. Nevertheless, thinking my daughter could deny herself to me for so long a time would be intolerable and shameful.

For a time, I believed Teresa was alive because I have been receiving money from an unknown benefactor. I know no one in America, certainly no one who would send me money. So I prayed it was Teresa.

Though I repeatedly asked Father Patrick Kelly to ask the benefactor to come forward, it was in vain. In time I doubted it was Teresa, for the child I gave life to and struggled against great odds to raise would never have denied herself to me. Therefore, I say Teresa Tozzi is dead to me, even if alive. So, please, let me remain in peace with my God and my faded memories.

The letter so overcame Teresa with remorse, she thought she would faint. Her innermost voice pulled at her to shout that she really was Annunziata's daughter. Unable to control her emotions, she unleashed a flood of tears.

Rocco, jubilant, stood and raised a fist heavenward. "I told you so." He pointed with an outstretched arm. "Just look at her, Judge. If she isn't Teresa, why would she be crying so much? That crazy woman is my wife! Throw her in an asylum..."

"Sit down!" the judge ordered, pointing his gavel at Rocco.

Reluctantly, Rocco sat, but mastery was written all over his face.

The judge tapped his index finger on a stack of briefs. Then, hopefully asked, "Has Reverend Patrick Kelly been contacted?"

"Yes, Your Honor, but he refuses questioning in this matter."

"Judge," Rocco shouted, "why don't you just ask her? You can see she's guilty."

"Well, young lady," the judge leaned forward as if hoping he'd get the right answer.

Teresa, almost overcome with tears, could say nothing in her defense.

"Young lady?"

"Your Honor, I'm....I'm...sorry."

"There you have it, Judge. Guilty!"

The judge, taking her response as an admission of guilt, shook his head in disappointment. "You are all dismissed, pending a sanity hearing." He struck his gavel, got up and headed for his chambers.

Newspapermen crowded around Teresa as Harry and Nick ran interference for her. They pushed and shoved through the crowd in the courtroom, along the long corridor and into a conference room.

Ben shook his head. "I was sure we had him until you practically admitted it!"

Nick put his arm around Teresa's shoulder, trying to calm her, not happy at the way Ben had conducted the case. "This isn't the time for this discussion."

"I wasn't prepared," was all she could say. "Isn't there something we can do?" Teresa asked, her eyes pleading.

"I wish I could say something comforting, but I can't." Ben shook his head, "If we can't get that letter struck, we could be in big trouble."

* * *

Teresa sat in the same seat in the same crowded courtroom, faced with the same reporters, but this time it was before the cold, calculating-looking Judge Stanford. What Ben had said to her about Judge Stanford hadn't been comforting, "Stanford's a Victorian who believes a woman's place is in the home and, even there, only the kitchen and the bedroom. If that isn't enough, he's a bigot who hates everyone who isn't white, Anglo-Saxon, Protestant, and he's a class snob." Added to her distress was that her mother's letter hadn't been struck. She tried to remain calm as the judge peered over his glasses at her.

"I have come to a decision, but first, have you anything to say, young lady?"

All morning her anger had brewed. The more she tried remaining calm the more she seethed. She stood, rocking with emotion: "Your Honor." Her voice was louder and shriller than she wanted it to be. It was as if another person were using her body and controlling her. "That man," she pointed at Rocco who sat so close she could smell his alcoholic breath, "is a cruel, lying murderer. I have witnesses who know he murdered people in West Virginia and..."

"Enough, woman! Your charges are not relevant."

"But I..."

"Sit!"

She sat, trembling with rage.

He shook his head in disgust. "We will have no more outbursts in this courtroom. Understand?" He readjusted his glasses and pointed at Teresa. "Let me inform you, young lady, life is not always what we desire. It can be harsh and unpleasant, but we must adjust, despite the inevitable harshness."

She stood again and stamped her foot. "No one has handed me anything, Your Honor. I came to America with nothing I worked hard, long hours for what I have...!"

"Don't interrupt me, and don't ever stamp your foot at me! You have not made a good impression on the court! Sit!" He pointed his outstretched gavel at her.

She sat.

Then, in a calmer voice, "Working, as you have been, is vulgar, unsound and..."

"Vulgar? Unsound!" she shouted. The strain of the past weeks had consumed her reserves. Out of control, she continued, "How dare y..."

"I said be quiet!" he roared as he struck his gavel. "Madam, you dare shout in my presence?" He shook his head in disapproval. "Very unseemly. Obviously you are a hysterical female." Then, as if talking to a child he said, "Don't you know hysterics are much ado about nothing?"

She was about to respond, but Ben gripped her arm.

"I can understand working in a factory to help support your husband. It is in keeping with your class," he shook his head disapprovingly. "However, venturing to become a business owner is very unladylike and certainly not in your class. The very fact that you got an education confirms this presumptuous behavior. As if that were not enough, you deliberately lied and hid from your husband." He clacked his tongue and shook his head. "Unforgivable! Your rebellion against your role in life, and your self-centeredness, have led to your nervous disorder." He pulled a handkerchief from beneath his robes and wiped his eyeglasses. "You have been deceitful and in the service of malevolent impulses. Further, you are introspective and desire solitude and independence."

Teresa, dismayed, pinched her lower lip between her teeth to keep from screaming.

"These unnatural desires," he continued, "are perhaps the most distinguishing features of female insanity. Therefore, I have decided to have you confined for an indefinite period at the Maple Crest State Mental Institution until you have come to your senses. The sooner you realize the error of your ways, the sooner you can get better."

Teresa cupped her hand over her mouth to stifle a scream. Her legs collapsed beneath her. She didn't even hear Rosa's scream. From a great distance, she heard the judge say, "In addition, all the properties that you claim to be yours will be your husband's to do with as he sees fit."

Rocco reveled in his conquest. His expression was hard, cold, cruel, calculating and triumphant.

Apparently Stanford didn't like Rocco either, for in the next breath he turned to Rocco and said, "Unfortunately, this country has become a dumping ground for unfit Roman Catholics, common laborers, and criminals. These United States have become the asylum of the world." He turned to Teresa. "I would have placed you in your husband's custody, but I believe it would be in your better interest to confine you for treatment. Case dismissed!"

# Chapter 23

Dreamlike, some inmates drifted through the sitting room as if looking for an elusive consciousness. Others sat dazed on olive-drab unupholstered wicker settees lining olive-drab walls. For Teresa, sobering realities were two massive nurses guarding two exits. Even more sobering was the officious middle-aged nurse who stalked the room. All three nurses' white uniforms stood in sharp contrast to everything else in the room.

The officious nurse motioned to Teresa to sit on a settee beside a continually swaying woman. Teresa sat as if given a royal command. She took an instant dislike to the thin-lipped nurse, who looked as stiffly starched as her alabaster-white uniform. Even her hair, pulled severely back in a tight bun, looked as if she had starched it. The white cap on her head almost looked glued in place.

However, what offended her more in the room was a zoo-like stench. What could be its source? The floor? No, the olive-drab linoleum was immaculate. The walls? No, again. They appeared recently painted with a high-gloss enamel that played havoc with her eyes. The narrow, barred windows near the ceiling with their olive-drab curtains were shut, so the stench wasn't coming from outside. The women's clothing? All were dressed alike, in a shapeless Mother Hubbard cotton dress. Her dress didn't emit the odor, so she presumed theirs didn't. Teresa turned to the woman sitting beside her. "What's that smell?"

The woman stopped her rocking and looked at Teresa as if Teresa had appeared from thin air. "What smell?"

"It smells like a zoo in here."

She sniffed the air. Then, with a flash of recognition, "Oh, you'll find out."

"Quiet!" The officious nurse stopped her marching, turned, and shouted at the woman beside Teresa as if she were deaf. "No talking, Goldie!"

"Yes, Nurse Davis!" Goldie shouted back.

Goldie began repeating, "Mary had a little lamb. Mary had a little lamb," increasing the volume and speed by degrees until she was almost shouting.

"Goldie!" Nurse Davis commanded, "I told you before. Quiet!" She shook her head in frustration.

Although the nurse's eyes were on Goldie, Teresa felt as if they were directed toward her. It offended Teresa. She wanted to stamp her foot at the woman, demanding treatment befitting a rational human being, but she merely sat. This was just another in a series of indignities she'd had to endure since she had been at the courthouse. How long ago was that...one hour? It couldn't have been much more, and yet it seemed a lifetime had passed.

Nurse Davis clapped her hands, demanding attention from all in the room. "All right, ladies, you know the routine. Line up by twos."

She herded everyone into the dormitory. Here, too, the walls were dark green. A dark-green cement floor stripped the room of warmth. Twelve cots, covered with green chenille bedspreads, lined each side of the room. Teresa didn't have much time to dwell on the decor, for Nurse Davis reentered the room pushing a metal tea wagon. Arranged neatly on the wagon's surface were small white paper cups and a clipboard.

"Line up, ladies." She clapped her hands rhythmically. "Come on! No lagging. Linda, stop pushing! Goldie, I see you trying to hide. If you aren't careful, I'll give you a double dose!"

When they had lined up to Nurse Davis' satisfaction, she began dispensing the cups. "Drink it, Susy, and be quick about it or I'll pour it down your throat! Do you hear?"

"No!" The gaunt woman replied, almost spilling the contents as she pushed the cup away. "I don't want any."

She grabbed Susy by the hair at the back of her head and yanked, forcing her to open her mouth. Nurse Davis poured the liquid down Susy's throat like a shot. Susy gasped and coughed until tears ran down her cheeks.

Nurse Davis pushed Susy aside and made a check mark alongside Susy's name on the clipboard. "Come on, Goldie, or I'll do the same to you."

Goldie screwed up her face and held her nose as the medicine went down.

The nurse repeated the ritual until she reached Teresa. Although Teresa knew she had to face the inevitable, she remained better than an arm's length away from the nurse.

"Come on, Miss Society Set, you're next." Nurse Davis' annoyance telegraphed.

"What is it?" Teresa asked suspiciously.

"Just a little cocktail before bed time," she answered without a trace of humor.

Teresa shrugged her shoulders. "I don't drink."

Goldie laughed.

The nurse's penetrating stare silenced Goldie. Then she looked directly into Teresa's eyes. "Don't be funny. You'll drink this paraldehyde, Miss High-and-Mighty and be quick about it. It'll help you sleep like a baby."

"I don't have any trouble sleeping."

"Oh, a wiseacre, are we?" The nurse adjusted her white cap as if it had disobeyed orders by slipping a bit to one side. "I don't have all night. Drink it, or we'll force it down your throat." She edged forward and held out the cup to Teresa.

Teresa moved back.

The nurse looked heavenward. "Why does Ward Five get all the wiseacres? Here!" she commanded.

Reluctantly Teresa took the cup and now knew where the zoo-like stench had originated; the little cup reeked of it. Holding her nose, she swallowed the dose in one gulp. It burned. She was about to ask for water to wash it down but changed her mind. It would only anger the nurse. Instead, she asked through a constricted throat, "When am I going to see a doctor or someone in authority?"

"When we are ready, Missy," she answered as if Teresa had affronted her authority.

"But I'm in here by mistake," Teresa persisted.

"The judge didn't think so." The nurse drew her lips into a tight, mirthless smile, revealing that she must have been following the trial in the newspapers with some malevolent pleasure. "When your time comes, I'll tell you, and not before. Go to bed!" She turned and pushed the cart out of the room.

Teresa had never felt so lonely, so abandoned, and so ill-fated. In that brief moment before sleep, she tried prayer, but the words wouldn't come. She tried to think of Nick, but he wouldn't come either. Blessedly, sleep came.

She awoke from a deep, sticky sleep, unsure of where she was. However, a sinking dread within her breast told her she was not safe at home. Suddenly the horror struck her. Despite the medication, a small voice within her said that she must fight to stay alive! Over the years she had worked relentlessly for what she had gained. Now, she knew she couldn't let things just happen to her, so for the next two days, Teresa went on a hunger strike, sure that she would get the authorities' attention. At last it happened.

Nurse Davis and a handsome, burly, blond orderly whom Teresa had never seen led her through an unfamiliar part of the institution. She tried to talk to the orderly, but he didn't respond. His reluctance didn't surprise her; what did was Nurse Davis' attitude toward him. The woman's eyes glinted with pleasure as she gazed at him. He didn't seem to notice.

They stopped at an unmarked door. Teresa thought triumphantly, *I'll show these people they can't push me around!*

"All right, Miss Society, in with you," she commanded in a tired voice and pushed Teresa into a room barely large enough for the examining table. The room stank of carbolic.

Teresa was so relieved to see a doctor waiting at the head of the table, she failed to notice the basin on the counter beside him. Alongside the basin was a long tube with a funnel attached to the end.

"Doctor, I've been wanting to see you for so long. You see, I..."

"On with you." He pointed to the examining table. "Quickly now, I have a very busy schedule."

"But there is nothing wrong with my physical condition, Doctor," Teresa insisted as she climbed onto the table, "or mental, for that matter. You see..."

"This is not an examination, young lady," the doctor stated flatly.

Teresa was about to speak again when the nurse and orderly pushed her down on the table and held her fast.

Her eyes bulged as the doctor forced the long tube up her nose and began to pour liquid into the funnel. The searing pain in the back of her nose almost choked her. She strained every muscle, attempting to get away, but they held her down.

His voice was cold and demanding. "The more you struggle the worse it will be for you. We're not stopping until we're through feeding you, so get used to the idea."

\* \* \*

It was cold, strolling in the quad behind Ward Five, but Teresa was grateful the snow had been late in coming. To be closed off by heavy snows from this modest path of freedom would have been intolerable. The quad, almost the size of a football field, had dormant yellow-ocher grass as lawn at its center. Wooden picnic tables were placed randomly on the lawn. A few evergreens along each of the four red-brick walls did little to break the monotony or ease the prison-like atmosphere. The walkway, too, reflected the prison atmosphere. It had no meandering curves for interest.

Teresa took a deep breath, trying to rid herself of the smell of paraldehyde, but it was impossible. The stench was within her now, a part of her, like her flesh. She stretched out her arms as if trying to capture the air around her. "It's good being outdoors. Even Nurse Davis can't keep me from that."

"Oh, yes, she can," Goldie said. For almost a week she had remained almost lucid. Goldie swayed in and out of comprehension with longer periods of comprehension as time elapsed. It pleased Teresa, not only because she was concerned for Goldie's well-being, but because Goldie was the only person in Maple Crest with whom she could communicate at all. "You must'a guessed Nurse Davis is the heavyweight around this joint. So stay on her good side and you'll get the best work."

"You mean there is better work than pushing a broom or a polishing machine around the rooms?" Teresa scoffed.

Goldie laughed. "And worst. You could be washin' and sortin' in the laundry room. Or you could be on latrine duty. I hate that the worst." She shivered at the prospect. "They think that by doin' work, you'll get better. I could never figure that one out. It's that kinda work that drives me nuts. Yep, like I was sayin,' Nurse Davis is the one who says if you get out of this here joint."

"What?" Teresa stopped in her tracks. Her fear almost overcame her.

"At least, it winds up that way."

"But she's no doctor!"

Goldie laughed. "She thinks she is. Anyway, she's the closest you'll come to one for a while. You're supposed to see a doctor twice a week, but you're lucky to see one once a month."

"What?" Goldie dismayed her.

"Yep. This dump's that overcrowded."

"It doesn't seem overcrowded."

"That's just Ward Five, at least right now." Goldie looked at her feet as they resumed walking. "The women's section's got thirty-two wards. I guess the men's section's the same. Some wards got patients sleepin' on the floor. Yep, Nurse Davis's the one who says who gets bumped up to Staff. That's where you get your walkin' papers. It's kind of scary, facin' those guys. They don't make it easy. But you gotta see a doctor first. I've been in this place for five years and I been there only once."

"Good God! I may never get out! I may even get a doctor like that stupid judge who thinks independence is grounds for committal."

"Settle back. You ain't got no choice. Try an' get a job that ain't too bad. I like workin' in the kitchen. You got to be near normal to work there. Whenever I work there, I'm happy 'cause sometimes I get a chance to see Clyde." She smiled proudly. "He delivers the bread here. All Clyde and me do is wave, because that guard at the door watches us like a hawk, but Clyde comes to see me on visitors' day. He wears a patch over his missin' eye. He lost his eye an' two fingers in the war, but I love him and...."

Teresa no longer listened. Was her only way escape? If so, how?

Later that evening, just before the paraldehyde took effect, she concluded she must get Nurse Davis to assign her to the kitchen. That might be her escape route if it came to that. However she would need outside help. But who? She hadn't heard from anyone. *Have they all forsaken me?*

\* \* \*

For three days Teresa flattered and helped the rigid nurse whenever she could, but Nurse Davis behaved as if it were all part of Teresa's duty. As she washed and waxed the floor and desk to a mirror-like finish, her mind wasn't on the white, neat, cold, impersonal room. Teresa's mind was on escape. Nurse Davis' sudden appearance in the doorway nearly frightened Teresa out of her wits. The rubber-soled shoes were the only soft thing that Teresa could find about the woman.

The woman eyed Teresa suspiciously for a moment and then composed her features. "Hey, Miss Society Set."

Teresa tensed, wondering, *What next? Calm down. You're acting suspiciously.* "Yes, Nurse Davis?" *Has anyone ever called her anything else?*

"You know a lot about sewing and fashion."

"A little, anyway." Teresa suspected an ulterior motive.

"I have a blouse that could use a pink collar. You know, something high." She placed her thumb and forefinger around her neck to illustrate. "Think you could do it?"

"I believe I can, but I'll need a needle and scissors. Is it permitted?"

The nurse looked her up and down. "You're not the dangerous type, or suicidal. So I can allow it, but only if you work in this office."

Then it occurred to Teresa that this conniving, vicious woman knew she was sane. Otherwise, would she permit Teresa to use scissors? *If she knows, why won't she get me released? Resentfulness? No. Why would she resent me?* Teresa swallowed her anger and tried to remain calm and impersonal. "May I see the blouse?"

It didn't surprise Teresa that the woman had the blouse hanging in the office closet. What did, however, was that she had selected a sheer, pink silk blouse. Then she remembered the orderly and guessed he motivated the nurse's desire to be feminine. "Good choice. It would just frame your face beautifully. Wait, let me show you." Teresa took a piece of paper from the wire in/out box on the desk's corner and sketched a collar. "What do you think?"

"Fine," the woman answered without showing appreciation, as though Teresa had merely filled out a medical form. "Can you make entire garments?"

"That depends. Not suits. I'm not a tailor."

The nurse unlocked the desk's bottom drawer and pulled out a pattern. "Can you make this?" The pattern was the typical straight-line skirt that Giustina had been making in the factory, the first garment Teresa had ever made.

"No problem, but I'll need a sewing machine, material, thread and a place to work."

"I've got the material here and there's a sewing machine in the utility room." She looked around the room and shrugged her shoulders. "I guess we can bring the machine into this office."

Teresa thought for a moment. She desperately wanted some solitude to plan her escape. "We could, but isn't there another place more private? How large is that utility room?"

"Small, and there's a lot jammed in there. We can't move it all out, but maybe you can squeeze in there."

Teresa smiled to herself. "Fine. The machine will be very useful for making the collar, too. Hand sewing is not my forte. There's just one other thing, Nurse Davis. If you want me giving it the attention it deserves, I'll have to be off the paraldehyde. I can't work in a fog." Teresa tried to look indifferent when she said that, but her heart pounded all the same.

Again Nurse Davis eyed her distrustfully, then the idea began to have merit. "All right. As I said, you're not the dangerous type."

Teresa set to work immediately, trying to organize the utility room. She moved, stacked and shifted brooms, mops, soaps, buckets and some mysterious items still in sealed boxes. Judging from the dust, these things had been in the room for years. It was frustrating; if she cleared one section, she cluttered another. Finally giving up, she just turned the sewing machine so that her back was to a grimy transom-sized window high up the wall. Exhausted, she sat at the machine and looked toward the door. She couldn't see it, and better still, no one could see her. Sewing for the nurse would prove to Nurse Davis that she was sane, if the woman had any doubts. If nothing else, making the garments might change the nurse's presumed hatred toward her.

\* \* \*

The following day, Teresa made the collar and attached it to the blouse. Although she worked quickly, it was the best work she had ever done. When she presented the blouse, Teresa could see the woman was pleased, but still she conferred no thanks. Teresa really didn't expect any, but to her distress, she still didn't have access to a doctor. She was convinced now that her only way out was escape.

The next day Nurse Davis called her into her office again and smiled, a smile that failed to reach her eyes. The woman stood by the closet's open door. On the shelf above her head were two bolts of black wool. "I have material for a skirt and a coat."

Teresa's heart sank. She guessed that the woman would have her as a captive seamstress.

Without another word, Nurse Davis handed her the patterns, turned her back on Teresa and retrieved the material from the closet. Turning her back on Teresa was another sign for her that Nurse Davis knew she was sane, for the woman never turned her back on any other patient.

* * *

Teresa was about to cut the skirt from the wool when she heard the closet door open suddenly. In her, distress, she miscued the pattern and ruined the wool! Her adrenalin rose.

"Hey, Miss Society Set, you in there?"

At first she was tempted to say nothing, but that wouldn't do any good. "Yes?" Teresa could tell the woman was annoyed about something. However, from where Nurse Davis was standing, she couldn't see Teresa, let alone the ruined garment.

"You're needed in the kitchen. One of my workers is sick. I hope it's not influenza. Don't want an epidemic in Maple Crest. Anyway, there's no telling when she'll be well enough to work in the kitchen again."

*The kitchen!* Teresa tried not to show her joy as she struggled to get out. Another sign that the woman knew she was sane, or why would she have her working around knives?

Confinement within the asylum's drab walls and the even darker utility closet had left her unprepared for the kitchen's glare. If anything, the noise in the white-tiled room bothered her more than the glare. With nothing absorbing the clatter of pots, pans and dishes, it verged on earsplitting. *Never mind,* she thought, *it won't be forever.* Quickly she added, *God willing!*

Teresa studied the room. There was only one possible exit, the double doors patrolled by a male guard. He wasn't much to look at, an elfin man with rounded shoulders and a pot belly, but he seemed an overwhelming obstacle to her. The windows? Steel bars blocked that route. The swinging doors behind her opened to the dining area.

Teresa determined that she needed help for the escape, but whom could she trust? The three women cooks weren't inmates. Although they had greeted her in a friendly way and had even handed her food to sample, she felt sure she couldn't trust them. Teresa was also uneasy about the two waitresses. *Goldie?* She watched Goldie mopping the floor and singing at the top of her lungs. *She'd never tell, but the poor woman's attacks are so unpredictable.*

Another problem was time. The sick inmate might return any day. Teresa hoped if she did the work of two and tried to be light-hearted and friendly, they would want her to remain in the kitchen after the other inmate returned. *Light-hearted? That would take some acting!* Teresa breathed an impatient sigh as she scrubbed a roasting pan they had handed her.

Then the question of outside help remained unsolved. As yet, no one had visited or even written her. *Why? Maple Crest isn't that far away. So much for undying love and devotion.*

Teresa dried the last pot and hung it on the rack above her head. She placed her white muslin apron on the counter beside the sink while Goldie waited for her at the door. Kitchen duties afforded them some freedom. At least they could go and come without supervision.

When they entered the dormitory, they saw Nurse Davis standing with her hands on her hips. "You have a visitor, Goldie. You, too, Miss Society."

"A visitor? Who?" Teresa asked.

"You think all I have to do is watch the visitors' room? All I know is it's a man."

A tingle of excitement returned. *Nick? Harry?* The same gnawing questions reappeared. *Why haven't they been to see me? Are they afraid of me now? After all, the court judged me insane.*

"Let's go, Missy."

"Yes, of course. I'm sorry. I don't want to add any more work to your already busy day. It's so unfair of me."

"Well, I'm glad somebody around here finally appreciates me."

"Everybody does, Nurse Davis." Teresa almost gagged at her chicanery. However, freedom had its price. "You should hear them talk about you."

"I'll bet." The nurse cast it off as a lie. Nonetheless, Teresa could tell ego had won out. "Tell me, Missy, when are you going to finish those garments?"

Teresa felt the knot in her stomach make its ugly appearance again. *The woman isn't going to let me work in the kitchen too long. She wants those garments. Then there's the miscued skirt to worry about. Think quick!* "I can work on them when I've finished my duties in the kitchen. There's still time before I go to bed."

The woman seemed pacified. In any event, Teresa was too excited to dwell on the nurse or the skirt. She put on her overcoat and went to the visitors' room. A blush of excitement filled her cheeks when she saw Nick. His obvious pleasure at seeing her thrilled her. However, his inability to hide the concern he felt at seeing her in the asylum distressed her. She tried, but failed, to show a smile.

They left the building and strolled in the quad. Hand in hand, they walked silently for a few minutes, each hesitant to be the first to speak and break the silence. It troubled Teresa. Had they grown apart that much? Was there no turning back for them? Others in the quad didn't show any signs of tension, or was it just her imagination?

Nick removed his glove so that he could hold her small bare hand in his sturdy one. Her hand felt so small and cold within his tight grasp. "I tried to visit you several times, but each time they turned me away."

She breathed freely again as her tensions melted away. "Oh, I'm so glad. I was afraid you didn't want to see me."

"Good Lord no, *mia cara.*" He squeezed her hand and pressed it to his lips. "Never that. How could you even think it?"

"Well, when I didn't hear from you, Harry, Rosa, or Ben, I..."

"Didn't you get my letters?"

"No."

He shook his head in dismay. "Harry tried to see you, but they wouldn't let him in either." The thought of Harry being on her mind perturbed him. Then he chided himself for being jealous. After all, they had been business partners. "Harry fired Ben and has gone to Judge Rivers, who has a private practice. That explains why you haven't heard from Ben. Rosa's been so upset about you, she's been calling me every day, asking if I've heard anything. Oh, I almost forgot. Delora sent you some cheese." He handed her a square fist-sized package which Delora had wrapped in butcher paper and tied with twine. "Rafaello wanted to send you some wine, but I told him they wouldn't allow it." Nick smiled, "He tried driving Delora and Liza up here once, but he got lost. Rafaello drove around for hours and finally gave up."

Teresa's eyes widened, "They never used the automobile since you left it for Ernesto. Delora has always been too afraid of it. Once she even hid the keys from him."

"She was willing to have him give it a whirl to see you. When he got lost, she told him it was an object lesson for him; only the young can drive automobiles." He laughed. "I think he was secretly glad she objected. It gave him an excuse not to drive. I'd have brought them along, but I didn't want to share you with anyone."

Teresa smiled in the midst of tears. She searched her coat pockets for a handkerchief.

"Don't cry. I can't bear it." He pulled a handkerchief from his flight jacket's pocket and wiped the tears from her eyes. "You never seem to have a handkerchief when you need it." He smiled.

"It's just that I'm so happy to see you and hear that my friends haven't forgotten me."

He tried to take her into his arms, but she pushed him away. "No, I think I still smell like paraldehyde, although I've been off it for a couple of days."

"I don't care if you smell like the exhaust from my Jenny. It wouldn't bother me, *cara,*" he assured her, but he bowed to her wishes.

As they sat on a bench, she unwrapped the package of creamy provalone that had aged enough to form cracks. "Oh, the dear lady! She remembered that I love provalone. The food in this place is terrible. I had the impertinence to offer to show the cook how to make tomato sauce, but she took offense. That ended my attempt at charming her into having me on kitchen duty indefinitely. I never know enough to keep my mouth shut."

Teresa lifted the cheese, held it to her nose and savored the aroma. "If Delora only knew what a savior this is. It has almost taken that noxious paraldehyde smell from me. I'll never get used to that awful smell, despite what Goldie says."

"Goldie?"

"An inmate. She's a good person." Teresa wrapped the package and got up.

He slipped her hand through the crook of his arm and squeezed her to him as they resumed their walk. Teresa interested him, not Goldie. "What did the doctors say? When are they releasing you?"

"Doctors?" She smiled a mirthless smile. "I haven't seen one yet."

"What? I can't believe it!"

"Neither can I, but there it is. Getting out of here legally may take months, years, or maybe never. The nurse in charge is impossible to get around. I know it must sound irrational, but I think she hates me."

Nick stopped and looked at her. "Why?"

"Maybe she's jealous of my business success, being foreign-born as I am. Maybe she's...Oh, I don't know. It's beginning to sound irrational to me, too. All I know, Nick, is that I can't take it here any longer."

Nick looked over his shoulder to see if anyone was within hearing. "Then, *cara,* the only thing to do is escape."

Teresa looked up at him and smiled. "I came to that conclusion, too." Then she stopped to reconsider. "I can't ask you to help. It could ruin you."

"It wasn't you who asked me, but I who suggested it. If you don't let me help you, I'd be more than offended; I'd be angry. Damn any consequences!"

"You love me that much?"

"More."

She squeezed his hand and wanted to kiss him, but held back.

He pressed her hand against his heart. "Tell me, *cara,* any idea how we can manage an escape?"

She looked around, making certain they weren't being observed. As quickly as she could, she told him her plans.

A smile crossed his face. "Mama was right when she said you've got gumption."

"Not gumption. Desperation or survival, but not gumption." *Funny,* she reflected, *I haven't once thought of Giustina since I've been here.* What surprised her more was that didn't she really care what Giustina thought of her. It was exhilarating.

The exhilaration added to her excitement about her plan and gave substance to it. She became more animated as she continued to speak. "Every day at eleven in the morning, Clyde delivers bread for the Gordon Baking Company. Maybe you can get a job with that company, or maybe you can talk Clyde into letting you ride with him."

"That's a cinch, even if I have to pay Clyde for the privilege."

"If you do manage it, have a change of clothes for me. The sooner I get out of these, the better."

"Rosa will give me something, I'm sure."

"Let's not get her involved. She and her family could get deported."

"I'll figure something out. What do we do after we get you out?"

"I don't know. I can't go back to my apartment or stay with Delora or with Rosa. They'll be sure to look for me in those places. Hiding forever is something I can't bear thinking about right now."

"I can fly you somewhere." He wasn't willing to give up his idea.

"We'll see. Anyway, Rocco's won, hasn't he? He's got my business, my money, and my identity. Wherever I go, I can't earn a living without papers."

"If you marry me, you won't have to worry about that."

"How can I marry you? I'm legally married to Rocco."

"Then live with me."

He tried to take her in his arms again, but she resisted. "No, I can't bear it. If you kiss me now, I'll collapse. The hard things make me stronger, but the gentle things make me weep."

"You haven't answered me. Live with me."

"They're sure to suspect you, when they look for me." She smiled a crooked smile. "Besides, my mother and the nuns have done too good a job. I can't do it, as much as I have often dreamed about what it would be like." Deep in thought, they remained silent as they walked. "Would you do another very big favor for me and hire a detective? I want Rocco followed."

"What?" She had amazed him. "Why?"

"Somehow I've got to get the goods on him. Find out where he's living and what he's been up to."

"Consider it done." His hand began to feel cold so he slipped it into his pants' pocket. "Oh." He stopped walking and pulled out a creased letter. "I almost forgot. This letter came for you."

When she recognized her mother's florid handwriting, a sense of uneasiness, no, more like irritation, almost made her hand the letter back to Nick. Then something made her open it.

My dear daughter,

Forgive me for all the pain I have caused you. I honestly thought I was doing the best thing to have you marry Rocco. So many Italian women had married and left for America that I thought you would be going to a better, happier life. I did not know how much anguish and trouble he would inflict upon you.

How could I? Even when he beat you, I thought it was the drink, nothing more.

When I heard you had died at sea, it threw me into a despair that even the Mother Church could not help. I prayed and lit candles for your soul's resurrection.

God answered my prayers. When I received the money from America, it lifted me from the depths of Hell, for I knew it came from you. Although I was overjoyed at your resurrection, it saddened me, too, to know you hated me enough to have me believe you were dead.

When I received the letters from the courts, I did not know how to answer them. Should I tell them, yes, it was you? Would that have helped or hurt you? If I told them no, what would that have done to you? Again I went to church for guidance. God told me to be vague. I tried. Did I succeed? Please, write to me and tell me I did the right thing and please tell me you have forgiven me.

Whatever you may think, my child, I love you. I kiss you. Mama.

When Teresa finished reading the letter, she thrust it into her pocket. Again she had to use Nick's handkerchief to wipe the tears from her eyes.

Nick didn't know how to comfort her. He simply placed his arm around her shoulder. "Anything I can do?"

"No." She thought for a minute, then said, "Yes. Would you please write to her and tell her I forgive her if she will forgive me? Tell her she did the correct thing in being vague in the letter and that I will write her as I can. I don't think she should know, just yet, what has happened to me, do you?"

Nick shook his head. "No."

When they continued their stroll, Teresa saw Goldie and Clyde sitting at a picnic table. "We're in luck, Nick; Clyde is here."

\* \* \*

Lightning illuminated every corner of the kitchen. Almost immediately, a rolling boom of thunder shook everything and everyone in the room. Teresa, already on edge, screamed louder than anyone else, but it did nothing to relieve her tension. For the hundredth time, she looked anxiously toward the doors and then toward the wall clock. One-twenty in the afternoon! Well past delivery time, but still no Nick! She avoided the guard's glance. He had looked at her once or twice, but in her anxiety she couldn't tell whether he was suspicious or interested in her. In either case, she shuddered at the thought. His long basset-hound face with all its crevices repelled her.

It had almost been a week before Nick could ride with Clyde in the delivery van, and two days before she and Goldie could work together. Each day Teresa feared the other inmate would return.

Teresa glanced at Goldie, who stood with her back to her. *Are you with me, Goldie?*

Teresa tried not to exhibit her anxiety, but it was torture for her. *I can't cope with this tension for another day!* Just when she thought she would scream without the cover of thunder, she heard a delivery van pull up to the doors. She held her breath. *Please, dear God, let that be Nick!* As if He had heard her, the door opened and Nick entered, carrying a huge wicker breadbasket loaded with bread. Teresa glanced at Goldie, who just kept scrubbing a huge copper caldron. To Teresa's dismay, Goldie began singing at the top of her lungs as if she were the only person in the room:

*"Over there! Over there!*
*Send the word, send the word over there..."*

It further alarmed Teresa that Goldie wasn't the least interested in where Clyde was. Why didn't Goldie look toward the door? *Jesus, Mary and Joseph, she's faded! Goldie, honey, look up,* but Goldie just continued to sing.

"Hey!" the guard asked Nick, "where the hell is Clyde?"

Nick laughed, "Hiding in the van."

Even mentioning Clyde didn't cause Goldie to respond.

Nick shrugged his shoulders. "Clyde doesn't want to get his feet wet with all this rain, I guess."

The guard smiled and bit into a roasted sweet potato, nearly devouring it whole. He swallowed hard and cleared his throat. "Tell Clyde he's missin' some good eats today just because he thinks he's goin' ta melt." His laughter shook his jowls. "That Clyde must have some cat blood in him."

"Me too," Nick laughed. "It's getting colder. The rain is starting to turn to sleet."

"Yeah," the guard agreed, "I felt that cold air when you came in."

Teresa's nerves were beginning to crack. *Forget the weather report and get to it!*

"Give Clyde one of these," the guard said. "I know how much he likes them." He picked up another sweet potato off the counter and tossed it to Nick.

Nick caught it as if he were intercepting a forward pass. He ran to the other side of the guard and lifted the potato overhead as if to throw it back, forcing the guard to turn away from Teresa. Seizing the opportunity, Teresa edged her way to the door. When she reached the door, she turned her head to look at Goldie at the far end of the counter. Goldie, paying no attention to her, picked up the copper cauldron filled with hot soapy water. *Goldie! Wake up!* But Goldie remained detached. *Dio mio, help me, please!* Teresa was beginning to give up hope. Then, just as if Goldie had been rehearsing it for weeks, she dropped the cauldron onto the floor. The cauldron's piercing clang as it hit the tiles was nearly earsplitting. Sudsy water scattered in every direction.

"Yeeeowww!" Goldie let out a howl that reverberated around the room.

It was so alarming that everyone, including the guard, ran to her rescue. Everyone, that is, except Nick and Teresa. Teresa opened the door and slipped out. Nick, carrying the empty basket, followed her and quickly jerked the door closed behind him.

The humidity, freezing rain, and a huge plume of vapor from the van's exhaust seemingly conspired to protect them from view. Nick pushed Teresa into the back of the delivery van, slammed the doors shut, raced around to the front and jumped in beside Clyde. He hadn't moved that fast since before his injuries. "Let's get the hell out of here!"

Teresa edged her way forward and kissed Clyde on top of his head. "Thank you, Clyde, I'll never forget you for this."

"My pleasure, Miss." His face colored a bright red as he assured her, "It's the most excitin' thing I done since the war, an' that's a fact."

"I hope it doesn't cost you your job."

"Na, Miss, my brother owns the bakery." Then he laughed. "Who cares what he thinks?" He gave a Bronx cheer. "He never went off to war like I done. I keep remindin' him of it most every day. I hold up my hand and wave it in his face to show him I ain't got all my fingers no more. Then I lift this here patch to show him my missin' eye." He laughed again, although Teresa detected resentment toward his brother.

Nick turned his head around. "There's a bundle of clothes in there for you, but keep low until we're out of sight of the asylum."

Teresa felt for the bundle. "If you two promise to keep your eyes forward, I'll change my clothes."

Nick turned to look at her just as a flash of lightning lit her face and knew that the realization of her escape would hit her soon. "I'll do my best, but it won't be easy," Nick laughed, trying to keep the mood light.

Teresa unwrapped the bundle. Another lightning flash illuminated the van's interior. It surprised her that her hands were shaking so much. The escape had been easier than she had imagined, too easy. Trying for some control, she forced herself to think. "Where did you get the clothes?"

Nick started to turn around.

"Eyes front!" Her voice sounded tearful.

"You drive a hard bargain, sweetie." Nick wanted to see if she was all right but knew he needed to sound normal. He laughed. "I got them from Liza. That kid's all right."

Teresa tensed at the idea of more people knowing about her escape.

As if he could read her mind, he added, "I didn't tell her we were planning this escape. No sense telling more people than necessary. I told her that you needed them at the asylum and she gladly gave them to me."

Her entire body was shaking now, but the cold seemed to be coming from inside her. She decided not to change, and just put on the black overcoat. It felt new. The coat was too long and wide for her. It even looked too large for Liza. The cold trapped within the overcoat transferred itself to her and increased her shivering. Teresa reached into the bag again and found, on the bottom, a crushed broad brimmed, black-felt hat which Nick had carelessly shoved in. She pushed out the crown and tried readjusting the brim to keep it from covering her eyes, but it flopped in waves around her head. The bones in her fingers ached from the cold, making it difficult to manipulate everything. She rubbed her hands together. "My hands are so cold."

"Look in the right-hand overcoat pocket. There are gloves in it. I bought them at the last minute. Hope they fit. And, oh, there's a scarf somewhere in that bundle, too."

She pulled out a pair of fleece-lined leather gloves and struggled to get them on. Although she finally managed it, she couldn't fasten the buttons at the wrists. "Perfect," she lied, thrilled at her first gift from him, apart from the flowers. She edged her way closer to him and gave him a hug. "Thank you, *caro mio.* How thoughtful. They're the best gloves I've ever had."

"How's everything else fit?"

"I don't know. It's too cold to change in here."

"No need to, Miss Teresa. I got me a bungalow not far from Maple Crest," Clyde reassured her. "That's where we're headin'. My Ma left it for me when she died. Guess she figured my brother got enough money without it. It ain't much of a place, but it's grand enough for me. Someday I hope to bring Goldie there after we get married."

"Goldie sends her love, Clyde."

"How is she?"

"Getting better every day. Oh, how good it is to get out of the asylum."

*"Mia cara,* how awful these past weeks have been for you." Nick squeezed the hand that she had placed on his shoulder and kissed the exposed wrist, failing to notice she hadn't fastened the glove.

When they had traveled about two miles from the asylum, Clyde swerved onto an unpaved, rut-dominated road. Teresa clutched Nick's shoulders to keep from hitting the van's walls and roof. "Sorry, Miss. I know it ain't a smooth ride."

"I don't mind, Clyde; it makes me know I'm still alive."

A hurricane lamp hanging on the side wall swung threateningly at Teresa when Clyde swerved into a driveway. He stopped abruptly behind Nick's automobile. Just in front of Nick's auto, almost hidden in a stand of overgrown hemlocks, Teresa could see a wooden bungalow. Clyde had boarded up the windows and front door.

"Don't let that there board on the door fool ya. Give 'er a yank and she'll come free quick enough." He reached into his pocket, pulled out a long key, and handed it to Nick. "Just drop it in that mailbox when yer through with it." With his thumb, he gestured over his shoulder toward a mailbox that teetered on top of a crooked wooden post. "I'll be 'round in a couple o'days to take the boards off and clean the joint up. Got me a feelin' Goldie's gonna be out soon." He reached behind him and took the hurricane lamp off the hook. "Yer goin' ta need the lamp because with them windows bein' boarded up like they is, there ain't much light inside. There's another lamp in the kitchen. When you leave, put this here lamp inside by the front door."

"Thanks, Clyde; you're aces." Nick pulled out some money from his wallet. "Please take this for your help."

"Hey, fella!" Clyde scowled and pushed Nick's hand away. "What do ya take me for? I did it 'cause I like you guys, see?"

They thanked Clyde again and ran to the bungalow as he drove away. In seconds they were inside. Teresa sagged against the entrance door, unable to take another step.

Nick, seeing her distress, firmly led her into the bedroom and thrust the clothing from Liza onto the bed. "You okay, *cara?*"

"What? Oh, yes, fine, fine."

Nick returned to the sitting room while Teresa sat hard upon the bed, trying to gain control. He looked around the place. Although it was musty and damp because it had been closed, the bungalow was neat and clean. The small living room had a flower-printed couch in front of a fieldstone fireplace. Stacked neatly in a box beside the fireplace were old newspapers. Above the fireplace mantel hung a print of an English hunting scene, complete with red-jacketed hunters, pointing dogs, prancing horses, and fleeing pheasants. Between the fireplace and couch was an imitation brown bearskin rug. In one corner sat an overstuffed chair and footstool. Tucked in the opposite corner was a potbellied stove.

Nick checked out the kitchen. It was a tiny kitchen, but orderly and clean. He returned to the living room just as Teresa appeared from the bedroom wearing a white cotton blouse with puffed dolman sleeves. The calf-length A-line black skirt fit loosely around her hips. It pained him to see her looking pale and exhausted, and yet it made him feel even more protective.

"How do I look?"

"Like a royal princess, my love."

Her laugh was brittle. "Not a princess, but at least the skirt's got a belt. I guess they're afraid we're going to strangle ourselves with our belts at the Crest and do them out of 'guests.'" She put on the overcoat. "Do you mind if we get going? I don't want to stay this close to the asylum another minute."

As they headed toward the city he asked, "What do we do now? If you haven't thought of anything, I've got a suggestion."

"You first."

"My first thought was flying to Pennsylvania to get far away from Rocco and Maple Crest, but with this weather, we can't fly.

So, my second thought is hiding out at Bob's place. He's got a small flat not far from the airfield. His landlord is away, so there's no problem there."

"Still, it wouldn't solve anything. We've got to find a solution. Rocco's been controlling my life for too long. Now it's my turn. Tell me, have you found out anything about him?"

"Well, I went to the Douglas Cramer Agency; Harry recommended it." He hesitated, not anxious to go on.

Teresa sensed his uneasiness. "Go ahead, tell me."

"You're not going to like this, but Doug says Rocco's living in your apartment."

"What? The nerve! Couldn't Harry kick him out?"

"He tried, but the lease is in your name," he shrugged, "and everything in your name is Rocco's."

"That lease won't be up for another six months!"

"Right. Anyway, the fool's been very busy making enemies. Apart from trying to undermine Harry and..."

"Undermine Harry!"

"Yes. And trying to wipe out Mama, too. Another thing you're not going to like is that he's just about ruined The House of Violetta. At first, business boomed when they sent you to Maple Crest. I guess people were curious because of all that notoriety. Once they had a sample of his coarse manner, business fell off like the plague."

"Oh, Nick, after all I went through to build the business. This is outrageous!"

"That's still not all. I don't know where he's finding the time, but Doug says he's also having an affair with Malespina's wife."

Teresa gasped, "Marietta?"

"If Malespina ever finds out, he'll kill Rocco for sure. The *Padrone* has many friends in powerful places, but I'll bet he'd take on that job for himself, with the utmost pleasure."

"Rocco likes living dangerously. Nick, I'm getting angrier by the minute!" Some steel was coming back into her voice, Nick was relieved to notice.

"He owes Malespina tons of money. That's where he got the money to bring you to court."

Her brows knitted into a frown. "Those two are birds of a feather, all right."

"Rocco's trying to delay paying off his debt to the *Padrone.*"

"I can't imagine Malespina being too happy about that."

"Neither can I." He feared for Teresa's safety and the establishment.

"Anything else?"

"Yes, and this is the dirtiest of all. Doug discovered that both Malespina and Rocco were kidnaping children from Italy."

"Then it *is* true!"

"It's true all right. It seems that Malespina had been sending Rocco to Italy for years to do the dirty work for him. Malespina has a dungeon of a place in the bowels of Five Points where he keeps the poor kids more or less captives. From what Doug says it's some dark, filthy cellar with no windows. For years, he had Rocco controlling these poor kids, but Rocco was too untrustworthy and mean even for Malespina's tastes, or maybe it was because too many kids died and that was ruining Malespina's profits. I don't know which."

"Those animals! It makes my flesh crawl! It's not for just me anymore. We've got to help those children."

"That's a tall order."

They grew quiet, each within his own thoughts, as they drove through the freezing rain that beat a tattoo on the auto's roof. Their breaths mingled and formed vaporous trails on the inside of the windshield. The wipers thumped back and forth in rhythm with Teresa's pulsing temples. Although they cleared a curved path across the windshield, it did nothing to clear her mind. It was the mist inside the glass that mirrored her thinking. Teresa wiped the glass with her gloved hand as if hoping it could clarify her thoughts.

Nick broke the silence. "Where to, *cara?*"

"First to the nearest telephone to call the detective."

# Chapter 24

It surprised Teresa that Nick selected the Spring Street factory for the phone call, but he was right. The factory was closed for the day because of Rocco's meddling. Giustina was at home in Totowa nursing a sick headache. That gave them all the privacy they needed. Teresa took her hat off and tossed it on the black woolen skirt that Giustina had neatly folded and placed on the desk. Despite the chill in the office, Teresa only felt the warmth of Nick's nearness. He helped her take her coat off and tried to embrace her, but she held back. She felt his annoyance. Teresa took his hand and kissed it, "Can you wait, *caro,* until I've done what I have to do and am finally free?"

Nick's frustration eased; he realized that Teresa needed to believe she wasn't helpless any longer. Still, he couldn't help himself. As she phoned the detective, he kissed the back of her neck and whispered in her ear, "Not a hint of paraldehyde. You're deliciously sweet and inviting as always."

The whisper of his breath on her ear shot through her, but she managed to get through a lengthy consultation anyway. As she hung up the phone, she turned around and faced Nick.

He gave her a quick kiss on the nose.

She laughed and held him at arms' length. "Doug has a man watching my apartment house right now. There's a woman with Rocco, but he doesn't know who she is. Anyway, Doug has to pull his man. Seems there's an emergency elsewhere."

"And Malespina?"

"They've lost track of him and so has everyone else in town, evidently. People have been clamoring at the store for the money he's been banking for them. I hope Elena isn't among them. Doug thinks the *Padrone* is either hiding somewhere or has run off with the money."

"Some detective Harry hired," Nick scoffed, unable to hide his jealousy of Harry's choice.

"It doesn't surprise me. Malespina's very cagey." Teresa took a small black address book from the middle drawer, thumbed through it and picked up the phone.

"Who are you calling now?"

"Marietta."

"Marietta? Why?"

"Maybe we can confront Rocco with her and get him to do what we want."

"Whew!" Nick shook his head. "I just rescued you and I want to keep you around for a long time. I hope we're not going into more danger than we can handle."

"It's worth the chance." Teresa gave the telephone number to the operator and absentmindedly toyed with the skirt on the desk. *I should give this skirt to Liza to thank her. No, it's too large. It would fit someone like Nurse Davis.*

"Nobody home?"

"Guess not." She hung up the phone. Teresa thought for a moment. "If Marietta isn't home and Malespina is missing, maybe they've run off together. If they have, then threatening Rocco with Marietta isn't going to work." She bit her bottom lip and picked up the phone again.

"Now who?"

"Harry."

Nick couldn't help feeling jealousy spiced with irritation. Fuming, he sat opposite her and stretched out his legs. His injured knee was throbbing. It hadn't for weeks. As he listened to Teresa's side of the conversation, he rubbed his knee. It didn't help.

"No, Harry, I'm not at Maple Crest. I've escaped."

"You've what?" His laughter stopped. "You shouldn't have! I've been working to get you a new hearing. Haven't you gotten my letters?"

"No. They must have been keeping them from me." Her rage toward Nurse Davis seethed.

"How did you escape?"

As briefly as she could, she recounted her escape.

It was maddening for Harry. While he had merely gone through channels to try to rescue the woman he loved, it was Nick who had again become the bold, dashing figure in her eyes. Envy and resentment formed a knot in his stomach. He forced himself to subdue his anger at himself and Nick to think rationally. "You must go back."

"Live without hope? Never!"

"There *is* hope. Judge Rivers said that under normal circumstances all it takes for a husband to have his wife committed is to declare her mentally ill. But in Rocco's case, since he's not an Anglo-Saxon Protestant, the courts may reconsider. It depends on the judge. Another thing," he went on, fuming all the time that Nick must be at her side as they spoke, "he believes your mother's letter can be struck. Anyway, it isn't going to help your cause to run away. You can't run forever."

After Teresa ended her conversation with Harry, she reflected, *Harry's been right about so many things, but I can't possibly go back!* Then it occurred to her that she should have told him about her plan to confront Rocco. *No. Why get him involved?* She got up abruptly and, without thinking, put the skirt that had been on the desk under her arm. "Let's go, Nick."

\* \* \*

It was dusk by the time they entered the lobby of her apartment building. With utmost trepidation, they headed for the stairwell door, but the stairs were roped off. A sign hanging from a rope read 'Closed for Repairs'.

Teresa moaned. "We'll have to use the elevator! That operator will call the police in a flash!"

"We've no choice if you're still determined to go through with this."

"I am," she said, although she wasn't quite as sure of herself as she had been.

"Then keep your hat brim down and scarf up. I'll keep his attention drawn to me."

"Not that one. He fancies himself a Casanova." Still, she did as Nick suggested.

They headed for the elevator at the rear and stared at the doors as if trying to gain strength from the geometric decorative patterns. "All set?" he asked.

She nodded assent.

Nick took a deep breath and rang for the elevator.

When the doors swung open, Teresa's body tightened.

"Floor?"

The voice was unfamiliar. Despite herself, she glanced from beneath her hat brim. A sleepy old man whom she had never seen before sat on the pull-down wall seat. She breathed easier. *At last things are going my way.*

"Penthouse," Nick said.

He faced Nick and shouted, "Speak up! I hate mumblers. Curse the day they was invented."

Nick leaned into the man's ear and raised his voice several notches, "Penthouse!"

"No need to shout, young man!" he shouted angrily. "Think I'm deaf? I ain't. All young folks think anyone older than them is deaf or stupid."

"Sorry. What's wrong with the stairs?"

"Ain't nothin' wrong. They're just paintin' them dad-blame walls and makin' more work for me. Ain't no reason why folks can't use 'em." All the way up, he mumbled to himself. He stopped the elevator abruptly and yanked on the lever to open the doors.

Teresa automatically reached into her pocket for the key, then remembered she no longer had it.

Nick waited before ringing, giving her time to change her mind. "Want to leave?"

"No."

He rang the doorbell. No answer. He knocked firmly and repeatedly on the door.

"Okay! Okay!" came Rocco's irate response from the apartment. "Hold your damn horses." They had to wait a minute or two before they heard his footsteps on the marble-tiled entrance floor. Teresa couldn't see Rocco peering through the peephole, but she could hear his indrawn gasp clearly.

When the door opened, Teresa's terror of him returned. Under any other conditions, she would have laughed at his bright red satin smoking jacket that clashed with his bright green satin pajamas. His hair had been plastered down, patent-leather slick, with pomade. He reeked of cheap cologne. Had she been calmer, she would have been upset to notice that the Duchamp painting was missing. Replacing it was an oil painting of a pseudo-Parisian street with streetlights wired to glow with the flick of a switch.

"What the hell?" Rocco came out of his trance and made a dash for the telephone beside the sofa.

Teresa, trying to control her voice, hoped he couldn't sense the terror within her. "Put that phone down, Rocco!"

Rocco obeyed her in spite of himself.

Teresa's seeming self-control had fooled even Nick as he stood in the open doorway.

The bedroom door behind Rocco slowly opened. Although Marietta tried to hide herself behind the door, Teresa could see that Marietta had stuffed herself into Teresa's white satin bathrobe. The idea of Marietta wearing her clothing disgusted Teresa.

Rocco's eyes formed narrow slits. "How the hell did you get out of the crazy house?"

With the lump in her stomach building, she exclaimed, "That's not your concern! What is, is that I know what you've been doing. Do the words 'kidnaping' and 'murder' sound familiar? How about 'deportation' or the 'electric chair?'" She didn't know if kidnaping children from Italy came under the heading of capital punishment in America, but she threw out the threat anyway. It struck home.

Rocco dropped the telephone receiver. "I'll kill you!" His face turned purple with rage.

"I thought so." His reaction gave her more courage than she had been feeling. "That's not all. What do you think Malespina would do if he found out you've been carrying on with Marietta?"

Marietta, astonished, stood in the open doorway. The housecoat spread open, revealing her black lace lingerie. Her breasts strained at the lace and ballooned above it.

Rocco's face displayed a mixture of fear and shock that Teresa was so well informed. He lunged for her. Nick grabbed him, and with his shoulder threw Rocco crashing to the floor. In an instant, Nick was on top of Rocco, all set to punch him, but Teresa pulled Nick back. Marietta ran to Rocco's defense.

"Not yet, Nick. Let him go for now," Teresa pleaded as she sought to restrain him.

Rage seethed within Nick. He wanted his own vengeance. Reluctantly he got up but kept his foot on Rocco's chest. Every time Rocco tried to get up, Nick pressed his foot down hard.

"Get your foot off me."

"Let him go!" Marietta, at a safe distance, demanded.

Nick removed his foot, but not before giving Rocco a final pounding with the heel of his shoe. He stiffened menacingly, keeping himself between Rocco and Teresa.

Rocco pushed himself off the floor and pulled down on his smoking jacket. It had hiked up under his armpits. "I'll kill you both," he repeated, this time with less conviction in his voice.

"Yes, Rocco," Teresa responded, taking courage from Rocco's obvious fear, "you could. You've killed before. I know all about Ubaldo and Peppi." Still trying to control her voice, Teresa waved her hand casually, "On the other hand, I could kill you. They wouldn't convict me. You said I was insane, remember?"

He started to say something.

"No, Rocco," she held her hand up, "you are going to give me a divorce, leave town, and return my business to me, or I'll tell Malespina what you've been up to. I'll give you two days' grace before I inform the authorities about your activities."

Rocco folded his arms over his chest. "Give all this up? Never! There is no proof, and who would care about a bunch of striking Italians? So go ahead!" He threw both arms up. "Tell the *Padrone.* Tell the police. They wouldn't believe you. All I'll have to say is that you're crazy."

"True. They wouldn't believe me, but they would believe the Douglas Cramer Detective Agency. I hired him when I realized you had the meanness in you to try to ruin my life." She smiled a dry one-sided smile. "No, Rocco, I won't be another one of your victims."

His eyes widened with surprise for a moment, then narrowed again. "Forget it! The detective will say whatever you pay him to say. I'll take my chances with Malespina. I owe him a lot of money. He's not going to do anything to me until he gets paid. One thing he loves more than Marietta is money."

"Maybe!" Malespina stood in the doorway behind Nick. His raincoat and derby were soaked through. A pearl and silver handled revolver in his hand glinted from the light above. Marietta screamed and tried to run for the bedroom door, but Malespina shouted after her, "It's too late to run, you *putana!*"

She stood riveted.

Malespina's nose was pinched white with rage. "I know what's been going on even before this moment. Too many of my 'friends' were all too willing to tell me about you, my devoted wife. How they enjoyed telling me." His eyes narrowed to mere slits.

Marietta's heart pounded. She slowly walked toward him with outstretched arms. "Please, Vittorio, wait!"

"What for?" He pushed her with his revolver. "Go to your lover, *putana!*"

She clutched her hammering heart. "No! Vittorio, don't! I can explain!"

"This is all the explanation I need." He waved his gun. "I am the *Padrone*. Are the two of you too stupid to know what that means? You two turned me into a cuckold and thought you could get away with it. Prepare yourself, my dear." He took aim.

Marietta shrieked, "No!"

The *Padrone* shot her in the heart.

Teresa gasped in horror but could do nothing to stop him.

As if he were hunting rabbits in the woods, he turned his gun on Rocco.

"Wait! *Padrone*, wait!" Rocco pleaded.

"Tell me, Rocco, do you recognize this revolver? It's yours. I'm letting you have it. No charge for the bullets."

"Don't do it, *Padrone!*" Rocco's voice rose in panic. "I have your money." He reached into his pocket and drew out some dollar bills. "See? We've been good partners and —

"Partners? When was that? Ha!" It was more an expletive than a laugh. "You told me yourself that this is the only way to handle a problem! For once I agree with you. "Take this!" He shot Rocco in the groin.

A pile-driving pain in the testicles streaked up Rocco's stomach. *"Madonna mia!"* Rocco screamed in agony and clutched his groin. "Kill me! Please, kill me! I can't stand the pain!"

Malespina picked up some money and slapped Rocco's face with it. "Thanks for the money. You're right; I value it more than Marietta." Then he placed the revolver in Rocco's mouth and fired. He picked up the money, shoved it into his pocket and placed the gun in Rocco's hand. Malespina turned to the stunned Nick and Teresa. "I've nothing against you two...yet. But..." In quick succession, he made a gesture over his mouth as if he were locking it shut and drew a finger across his throat. "You have been witnesses, so that you know I mean what I say." Then he walked out.

Teresa and Nick, knowing they couldn't ignore the warning, stood immobilized. Nick regained his senses first. "We've got to get out. Fast! That elevator operator may be nearly deaf, but somebody in the building must have heard those shots."

Teresa still didn't move. It was a nightmare beyond anything she had ever imagined. Suddenly she began screaming, chilling Nick to the marrow.

"Teresa!" He yelled right in her face, trying to bring her to her senses, but she continued screaming. He shook her shoulders. No effect. Reluctantly he slapped her face.

She stopped screaming and, for an instant, looked as if she were going to faint.

Nick, seeing her eyes beginning to turn back, slapped her again and shook her shoulders. "Pull yourself together! We don't have time to waste."

She began crying but failed to move. "I can't breathe. I can't breathe. I'm falling apart."

"Get hold of yourself! Let's go!" Nick took her by the arm, yanked her out the door and pulled her to the elevator. He rang for the elevator operator.

"Nick! We can't use the elevator!" Teresa said in near panic.

"I know! I'm just getting him to move up while we take the stairs."

"Oh, Lord, I'm sick to my stomach!"

\* \* \*

Teresa lost track of how long they rode around in Nick's automobile, trying to decide what to do. Nick stopped once to allow her to throw up. By the time her nausea had left her, the sleet had turned to wet snow, cutting visibility considerably. Yet, in their state of tension, they hardly noticed.

It was Nick who was the first to become conscious of the weather. "We have to hole up somewhere. The snow is caking the windshield." It was the first time he was glad his mother had chosen a closed-in vehicle. Having snow falling in on his girl would have been disturbing under the best circumstances, but now it would be impossible. "Any ideas?"

Tears still streamed down her face, but she was more nearly in control. "I don't know. The bungalow? I..." Her voice trailed off.

"The bungalow it is, then."

It took longer to get there than they had expected since Nick made frequent stops to clear the windshield. At last, he pulled into the driveway. The headlights illuminated snow-cloaked evergreens, silhouetting them against the brown clapboard bungalow. It was such a welcome sight, it seemed a palace to them.

Nick retrieved the key from the mailbox, trudged around the auto, handed Teresa the key and swept her up in his arms. He ignored the pains in his arm and knee as he carried her to the front door. She trembled in his arms, but he wasn't sure whether it was his influence or the evening's horrifying event.

"Put me down, Nick. I can manage from here."

"Not on your life. Can you pull the board off the door?"

Teresa pulled. It came off easily. She unlocked and opened the door. Nick placed her down gently just inside the doorway. He stamped the snow off his feet on the wooden stoop, reached inside for the hurricane lamp, and lit it.

The bungalow was colder inside than it had been earlier in the day. Without taking off her coat, she sat on the sofa struggling to control the persistent shaking of her limbs, but the more she tried, the more she trembled. She stared at the cold ashes in the fireplace and almost felt as if they were a commentary on her life.

Nick tossed some logs and kindling into the fireplace. He crumpled a few sheets of the old newspapers and tucked them between some logs. Nick almost pitched in a pine cone resting beside the logs, changed his mind, took a wooden match from a box on the mantel, and lit the newspaper. In a few minutes, he had a roaring fire, but the darting flames didn't stop Teresa's trembling. Instead, they magnified her leaping nerves.

Nick turned. Seeing her anguish, he wanted to take her in his arms to comfort her but instinctively felt he shouldn't. Instead, he took off his coat, held it in front of the fire for a minute and wrapped the warmed side around her legs. After lighting the potbellied stove, he glanced at Teresa. Satisfied she was all right, he strode into the kitchen.

He rummaged through the cupboards and found several soup cans, some brandy, a couple of shot glasses and mugs. "This brandy should do the trick," he called over his shoulder. His hands were still shaking from delayed reaction. It surprised him that they should be shaking now after all the carnage he had seen during the war.

He poured some brandy into a glass and took a swig to steady his nerves. Then he poured some for Teresa, turned and saw a gray enamel coffeepot on the black cast-iron stove. Above the pot on the stove's metal shelf he found a canister containing some coffee beans and a coffee grinder. Nick shook some beans into the grinder and milled them. "Lucky for us this kitchen has an indoor water pump," he called to Teresa, more to hear his own voice than to inform her. Then it occurred to him that the coffee wouldn't boil unless he lit the stove. He set to work lighting the stove. *My hands might be shaking but my head is still on straight,* he thought wryly. Nick started for the living room, returned and pumped some water for Teresa, knowing she could use it.

By the time he reentered the living room, the room had lost its cold, musty odor. A cozy, woodsy fragrance now filled the room. The firelight cast a spell-like radiance around Teresa, still sitting on the couch. She took his breath away. He stopped for a moment to stare at her. In the darkened room, lit by the fireplace, a soft glow surrounded Teresa like an aurora. When she lifted her legs and wrapped her arms around them, it broke the spell. He held the glass out to her. "Have some water. You must need it."

She swallowed it all without stopping, surprised she was so parched.

Nick took the glass from her and handed her the brandy. "This will help calm your nerves." At a loss at what else to do to help her, he threw a pine cone into the fire and sat beside her. He kicked off his shoes and stretched out his legs to warm his feet. "I think you'll warm up faster if you take off those coats, *cara.* The fire and the potbellied stove are doing their job."

Teresa didn't move, as if she hadn't heard him. She took another sip of brandy, felt it burn on the way down, but it didn't warm her or calm her nerves. The horror still clung to her like a claw.

Nick removed the coat from around her legs. "Get up, honey." He brought her to her feet as if she were a child, removed the other coat and sat her down beside him. Nick put his arm around her shoulder and rubbed her arms a few times, trying to give Teresa some of his heat. Then he held her so close he could almost hear her heart beating.

They stared into the crackling fire and watched the leaping flames. Their silence filled the room more than a crowd of rowdy people could have. Even the bursting pine cone did nothing to break their silence.

The aroma of coffee drifted into the room. Nick padded into the kitchen, found a couple of mugs, poured a jigger of brandy into the bottom of each mug and filled the mugs with steaming coffee. "Hungry?" he called to her. "There's some soup here."

"No. Too upset to think about food."

He returned to the couch, handed Teresa the mug and sat beside her. "You're so quiet. What are you thinking?"

"So many things." She warmed her hands around the mug and continued to stare into the fire. "I'm sorry I got you into this mess."

"You didn't get me into anything; I went on my own accord."

"Poor Marietta. She didn't deserve to die. Whatever she was, she was no murderer, no kidnaper, no exploiter."

"We don't know what she knew about the children and her husband's other businesses, but she knew she was playing a dangerous game with Rocco. She made her own choices, just as I'm doing now, choosing to stand with you."

"Still, such bloodshed." She closed her eyes as if that could block the image that had burned itself into her mind's eye. Again she heard the slaughtered animals' cries, coupled with Marietta's scream.

"I know it will stay with you for a long time, but with time it'll subside." At least he hoped so, for he seldom had a night without battling his own nightmares. He'd awaken screaming and trembling with cold sweats.

Teresa heard the pain in his voice as he relived battle horrors. She forced herself to shake the memory of the carnage out of her head, knowing they both had to focus on the future, not the past. "What are we going to do now, Nick?"

"Right now, the only thing to do is to wait until it stops snowing." He pulled her even closer. "Meanwhile, let's try to shut out the world. There's got to be some place in all this for us. Don't you think we've waited long enough, gone through enough, to deserve some happiness?"

Snuggled in his arms and warmed by the fire and brandy, it was almost easy to forget. *Why not? Haven't I suffered enough? Hasn't Nick? It's about time to think about our needs.*

Nick raised her chin. His lips hovered above hers. Gently he kissed her on the mouth. Slowly the pressure of his lips increased. Her lips opened to him. "My dear, darling," he said, remaining only a kiss away.

"Oh, Nick, I love you so much. Until now, I've always been alone. When I lost you, I thought I wouldn't survive. Yet

somehow, through all these years, you were always with me, *caro*.
One moment with you makes all the bitter memories vanish." She
brushed the lock of hair away from his eyes and kissed his brow.
Teresa felt her reserve slip away. Almost before she knew it, they
were naked and on the bearskin rug. His lips felt like fire as he
kissed her nose, her eyes and then her mouth. She returned her kiss
with such ardor it thrilled them both. His lips brushed her throat
and glided slowly down to her breasts, radiating heat throughout
her body. A strong desire rushed through her. She embraced him
and lifted herself to him. "Nick, please. I long to give myself to
you."

Nevertheless, as hungry for her as he was, he took his time
before he entered her. Her entire body screamed with excitement as
he moved forward again and again. A soft moan escaped her lips.
The two, finally spent, lay exhausted, locked in each other's arms.
"Nick, *mio amore,* somehow I knew it would be like this."

"I never knew it could."

They remained on the rug, still wrapped in a glow. After a
long while, Nick slept in her arms, his first peaceful sleep since the
war. The fire in the fireplace went down, bringing a chill to the
room.

She slipped away from him, added a split log to the fireplace
and to the potbellied stove. Then she tiptoed into the bedroom,
collected a pillow and a blanket and returned to the living room.
Teresa stopped for a moment and looked around. *Why does
everything in this room seem so wonderful?* Teresa stood beside Nick,
gazed down at his powerfully-built body and knew the answer.
*Nick. Funny, why hadn't I noticed that little-boy quality about him
before? Does sleeping do that for a man, make him seem vulnerable?*
Teresa smiled. How she wanted to kiss him but was afraid to waken
him. Ever so carefully she placed his head upon the pillow. After
warming the blanket by the fire, she placed it over him and slipped
in beside him.

Half-awake, Nick smiled and drew her back to him until he
felt the entire length of her body against him. He placed his hand
on her breast, kissed the back of her neck and fell asleep again.

It surprised her that she didn't feel guilty about having given
herself to him without marriage. All she felt was extreme joy.
Teresa couldn't sleep for fear she would wake and find him gone.
That would be something she could never live through again. She
just lay there, trying to memorize each curve of his body, as if

implanting the memory would make him permanent for her. She felt warm, safe, desirable.

It was morning when he awoke. He turned her over on her back and lifted himself on one elbow to gaze into her eyes. "Why did you let me sleep? I don't want to lose a single minute of being with you. Each minute is precious, vital. I'm so afraid fate will take it from us."

"Don't even think it!" A strong premonition struck her, almost crushing her. She shook it off with an effort. "How could I waken you, *mio amore?* It was delightful just being so close to you. I felt so safe, so wanted, so loved. Nick, when I was a little girl in Italy, I thought the world would be Heaven if I could only be alone. Now I know to be without you in this world would be absolute Hell. Oh, Nick, kiss me."

He didn't need a second invitation. Nick's first kiss was soft, moist, then breathless, then urgent. She opened her mouth with a whimper. A mutual shudder ran along the length of their bodies. For the second time he possessed her. This time it was even more beautiful for them than the first time. Reluctantly they parted.

After a while, still in a daze, she asked, "What time is it?"

"I haven't the foggiest. With these windows boarded up it could be the middle of the night." Nick sat up to collect his jacket that he had tossed on the couch hours before. He reached into its pocket and pulled out his pocketwatch. "It's 5:35 in the morning."

She got up quickly and went into the bedroom to dress.

"Where are you going? Come back and lie down beside me."

"I've got to go back to the asylum," she called back.

"Asylum?" It was as if she had thrown cold water over him. "Why? You're a free woman now."

"Not yet. Harry is right. I must go back to clear myself of the insanity charge and bring my life finally under control. For too long I've been living in shadows. The only way to come out is to return to the asylum and take my chances with Judge Rivers. Somehow I trust him."

"It may take months...maybe never! How can you even begin to trust these judges? And what about that psychopathic place? It's a miracle you escaped once. Do you think you can, twice?"

"Maybe not. Anyway, I've decided. Nick, I'm not concerned only about me," she said as she returned to the living room. "You'd get into trouble for helping me and..."

"I can take care of myself. I'm a survivor." Then he noticed the way she was dressed and frowned. "Why on earth are you wearing those institutional clothes?"

"If I go back wearing the clothes Liza gave me, there would be too many questions to answer. It could even connect me with the murders and..."

*"Cara,* I still think you're making a mistake."

"Maybe so, but I've decided."

"I knew something was going to separate us. I felt it," he said through clenched teeth.

"Somehow I don't think it will be long before we will be together again, this time for always. Something in the way Harry spoke makes me believe that Judge Rivers will be the answer for us."

Nick scoffed, "Harry said that about Ben, too, not to mention the detective agency."

Nick's remark brought her up sharp; for a minute he almost changed her mind. Then she shook her head. "This time I really believe it's different."

It annoyed him that she valued Harry's word over his. However, seeing her determination, he reluctantly asked, "How are you getting back in?"

"I don't know. Maybe brazen it out and go right through the front door." She smiled as his mouth hung open in disbelief.

"Sounds absurd to me." He was annoyed and wanted to strike out. "If it works, then what?"

"I'll have to wait and see." Her mind was too active with ideas to notice his pointed remark. Then she had another thought that had nothing to do with her predicament, but she hesitated to ask him, not sure she wanted to get Nick further involved. "Nick?"

"Yes?"

"Could you please have the detective make some phone calls? Something should be done to help those kids Malespina's got trapped like slaves. Be careful, though. I don't want Malespina finding out. There's no telling what he might do."

"They'll just send them to an orphanage. From what I hear, it's no bed of roses there." He shook his head skeptically.

"Maybe not, but anything's got to be better than what they've been through." She thought for a minute. "Do you think we can get them reunited with their families in Italy?"

"Slim chance, even if they could tell us where they came from in Italy." He saw the disappointment in her face and felt guilty for being angry with her. He smiled and tried to reassure her. "Okay, *innamorata,* I'll give it my best."

She blew a kiss from across the room. When she saw the hungry look in his eyes, she laughed and ran into the kitchen. "Let's see if there's anything to eat in here."

Nick reached down for the pants he had thrown over the arm of the sofa the night before. As he dressed, he could hear her opening and closing the cupboards. It sounded so wonderfully domestic to him. He began fantasizing about how beautiful their life would be when they were married.

"We're in luck," she called to him, "there's some farina here and even some honey. No milk, of course, but that should do us. Oh, yes, the soup. Would you like some soup instead?"

"Both," he called back and laughed, realizing suddenly that he was famished.

She found herself humming, despite the horror of the evening before and the ordeal that lay ahead of her. Her heart was full of love for Nick; nothing else mattered. Visualizing Nick by her side, or waiting for her, she could survive anything, no matter what.

He sat on the couch and began to tie his shoes. Uneasiness crept over him. "Another thing bothering me, *cara,* is that I may not be around for a couple of weeks to get you out of any trouble. I may have a job delivering airmail. It will be our first big break." He didn't want to tell her that it wasn't the mail but the army that wanted him as flight instructor. Then he shook his head and drew his lips into a hard line. *Damn! Why did it turn up just now?*

"How can you fly in this weather?"

"We'll just wait until it clears up, that's all. As I said before, I'm a survivor."

Although she felt a pang of regret that he would not be near, she did her best to reassure him. "Don't worry, *amore mio,*" she called back, "I'm a survivor, too. But I'll miss you, dreadfully." She reentered the living room and sat on the couch beside him. "I can't believe we're finally together. Oh, Nick, I don't know what I would do without you. You are my life. The thought of being away from you for even one instant is heartbreaking."

*"Mia amore,* when you need me, just close your eyes. I'll be there, wherever you are. You will feel my presence, for I'll be

thinking of you at the very same moment. Nothing lasts forever, not even separation. I'll fly back to you in a wink."

"I still worry about flying. I can't help it."

"Now it's my turn to say, don't worry about me. If my number wasn't up with all that happened to me at the front, I'm invincible."

"Nick, don't say that." She crossed herself to ward off the evil spirits. It had been some time since she had performed that ritual.

He smiled and kissed the palms of her hands. "Do you know how much I love you? In no time we are going to be married." He didn't want to bring Harry into this conversation, but in spite of that he found himself saying, "I think Harry will help arrange the wedding for us, don't you?"

"Dear, sweet Harry. It pains me to think of how much I've hurt him."

"Harry cares for you and wants you to be happy. I think he feels sad about us, but he knows you really belong with me."

# Chapter 25

It was a bold move, but Teresa hoped that everyone at the asylum would be too preoccupied with eating lunch to be concerned with her. She pulled Liza's coat tightly around her to bolster her courage, squared her shoulders and entered through the front door. The same guard who had been there when she had first arrived at Maple Crest sat at his desk munching a sandwich. Between gulps he turned pages of a detective magazine. A chill ran the length of her body when he looked up. "Nurse Davis," she said as calmly she could.

"Know how to get to where she is?" he asked, apparently taking her for a visitor.

"Yes." She breathed a fraction easier.

Reluctantly he put down his sandwich, grabbed the keys, unlocked the door and stood aside to allow her to go through the gaping passage. "Wait!" he said. "Haven't I seen you before?"

She stopped suddenly. "I don't know, have you?"

The guard looked at her again for what seemed forever to her. Then the skirt tucked under her arm caught his attention. "Whatcha got there?" He pointed to it as he sucked a particle of food from between his front teeth.

"Oh, it's just a skirt for Nurse Davis that she ordered."

"Let's see it," he insisted.

She unfolded it, blocking her face with the skirt, while he examined it. "I'm her seamstress."

He shrugged his shoulders. "Okay. Guess that's where I seen you before."

Her heart started to beat again. *Dear God, am I doing the right thing?* She began praying she wouldn't encounter anyone in the long corridor. For the moment, she was lucky; the long corridor was empty. The utility closet was near the end of the corridor. If she could get there before she encountered anyone, she might have a chance to succeed. Again luck was with her. Teresa opened the door to the utility closet, took her coat off and tossed it in, barely missing the mops and brooms. She took a deep breath, adjusted her dress and refolded the skirt. *Now for Nurse Davis. Lord stay with me. What can she do to me? Knock me down to a lower ward. God, I hope not.* Then the thought of solitary and what Goldie had said about it struck her. She shivered as she rounded the corner. With her heart pounding, she entered Nurse Davis' office.

The nurse shot to her feet. Her face nearly purple with rage, she hissed, "Where the hell have you been? I've been searching the place for hours! Thank God no one else knows you were missing. Do you realize how much trouble I would have been in? You would have destroyed my spotless record. You'll pay for the anxiety you've caused me!"

Teresa tilted her head to one side and smiled apologetically. "I'm sorry I put you through all that anxiety, Nurse Davis. It was careless of me."

"It certainly was!"

Teresa could see that the woman's attention had been drawn to the skirt. *Well, here goes, for better or worse.* "Did you look in the utility room?"

She placed her hands on her hips. "Of course! What do you take me for, a fool?"

"Of course not, but that's where I was. I was working on this skirt and fell asleep behind all those boxes and things. The air gets very stuffy in there. I tried to open the window but it wouldn't budge. It must be painted shut."

"Why didn't you answer me when I called to you?"

"I didn't hear you. I must have been asleep. At least I think I was. Maybe I passed out from the poor air circulation in the room."

"Are you trying to tell me you were in that room all this time? Impossible!"

"I left a couple of times to go to the lavatory, but yes, I was in there all the time." Teresa could see the woman wasn't convinced. She laughed. "I confess. You caught me. I escaped, and because I missed the place so much, I decided to force my way back in." She laughed again to show the absurdity of the idea. "I was working on the skirt and got so interested in it, I simply forgot the time." She held up the skirt.

Nurse Davis's relief at finally finding Teresa, not to mention the garment, overcame her anger a little, and her common sense a lot. "Let's have it," she said, and snatched the skirt out of Teresa's hands.

"You've been so kind, so thoughtful, and so patient with me that I only want what is best for you. I hope it fits you."

The woman held the skirt up to her waist to see if it would fit just as the burly orderly entered the room. Nurse Davis' expression quickly changed. She looked like a schoolgirl with a crush on the teacher. It wasn't lost on Teresa.

"I see you found her," the orderly stated. "Where was she?""

Teresa answered before Nurse Davis had a chance to, "I must have passed out in the utility closet. If it hadn't been for our clever Nurse Davis, I could have smothered in there."

"Hey!" he said, already bored with the subject, "where'd you get the skirt?" Amusement lurked in his eyes. "You got yourself a beau?" He laughed as if the idea were preposterous.

"Why not?" Nurse Davis bristled with resentment at his scepticism.

Now the woman became even angrier. Her resentment turned on Teresa. "Get back to your duties in the kitchen and be quick about it. This is the last day for you there. Tomorrow my other worker will be back on duty."

As Teresa started to leave, the nurse shouted after her. "Don't think I'm letting you off easy, Missy. Not by a long shot. I'm not through with you yet!"

\* \* \*

The next day, as Teresa was washing the lavatory floor on her hands and knees, Nurse Davis walked up behind her. Her eyes glowing with delight as if she had uncovered the most delightful bit of gossip, she waved a newspaper in Teresa's face. "Hey! The police found your ever-lovin' husband dead as a door nail."

Teresa didn't know how she should react. She knew she shouldn't appear upset by his death after what he had done to her, but not happy either. Teresa rose to her feet and pretended surprise. "What? Let me see that!" She wiped her hands on her apron.

"Here, read it for yourself. Page three." She laughed and walked away, fully satisfied with herself.

Teresa's hands shook as she quickly turned to page three: *Notorious Woman's Husband Found Shot*

*Rocco Martello, husband of Teresa Tozzi Martello, the well-known couturier from The House of Violetta, has been found by the police shot to death. In an apparent murder/suicide, he was found with the lovely Marietta Malespina, wife of Vittorio Tomaso Malespina. Mr. Malespina has been missing for several days and has aroused suspicion because of his mysterious absence.*

*Teresa Martello's husband had her committed to Maple Crest, the asylum for the insane....*

Teresa didn't know if she should feel relieved that she wasn't a suspect in the case or angry that she was again in the newspapers. She didn't like the article calling her the "notorious woman". Nor did she like their reminding everyone that she had been committed.

All she knew was that she wanted desperately to call Nick for reassurance, and Harry, about the impact it might have on her case. Frustrated, Teresa crumpled the newspaper in her hands and threw it into the wastebasket.

\* \* \*

For the next four weeks, Nurse Davis had Teresa doing the worst job in the asylum, cleaning the loathsome lavatories, a job she hated doing even at home. She even had Teresa back on the dreaded paraldehyde. This time the medication seemed worse to her, but she was relieved she hadn't been sent to solitary or knocked down to a lower ward. The visits by Nick and Harry and the gifts of flowers and candy for the nurse may have helped her.

At the end of the fourth week, the woman suddenly became almost cordial, so much so that Teresa became suspicious. Still, despite her suspicions, Teresa didn't dwell on it, for she had another concern. She had skipped her period. Teresa tried to shrug it off as stress, or paraldehyde. She couldn't ask Nurse Davis about it, for if she was pregnant, apart from the scandal, her pregnancy would reveal that she had been out of the institution when the murders had been committed. She couldn't ask Goldie, for they had released Goldie. *Lord, what if I'm pregnant? I must escape again.* This time, however, it would be almost impossible, with Goldie gone and no access to the kitchen. She must have solitude and get off the paraldehyde to think. *The utility room.*

As Nurse Davis escorted her to the visitors' room, she decided to ask, "How would you like me to make you that overcoat? The material is still in the utility room." Teresa could then substitute Liza's coat for the one she was supposed to make, and get rid of the paraldehyde and drudgery. How she was going to get rid of the material later she hadn't figured out yet. She knew there was no rush, for the woman never entered the closet. It was Teresa's conviction that the woman suffered from claustrophobia.

The woman smiled. "I was just thinking the same thing."

Her smile came as a surprise to Teresa. It was the first time she had done so. "Then get me some black satin lining and buttons. I'll have it for you in a day or two."

"I've got them."

"Take me off the paraldehyde, too."

"Fine." She smiled again. "Only this time, don't disappear on me. I'll be watching you."

Harry's smiling face greeted them as they approached, turning the gray skies bright for Teresa and Nurse Davis. He was resplendent as always in his well-tailored gray overcoat and pearl-gray homburg. Under each arm he had a large box tied with a wide blue ribbon. "Hello, Nurse Davis. I've never seen you looking lovelier." He placed one box down and kissed the woman's hand without showing the least revulsion.

"Oh, Mr. Goldstein, thank you," she almost giggled.

"These samples crossed my desk today. When I saw them, I thought of you. Perfect with your blue eyes."

"My goodness, for me? What are they?"

"A light blue suit and a matching woolen overcoat. Would you please try them on? I'd love to see you in them."

"Why, of course." She fairly beamed in anticipation.

"Perhaps you will allow me to help you carry them in. The box with the coat is heavy."

"No. I can manage." She placed one box under each arm, spun on her heels and carried them with ease as she disappeared through the doorway.

Teresa and Harry turned and walked out the door to the quad. A stiff Canadian wind greeted them. Teresa turned her face to the gray sky and closed her eyes for a moment, shielding them from the sharp wind. "Bringing those gifts for Nurse Davis was sweet of you, Harry."

"My intention was twofold, to make life easier for you in this dreadful place and to get her out of our hair."

"Yes, she is always around when you're here. She never does it with other visitors. I think she's got a crush on you."

Harry just laughed.

"Feels as if it's going to snow," she said, afraid to ask what he had found out about her release.

"I hope not. I can do without snow. Has Nurse Davis scheduled a visit to a doctor yet? There's a new doctor on staff."

"No. Maybe she never will, now that she's got a seamstress as a slave." Finally, unable to wait any longer she asked, "Do you have any good news for me?"

"I think so. I didn't want to say anything just yet to get your hopes up, but I can't hold back. Judge Rivers was livid about your not even seeing a doctor for evaluation because of Nurse Davis. I think he's doing something about it."

"Oh, maybe that's why she's so changed in her manner toward me."

"Anyway, he's still trying to get some action through the courts, but it's slow going."

"Rocco's death hasn't helped in any way?"

"The Judge says it could, because it revealed his character. But," he shook his head, "if you can get her to have that new doctor examine you, you'd be out in a jiffy."

Teresa shook her head, "I'm getting too impatient to wait much longer. It may be time for another escape attempt."

"Don't do that! Be a little more patient."

"It's easy to say. You're not the one in here. Patience is something I no longer have."

Harry blushed. "I'm sorry. It was thoughtless of me."

"It's my turn to say I'm sorry. It was thoughtless of me, Harry, but sometimes I think I will *really* go mad if I stay here another day. That woman -"

"Shhh, there she is."

They had turned the corner and were facing the entrance door. Nurse Davis, in the light blue overcoat, almost promenaded as if she were on a showroom runway. "It fits perfectly!" she beamed.

"How lovely!" Harry said.

"Oh, yes," Teresa said. "Let's go in so we can see what the suit-dress looks like on you."

They quickly entered the waiting room where the woman removed her overcoat.

Harry took the woman by the hand and swung her around. "Wonderful. I'm so glad I thought of you when I saw the ensemble."

"The only thing it needs," Teresa chimed in, "is a pair of shoes and a hat to match. I know just the place to get them. They have almost everything, and if they don't they can make it up in no time."

"Where?" the woman, now in a state of near-ecstasy, asked. "I'll go there this Saturday."

"Oh," Teresa said, "I'm sorry, but it's only for people in the trade. Harry, you know "Myer and Son's. Maybe you can get them for her." Sam Myer and Son's was a code name they used to appease an impossibly demanding client.

"I wish I could," he said, picking up her meaning, "but I had words with Sam. Sorry. You're the only one he ever listened to, anyway."

"Well," Teresa said, "I guess that's that, then. Too bad. Nothing else will do."

The disappointment on Nurse Davis' face was a joy for Teresa to see. "I'm sorry to say visitors' hours are over, Mr. Goldstein."

Harry kissed Teresa on the cheek, gave her a hug and left. Nurse Davis led her first to her office to retrieve the material and then to the utility room.

Teresa entered the room, squeezed past the clutter, sat at the sewing machine, placed her head in her hands and wept. This time, the room was not a retreat, but an insufferable prison.

For the next week, she pretended to work on the overcoat and tried to plot an escape, but nothing came. Apart from that, there was nothing else to keep her mind occupied. The coat only needed to have the buttons replaced with those that the nurse had supplied. Disposing of the old buttons was easy. She flushed them down the toilet, but the material was another matter. Every time she left the room, she took bits of the material and threw them into the waste containers. Only a few pieces were left, but they could have been thought of as cutting waste. "I can't stand another day of sitting here!" She gathered the coat in her arms and trudged over to Nurse Davis' office. "The coat's finished." She held it up for inspection.

The woman's face brightened. "Oh, good." Almost ignoring Teresa, she took the coat from her and tried it on. It fit perfectly. Then, as if she had just remembered, she said, "I was just about to call you. There's a new doctor on staff. He wants to examine you this afternoon." She grimaced, obviously not thrilled with the new doctor's usurping authority.

* * *

Teresa wondered what had caused the interview; Judge Rivers or the new doctor's new broom policy. She didn't care. All that was important was that she now faced a real doctor in his mahogany-paneled office.

"Good afternoon, Teresa." He smiled and approached her with his hand extended. "I'm Doctor Fritz Becker."

She took his firm hand in her trembling one. "Good afternoon, Doctor."

Despite his attempt to look older with his Sigmund Freud-like mustache, beard, tie, and glasses, the Doctor looked like a youngster fresh out of college. He adjusted his white coat over his black three-piece suit. She observed, she didn't know why, that his baggy trousers needed pressing. All she knew was that she was searching for the words to convince this man that she had been committed by mistake. Then she noticed, alongside a large cigar in the marble ashtray, a worn copy of Freud's *Interpretation of Dreams*. On Harry's recommendation, she had read it about a year ago. This could be her access! "Has anyone ever told you that you look like Sigmund Freud?"

His eyes opened wide in surprise. "You know about him?" He gestured to a chair opposite his desk.

"Of course. What a wonderfully brilliant and enlightened man he is."

"Have you ever met him?" he asked, his interest piqued.

She smiled and shook her head. "I'm sorry to say no. I know he came to this country in nineteen aught nine, because that was the year I came to this country. He lectured at...let me think," she closed her eyes for a second, "Worcester College in Massachusetts, I believe."

"Right you are! That was my college."

"My goodness, you were at his lectures?" It also meant that he was older than she, but he didn't appear to be.

"Every one of them."

"How fortunate."

"Do you mind if I smoke?" he asked, pointing to the cigar. Gray smoke curled in the air.

"No, not at all. Cigar smoking always reminds me of my father, although he died when I was very young." She thought that would get his attention. Her father had never smoked.

He wrote something down. "What do you remember about your father?"

"As I said, not much. He was a kind man, but seldom around."

The doctor wrote something down. "And your mother?"

"A good, hard-working soul."

He wrote again. Then as an afterthought, "What do you know about Freud's work?"

She smiled modestly. "Not much, I'm afraid, although I'd like to know more. Perhaps you could tell me what books to read, but I know you are far too busy to do that." She hoped she didn't show her resentment toward him for not having seen her before this.

"I'm terribly overbooked. I've tried to have them engage more doctors. However, money is short and being a new man here..." He shrugged and reddened, embarrassed at having said more than he should about his own problems. He picked up the copy of *Interpretation of Dreams* and riffled the pages with his thumb. Realizing what he was doing, he put it down. "But, I'd be happy to make a list for you. Can you read German?"

"A little."

He leaned back, placed his two hands together as if he were praying and gazed out the window for a moment. "Talking therapy is new and exciting. Not many people understand it. Still fewer accept it." Then, as if he had been called back from a visit to Doctor Freud, he turned his attention on Teresa. "Tell me something about yourself, Teresa."

"There isn't much to tell."

"I'm sure there is more than you think. Let's start with your arrival in this country."

As briefly as she could, she related the story of her life.

He got up when she finished, took her hands in his and raised her to her feet. "My dear, if I could meet that stupid judge, I would have him committed. I hope you can forgive the injustice. I can't. I'd take it upon myself to release you, but we must go through Staff." He saw her face fall in panic. "Don't worry. It's just a formality. They rubber-stamp whatever I say, but they have to justify their position. They are meeting next door right now. I'll set up the appointment. It shouldn't take too long. Pack your belongings. You'll leave when you find the means of travel. It's been a pleasure meeting you." Then, as an afterthought, he flipped his pad open and handed it to her. "Give me your forwarding address and I'll send you a list of books to read. Be sure to write me, will you?"

"Of course." As she wrote out her address and he filled out the form for her dismissal, all she could think of was Nick. "May I use your telephone, Doctor?"

"Certainly."

Where would Nick be? Flying? Giustina's? She didn't want to call Giustina. Giustina hadn't talked with her since the day she had been at the courthouse. She tried to get in touch with Harry, but he wasn't at his office. She was beginning to worry she'd have to spend another day in the institution. She couldn't wait. Then she remembered the Teterboro hanger number.

Bob answered the phone. "Hey, Nick," he yelled, "Teresa's on the line."

When Nick answered the phone, her excitement over the news she had to tell him exceeded only that of hearing his voice. "They're releasing me," she said calmly, although her insides were jumping with joy.

"Releasing?" He shouted with joy into the phone.

"Will you come and pick me up?"

"What a question, my darling. Just look out your door. You'll find me there!"

* * *

"Liza!" Teresa, a bit miffed at seeing Liza in the driver's seat of Nick's auto when he picked her up, tried not to show it. She had fantasized that she and Nick would relive their romantic moments at the bungalow, forgetting that Goldie and Clyde would probably be there. Then she felt guilty at her ingratitude. *After all, Liza did give me clothes to wear for my escape.* Nevertheless, the yearning to make love to him throbbed throughout her being.

Nick gave a rebel yell, grabbed Teresa and lifted her high in the air, causing several visitors entering the building to turn and stare. "Darling, at last!"

Although she asked him to put her down, she wanted to remain in his arms for the sheer joy of it. When he put her down, she thought of Liza. *Why am I being so selfish? Nick and I will have a whole lifetime to make love to one another.* She kissed and embraced Liza when she emerged from the auto. "Thank you for the clothes."

"It was nothing. Nick's been teaching me to drive. He didn't want to waste any time driving me home." She was about to get behind the wheel again but changed her mind when she saw the disappointment on Nick's and Teresa's faces. She climbed into the back.

Nick's face reddened at having shown his feelings. "You don't mind, do you, Liza?"

"Not at all. I can use the break. It was a long drive up here."

Nick held the door open for Teresa as she climbed in. He dashed to the front of the car, cranked it up, practically jumped in, sat beside Teresa and took her hand in his. How desperately he wanted to take her into his arms and hold her until she was a permanent part of him. *Why the devil did I bring Liza along with me? Bob could have taken her home. Teresa and I could have made love at the bungalow.* He sighed. *Well, we'll have plenty of other times.* The thought didn't satisfy his immediate desire. "After I spoke to you, honey, I called Harry to see if he could set the date for our wedding service at the church. He said for some reason he had forgotten to cancel the date he had set for your wedding to him. So, my sweet, in three and a half weeks you'll be mine forever. I tried to get Harry to move it closer, but it couldn't be done. I didn't know you were to marry Harry in a Catholic church. As far as I knew they wouldn't allow mixed marriages."

"Harry was willing to convert for me."

Nick gave a low whistle and felt new respect for Harry's love for Teresa. "Boy, that's quite a thing for him to do. I don't think I could do such a thing."

"He's an exceptional man. I tried to talk him out of it, but he said he wanted to do it so that our marriage would be complete."

Nick felt guilty for all the things he had thought about Harry. "He said the wedding gown is almost ready, just a couple of fittings for you and it's done."

Teresa smiled for him and squeezed his hand. "Three and a half weeks seems forever to me." She was about to lean over and kiss him on the cheek, then remembered that Liza was in the back seat. They remained quiet for a mile or two, staring at the snow-covered landscape without seeing it. Then the thought of Liza returned to her. "Why this sudden urge to learn to drive, Liza?"

"I want to drive an ambulance in France."

"Liza!" Teresa didn't bother to hide her annoyance at Liza's lack of regard for her parents. Her annoyance was tinged with not being able to be alone with Nick. "You can't do that to your parents."

"You went off on your own," Liza scoffed. "Why can't I?"

"The situation was entirely different. Your parents haven't insisted that you marry someone whom you hate, a man who is violent and obnoxious. I didn't come to this country willingly. When I assumed another identity, I acted without thinking. Although I wouldn't have gone to Rocco under any circumstances, living a lie is no answer. I gave my mother more pain than I should have. Inevitably we have to come to terms with what we do in life. We must pay the piper."

Liza scoffed. "Save me from those platitudes. I'm all out of thread and can't sew a sampler."

"It may be a platitude, but platitudes have stood the test of time. Please, Liza, don't add to your parents' suffering. Worrying about Ernesto is more than they can endure."

"We all have our own needs and inclinations we feel we must follow."

Teresa ran out of arguments. She sighed and shook her head.

They fell into silence again, each of them with his own thoughts and desires.

It was Teresa who broke the silence. "Tell me, Nick, what's been happening? They've insulated me at Maple Crest."

"Do you know Rocco and Marietta are dead?" Nick asked Teresa knowing all too well that she knew. But he had to keep Liza ignorant of the fact that Teresa had known, for the only way that Teresa could have known was if she had escaped.

"Yes. Nurse Davis was only too happy to wave the newspaper under my nose."

"Well, apparently Rocco had some papers in your apartment implicating Malespina in the kidnaping of Italian children and keeping them as slaves. The papers even told where the kids were being kept. The police raided the place and put the kids in an orphanage."

"Thank God! And Malespina? What's happened to him?"

"The police can't seem to find him."

"That's dreadful! Don't tell me the beast will get away with it?"

"Who knows? All I know is that when they searched his store they found the illegal numbers and other gambling in back, along with the pigeons that carried the racing results. Anyway, the store is closed, and all the money that he had in his bank has disappeared. Poor Elena lost all her money."

"That's terrible! What a double-dealing thief Malespina is!"

"Enough about him," Nick said. "Now that the doctor has given you a clean bill of health, it'll be a snap for Judge Rivers to clear your name."

"I hope so."

They fell into silence again.

It was Nick, this time, who broke the silence. He hated to say what he had to say, knowing how much Teresa feared flying. "I'm off in a couple of days. The army wants me as an instructor."

"What?" It was as if he had thrust a cold knife into her heart. "In this weather?"

"It's cold, but we'll be flying low, so we won't get any ice on the wings. It's perfectly safe, *cara*. You worry too much."

"How long will you be away?" she asked, not really reassured.

"I'll be home the day of the wedding."

"Will you be around for a couple of days?" she asked hopefully.

"Yes, *cara.*"

It was as if they could read each other's minds; they would still have their moments of lovemaking. They smiled and squeezed each other's hands, sending a flame surging through each of them.

# Chapter 26

Although Liza looked lovely as the maid of honor in her pink silk-crepe gown, the guests craned their necks to peer around her to look at Teresa. Rosa had been Teresa's first choice as maid of honor, but Rosa had placed her hands over her face as if hiding from the very idea. "I can't, not in my condition. You know the public can't see me this way. I'd make a spectacle of myself by walking down the aisle. No! No! I simply can't; please don't ask me!"

"Then sing at my wedding, please. You'll be on the organ loft. No one will see you there. I want you to sing *Ave Maria,* for me."

The pleading in Teresa's eyes had made her relent. Now, waiting on the organ loft for her friend, she was so happy for Teresa, she didn't think of her own embarrassment.

As for Liza, it was with mixed feelings that she led the way down the aisle. She was happy it was Teresa's wedding, for she had learned to love and admire Teresa, but she was heartsick that it wasn't her own wedding. As she drew closer to the altar, she thought about her lost love, whom she almost saw standing at the altar. The pressures of her family and friends weighed heavily on her. She wanted desperately to go to France to do her share in the war effort as her brother was doing. *Was it selfish,* she wondered, as Teresa had suggested, *to think only of my desires?* She breathed a sigh of sadness and frustration as she looked from side to side at all the smiling faces in the church. Looking as happy as the rest was difficult for her.

Almost everyone else in the church smiled contentedly; everyone, that is, except Giustina and Harry.

Giustina didn't believe any woman was good enough for Nick, especially not this one. She counted a long list of negatives. Teresa had been married before, lied about it and about who she was. Then she had been in a mental institution! Worse yet, Giustina was sure Teresa and Harry had carnal knowledge of each other. Perhaps she could forgive Teresa for some of her transgressions if only Teresa hadn't betrayed her twice by leaving

her after she had spent time and money training her. Still, fearing
the loss of her son, she remained silent about the wedding.
However, it didn't stop her from praying. She prayed at church and
at home morning and night. She prayed and prayed, until her
knees and back ached, that somehow the marriage wouldn't take
place. Even now, as she looked down the aisle, she prayed. *Please,
Dio mio, don't let this marriage take place!*

Across the aisle stood Harry. No one noticed him. Harry,
stone-faced and as pale as Teresa's gown, looked only at Teresa. For
him, the altar was a sacrificial table on which they were offering his
heart. This should have been his day, his bride, and his joy. Teresa
was wearing the gown that she would have worn at their wedding.
The wedding was taking place in the same church that was to have
been theirs, the reception hall the same, the band the same. Only
the groom was different. He had known they wouldn't permit him
to marry in a Catholic church without converting, so he had been
willing to, to please her. Had his parents been alive, they would
have died on the spot with his proposed conversion. The thought
plagued his conscience, but his love was such that he'd willingly
suffered the pangs of guilt. It was his offering to her. Now that she
was marrying Nick, he decided he'd have to do penance and
reparation. *I can't stay in New York with her as another man's wife.
When she's back from her honeymoon, I'm going to France as an
ambulance driver. She can handle the business without me.*

In the vestibule, absorbed in her own jubilant thoughts,
Teresa stood resplendent in her white satin gown trimmed with
tiny white pearls. Her headdress of voile, stiffened with sugared-
starch, reached out more than a hand's length and circled the back
of her head. Her face glowed with an excitement the veil couldn't
hide. A gossamer veil cascaded down her back and swept out along
the wide train as if trying to amass all the joy in the world. She
carried a huge wedding bouquet of white roses, baby's breath, and
white satin spiraling ribbon streamers which fell nearly to her feet.
*Yes,* she thought, as she looked down the aisle, *the only way to
achieve great happiness is to open one's heart completely. Nick, my love,
I open it to you and only you.* Her heart skipped with great joy. *At
last I will be his wife!*

Beside her, acting as father of the bride, Francesco looked at
her and smiled broadly. She squeezed his hand so hard it almost
made him wince. Nevertheless, he was so grateful and happy for

Teresa, who had given him the opportunity to get an education, that he ignored the discomfort.

On the balcony above Teresa, the pipe organ began the wedding march, filling the church with its deep full tones and her heart with joy. As she began her walk down the aisle, she caught a glimpse of Harry. The pain in his eyes dug deeply into her heart. *Why did I cause him this pain? He loves me, but I hope that eventually he will come to realize that I do love him, love him dearly, but as his very best friend.* His pain was the one lamentable thing to mar an otherwise perfect day. Harry saw the pain in her eyes and smiled to reassure her that it was all right, that he was all right. How she wished she could be two people, for she loved Harry, too.

Teresa looked down the aisle. Everyone was there, Delora, Rafaello, Elena, Goldie, and Clyde. Father Patrick Kelly waited at the altar. But no Nick. *Where is Nick?* Her eyes strained to see him; they darted first to one side of the altar then the other. She looked as far as she could into the transepts on either side, hoping he would be just emerging, but she couldn't find him. Nor could she find his best man, Bob. A sudden chill ran through her. Since Nick had taken her home from the asylum, she hadn't seen him, nor had she heard from him. To her regret, they had never had their rendezvous at the bungalow, nor had she had the chance to tell him that she was pregnant. Where was he? Had he changed his mind now that he had possessed her? She flushed from head to toe at the thought.

Now, the aisle seemed to grow ever longer and the apse ever further with each step. She wanted to run to the white marble railing to see if he were somehow missing from her line of vision. Yet, she was too afraid. What if he wasn't there? Losing him again would be too much for her to bear. *Haven't I suffered enough?*

Teresa's heart beat wildly. No longer did she hear the organ as it piped the wedding march. All she heard was her mother's voice from the past spinning within her head,

*"Love is not for you!"*

But as she approached the white marble railing, she saw Nick's smiling face greeting her as he, resplendently dressed in white tie and tales, emerged from the apse. With the sight of him, her fears slipped away as did her mother's maddening voice. Teresa now knew beyond all doubt that their life together would be as strong and a pure as the white Carrara marble from the limestone massif of the Apennines. At last she found her love and it was Nick.

# About the Author

After attending the Academy of Arts in Newark, New Jersey, and the Art Students League of New York in New York City, I had a one-woman exhibition at the Perdalma Art Gallery on 57<sup>th</sup> Street in New York City. As an Electro-Mechanical Designer, I helped design the Comsat (a communications satellite), the flight control systems for the Concord, the 747, and the DC10. I studied classical guitar with the internationally renowned classical guitarist, Rolando Valdes-Blain. However, over-practicing ruined my left hand. To strengthen my hand, I switched to the theater organ and then to the piano. Unfortunately, they didn't help me enough to allow me to resume playing the guitar.

After I married Lou, he convinced me to attend William Paterson University to study writing. While there, I achieved the distinction of outstanding senior in the Humanities Honors Program.

I owe my interest in writing to my father, who told the best slice of life stories at almost every dinner meal. My short story "Tunnel Vision" earned First Prize in the Emily Greenaway Creative Writing Award (1989). In 1991, my short story "Wolves" earned their Honorable Mention. My short stories have appeared in *Essence Magazine, Footwork* (a Paterson Literary Review), and *Avanti,* (an Italian-American publication).